David Mason wa‌‌‌‌‌‌‌‌‌‌‌‌‌‌‌‌‌‌‌‌‌‌‌‌‌‌‌‌‌‌‌‌‌‌‌‌‌
He was commiss
He was seconde
Southern Arabia
during the Dhof
the Transglobe Expedition (1979 to 82), the first surface journey round the world on its polar axis. He has travelled extensively, and is a keen linguist, speaking Arabic, French and German, and currently studying Russian. He now lives in Oxfordshire and is married with four children. He was the High Sheriff of Oxfordshire from 1994 to 95 and is the author of the international bestseller *Shadow Over Babylon*.

LITTLE BROTHER

David Mason

CORGI BOOKS

LITTLE BROTHER
A CORGI BOOK : 0 552 14302 2

Originally published in Great Britain by
Bloomsbury Publishing Plc

PRINTING HISTORY
Bloomsbury edition published 1996
Corgi revised edition published 1997

Copyright © David Mason 1996, 1997

The right of David Mason to be identified as the author of this work has been asserted in accordance with sections 77 and 78 of the Copyright Designs and Patents Act 1988.

In this work of fiction, the characters, places and events are either the product of the author's imagination or they are used entirely fictitiously.

Condition of Sale
This book is sold subject to the condition that it shall not, by way of trade or otherwise, be lent, re-sold, hired out or otherwise circulated in any form of binding or cover other than that in which it is published and without a similar condition including this condition being imposed on the subsequent purchaser.

Set in 10/11pt Plantin
by Phoenix Typesetting, Ilkley, West Yorkshire.

Corgi Books are published by Transworld Publishers Ltd,
61-63 Uxbridge Road, London W5 5SA,
in Australia by Transworld Publishers (Australia) Pty Ltd,
15-25 Helles Avenue, Moorebank, NSW 2170
and in New Zealand by Transworld Publishers (NZ) Ltd,
3 William Pickering Drive, Albany, Auckland.

Reproduced, printed and bound in Great Britain by
Cox & Wyman Ltd, Reading, Berks.

Contents

Author's note	6
Acknowledgements	7
Prologue	9
Part One	13
Part Two	129
Part Three	273
Map of North Korea	274
Part Four	389
Map of Yŏngbyŏn	390

Author's Note

The acronym IRIS is, to the best of the author's knowledge, fictitious; its concept, however, is not. A computer program with precisely these capabilities is being developed for the British security services. Even while still at the development stage, this program played a crucial part in enabling the British police to identify two suspects in a horrific and highly publicised murder case. Both suspects were subsequently convicted. By the time this book is published the development of this program will be complete and it will be a reality. The construction of a weapons system as described in this book will then be perfectly feasible.

Acknowledgements

Many individuals who helped me with my first book, *Shadow Over Babylon*, also assisted with this one. The advice and encouragement of Jock Tillotson, Patrick Mavros and numerous other friends have meant a very great deal to me. My secretary, Sarah Wint, helped with research and at the same time somehow managed to keep me aware of what else was going on in the world. Dr Michael Kenworthy Browne and Jean Dunsby put me straight on a number of details; so did Martin Jeacock and Jane Corbin in their different fields. My brother Robert Mason gave me an idea central to the story, as did Peter and Youngin Hyun, and Adam Sack. Crispin Gascoigne was instrumental in bringing about something of an adjustment to my schedule. In a slightly different sense, so were Richard Bethell and a number of new friends overseas.

Brigadier David Morgan, OBE, Commander of Commonwealth Liaison Mission and former Defence Attaché at the British Embassy, Seoul, showed great forbearance and was a mine of information and experience; and once again, I must confess boundless admiration for the amazing Dr Dave Sloggett, whose scientific knowledge and expertise seem unlimited.

Nigel Newton and David Reynolds, among others at Bloomsbury, were extremely patient. Vivienne Schuster's encouragement was unflagging. I am particularly grateful to Peter Mayer, Robert Dreesen and John Paine, whose wise editorial advice and guidance have been immensely helpful.

In addition to those named above, there were almost

as many others whose names I cannot publish. They know who they are, and I hope I have managed adequately to convey to them how very grateful I am.

Finally, I must acknowledge the stoical fortitude of those with whom I come into daily contact – in particular my wife Monique, our daughters Natalie, Catherine and Chantal, and our son Michael.

Prologue

The man stood in the shadows of Potsdamer Platz, a little distance away from the grass mound marking the apocalyptical wreckage of Adolf Hitler's death-bunker. He had been standing there for a long time, watching and thinking. He showed no sign of interest in the bunker itself, nor in the hideous episode of history it represented. His pale eyes, red-rimmed with fatigue, were elsewhere; his mind was considering the implications of the new event in history being enacted right in front of him.

He was tall, fair-haired and slightly built, with a bland, unlined, almost featureless face. His height was really his only distinguishing characteristic. He had had little sleep in the past few days, and knew he would have little time for rest in the days to come, but he thrust all thoughts of tiredness from his mind. His whole attention was fixed on the crowd of people streaming past him. His face registered no expression at all.

The crowd was large but orderly, the people keeping in line as they filed past. As always, they were patient and well-disciplined. In many ways the sight was unremarkable but for who these people were, and where they were going. In only one respect, probably undetectable to those who did not know them, was there anything unusual about their demeanour.

The man in the shadows knew the character of these people very well indeed, and he recognised their new mood. It did not come as a shock to him – he had been expecting something like this for months now, and he had already seen signs of it elsewhere in the four weeks leading up to this day; but he had never seen these expressions on their faces before. Where previously there had been nothing but slack, inanimate resignation, he could now see excitement. The new mood was carefully restrained and controlled, but it was there – he could see it in their eyes. Those eyes, that had until now been dulled by twenty-eight years and ninety-one days of servility, fear and suspicion, were now alight with hope and energy.

It was 9th November 1989. The Berlin Wall had finally been breached. The man standing in the shadows had come to see it, to watch the East Berliners heading westwards like moths towards the bright, seductive lights of the Kurfürstendamm. As they crossed over, they would each be handed a 100-Deutschmark gift, courtesy of the *Bundesrepublik* government. They would gape at the rich variety of goods on display in the shops, symbols of the beckoning lifestyle that few of them had even dared dream about. Then they would return later in the evening, clutching carrier bags containing perhaps just a few oranges, or chocolate bars – simple things unobtainable in the East, and emblematic of their new-found freedom. Their lives would have been changed forever by what they had seen, and there would be a fire in their minds, a refusal to go on tolerating the old, repressive ways of the DDR. That fire would catch in the tinder of their imaginations and burst out like a forest blaze. From then on, the spectator in the shadows knew, no power on earth would be able to extinguish it.

It was all over, he realised. An irresistible, irrevocable process of change, a seismic, unstoppable political force, had been unleashed. He had known for months, ever since the Hungarian experience back in May, that it would happen here too, sooner or later; and now it had. Here in East Berlin, things still appeared orderly and under control; but later, he knew, would come the recriminations, the impatience for change boiling over into riots, anarchy and revenge attacks on the old ways, the old institutions.

At Gorbachev's prompting Erich Honecker had already gone, replaced as DDR President by the moronic Egon Krenz, a weak, blubbering, horse-faced buffoon who was already capitulating to one inevitable demand after another. Krenz was trying to give the impression that he was the great beneficial reformer, that it was his initiative that was responsible for the recent pace of change. But no one, not even the dullest Party ideologue, was fooled by his drunken, self-justifying ramblings.

The man in the shadows had known what would happen, but few others in authority – even now – appeared to have understood it. The hierarchy would cling on, hoping to salvage something, to restore some semblance of order; but power had irretrievably slipped from their hands. From Krenz downwards, they would soon be swept aside by the tide of history. Even the previously implacable General Mielke was showing signs of panic, making token concessions which he thought he would be able to rescind later. *Idiot*, thought the man in the shadows. *Mielke should be here to watch this. Then he would understand.* Mielke, he reflected, had not been in Leipzig the previous month. Had he been, he would have seen the security police, who had savagely put down a peaceful demonstration by twenty thousand people on 7th October, cave in and take no action two days later against a demonstration by more than three times that number. In the thirty days since then the thing had snowballed, its gathering momentum propelling it ever faster towards the inevitable outcome.

There was little time to waste, thought the man in the shadows. There was no longer a future for him or his kind here. Soon he would be a pariah among his own people. At best, he might hope for immunity from prosecution in return for what he knew – if he was lucky.

After that, he would be on the scrap-heap. Who would employ him? He would be lucky to get even menial work. No – the future for him lay elsewhere, in the rump of the organisation, if it could be salvaged. It was just a matter of where to go, of how to set up the move, and of what to do once there. He would need assistance in acquiring and establishing a new base for the organisation, but after that . . .

Colonel Gerhardt Eisener of the *Staats Sicherheitsdienst* stepped out of the shadows and walked back towards the headquarters in Normannenstrasse. There was not much time, he realised, but he knew what needed to be done.

PART ONE

1

Graham Wiggins was not as observant as he liked to think he was. His powers of observation and recall were perhaps no better than average. He would afterwards maintain, with some justification, that there was no particular reason for him to suspect that anything unusual was happening that Saturday morning until he heard an unusual noise and turned round to see what it was.

From the point of view of the police, who subsequently interviewed Graham Wiggins at length, it was a pity that he had not noticed a few more details beforehand. Accurate descriptions of the occupants of the white Transit van would have been useful, and it might have saved a little time if he had been able to identify or describe the older of the two pedestrians. In fact, as the police would later realise, what Graham Wiggins noticed – or failed to notice – made no difference to the way things eventually turned out.

It was a Saturday morning in Oxford City Centre. Saturday, thought Graham Wiggins later, shaking his head. You didn't expect things to happen on a Saturday, did you? Sunday: now that was a different matter. Lots of things happened on Sundays. Or Fridays. Or Mondays. Even on Thursdays sometimes; but not really on Saturdays. Saturday was . . . well, it was neither one thing nor the other, was it?

So Graham Wiggins was walking along the High Street on a Saturday morning, not expecting anything unusual to happen. And of course, something did. And when it happened, he didn't see it. Not to start with, anyway – not until he turned round.

The old man was walking towards him; Graham Wiggins didn't even give him a second glance. Two steps behind the old man was a smartly-dressed fellow in his thirties. Then came the white van, a Ford Transit.

The white Transit was driving very slowly. Its side-loading door was open, but this did not register with Graham Wiggins at the time, and he didn't notice the two men in overalls standing inside, holding on to a grab rail. Graham Wiggins walked past the old man, then the younger, smartly-dressed one; then the van. It wasn't until he was about ten yards past the van that he heard the noise.

It was a sort of thud, not very loud, but there was something slightly unusual about it. Graham Wiggins only just heard it. He turned round to see what it was.

The younger of the two pedestrians, Graham Wiggins saw, was now lying on his back on the pavement. Two men in white overalls were helping the old man into the Transit van, through its open side-door. One of them said something. Graham Wiggins wondered briefly why the younger man was just lying on the pavement, but he stood and watched as the old man was helped into the van. The two men in white overalls climbed in after him and slid the door shut; then the Transit pulled away from the kerb. There was no revving of the engine or squealing of tyres; the van just drove off down the High Street perfectly normally.

The younger man was still lying on the pavement, not moving. Graham Wiggins liked to think of himself as a helpful citizen, but if he had been honest with himself he would have admitted that it was more curiosity than anything else which made him walk back to see what was wrong with the man. He looked down at his face. The eyes were wide open – in fact they were bulging out of their sockets. Puzzled now, Graham looked up again at the departing van, just in time to see it reach the traffic lights at the Carfax, at the top of the High Street, and turn left round the corner into St Aldates. Then he looked down again at the man's face. The man still hadn't moved. He saw a small smear of blood on the pavement underneath the man's head.

Graham Wiggins' thoughts were by now confused, but if he thought anything at all it was that the man must have had a heart attack and gashed his head when he collapsed on to the hard pavement. He had never seen a dead man before, but this man looked pretty dead to him. He didn't know what to do, so instead of feeling for the carotid pulse beneath the jaw, he did what he had seen actors do in films. He undid the button on the man's jacket and bent down to put his ear to the chest to listen for a heart-beat. That was when he saw the shoulder-holster under the open jacket, and the pistol that was still in it.

Graham Wiggins looked up from the body, saw a man coming out of a shop nearby, and did the other thing he had seen actors do in films. This time, he got it almost right. 'You! Call the Police! Quick!' he yelled urgently.

Five minutes later, Graham Wiggins was feeling quite pleased with himself. It had been gratifying to see how quickly the police had responded to the call-out he had ordered. Six uniformed officers were already on the scene, two of them holding back a gathering crowd of onlookers while two more dealt with traffic; the fifth was erecting a flimsy screen around the body and the sixth was asking him, Graham Wiggins, exactly what he had seen.

'I saw the whole thing, officer,' he said in a loud voice. Apart from the body behind the screen, Graham Wiggins realised, he was the centre of attention. 'The whole thing.'

It did not take the officer long to realise that Graham Wiggins had actually seen very little. Politely, he cut the interview short, telling him that it might be necessary for him to come down to the station later to make a statement. Would he mind waiting?

Graham Wiggins didn't mind at all. In fact, he had every intention of waiting. This was the most important thing that had happened to him for a long time, and he was in no hurry whatever to leave. He was the prime witness to a murder, wasn't he?

What particularly pleased Graham Wiggins was his own reaction to what had happened. He felt perfectly calm and composed, despite having seen his first dead body. Ice-cool, he told himself. No shakes, no hysterics, no dry mouth; nothing like that. Ice-cool. Ignoring the policeman's request that he wait behind the tape that had been strung across the pavement to keep onlookers at their distance, he instead moved closer to the body and did his best to look important.

The police were no longer paying any attention to him. Two minutes later, this minor lapse on their part led to Graham Wiggins overhearing something which might, in any other circumstances, have given him a story he could have told and retold for years.

Another man had arrived on the scene. Plain clothes, but obviously a policeman, Wiggins realised. A senior one, too. CID, probably. Maybe even Special Branch. The man bent over the body behind the screen and then straightened up. His back was turned, so Graham Wiggins couldn't see what he had in his hand. Probably that Walther pistol, he thought.

Graham Wiggins wasn't to know it, but the pistol was a Glock 17, and in any case that was not what the plain-clothes man held in his hand – it was the dead man's wallet and identification. Edging closer, Wiggins saw the plain-clothes man reach for his radio and heard him speak.

The phrase 'MPG officer' meant nothing to Graham Wiggins, but the phrase 'one of ours' certainly did. So the dead man was a policeman! He waited to hear what would be said next. In the distance he heard the wailing of a siren that advertised the rapid approach of an ambulance from the John Radcliffe Hospital.

After a few seconds the plain-clothes man's radio squawked a reply. Graham Wiggins didn't understand some of the jargon, but he distinctly heard the name 'Sir Reginald Hislop'. For a couple of seconds his mind went blank with surprise, and then he began to piece it together.

That old man . . . Yes, come to think of it, that was who the old guy was! Sir Reginald Hislop! And the dead policeman must have been on bodyguard duty! 'Jesus!' he exclaimed aloud.

The plain-clothes man, Detective Chief Inspector James Napley, heard Graham Wiggins' exclamation. He turned round and saw Graham Wiggins standing just feet from him. 'Who the hell are you?' he asked.

'I saw the whole thing!' said Graham Wiggins excitedly. 'It was Sir Reginald Hislop who was driven away in that van!'

DCI Napley bit back his annoyance. 'Keep your voice down,' he said evenly. 'Now, just tell me what happened.'

Two minutes later, DCI Napley had extracted as much information as he knew he would get, and Graham Wiggins found himself being firmly escorted away to St Aldate's Police Station, only a quarter of a mile away. 'Make sure he doesn't speak to anyone at all until I get back there, understand?' Napley called after the escorting officer.

Graham Wiggins walked in silence, bemused but still in a state of some excitement. Eventually he found his voice. 'What does MPG stand for?' he asked the escorting officer.

'Mobile Protection Group,' said the policeman.

'What's that? Bodyguard duties, is it?'

'Sort of,' said the officer.

'So your dead colleague was looking after Sir Reginald Hislop, was he?' asked Graham Wiggins. 'Why would that old has-been still rate a bodyguard? He's history.'

'All former British Prime Ministers have them. Sir Reginald Hislop's no exception. Now listen, Mr Wiggins,' said the policeman. 'You heard the DCI. Keep your voice down, OK?'

Jesus, thought Graham Wiggins, recalling years gone by. He could only just remember the old days, when Hislop had been in power. Old Reginald Hislop. He'd dropped right out of circulation since then, of course. Never in the news at all, these days. Stop ten people in the street, and probably half would never even have heard of him. But now it looked like he'd been . . . Yes, he'd been kidnapped! A former British Prime Minister! Kidnapped!

2

In the early hours of that same morning, Saturday 24 April 1993, two men had driven a dark blue G-registration Ford Iveco tipper lorry through the relatively empty streets of the City of London, into Bishopsgate. Parking the lorry on the double yellow lines just to the south of Bishopsgate's junction with Wormwood Street, the driver climbed down from the cab. A twenty-five year old man, he lit a cigarette and casually looked around while his passenger, an older man of thirty-four, lingered in the cab for a minute or so longer. In the footwell of the lorry's cab, out of view of any passing pedestrian who might have been watching (none were), the passenger carefully extracted a small cylindrical dowel rod from each of two identical items known as TPUs – Timing and Power Units. One TPU would probably have sufficed, but they had been known to fail and the fact that there were two, one acting as a failsafe back-up, made sure of things. When the passenger had pulled both dowel rods clear, he too dismounted. The two men locked the cab and departed on foot.

They headed north to Liverpool Street Station, only a few minutes walk away. At the station the older man was seen to make a telephone call from a public callbox at about 8.40 a.m.; then, for all practical purposes, the two men disappeared. It is not known what route they took from Liverpool Street Station, or which method of transport they chose – British Rail, London Transport underground, or bus (the other possibilities, such as private car, taxi, or continuing on foot, were later dismissed as being less likely) – but their movements were never traced.

The significance of the telephone call made by the older of the two men was only realised more than half an hour later, at 9.17 a.m., when the switchboard buzzed at the headquarters of the Sky Television satellite broadcasting company. The caller did not identify himself but simply informed the Sky switchboard operator that a large bomb had been planted in Bishopsgate, in the City of London, and would explode within the hour.

Seven other news organisations received similar calls over the following ten minutes, but the call received by Sky was in one respect more significant than the others. Following a recent spate of nuisance calls, the company had installed a brand-new American-made PABX system which, when used in conjunction with the new British Telecom 'System X' digital switchboards, had the facility to trace the origin of any telephone call almost instantly. The call was swiftly traced to a public call-box in the tiny South Armagh village of Forkhill, near the border with Eire; it was later correctly assumed that the caller had himself almost certainly been telephoned from Liverpool Street Station by the blue Iveco lorry's passenger and that he was simply passing the message on.

To the Metropolitan Police, bomb warnings are

nightmares with which they have to live almost daily. The majority turn out to be hoax calls, but every single one has to be taken seriously, even those not prefixed by a terrorist organisation's 'code-word'. In the case of this particular alert, there were eight calls, all warning of the same incident, and all prefixed by an IRA code-word. When Scotland Yard's Bomb Squad learned from Sky that the origin of the call had been a Forkhill public phone-box, it simply reinforced their impression that this warning was more likely than most to be genuine.

No time was wasted by the police in passing on the warning and, as far as possible, in clearing the area around the lorry. The evacuation task was rendered slightly easier by the fact that it was a Saturday morning and that the City was therefore relatively (although by no means completely) empty.

The decision as to whether or not to evacuate a building during a bomb scare is always an appallingly difficult one. Quite aside from the massive inconvenience and disruption that a large-scale evacuation causes, the police are well aware that a terrorist bomb rarely explodes at the time given in the warning – if, indeed, any warning time *is* given. Many terrorist devices are deliberately set to explode earlier than indicated, with the precise intention of causing casualties to those who would have been relatively safe indoors but instead had rushed outside and were hurrying away from the scene.

In this particular case, the Police got the balance right. The buildings nearest to the suspect bomb, and therefore most at risk, were rapidly emptied through rear doors, while in other buildings a little further away the occupants were advised to stay inside but keep well away from windows and, where possible, to move into basements and cellars.

Unfortunately, and through nobody's fault, the Police were less successful in finding a qualified

Ammunition Technical Officer – more commonly known as a bomb disposal expert. There were three qualified ATOs on the availability list that weekend but of these three, one had already been called out and was elsewhere investigating another suspect object (which in the event turned out to be harmless), the second had been taken ill with severe food poisoning only hours before, and the third, unaware of the illness of his colleague, was at home twenty miles away outside London – too far for him to get to Bishopsgate in time to have any hope of dealing with whatever device, small or large, happened to be in the dark blue Iveco lorry.

The device, although no one other than those who had assembled and planted it could have known this at the time, was very large indeed – far bigger than anything previously constructed by the IRA. Similar materials had been used in five earlier bombs. The first, just over a year before on 10 April 1992, had exploded in St Mary's Axe, close to the Baltic Exchange. A coded telephone message had warned of an imminent explosion outside the Stock Exchange, but this warning had proved incorrect. The Baltic Exchange bomb, in a cargo van containing what was later estimated at 1200–1500 lbs of an improvised explosive known as ANS, had devastated the surrounding area and caused havoc in the City of London. The blast damage and disruption to business had caused damage amounting to hundreds of millions of pounds. Later that same evening, a similar explosion had occurred beneath a road flyover at Staples Corner in North London. The scale of these two attacks was a quantum leap ahead of anything previously attempted by the IRA on mainland Britain.

The following three attacks failed, due to a surprising degree of ineptitude on the part of the IRA bombing teams. On the eve of the City of London Lord Mayor's parade, a box-bodied heavy-goods vehicle was stopped by police at Stoke Newington. The two occupants shot and nearly killed one of the police officers, but an arrest was made. Examination of the vehicle revealed a one-ton bomb, fully prepared but not armed.

The next attack was an attempt by the IRA to blow up the Canada building at the recently-completed Canary Wharf complex. This too failed, but for a different reason: there was an elementary fault in the explosive detonating train of the one-and-a-half ton bomb. The main charge failed to detonate and was defused. A spokesman for the Provisional IRA High Command issued a statement describing Canary Wharf as 'a prime economic target, symbolic of the Thatcher years. Let's face it,' he went on to say, 'if someone was to bring down the World Trade Center towers in Manhattan, it would be a severe blow to American prestige.' This was a chilling foretaste of what was to come only a few weeks later, when just such an attempt was made on the World Trade Center by an extremist Islamic group.

There was another basic fault in the next device, a 3000 lb bomb in a Transit van parked on the Tottenham Court Road near the Centre Point building. It too failed to detonate.

The pattern in all five attacks had been the same. All had utilised panel vans or trucks which had been stolen and given new registration plates. In each case the plates were of identical vehicles which were in legitimate use elsewhere, to confuse vehicle computer checks. All had used main charges of up to 4,000 lbs of ANS explosive. ANS is a mixture of ammonium nitrate-based fertilizer blended with sugar – in this case, icing sugar. The ANS mixture is rather less stable than the better-known ANFO (ammonium nitrate/fuel oil) but it is more powerful and has the advantage of being relatively odourless.

All five bombs had used similar booster devices, connected in each case by detonating cord to three commercial electric detonators of American origin, initiated by a pair of IRA-designed TPU timing and power units. Detonating cord resembles plastic washing-line; about a quarter of an inch thick, it is packed with high explosive and can be cut to any required length. It can be handled safely, requiring a detonator to set it off; when it explodes, it does so with a force sufficient to ignite any other explosive with which it is in contact.

A critical element to the success or failure of any bomb is the size and configuration of the booster device, which actually detonates the main charge. The features of the booster devices used had of course been established from examinations made of the three previous bombs that had failed, but such information is kept closely guarded to avoid teaching other subversive organisations how to follow in the Provisional IRA's footsteps. The booster devices were buried deep within the main charge of ANS, and the detonating cord ran from there into the front of the vehicles, to the electric detonators.

An electric detonator is a thin aluminium cylinder, typically 5mm in diameter and 5cm in length, closed at one end and with a pair of thin electric wires protruding from the other. These wires are connected to either end of a small, very fine length of wire coiled into a simple filament inside the slim cylinder. As with a light bulb, this delicate filament is designed to heat up instantly when electric current is passed through it. Unlike a light bulb, however, the filament is not surrounded by inert gas to prevent combustion – in fact, the reverse is the case. The cylinder is packed with a highly volatile, sensitive and unstable chemical compound which ignites with a sharp crack when heated by the filament. It is in fact capable of exploding with enough force to shred the hand of anyone unwise enough to treat it with insufficient respect.

The two TPU units used for each bomb were purpose-built IRA devices. Essentially, the TPU unit consists of a battery-driven electronic time-clock with a preset delay, a power-pack and, to make tampering more difficult, a mercury tilt switch anti-handling device. At the prescribed time, the timing device closes an electric circuit, allowing power to flow through into the detonator, setting it off. The explosive chain reaction then begins: detonator, detonating cord, booster, and finally main charge; but the effect is virtually instantaneous. All that was required to start the clock running was for the dowel rods to be extracted from the two TPUs, which was what the lorry's passenger had done just before leaving the scene.

At 10.25 a.m. the digital timer on the first TPU activated itself precisely on schedule and within less than a millisecond an electric current surged through the wire to the electric detonator, which instantly set off the huge explosive charge.

The size of the charge was later calculated as being larger even than its five predecessors. For a number of reasons it was not possible to be absolutely precise in this calculation, and of all the observable effects of the blast perhaps the least helpful was the size of the crater that had been blown in the road. The crater was thirty-six feet across and nearly twenty feet deep; but the construction of roads varies widely, particularly in city streets – the surface and subsoil are not homogeneous due to the sewers, water-pipes and numerous other service ducts that run beneath them. Not only that, but the configuration of the bomb – its shape, and the exact positioning of the boosters within the main charge, which would have affected how much of its force would have been directed downwards into forming the crater – was unknown.

More helpful was the general estimate that could be made of the explosive charge's efficiency. ANS has an efficiency of 50–80 per cent of that of tri-nitro-toluene (TNT) – and extensive testing of TNT has been carried out over many years at the Ministry of Defence Trials and Evaluation Establishment at its huge Shoeburyness range. These trials have provided a set of results that are used as a standard; the effects of varying sizes of TNT explosions on different structures are known, and these could be extrapolated into equivalent figures for various improvised explosives of different efficiencies. In this case, the damage caused to structures close to the point of detonation of the Bishopsgate bomb indicated that as much as three or four tons of ANS could have been carried in the Iveco tipper-truck, exceeding by a long way anything previously experienced on the British mainland.

The overall effects of the bomb on the wider area were consistent with this figure. The devastation was awesome. The blast was of a size and force sufficient not only to smash windows and scatter debris over a radius of over 500 metres and send a huge mushroom-cloud of smoke high into the sky above the City of London, but to cause massive structural damage, later estimated at up to £1bn, to dozens of buildings and completely flatten one of them – the oldest of them all, the tiny medieval church of St Ethelburga-the-Virgin. The ancient church had survived the Great Fire of 1666 and the Blitz, but now it had been reduced to a pile of rubble.

Perhaps the most spectacular architectural casualty was the National Westminster Bank tower, at six hundred feet the second tallest building in London. For the 100 staff still inside the tower when the explosion detonated just fifty yards away, it proved a terrifying experience. The huge building was rocked to its foundations and most of the 2300 windows, a total of three acres of plate-glass, were shattered. Four hours later it was still deemed unsafe for the occupants to leave the tower, with lethal shards of glass still tumbling from their frames to join the rubble on the street hundreds of feet below.

Forty-seven people were injured in the blast, many

seriously. Most were victims of flying glass and other debris, but some had simply been picked up by the force of the shock-wave and flung across rooms against walls. Others had been injured when parts of ceilings collapsed on top of them.

One man died. Edward Henty, a cheerful and hardworking photographer on assignment with the London-based *News of the World*, was in the street only a few yards from the Iveco lorry when the bomb went off. It was the day before Henty's twelfth wedding anniversary; he died instantly, but such was the devastation caused by the bomb-blast that his body was not found until five hours later.

It is sometimes said that a little good comes of every event, however appalling its consequences may initially appear to be. There was nothing immediately apparent in the case of the Bishopsgate bomb to offer anyone – other than the IRA, who exulted in the success of their mission – even the smallest crumb of comfort. One consequence, however, despite being of such apparent insignificance as to pass completely unnoticed at the time, would soon set in motion events that would affect the course of history.

In the anonymous office of a partner in an investment management firm on one of the floors of No 99 Bishopsgate, part of a steel window-frame had been wrenched from its structure and flung inside the room by the force of the blast. The twisted piece of steel struck a metal box sitting on a desk in the investment manager's office, shattering the lock on the box and strewing its contents, a sheaf of papers, onto the floor.

The box was of the type used for the safe-depositing of valuables; made of thin-gauge steel, such boxes relied for their security not on their construction, which was somewhat flimsy, but on where they were kept – usually in a high-security vault or strong-room. This particular box had been withdrawn from the strong-room the previous afternoon and opened by its owner, an overseas client of the investment management firm. The client had taken it away and spent some time alone, reviewing and amending a few of the documents it contained; by the time he had finished his work, the time-lock on the strong-room door had been activated and it was too late for the box to be replaced. Annoyed, the client had locked the box and left it with the investment manager, not unreasonably assuming that it would be safe in his custody. The investment manager, unaware of the contents of the box, had promised his client that he would return it to the safety-deposit the following morning at 10.30, when the time-lock would once again allow access to the strong-room.

Had the building been in a fit state for the investment manager to enter it that Saturday morning, he would have dutifully gathered the papers together, locked them into a replacement box and informed his client of what had happened; but the Iveco lorry had been parked right outside No 99 Bishopsgate and the building had taken the full force of the bomb-blast. It had immediately been condemned as structurally unsafe, and access was for the time being prohibited.

The smashed window of the investment manager's office gaped open to the elements; the documents lay where they were, scattered on the floor, surrounded by fragments of broken glass, covered in a light film of dust.

3

Detective Chief Inspector James Napley of the Thames Valley Police put down his telephone and sat for a moment in silence. He was a calm, unflappable man who took most things in his stride, but he had been badly rattled by what had happened.

Like most good policemen, Napley had developed a nose for trouble, and he had somehow known straight away, even before learning any details, that the investigation into the incident in Oxford High Street was going to be no routine affair. Now, except for the policework that would be involved in trying to trace the van and its occupants, the matter had been taken out of his hands – the Security Service, MI5, were already involved and he was to pass the baton on to them.

Napley was soon to demonstrate just how good a detective he was. After reporting to his boss, Mike Chalmers, the Chief Superintendent in charge of the Oxford City Police Area, Napley calmly lit a cigarette, sat back in his chair and stared out of the window, not looking at anything in particular, a thoughtful expression on his face. Apart from occasionally drawing on the cigarette, he remained immobile for nearly five minutes; then he stubbed out the cigarette and went down to the incident room.

'Bill,' he said quietly to a uniformed Inspector, 'I think we may be able to save a bit of time here. I suggest you get a couple of your bodies over to the Westgate car park. There's a good chance they'll find that white Transit van there, probably on the top floor of the multi-storey section.'

Inspector Bill Walston gave him a surprised look, but he knew Napley well enough to realise there would be a good reason for the DCI's hunch. He gave the order, and the two police officers on patrol who happened to be nearest to the car park received their instructions over the radio. They were there three minutes later, and five minutes after that there was a call from one of them, PC Donald Brown, to say that there was indeed a white Transit van parked on the upper level, which was otherwise largely empty of cars. He gave its licence-plate number. Less than a minute later, the Driver and Vehicle Licensing Office computer database in

Swansea yielded the information that a van with that registration number had been reported stolen a week before. It was 10.58 a.m.; barely twenty minutes had elapsed since the incident in the High Street.

Walston needed no further instructions; more police officers were soon on their way to the car park, where they would spend the rest of the morning questioning shoppers emerging from the adjoining Westgate shopping centre and heading for their cars. Had anyone seen the Transit enter the car park at about 10.45 a.m.? Had anyone noticed another car or van leaving shortly after that time? There were only two positive answers to the first question, but neither of the respondents was able to elaborate or provide any useful information. In answer to the second question, however, many people said that of course they had seen cars leaving – but none of them could remember details. Why should they? Cars came and went all the time, didn't they? It was a busy car park, and it was Saturday morning, wasn't it?

Meanwhile, swarms of fingerprint experts, forensic scientists and photographers had descended on the Transit van and were examining it in minute detail. Numerous clothing fibres were found, as expected; it would take days for all of them to be analysed and for this reason they were of little immediate use; but there were also ten hair samples, eight of which were grey in colour and the other two brown. Most promising of all, there were two full hand-prints, right and left (the left one was rather smudged) on the metal floor in the back of the van. Everything else in the van had obviously been wiped clean.

'Where did you find those grey hairs?' asked Napley.

'In the back,' reported the analyst. 'The brown ones were in the front.'

'Right,' said Napley. He turned to one of his Detective Constables. 'Brian, I want you to come with me. We're going to pay a call on Lady Hislop.'

In the car, Napley had a further thought and radioed

the St Aldate's Police station and was put through to Chief Superintendent Chalmers. 'Sir, has anyone told the old lady yet about her husband going missing?'

'Not yet, Jim,' replied the Chief Superintendent. 'We still don't really have anything concrete to tell her, although she may start to worry fairly soon, when he doesn't turn up. I was going to give it another half hour, then go to see her myself.'

'I'll save you the trouble, sir. I'm on my way there now.'

Chalmers was relieved; he was used to the distressing task of breaking bad news to people and wherever possible he shouldered this burden himself in important cases, but he now had a major incident on his hands. Many dozens of police officers were already committed to it, and he could scarcely afford to absent himself for what was in effect a social call, however important. He thanked Napley warmly.

Lady Hislop answered the door herself. She appeared tired and rather careworn, but she gave Napley and DC Brian Taylor a friendly smile when they introduced themselves and she welcomed them into her house. Napley was immediately struck by her genuine, unassuming nature. *What a nice woman*, he thought, as she went off to make them a cup of tea.

A few minutes later, Napley gently broke the news to her. Lady Hislop crumpled a little in her chair, but there were no tears; for a minute or so, she remained silent, lost in her thoughts. Napley's heart went out to her. She trusted us, he thought, and now we've let her down. We failed to protect her husband.

The small, quiet voice, when it came, startled Napley. 'I won't ask why or how this can have happened, Chief Inspector. I've never really understood any of these things. I've just had to accept them for most of my life. Lots of horrible things happen . . . But I thought all that was in the past . . .' Lady Hislop shook her head gently; then she continued, talking in a sad, resigned voice, as much to herself as to Napley. 'It's just that I can't see any sense in it. After all these years . . . You see, we don't do much any more, these days. We hardly go out at all. We live a nice, quiet life . . . My husband has become a little forgetful, you see, and I'm rather glad that we are mostly left alone to get on with our lives, in peace and quiet.' She was shaking her head in bewilderment, unable to grasp why anyone would want to kidnap her husband. Suddenly she looked up at Napley, the beginnings of tears in her eyes. 'Oh, but I am being so selfish. I'm so sorry to hear about young Colin! What an awful thing! He was so nice and kind to us!'

Napley was perplexed for a second or two; then he realised she was referring to the dead Protection Group officer whose job it had been to provide security for her husband. He changed the subject. 'Lady Hislop, you are very considerate, and I am very sorry indeed about all this. You have my assurance that we will be doing everything we possibly can to find your husband.' He paused. 'But there is one thing you might be able to help us with, if I might ask a small favour. I hate to intrude, but it could just help.'

She gave a wan smile, looking a little uncertain. 'Yes, of course. But what . . .?'

'Could we have a quick look round your husband's bedroom? We might just find something that could be of assistance.'

'Of course,' said Lady Hislop, rising to her feet.

She led the way up the stairs, and opened a door. 'Please – go on in. I'll wait downstairs . . .' The door closed; Napley and Brown heard her footsteps retreating slowly down the stairs.

Less than a minute later, Napley had what he had come for; he carried it downstairs, sealed in a plastic evidence bag. He held it up to her. 'Lady Hislop, we haven't disturbed anything in the room at all, but would you mind if we took this away for examination?

I promise to return it to you within a day or two.'

She looked puzzled, but smiled at him and nodded. 'Oh yes, I am sure that will be all right, Chief Inspector. And thank you for coming to see me. If there's any news . . .?'

'I will let you know straight away, Lady Hislop. And it is you who has been kind. Thank you for the cup of tea, and for your help – thank you very much indeed. And I am so sorry about what has happened.'

She gave a little, sad smile as Napley and Brown left; the door clicked shut behind them.

An hour later, Napley learned that forensic analysis had confirmed that the grey hair samples and right hand-print taken from the Transit van were a perfect match with the hairs and fingerprints found on the hairbrush he had taken from Hislop's bedroom. There was no longer any doubt.

'By the way, sir,' DC Taylor asked him. 'How did you guess about the van being on the top floor of the Westgate car park?'

Napley grinned. 'Nearest and best place for a switch, wasn't it? I reckoned the kidnappers would want to change vehicles as quickly as possible. The van was seen turning left at Carfax into St Aldate's; that would take them right past this station, and the Crown Court too, would you credit it. Cheeky bastards,' he muttered. 'They obviously planned it well, and had everything in place. I mean, they wouldn't race off down towards the Southern Ring Road, or something stupid like that, would they? No. They would switch cars. The Westgate multi would be ideal – turn right just past the Crown Court into Thames Street, and the car park is only a quarter-mile further along on the right. The top floor was most likely to be empty, with less chance of anyone seeing anything going on. Logical. No more to it than that.'

A little later, Napley was summoned upstairs where he found Chief Superintendent Chalmers in conference with a small, dapper man in his sixties wearing a military tie. Chalmers introduced him as Colonel Goodale of MI5.

'Retired, actually,' said Goodale, smiling as he shook Napley's hand. 'But I've been pressed back into service to help deal with this matter.'

They un-retired you pretty bloody quickly, thought Napley, meeting Goodale's eyes. He noticed that they were an unusually bright, penetrating blue. In appearance, he decided, Goodale bore a striking resemblance to the actor Sir John Mills. Even the voice was similar. 'Good to meet you, sir,' he said politely.

Chalmers cleared his throat. 'Colonel Goodale has some ideas about what the press should be told about this,' he said. 'Colonel?'

Goodale swiftly outlined his thoughts. There must be no public mention of Sir Reginald Hislop, he said firmly, nor indeed of any 'old man' at all. The police officer who had been murdered was to be identified not as belonging to the Mobile Protection Group but instead to the Drugs Squad, working undercover on an investigation into a major international drugs ring. Operational security, including the personal safety of other plain-clothes officers working on the case, would be the pretext for not releasing any further information for the time being, but the fact that the officer had been shot dead could be disclosed truthfully. Could Napley think of any objections?

'No, I don't think so, sir,' said Napley. 'In fact, that story could work pretty well. I've got one witness downstairs in isolation who says he recognised Hislop, but he's all mouth and trousers. He claims he saw everything, but I can turn that to our advantage. He didn't actually notice very much at all. He'll keep quiet all right, if I tell him his life would be in serious danger if he went blabbing off about it and the criminals found out. I'll put the fear of God into him before I let him go.'

'Fine,' said Goodale. 'Is there any other possibility of details leaking out?'

'I don't think so. I sent one of my men with the ambulance to keep gossip at the JR hospital to a minimum. If we were trying to cover up the shooting there'd be a problem, but this story should fit all right. And I don't think Lady Hislop will tell anyone. I asked her to say nothing about it for the time being, and in any case she didn't strike me as someone who would make a fuss.'

Colonel Goodale nodded. 'I know her quite well. She's a very private person, and she'll keep things to herself. Now,' he said, 'is there any news on the weapon that was used?'

'Nothing precise yet, sir. There was a small entry-wound at the back of the victim's head, and no exit-wound. X-rays have shown a single, small-calibre bullet still in there, a .32, or something like it. It will be extracted and sent for analysis, and then we'll know more. The pistol itself must have been silenced, as there was hardly any noise.'

'I see,' said Goodale thoughtfully. 'Could I ask you to let me know as soon as you have the analyst's report on that bullet? I would be interested to hear if there is anything unusual about it.'

'Unusual, sir?' asked Napley. 'What sort of thing do you mean?'

'Well,' said Goodale, 'in particular, I'd like to know whether or not the bullet bears any rifling marks from the weapon that fired it.' He produced a card and handed it to Napley. 'Here's my telephone number. Ring me as soon as you hear anything, would you?'

'Certainly, sir,' said Napley, puzzled. What was the man talking about? All pistol and rifle bullets bore such markings. He looked curiously at Goodale, but the MI5 man's bright blue eyes were steady and unwavering. *He knows more than he's letting on,* thought Napley intuitively.

'Well, thank you, gentlemen,' said Goodale. 'I think that covers everything for the time being. Now, I'm afraid I must be getting back to London.'

4

Gerald Cusak was in a hurry. Already five minutes late for rehearsal, he cursed to himself as the bus ground its way through the heavy traffic. He knew he should have foreseen the traffic problems the wretched bomb would cause, and come by underground to Moorgate station. He looked up, frowning, and saw that a young woman sitting opposite him was gazing at him with interest. When she realised he had noticed her look she quickly dropped her gaze.

Gerald was used to that sort of thing. A dark, good-looking man in his early twenties with strikingly deep, expressive eyes, he was well aware that women were attracted to him. He smiled and waited for her to look his way again. She did so less than a minute later. Their eyes met; he held the look, while she blushed and hurriedly dropped hers. *It never fails, Gerry,* he thought to himself. One of his first directors had given him the tip: 'Either frown or smile,' he had said. 'You've got a glorious smile and such a wickedly dark, soulful frown. But what an *awful* shame that you waste it on the girls . . .'

Hmm, thought Gerry appreciatively. This one was pretty, and maybe . . . then he frowned again. *Dammit*, he thought savagely. *No time*. He looked around. The bus was now at a standstill in clogged traffic. The hell with it, he decided. Thrusting his way to the exit at the back, he jumped off and started to run along the pavement in the direction of the Barbican Centre, vaguely aware that there seemed to be rather more litter about than usual. Behind him on the bus, a young woman was left wondering what on earth she had done wrong.

As he ran, a movement caught his eye and he glanced up. A few hundred yards away, the NatWest Tower was clearly visible, high above the skyline. He could see the extent of the damage the bomb had caused – the shattered windows gaped open, dark instead of silver. But there was something odd. There was movement at the windows where there should have been none. Then he realised what it was. The east wind was now gusting strongly; it was obviously blowing right through the tower, and the vertical hanging blinds were now fluttering out of the broken windows like streamers. As he watched, a sudden strong gust hit the tower; the streaming blinds whipped violently, and a vast cascade of papers began to pour out of the windows like confetti. Millions and millions of pieces of paper, confidential documents that had been sitting on desks in the tower, now blowing out and away, all over London . . .

Ye gods, thought Gerald, pausing for a moment in astonishment at the spectacle. *So that's what's caused all this bloody litter* . . . Then he cursed to himself. *No time to stand about gawping.* He started running again.

The young actor was just turning the corner into Chiswell Street when something blew into his face. Momentarily blinded, he collided with another pedestrian and both went crashing to the ground in a tangle of limbs.

'You stupid clumsy bastard!' yelled the other man with feeling. 'Why can't you fucking well look where you're going?'

'I'm very sorry,' said Gerald. He stood up, nursing his left wrist. The palm of his hand was grazed. He held up the piece of paper, now crumpled in his grip. 'This suddenly flew into my face, and I couldn't see. I'm sorry.'

With that he set off at a run again. Two minutes later he arrived, panting, at the theatre. To his relief, he found he was not the last to get there – he had even beaten the director to it. He relaxed.

Three hours later the rehearsal finished, and Gerald and four of the other actors went off for a drink. The wind was still gusting strongly as the five of them left the Barbican Centre; Gerald turned up his collar and thrust his hands into his coat pockets. He felt something. *What . . .? Oh yes,* he thought, *that bloody piece of paper.*

Inside the pub, he pulled it out and examined it. It was in fact three pieces of paper, very light airmail quality, stapled together. There were some corner sections of other sheets which had obviously been torn away. The pages he had were numbered one, five and six; pages two, three and four were missing. Placing the pages on the bar, Gerald smoothed them out with his hand and started reading.

'Hey, wake up, Gerry! I asked, what's yours? Aren't you joining us?'

'Oh, sorry, Giles,' said Gerald. He looked up and flashed his smile. 'Straight Scotch, please. Very kind of you.'

Giles Smallpiece gave the barman his order, then turned to Gerald again. 'What's that you've got there that's so interesting?'

'Document of some sort,' said Gerald, folding it up and pocketing it. 'Bloody thing blew into my face this afternoon. Nearly caused a nasty accident. Just wanted to see what it was – load of gibberish, as far as I can make out.'

'Oh,' said Giles, losing interest. 'Hey,' he said conspiratorially, changing the subject, 'what did you think about Julia's performance today? She seemed a bit out of it, if you ask me. I hope she's not *on* something, if you see what I mean.'

Gossip and small talk about the play, the cast and that day's rehearsal continued for half an hour, but Gerald's mind was not on it. He took early leave of his companions, who looked as though they were settling down to a long session, and set off back to his flat. As he left, he realised with a sense of guilt that he had not bought a round of drinks; behind him in the pub, he guessed, Giles was probably asking the same question about him as he had about poor Julia.

He walked home, trying to decide what to do. He had not been entirely truthful with Giles about the document. He had skimmed through it rapidly and, although most of it had made little sense to him, a few things had unsettled him. For one thing, at the top of page five were the words 'MOST SECRET' in heavy capital letters. On pages one and six, in the same place, something had been deleted with correcting fluid – probably the same words, thought Gerald. The Tippex artist had probably just neglected to blot them out on page five. Plenty of other words had also been Tippexed out all through the document, and different words typed over them. Gerald wondered what on earth lay beneath all that Tippex.

The other thing that bothered the young actor was the hand-written note at the bottom of the last page. But it was not what it said that intrigued him – in fact, he could not understand a word of it. What was odd was that it was written in some foreign script. To Gerald, it looked like Arabic. What was an Arab doing, scribbling notes on a secret document?

John Geraghty grumbled to himself as he went to answer his doorbell. *No sooner back off duty after a hard day chasing villains*, he thought, *than some bugger comes round to disturb you*. He undid the latch and opened the door to see his neighbour from the flat upstairs.

'Oh, hello,' he said. He liked Gerry because he was never any bother – no loud music, noisy parties or any nonsense like that. Quite a procession of girls, of course; but he could understand why. Good-looking young fellow. Nothing wrong with that. At least it wasn't boys. Geraghty smiled at him. 'What can I do for you?'

'Look, I'm very sorry to bother you, John,' said Gerald apologetically, 'but I've found this piece of paper and there are a couple of things about it that worry me. I thought you'd know what to do about it.' He handed over the document.

Geraghty looked bemused at first, but his face cleared as his neighbour explained how he had come across it. 'I shouldn't worry, Gerry. You should have seen the bloody mess in the City today – it's stuff that's blown out of broken windows from the bomb. Some places were knee-deep in bumph. Squads of poor buggers have spent most of the day trying to clear it all up. I'll get rid of this one for you, if you want. Thanks for handing it in – nice to see a bit of public spirit.'

'No problem, John,' said Gerald. 'But I think someone ought to take a good look at it. I mean, look at this bit here . . .'

Geraghty's face began to crease into a frown as he scanned through the document. 'Yeah,' he said. 'You may be right.' Then, with an effort, he smiled. 'OK. Now look – don't you worry about it any more. I'll deal with it first thing in the morning. If I hear anything, I'll let you know. And thanks again. Good of you to help.' Geraghty closed the door on his departing neighbour and returned to his chair in front of the television. He had had a tough day and all he wanted to do was relax.

Yet he found his mind only half-concentrating on the programme. That document nagged at him – it was a bit of a mystery. He picked it up again and read through it in detail. It seemed to be a report about the relative suitability of a number of well-known companies to undertake an unspecified contract. The stupid thing was, he could see no possible connection between any of them. Why, for example, would IBM, Tesco and Courtaulds, to name just three, be competing for the same job? Computers, food retail and textiles? It didn't make sense. 'Com Union' probably referred to Commercial Union – that added insurance to the puzzle. Then there were lists of names, addresses and telephone numbers – again, none of them making much sense. Did Tesco have a base in Germany, and IBM in Belfast? Maybe, but it seemed an odd way to get hold of those companies when they were well represented in London. Then there was this 'MOST SECRET' heading on page five. It would be interesting to see what was underneath all that Tippex, thought Geraghty, moving the document about in the light. Then something struck him – of course, all those company names and other incongruous references had been typed over the Tippexed original words!

Geraghty's interest was now definitely aroused. He switched off the television and went over to his desk. Laying the document flat on the blotter, he took out a pocket knife and carefully began to scrape away at one of the lumps of Tippex. He was surprised how hard it was – the stuff had set like concrete . . . Damn! He had torn the paper. He realised that scraping it off wasn't going to work and sat back in his chair to think, reaching automatically for a cigarette and his lighter. The action triggered off a memory – a mate in forensic had once told him how easy it was to read what lay underneath a crusted layer of Tippex, if you knew how. Geraghty's policeman's instincts were warning him not to tamper with the document any further, but curiosity overcame discretion. Rummaging in the desk drawer, he found his can of lighter fuel. Then he went into the bathroom, where he took a small ball of cotton wool from the medicine cabinet. In the kitchen he grabbed a large china plate. Armed with these, he set to work back at his desk.

Using his knife, Geraghty carefully unbent the staple, separating the pages and laying two of them aside. Placing the first page face down on the plate, he squirted some of the lighter fuel on to the cotton wool pad and began dabbing away at the back of the paper. The Tippex on the front remained unaffected, but beneath it he could now see the original typed words in reverse image. When he had moistened the whole page he took it into the bathroom, held it up to the mirror and began to read.

Ten minutes later, John Geraghty was a shaken man. He had finished treating all three pages, and had read their contents. The document now lay on his desk, the lighter fuel gradually evaporating away, the paper slowly returning to its normal opaque state. Geraghty's concern had mounted as he read; he was still not entirely sure what the document represented, but some of the previously hidden words had leapt out at him. Beneath the word 'IBM' was 'IRA', beneath 'Com Union' was 'Abu Nidal'. 'GKN' was now 'KGB', 'Stena' was now 'Stasi', and 'Courtaulds' was 'Securitate'. There were a number of other examples; the person with the Tippex had obviously picked at random companies with names the same length as those of the organisations hidden beneath.

The document now appeared to be an assessment of the suitability of these various organisations to do a particular job. A figure of five million US dollars was mentioned as a suggested inducement. It was the first Geraghty had heard that any of these organisations might consider undertaking commercial work for a third party, rather than operating strictly within their own national or ideological interests. Thoroughly alarmed, he sat back and wondered what to do; then he came to a decision. He would ring his boss at home and tell him he needed to see him straight away. He reached for the telephone and dialled the number.

Five minutes later Geraghty slipped on his coat, stuffing the can of lighter fluid and a fresh ball of cotton wool into a side pocket. Then he left his flat and descended the steps to the street. Secure in his inside breast pocket was the document, now dry but still giving off a faint odour of petrol – three sheets of paper that the wind had blown out of an anonymous investment manager's office in the shattered remains of 99 Bishopsgate, and which had come to him by the purest chance.

Shivering slightly as the cold night air hit him, Detective Constable John Geraghty set off down the street and disappeared into the darkness.

5

The small car drove slowly up to the heavy steel gate set back from the road. The driver switched off the engine and climbed out. He was in his forties, tall and lean, with black hair greying at the temples. He wore sunglasses and a lightweight suit. Pausing by the car for a moment to light a cigarette, he drew deeply, snapped his lighter shut and replaced it in his jacket pocket, then walked up to the buzzer on the left-hand gate-pillar. There was a small speaker grille next to the buzzer, and a video-camera lens mounted high above, on top of the pillar. He pressed the buzzer and waited.

'Yeah?' came a tinny voice from the speaker after a couple of minutes.

'My name's Howard,' said the visitor. 'I have an appointment to see Mr Cowgill.'

'What's your business?' asked the voice abruptly.

'That is between Mr Cowgill and me,' answered Howard evenly.

'Oh, very funny,' sneered the voice. 'Ha bloody ha. Stand back from the gate so I can see you.'

Howard took a couple of steps back and stood looking at the camera.

'Take your glasses off.'

Howard removed his sunglasses and put them in his

pocket. His dark eyes glittered, narrowing against the bright midday Mediterranean sun. He took a last drag on his cigarette and flicked it away. *The fellow probably isn't very impressed with my car,* he thought impassively. *His attitude might have been different if I'd shown up in a big flashy one.*

'OK, wait there,' said the voice. 'I'll be down in a minute.'

'Be quick about it,' snapped Howard. 'I'm not used to being kept waiting by hired help.'

There was nothing for a moment, then the speaker went dead. *That should make things more interesting,* thought Howard. *I wonder what effect that last remark will have.*

Howard studied the property through the heavy bars of the electric sliding gate. The pillars were large and built of solid stone, he could see, and the gate would be strong enough to stop a truck. That wall either side was concrete, ten feet high, with shards of broken bottle-glass cemented into the top. On the other side of the gate, a gravel drive stretched away uphill for nearly a hundred yards, before curving round to the right and out of view. Howard could just see one corner of a large two-storey villa behind a screen of tall cypress trees.

Five minutes later came the sound of a dog barking. A heavily built man appeared, walking down the drive. He was wearing a dark blue double-breasted suit. Clipped to the breast pocket of the suit jacket was a small radio transceiver with a stubby antenna. In one hand the man held a thick leather leash and the dog, a large Rottweiler, was straining forwards, barking furiously. The man held the leash easily, controlling the powerful dog with little apparent effort.

Howard watched the approach of man and dog. As they drew nearer Howard could see that the man wasn't just heavily built – he was massive. At six feet, three inches Howard was tall, but this man dwarfed him. Six feet five at least, thought Howard, and he must weigh nearly twenty stone. None of it spare fat, either. Solid muscle and steroids. There was a bulge visible beneath the left armpit of the man's jacket. Despite his bulk, Howard could see that he moved lightly on his feet. An ox of a man, but not a particularly clumsy one, he decided.

Twenty yards from the gate the man unleashed the dog, which pelted forward and threw itself at the bars, redoubling its barking, straining to get at Howard.

'Jake!' snapped the big man as he reached the gate. 'Quiet! Sit.' Obediently, the dog moved to one side and sat down. It continued growling menacingly, its eyes never leaving Howard, its muscled body trembling with suppressed energy.

The man was scowling, his jaw clenched. He held out his hand. 'Let's see some ID, mister,' he said flatly.

Howard gave him a wintry smile. His earlier jibe had had the predicted effect; the man was clearly angry, trying to control his temper. Howard pulled out his wallet and extracted his driving licence, handing it through the bars. He said nothing.

The man studied the licence briefly and pocketed it. 'Get back in your car. Pull through the gate into the lay-by, then switch off and get out.' There was a hum as the electric gate slowly slid back.

Howard followed his instructions. As he parked the car in the lay-by and got out, the gate was already closing behind him again. The dog remained where it was; the man approached.

'Turn round, sunshine. Spread your hands on the roof.'

Howard turned to comply. He felt a hard shove in his back, and his chest banged against the car. He resisted the temptation to retaliate. He was quickly searched, a pair of powerful hands running roughly down his body. Close to, the big man smelled of beer and garlic.

'OK, let's go,' said the man, stepping back. 'Walk in front of me up the drive.'

'My briefcase,' said Howard.

'What's in it?'

'Papers.'

'Get it out of the car. Put it on the bonnet, open it where I can see and then stand back.'

Howard complied; the man riffled through the contents and then snapped it shut.

'OK. Get moving. And watch yourself, or it'll be a pleasure to set the dog on you.'

Howard said nothing. He walked slowly up the gravel drive, the man and the Rottweiler following close behind. The dog's low growling continued threateningly. The man spoke briefly into his radio. 'We're coming up the drive now.'

As Howard rounded the bend in the drive the villa came into view. It was a mixture of modern and ersatz old-Spanish architecture, built, Howard guessed, of concrete block-work disguised by paint that was supposed to give an impression of the local orange-tinged stone. The colour was wrong, too vivid, and the overall effect was garish and vulgar. There were cream-painted security shutters on all the windows and doors; Howard guessed they were steel ones. Steps led up to a verandah shaded by a large blue awning, beneath which he could see a glass sliding door leading into the villa's interior. Two men in identical dark suits stood on the verandah watching; although neither was quite as large as Howard's escort, they were solidly-built and unsmiling. Both were armed with Ingram M10 9mm sub-machine-guns.

'Up the steps,' said the big man.

The barrels of the two Ingrams followed him as he mounted the steps. In the centre of the verandah was a white cast-iron table and two upright matching chairs. 'Sit down,' said the big man. 'And wait there. Jake, sit.' He disappeared inside, leaving Howard with the two armed guards and the Rottweiler.

Howard sat down and carefully reached inside his

jacket. He saw the muzzles of both sub-machine-guns twitch in warning; he smiled and pulled out his pack of cigarettes, opening it and lighting one.

'Put that out,' said one of the guards, gesturing meaningfully with his gun-barrel. 'The boss doesn't allow smoking.'

Prick, thought Howard, wondering whether to make an issue of it. He decided not to. He drew once on the cigarette, then flicked it away over the edge of the verandah, saying nothing.

Half an hour later he was still sitting there; he had heard muffled voices coming from inside the villa, a raucous laugh and the sound of a woman giggling, but otherwise nothing. He looked at his watch and sighed. He had already come to a decision about this contract. His appointment had been for twelve forty-five; it was now a quarter past one. The dog was now lying down, but its eyes were still fixed on Howard.

The big man appeared again. 'Jake,' he said. The dog rose to its feet instantly and padded over to his side. 'You,' he gestured at Howard. 'Come with me. Mr Cowgill's ready for you now.'

I doubt it, thought Howard as he stood up. He followed the big man inside; behind him came the two armed guards. Together they mounted the stairs to the first floor. The big man knocked on a door at the top of the stairs, and a muffled voice called, 'Come.'

'Wait here,' said the big man, opening the door and disappearing inside.

Sod this for a game, thought Howard. *I've had just about enough of this bullshit. I'll give him thirty seconds.*

The door opened again almost straight away and the big man jerked a meaty thumb at Howard, gesturing at him to enter. The Rottweiler followed Howard into the room, the two armed guards remaining outside. The big man shut the door and stayed next to it with the dog.

It was a large, airy room. The walls were painted a

pale yellow and covered with poster-size photographs of a tanned and fit-looking man with sandy hair, in his early fifties, and a platinum-blonde woman of about thirty-five in a variety of poses and swimwear, skimpy scraps of cloth designed to show off her large breasts and posterior to maximum effect. At the far end of the room was a large double bed. On it was lounging the man featured in the photographs. He was wearing a short green towelling robe; his sandy hair was thinning and carefully combed back. On his right wrist he wore an ostentatiously heavy gold watch. He no longer looked quite as fit as the photographs showed him, and Howard guessed they had been taken five years or more before. He was eating from a bowl of fruit beside him on the bed; he made no effort to rise.

'Nice, huh?' he said, gesturing at the photographs. 'Me and Gloria, my wife.' He paused to put two large grapes into his mouth. 'So. You're Ed Howard, yeah?'

'That's right, Mr Cowgill,' said Howard, setting his briefcase down on the floor beside him. There was a distant sound of splashing from a pool outside; Howard guessed that the woman had gone outside for a swim. 'You sent me a fax a fortnight ago asking me to come and advise you about your security arrangements.'

'Yeah, I did,' said Cowgill. 'Well, you know how it is, eh? My line of business, living abroad for this and that reason, know what I mean?' He chuckled easily, eating another grape. 'Fact is, I've been getting a bit of, shall we say, unwelcome attention recently. You know, telephone calls and so on. Had me going a bit at first, I don't mind telling you, so I asked around. Your name was mentioned.'

'Could I ask who recommended me?'

Cowgill tapped the side of his nose with a forefinger and grinned. 'Ask no questions, eh? Doesn't matter. I just heard, like.' He laughed.

Howard nodded, saying nothing.

'Fact is,' Cowgill continued, 'I got to thinking again,

later. I reasoned that maybe I'd got a bit too jumpy at the time. After all, I've got Frank and Jake here, and Ronnie and Kev outside. Frank's been with me for years, haven't you, Frank?'

'Yeah,' said the big man at the door.

'Good lad, Frank is. Kev and Ronnie, too. I pay them well. Loyalty, see? I mean, one word from me to Frank and . . .' he snapped his fingers, 'know what I mean?'

'Of course,' said Howard, keeping his voice light.

'So, I'm not sure I'm going to need you after all. Sorry for dragging you out all this way, but when all's said and done, I think my security's good enough as it is. Don't you agree?'

'No,' said Howard.

The thin knife flashed through the air. It buried itself deeply into the wooden headboard of the bed, half an inch from Cowgill's neck, pinning his towelling robe to the board. A split-second later a second knife followed it, pinning the robe similarly on the other side. Cowgill was too stunned to move, but the Rottweiler leapt forward, charging at Howard. A third knife appeared from his sleeve. Dropping to a crouch, Howard drove the blade hard into the dog's chest, slicing through its lungs and aorta. With its feet failing to grip properly on the tiled floor, it had made an easy target. It fell dead.

The big man was already hurling himself forward. Howard sidestepped him easily and brought the edge of his hand across in a crunching, steel-hard chop to the side of the big man's neck, just below his ear.

Dream on, Frank, thought Howard as the big man collapsed unconscious. Howard now moved towards the door and stood to one side of it.

'Help!' croaked Cowgill weakly. Then he recovered his voice and let out a scream. '*Help!*'

The door burst open and the two armed guards piled through. Kev was felled by a blow similar to the one inflicted on Frank, and Ronnie received a thudding short-arm jab to his windpipe. He went down, gasping for air.

With one eye on Cowgill, Howard picked up both the Ingram M10s, slinging them over his shoulder. He heaved Frank's heavy body over on to its back and pulled the big man's pistol from its shoulder holster. It was a 10mm Smith & Wesson model 1006. Checking it, he saw that a round was chambered. He retrieved his driving licence from Frank's pocket, put it back in his own and then rose to his feet, levelling the big pistol at Cowgill.

'No,' he repeated calmly. 'I don't think your security's good enough. In fact,' he continued, 'I can think of at least a dozen things wrong with it that I've noticed so far, and these gorillas here are just three of them.'

Cowgill was frozen with fear. 'D-don't!' he croaked. 'P-please don't sh-shoot . . .' he raised his hands slowly. 'I'll . . . I'll pay! Whatever you want! I'll pay! Just don't . . .'

'Shut up,' snapped Howard, his voice menacing. His eyes glittered darkly at Cowgill. 'Come over here.'

Cowgill struggled to comply, but his robe was pinned fast to the headboard by the two knives. 'I c-can't!' he whimpered.

'Get up!' Howard's voice was like a whiplash.

Cowgill had no option. He struggled out of the towelling robe and got to his feet, naked. He suddenly looked shrunken, grey and flabby. 'Please don't . . .'

'Over here.'

Cowgill advanced fearfully, his hands high. Howard scythed his legs from under him with a kick. Cowgill fell heavily to the tiled floor next to the dead Rottweiler, sprawling in a pool of its blood.

'Face down.'

Moaning in fear, Cowgill turned over and lay spread-eagled. Howard lit a cigarette and watched him for a minute, inhaling deeply. Splashing noises were still coming from the pool outside; the woman had obviously heard nothing. Bending down, he pulled the knife from the dog's body and carried it over to the bed. He pulled the two other knives from the headboard, wiping the bloody one clean on the green towelling robe, then replacing all three in the soft chamois-leather sheath strapped to his left forearm. He stood looking down at Cowgill.

'Now just you listen, you pudgy little piece of dirt,' he said contemptuously. 'As you no doubt now realise, you've made a series of very bad mistakes indeed. In the first place, I didn't much like the tone of your fax. I'm not used to being summoned to meetings – I prefer to be asked. Politely. In the second place . . .'

The injured Ronnie was wheezing and moaning, clutching at his throat and trying to sit up. 'Belt up, Ronnie,' said Howard. He kicked him on the side of his head and he fell back unconscious.

'As I was saying,' Howard continued, 'in the second place, I don't like being pushed around or kept waiting. Especially by stupid, incompetent apes like Frank, or dirt like you. Third, I don't like guns being pointed at me. And I especially don't like being threatened or attacked by dogs. Someone I know was once scarred for life by a dog just like this one. But those are minor matters, really.' He pulled on his cigarette. 'You see, my real objection to doing business with you is this. I know who you are, and I know how you made your money. I also know you hurt a large number of innocent people making it. You're worse than just bent. You're a nasty, vicious crook of the worst type. And I don't do business with crooks, especially ones like you. Do you understand?'

'Y-yes,' whimpered Cowgill.

Howard rapidly unloaded and field-stripped the two M10 sub-machine-guns. He removed the bolts and pocketed them, then threw the now-useless weapons aside. They clattered across the tiled floor and disappeared out of sight under the bed.

'This time, you live,' said Howard. 'But from now on, you're retired. If I hear you've started up in business again, I'll be paying you another visit. Just bear that in mind.' He dropped his unfinished cigarette onto the floor next to Cowgill's face, picked up his briefcase and turned to leave, pocketing Frank's pistol. 'Now, you'd better call that tart of yours back in here to help you clean up the mess. And don't worry, I'll see myself out.'

As he drove out of the gate three minutes later, Howard thought he heard a woman's voice begin to scream hysterically.

6

The door opened without warning and a man's face appeared. He beckoned urgently. 'Come quickly, Gerhardt. I think he's waking up.'

Colonel Gerhardt Eisener rose to his feet and followed. 'I am surprised to hear it, comrade General,' he said calmly. 'He is still heavily sedated, as you ordered.'

'But he's not lying still. And he's started muttering in his sleep.'

Eisener decided not to argue. His commanding officer had been specific and insistent on the question of sedation, and Eisener knew from long experience that it was counter-productive to argue with him. 'Perhaps I should fetch comrade *doktor* Linden to see,' he said.

'No. I want you to deal with it, not her.'

Eisener decided not to argue about that either, despite the fact that Anna Linden was a qualified doctor and he himself was not.

At the end of the short corridor General Erfurt pushed open a door and entered, followed by his second-in-command. It was a small single bedroom. On the bed lay an old man with two days' growth of stubble on his face, dressed only in a hospital gown.

Eisener could tell straight away that although the old man on the bed was not completely motionless, he was still a very long way from consciousness. Nevertheless, for the benefit of his commanding officer, Eisener went through the motions of checking his pulse and lifting an eyelid. It was most unlike the general, he mused, to show any signs of nerves or anxiety; Erfurt was normally a solid, determined and forceful character and Eisener had never seen him even flinch, let alone buckle, under stress. Nevertheless, ever since their arrival in England a few days previously, the general had seemed more wary and on edge than usual. To some extent, thought Eisener, he had fair reason to be so; if he had been recognised . . . But the possibility of that was so remote as to be not worth considering. For a start, Erfurt's appearance was . . . well, he looked more like a retired manual labourer than a general.

The contrast between the two men was marked. Eisener was tall and slim and in his forties, while General Erfurt was stocky, powerfully built and in excellent physical condition for a man of sixty-eight. The general kept himself in good shape with a rigorous daily programme of physical exercise. His once dark hair had long since turned iron-grey and was cropped short; only the heavy, brooding eyebrows above the deep-set dark eyes retained their original colour.

In common with those of many dark-eyed people, the general's moods and thoughts were difficult to read. There was nothing about him that made it immediately evident, to people who did not know him, who or what he was. His bodily strength was obvious; but then many men, from a wide variety of backgrounds, were physically strong. In many ways, the general relished the classless anonymity of his appearance. He was fully aware of it and had many times used it to his advantage.

Often, as a result, people had assumed him to be a man of crudely muscular attributes, a mere thug; most of them had later bitterly regretted their mistake. The general had a first-rate brain; he was a shrewd, cunning and clever manipulator of others, with a talent for organisation and a ferocious determination that had inexorably brought him success throughout his long career.

Certainly, Colonel Gerhardt Eisener had never made the mistake of underestimating his boss. He had been a protégé of the general's for over twenty-five years, and for the last ten he had been the older man's right hand. The two made an unlikely combination, Eisener knew. The general was dogmatic, formal and unbending, whereas he, Eisener, was more flexible and perhaps more calculating – though certainly no less ruthless – than his commanding officer. The difference lay in what the two men chose to keep from others. The general always concealed his thoughts and, where it suited him, his intelligence; but he never covered up his uncompromising, pugnacious nature. Eisener, on the other hand, had never tried to hide his own intellect, but he had always preserved one facet of his character from all his colleagues, including the general. All would have characterised him as the ideal second-in-command, a somewhat faceless but extremely efficient behind-the-scenes man, utterly loyal to the general. Not one of them had ever guessed – in fact they would have found it difficult to believe – that he was possessed of an intense personal ambition. Eisener knew the general better than anyone; and he knew that while the older man appreciated brains in his subordinates, personal ambition was regarded with nearly as much disfavour as dissenting views would have been. Eisener had therefore simply concealed his true nature. In many ways – initially, at any rate – it had suited him simply to attach himself to the general's rising star. Latterly, he was well aware, he had become almost indispensable.

The general had had his uses too, Eisener

acknowledged to himself. Without his influence, it would never have been possible to effect the organisation's safe transfer out of East Germany. Eisener had put the idea to him the day the Wall had come down, and Erfurt had been remarkably receptive. He had immediately seen the advantages of Eisener's idea to preserve the operational capability of the department. Eisener had presented it as a matter of ideological necessity – if the department could be kept alive and effective, with its worldwide network of agents largely untouched, it would not matter where its headquarters were actually based, as long as that base was secure and communications were reasonably good. The department would be able to continue its valuable work of undermining capitalism. Socialism, said Eisener, would live on. The general had grasped at this prospect with enthusiasm.

Eisener himself had little time for ideology. Naturally, he had been careful never to give the general – or anyone else – cause to suspect it. In truth, he thought, it hadn't really mattered too much in the old days, while the *Republik* was still intact. Then, there had been no alternative but to toe the Party line. Any desire for personal wealth, or for the freedom that people in the western democracies took for granted, would have been futile. The wealth and freedom of the West had been glimpsed by the privileged few who had travelled abroad and seen these things for themselves. Only those considered utterly reliable were ever selected for travel or postings there; most returned boiling over with indignation at the 'decadence' they had witnessed and, more often than not, spluttering loudly in their indignation about the riches and privilege they had seen – ironically, in a manner likely to encourage aspirations to these things rather than contempt for them. Eisener himself had travelled enough to have realised that those living in the West, for all their 'decadent' tendencies, enjoyed a better life than anyone did in the East.

'As you say, comrade General, he is showing signs of stirring. I think he will soon be ready for his next medication. I will go and prepare it.'

'Good. I don't want him waking up here. In fact, I want him kept fully sedated until we get him all the way back to base. You are sure it can be done?'

'I believe it should be possible, comrade General,' he replied. The only problem, he reflected privately, would lie in the general's idea of sedation – to him it meant nothing less than the patient being fully comatose, completely immobile and totally unresponsive. Eisener knew that to maintain a patient in such a condition for days on end, using drugs to do it, carried grave risks – especially for an old man such as this. The trick would be to keep him as lightly sedated as possible, allowing him to move his limbs, sit up and even appear to wake up from time to time. As with a patient apparently awake in post-op recovery the old man would have little or no memory of it later and besides, from what Eisener knew of this case, it wouldn't alter the eventual outcome even if he did.

Five minutes later, Eisener withdrew the hypodermic needle from the old man's arm, dabbed the mark with an antiseptic wipe and applied a small plaster over the spot. 'There,' he said. 'It will take another fifteen minutes or so for it to take effect.' The syringe had contained 5ml of distilled water, but the general was not to know that. The next proper dose would be administered in three hours' time, as planned.

'Fine,' said Erfurt, satisfied that things were being done in accordance with his wishes. 'Now, have all the arrangements been made for departure?'

'If you come next door, comrade General, I have all the papers there and will go over the details with you. I hope I have overlooked nothing.'

At nine-thirty that evening a blue Nissan van drove out of London, heading south-west along the M3 motorway towards Southampton. Eisener, driving, marvelled at the ease with which one was able to move around England unchecked. *The British make things so easy for themselves,* he told himself, *but so difficult for their own authorities.* The safe-house they had just left was a case in point. Where else but in a western city, he wondered, could one find accommodation with such ease and with a garage integral to the house, where one could load and unload a vehicle unobserved? It was absurd – an ideal cover for criminal activity. So easy . . .

Beside him in the passenger seat, General Erfurt was restless. 'Everything is ready on the ship, you say?' he asked for the third time.

'Everything,' confirmed Eisener patiently. 'The usual accommodation module has been loaded into the hold and fitted out as required, and you will not be disturbed. Our people in Tangier are on standby, and everything is in place awaiting your arrival. The aircraft will be there tomorrow night and will wait for you. There should be no problems with the Tangier authorities – or at least, none that a wad of US dollar bills will not solve. The flight plan and refuelling stops have been filed and cleared, and the aviation fuel already paid for.'

'I don't know why we couldn't have gone via Leningrad or perhaps Murmansk,' growled Erfurt morosely. 'In the old days . . .'

'You are right, of course, comrade General. But unfortunately things have changed. When Gorbachev threw us to the wolves, facilities were withdrawn, as you know; and his successor . . .' Eisener shrugged. 'On the whole, I am confident that this is a safer option.'

'And you are clear about what you are to do once we have sailed?'

'Yes, comrade General. The burglary is scheduled for tomorrow night. I completed the reconnaissance yesterday. Security there is very poor, and there will be no problems.'

'Good,' said Erfurt. He was silent for a minute, then he twisted round in his seat and pushed back the sliding partition hatch into the rear. 'How is he?' he called over his shoulder.

'He is sleeping soundly, comrade General,' replied a woman's voice. 'I will make sure he stays that way.'

'Fine. You'd better change into the, ah, the clothes you're going to use, comrade *doktor* Linden. We'll be there before long.'

'I already have them on under my coat,' replied the woman.

Erfurt nodded curtly and closed the hatch. He wrinkled his nose at the strong smell of perfume that had wafted through from the rear. 'Is it just the one guard she has to . . . to distract, Gerhardt? Or may there be more than one?'

'Just one,' Eisener replied. 'When he hears what she proposes for him, I very much doubt he will raise any objections. All we will need is ten or fifteen minutes, to get past the gate into the dock, drive to the ship and unload, and for me to drive back out again afterwards. Comrade *doktor* Linden will make her own way to you when she has completed her task and I have left.'

'Disgusting,' muttered Erfurt. 'A doctor, prepared to behave like that.'

Eisener's expression did not change. He had a brief vision of Anna Linden's long legs wrapped round the dock gate's night-watchman. The man would not be able to believe his luck. 'One of the earliest things you taught me, comrade General,' he said softly, 'was the need for all operatives to be compliant and versatile.'

7

'Right! Just two or three questions before we decide what we're going to do about this.' Commander Gordon Scott of the Metropolitan Police Special

Branch looked around the large table and smiled. One or two of those present groaned inwardly; the smile was not a good sign. The commander was a large, affable-looking man who was on the whole genial in his approach, but he rarely smiled while discussing serious matters. When he did, the smile usually presaged a blistering dressing-down for some unfortunate subordinate. 'I don't mind who answers these questions,' he continued, 'so if any of you have any useful information, let's have it. First: how much of this bloody paper is there, and what has been done with it?'

There were a few hesitant looks; then a chief superintendent about halfway down the table leaned forward and spoke up. 'I can only speak for my patch, sir, but I'd say we've collected about a ton and a half so far. It's all been bagged up, and at present it's occupying a couple of my custody cells until we get instructions about what to do with it.'

Opposite the chief superintendent another man was nodding. He chipped in: 'If anything we've got more – maybe two tons. But frankly, sir, I doubt whether we've got half of what there was. A lot of it was chucked into dust-carts, skips and bins. People were picking it up everywhere. Some of it was handed in, but I dare say a lot wasn't. And from what I've seen, there's plenty more still inside the buildings – it's still blowing out every time there's a gust of wind.'

Commander Scott was nodding. His second and third questions had already been answered in as much detail as he could reasonably have hoped for. 'Anyone else?'

Three more hands went up. It was evident that the litter problem was a widespread one.

'All right,' said Scott. 'Here's what I want to happen. I want all the bags centralised here at the Yard. And with every two bags,' he continued, 'I want you to send a body. I don't care whether he or she is uniformed or admin staff – it doesn't matter. If you've got fifty bags,

I want twenty-five bodies to come with them. I don't mind where you get them from – borrow them if you have to. They'll be briefed on what to do when they get here. Get them and the bags here by two o'clock, and they should be finished by close of play today. OK?' Scott looked around, the warning smile once again on his face to stifle any protest anyone might have been considering making. 'Good,' he said finally. 'Thank you all for coming.'

The senior police officers round the table rose to their feet and filed out of the room. Scott and Colonel Max Goodale remained behind. Scott turned to him. 'What do you think the chances are, Max?'

'Not good,' replied the MI5 man calmly, 'but it's worth a try. I don't suppose you —' He was interrupted by a knock on the door.

A clerk entered. 'You wanted to see Geraghty, sir. He's here.'

'Good,' said Scott. 'Send him in.'

Thirty seconds later, a distinctly apprehensive Detective Constable John Geraghty was ushered into the large room. Commander Scott gave him a swift glance of appraisal and waved him to a chair. 'Come and sit down, Geraghty.'

The detective had felt nervous when he had received the summons to New Scotland Yard, and he had experienced a feeling of sick dread when he heard who wanted to see him. Now he sat down and waited for the bawling out he fully expected to get.

Commander Scott's voice was calm and neutral in tone. 'This,' he said, 'is Mr Smith.' He paused to allow Geraghty to absorb this scant information, well aware that any elaboration would diminish its effect. He continued. 'Mr Smith and I would like to know, in your own words, exactly how you came by this document. Please do not omit any details.'

Geraghty cleared his throat and began, wondering as he did so who the hell 'Mr Smith' might be and where he fitted into this. He had mentally prepared his report in what he considered to be concise and clear language; but as he recited it he realised that he was sounding stiff and formal, like a young constable giving evidence in his first court appearance. He was soon interrupted.

'For the moment, Geraghty,' said Scott, 'we will leave aside what you did yourself when you were handed the document. What I want to establish are the exact circumstances in which your neighbour came across it. He told you it blew into his face?'

'Yes, sir,' said Geraghty, taking a deep breath. He looked up, squaring his jaw. 'I thought you might want to hear the full story, sir, so I took the liberty of bringing Mr Cusak along with me. He's waiting downstairs, if you would like to talk to him.'

'I see,' said Scott. 'Well, since he's been good enough to come along, I suppose it might be useful to have a word with him. Go and ask him to come up here, would you?'

Geraghty left the room, appearing a few minutes later with Cusak. Over the next quarter of an hour Scott gently coaxed details out of the actor, until he was satisfied he had the full story. 'Mr Cusak,' he concluded, 'you have been immensely helpful – possibly more helpful than you will ever know. I am very grateful to you. The papers you found are likely to help us with our investigations into a criminal conspiracy, and the information they contain could prove to be most valuable. I would, however,' Scott added, allowing a note of warning to creep into his voice, 'urge you for your own safety not to discuss anything you have read in that document with anyone else. At the moment, no one knows of your part in this. Please keep it that way, would you?' Then Scott turned to his colleague. 'Mr Smith, do you have any questions you would like to put to Mr Cusak?'

Colonel Max Goodale shook his head slowly, without

speaking, so Scott stood up and shook the visitor's hand. 'Thank you again for coming, Mr Cusak. DC Geraghty will show you out.' With a smile on his face he said, 'We'll see you back here in a few minutes, Geraghty!'

'I think that was useful, Max,' said Scott when the two of them were alone again. 'There's no further doubt in my mind. This is genuine – it's not a stunt.'

'I agree,' said Goodale. 'Most actors make rotten liars. It's only when they've got a script that they can convince an audience of something that isn't true.'

Scott was still nodding when Geraghty came back. The detective constable realised uncomfortably that there was now something a little different about the commander's smile, and this time he was not invited to sit down. *Oh Lord*, he thought, *here it comes*. He braced himself.

'So, Geraghty,' began Scott, 'you tried scraping some of the Tippex off with your penknife, did you?'

'Yes, sir. I was about to explain –'

Scott interrupted him, a hard edge to his voice. 'And you tore the paper, did you? And then you soaked it in lighter fluid, did you?' he continued relentlessly, not giving his victim time to answer any of the questions. 'And I don't suppose you bothered to wear gloves while you did this, did you? Nor do I suppose,' Scott continued, his voice now raised in unmistakable anger, 'that you even considered contenting yourself with just one bloody page, rather than all bloody three, did you?'

Scott, who had been pacing round the table, leaned across it and stared hard into the detective constable's face. 'Well, Geraghty?'

Standing rigidly to attention, his eyes fixed in front of him and not daring to meet the commander's, he muttered miserably, 'I'm very sorry, sir.'

'I should bloody well think you are!' snarled Scott. 'By your clumsy and amateur interference you've destroyed just about every bit of evidence there may have been on that document. You've wiped it all off with bloody petrol, for God's sake, leaving your own great big oafish fingerprints there instead.'

There was a long pause, then Scott sat down again. When he spoke, his voice had lost its hard edge. 'Yes, Geraghty,' he said. 'By your actions, you've destroyed just about every bit of evidence there might have been on those three pieces of paper. Everything, that is, except the most important bits.' He paused, reflecting. 'The paper has been identified, of course. Not that that will be any help – it's widely available. The typewriter has also been identified; but it's a cheap, popular model, so we probably won't get anywhere with that either. However, by far and away the most important thing is that we have the document itself. And I have to admit that we wouldn't have got that unless you had acted as you did. So,' Scott stood up, a friendly smile now replacing his predatory one, 'you can forget the bollocking I just gave you. Your failure to follow proper procedure this time will be overlooked. I'm going to give your boss a good report on you – a damned good report. Well done, Geraghty!'

The commander proffered his hand to the astonished detective constable. Numbed, Geraghty managed a weak smile, shook hands, muttered a hasty 'Thank you, sir,' and two minutes later was on his way downstairs, still not quite sure what had hit him. The senior Special Branch officer and the man from MI5 remained behind in the meeting room.

'There's plenty more for us to do, Max,' said Scott, 'but essentially we reckon that this is as much a job for your department as for mine. The Commissioner agrees. It shouldn't take long to go through all those sacks of paper. I sent out for some samples of the same stuff, so that everyone can see what we're looking for. It's a light airweight paper, and the three missing pages should be covered with Tippex like these ones we've got here. That will save a lot of bother . . . Anyway,' he said, changing the subject, 'let's see if we agree about what we're dealing with, shall we? Shall I start?'

'Go ahead,' said Goodale.

'OK. We're pretty certain this is a report typed by an "illegal" agent for the benefit of a foreign-based organisation. He – and our experts do think it's a man, from the handwritten footnote – researched, prepared and typed it up here. Obviously it was done in private, and equally obviously the person who wrote it did not have access to any embassy facilities – otherwise it wouldn't be sitting here in front of us. A photocopy would have gone off in some diplomatic bag, and this original would be safely stored in some embassy vault or, more likely, shredded. In fact, one wonders why this copy was kept at all. Some form of personal insurance policy by the writer, perhaps, and we'll never find the bugger now. But the point is, no embassies were damaged in the bomb-blast – there aren't any in the Bishopsgate area. This has to have been an independent effort.'

Goodale silently nodded his agreement with this conclusion.

'Before we move on to the actual content of the document,' continued Scott, 'I'll give you our thoughts on its writer and its possible intended destination. We have no case on record of an "illegal" producing an independent assessment such as this. Normally someone like that would pass information to his resident controller, and the thing would then be dealt with via embassy facilities. That way no one would be any the wiser, GCHQ etcetera permitting. That could narrow the field quite a lot, unless I'm wrong. It's a big assumption, but what we could be dealing with here is a report to an unfriendly government, or a major non-nation grouping.

'As far as governments are concerned, there are currently only four which don't have diplomatic representation here. Those four are Libya, Iraq, North Korea and Bhutan. As for non-nation groupings, the two most obvious ones are the Palestinians and the Kurds. Also, we felt we couldn't ignore those countries which do have diplomatic relations with the UK but of a somewhat strained nature. In that category we'd have to include places like Syria, Iran, Pakistan and Sudan. And of course there are plenty of other African shit-heaps – but you'd be more up-to-date on that stuff than me.'

'Indeed,' responded Goodale. 'Nigeria and Angola, to name but two.'

'Now to the question of what all this is about,' continued Scott. 'Again, we've made a few sweeping assumptions here. For the sake of brevity I'll leave out the reasoning which led us to make them. I am confident,' he smiled at Goodale, 'that you will point out any defects in our conclusions.

'First, although we only have half the document in our possession, it's clearly a well-informed, well-researched, detailed report which discusses the relative inclinations and capabilities of most of the major organisations which have at one time or another been engaged in the destabilisation of foreign governments, among other things. Broadly speaking, these organisations fall into two categories – terrorist groups and official intelligence agencies. Interestingly, the purely criminal groups who might otherwise be considered forces to be reckoned with, such as the Mafia, don't rate a mention.

'In the terrorist category the document lists most of the obvious ones, such as the IRA. In fact, it's more interesting for the groups it excludes than for those it mentions. None of the incompetents, poseurs or Walter Mitty types, such as Carlos "The Jackal", feature at all. Nor do the semi-competents – most of whom are so wrapped up in their own ideological idiocy that they'd be unlikely to consider outside commercial work.

'The official agency list is far more interesting, and equally revealing. I don't know who wrote this report, but I'd like to get my hands on him – in our view, he's hit the nail smack on the head. What he says goes along with our own thinking, most of it passed to us from our opposite numbers abroad. For example, there's mention of the Russian KGB. Why? What uninformed outsider would imagine that the KGB might contemplate commercial work? But the fact is, as you will know, that they are now actively seeking it. They've been excluded here only because in the writer's opinion they would turn down the particular job he has in mind. We think this man knows what he's talking about.

'Glossing over most of the others in the pages we've got here – and God knows what's in the other three – what the report boils down to is a clear recommendation in favour of one particular group. Again, the writer demonstrates an insider's knowledge. He recommends an organisation which every westerner thinks is now defunct. Everyone is under the impression that the former East German Secret Police, the *Stasi*, has been disbanded, its members mostly now in prison awaiting trial for treason or other offences. But it isn't true, of course. You probably know that as well as I do.'

Goodale grimaced. 'Unfortunately, you're right. It isn't true. The *Stasi* was within my area of expertise when I was serving, and when it became clear that they were involved I was called back out of retirement, because of what I know about them.'

'Do you mean to say they've been more or less ignored by MI5 since you retired?'

'It's not quite as bad as that,' said Goodale, hunching forward in his chair. 'But you're not far off the mark. You see, the problem really began in 1989, when the Berlin Wall came down. To put it in a nutshell, the Foreign Office gave too much credence to reports of the *Stasi*'s demise. One can understand how the media were led up the garden path, what with lurid stories about witch-hunts being conducted against former *Stasi* members and sympathisers, files being ransacked, prosecutions being brought and all the rest of it. But frankly the FO and ministers should have known better. It was dangerous and short-sighted nonsense.' He paused, frowning. 'Anyway,' he continued, 'MI5, and I believe SIS too, were instructed to cut back – in other words, largely to forget about – the *Stasi*. As far as our political masters were concerned, they were no longer a threat. The files are all still there, of course. But they haven't been kept fully up to date.'

Goodale sighed. 'All along, I was afraid something like this would happen,' he said quietly. 'In fact, I was almost certain it would, eventually. The most dangerous members of the *Stasi* were never caught. Their network is still largely intact; they just went underground, that's all. They reorganised themselves eventually, and now we're beginning to pay the price. They have become the most capable, best-organised, least choosy, most commercially-minded and most efficient freelance operators in the world. It was pretty well inevitable that they would, with all the assets they had at their disposal, both physical and financial. You should see the files we have on Grossman, for example, or Wenzel, or Swager – they would give you an idea of how good some of their players were. Or, perhaps more to the point, you ought to take a look at Erfurt's file,' he added, frowning darkly. 'That old bastard will be mixed up in this, one way or another. He and his sidekick, Eisener. I'm certain of it.'

Scott was studying Goodale's face keenly. The MI5 man's bright blue eyes had flashed with intensity as he mentioned the last two names. He considered asking Goodale for more details about them, but thought better of it. 'Well, Max,' he said, 'what you've just told me rather proves the point I was making. You and I know the *Stasi* is still alive and kicking, but how does the man who compiled this document know it? Out of all the organisations he mentions, he seems to have picked the most professional one of the lot.'

'He certainly does. But I'm sorry. I rather went off at a tangent back there. You were summarising the conclusions you had reached about the document itself. Please go on.'

In Scott's opinion, Goodale hadn't gone off at a tangent at all – what the MI5 man had said about the *Stasi* was highly relevant. He was silent for a moment, then he glanced back down at his notes. 'Our second conclusion,' he said, 'may seem an obvious one, but it's this. Again, it's based on an assumption and we have no evidence to support it. But our reasoning was fairly straightforward: you don't consider a shortlist of candidates like the ones in this document if the job you want done is strictly legitimate and praiseworthy – such as helping the nation's little old ladies across the road or guarding the Bank of England. Add to that the fee being talked about – five million US dollars – and we're clearly looking at a very big job. Our conclusion is that the *Stasi* has been hired to perpetrate an act of major and far-reaching importance, and that because of the clandestine way in which the document was prepared, and the nature of the candidates considered, this act will be highly illegal.

'The third conclusion follows on directly from the second. It's perhaps even more obvious – nevertheless it's an assumption which I think we must make, as it will determine what action we take. The job they've been hired to do will be fundamentally against the various national interests of all western democracies. If this is correct – and I'm sure it is – it follows that we must do our best to thwart it.

'And now our fourth and final conclusion. This one's very much a shot in the dark – in fact it's guesswork. We do, however, have some pointers. The first of these is the handwritten footnote, which our analysts have identified as being in Arabic. It's their opinion that the footnote-writer and the author of the document are the same person – some of the phrases used are the same. The footnote is an obvious later addition – it merely records that the writer has learned that the copy was received, and its conclusions accepted and acted upon. We therefore think that this man was probably reporting to an Arab government or organisation, disguising it for onward transmission, probably by fax, to look like a harmless commercial report written in English if it was intercepted. We don't know why he didn't just retype the bloody thing instead of all this messing around with Tippex, but no doubt he had his reasons – which is just as well, or it wouldn't be sitting here now.

'We've ruled out some of the obvious candidates. Libya has had the stuffing knocked out of it and is currently under immense international pressure because of its part in the Lockerbie air crash. Syria, which also had a hand in that bombing, can hardly believe its luck that the heat has been taken off it and all the blame put on Libya. Quite apart from that, Syria has plenty of reasons to behave itself nowadays. Ever since the Americans bribed that bugger Assad to join the Gulf War coalition, or at least not to oppose it, he's seen the benefits of being welcomed back into the international community. We think he's anxious to keep his hands clean, for the time being at least.

'As for the Palestinians, they'd use their own people – it's as simple as that. As you know, there are plenty of Palestinian terrorist groups. Some of them have been around for a long time and have been reasonably successful. The most obvious ones are mentioned in the document, but it's interesting that their various faults and weaknesses are listed in what most Palestinians would consider brutally insulting terms. So we don't think it can be them.

'In our view that leaves just one possibility – Iraq. The Iraqis fit the picture on a number of counts. First, their capacity to operate outside their own borders is now non-existent – all their overseas agents were rounded up and sent packing in 1990–91. They've got no one left, and the minute one of their people surfaced in the West he'd be picked up and hoofed straight back out of play. If they want any dirty work done abroad, they have no option but to hire outside help. Furthermore, they've always been good at buying knowledge and expertise of the kind this document contains. And there's plenty of dirty work they might want done. Perhaps at the top of their list would be the destabilisation of a neighbouring country, from which they could almost certainly profit. One of Iraq's neighbours is ripe for toppling, and it wouldn't take much to plunge it into chaos – maybe a political assassination or two, a few bombs scattered about, some religious sabre-rattling, that sort of thing. And I'm not talking about Kuwait. I'm talking about Saudi Arabia. It may be a wild guess on my part, but I shudder to contemplate what a few *Stasi* professionals might manage to do there. I don't think the possibility can be ignored.' Scott leaned back in his chair and folded his hands in his lap. 'Anyway, there you have it, Max. I'd be interested to hear what you and your people think.'

Goodale had been listening quietly, making occasional notes as Scott expounded his theories. Now he looked up from his notepad and spoke. 'You make a number of very interesting points, Gordon, some of which we hadn't considered. On the whole, I agree with what you say. In particular, your first three conclusions are absolutely in line with our own. Your fourth is absolutely fascinating.' The MI5 man paused for a moment. 'As I say, absolutely fascinating. Unfortunately, I'm afraid it may be based on a false assumption.'

'Oh?' Scott was surprised, but did not appear in the least offended. His expression was one of genuine interest. 'Really? Where have we gone wrong?'

'It's only a tiny detail, you understand,' said Goodale. 'Quite easily missed. But it makes a fundamental difference to the analysis. You see, we think that although this footnote was handwritten in Arabic, it wasn't written by an Arab.'

Scott had picked up a photocopy of the page in question and was studying it. 'Well, I wouldn't know,' he muttered. 'It's all scribble to me.'

'Me too,' said Goodale. 'But our language expert was quite categoric about it, once he spotted the clue. You see, the script of the writer's native tongue is very similar to Arabic. In fact, they have a common origin – there are even some common words. But there are certain distinct differences. If the writer had written in his own language, no doubt your linguist would have spotted it immediately. But it's written in Arabic, so he didn't. Luckily, our man did. The writer made two very small but distinct mistakes with a couple of accents. Actually, they aren't accents; apparently, they denote different consonants. Here, let me show you.' Goodale reached across and indicated a word on the second line of the footnote. 'You see this accent that looks like a French circumflex? In print it's shown as three small dots in a triangle. In handwriting it's common to join the dots, just as here. In Arabic they denote the consonants "th" or "sh", according to the shape of the character beneath them.

'Now there are only two Arabic script characters which have the three dots, or circumflex, above them. And this,' Goodale tapped it with his forefinger, 'isn't one of them. It's interesting – the word is almost identical in both languages, but it has a slightly different pronunciation. In Arabic it's pronounced with a "z" sound and has just one dot above it. In the writer's native tongue it's pronounced with a "zh" sound and has three – in other words, this circumflex. You can see he's used exactly the same word down here. Sheer force of habit, I suppose.' Goodale leaned back in his chair.

Scott studied the script for a few seconds. He could see what Goodale meant – the two sets of characters were the same. 'OK,' he said, intrigued. 'You've got me, Max. What language are we talking about? Kurdish or something? Or could this simply be some dialect of Arabic?'

'No,' said Goodale, shaking his head. 'Arabic is written the same everywhere, whatever the dialect.' He smiled. 'Or so I understand, anyway . . . No, we're certain about this. This word is definitely written in Farsi – which makes the man who wrote it an Iranian.'

8

Gerhardt Eisener walked quickly along the deserted streets of the industrial estate on the southern outskirts of the Berkshire town of Bracknell. He was wearing jeans, trainers and a loose-fitting black leather jacket. The streets were well-lit; bright quartz-halogen security floodlights blazed down from the corners of boxy, ugly buildings. He rounded a corner; in front of him, at the end of a cul-de-sac, was a sprawl of single-storey office buildings inside a high, chain-link fence. The main gate was closed; it was a substantial double gate with heavy hinges, and the man could see as he approached it that the hardened-steel security bolts were rammed home into their sockets in the ground.

Just inside the gate, on the right, was a small yellow fibreglass cabin. Eisener could see a security guard sitting inside, his uniform hat pushed back on his head, reading a newspaper. *Good*, he thought, and walked straight up to the gate. On the right-hand gate pillar was a bell-button on a steel box; Eisener ignored it and instead rattled the gate loudly, calling out to attract the security guard's attention.

The guard heard the noise and turned his head; he saw Eisener standing at the gate, smiling and waving at him. The guard frowned briefly, squared his cap on his head and rose from his chair. *What the hell,* he wondered, *was this bloke doing wandering around here at three in the morning? Probably pissed,* he thought sourly. He opened the door of the cabin.

'What's your problem, mate?' he called, standing in the doorway.

'Sorry to bother you,' said Eisener, 'but I can't find my car. I left it outside the Post Office depot, and all these streets look alike.'

'Oh.' The guard ambled across to the gate. 'Yeah, well, what you want to do is go back up there, turn first right, then—'

There was a soft thud as the bullet from the silenced pistol hit the guard in the throat. It missed the windpipe but severed the carotid artery on the left side and smashed into the fourth cervical vertebra. The guard jerked convulsively and collapsed; the sound of his body falling was not loud, but there was a clinking noise as a bunch of keys fell from his lifeless fingers. Bright red arterial blood sprayed from the wound, splashing down on the tarmac; Eisener stepped back to avoid being showered. He replaced the pistol in the shoulder-holster inside his leather jacket. From a breast-pocket he withdrew a small two-way radio and spoke into it briefly; within seconds he heard the low growl of an approaching car. A dark-coloured Range Rover turned the corner and slowly drew up in front of the gate. Apart from the driver there were two other men visible, both in the rear of the vehicle.

'He may have saved us some trouble,' said Eisener to the driver. 'He's got keys. We may not need the jack and cutters.'

He put on a black balaclava and a pair of thin gloves, then took a long-handled grab from the front of the vehicle and started to fish about on the ground just beyond the gate. The jaws of the grab closed round the large key-ring and he pulled it towards him, the keys clinking as they dragged along the ground. He wiped the worst of the blood off with a rag. Examining the lock on the gate, he selected an appropriate-sized key and inserted it. It turned; he levered up the bolt. When both gates were open, the driver moved the Range Rover forward inside the compound, avoiding the pool of blood. Eisener shut the gates behind them, dragged the body of the guard out of sight round the back of the cabin, then climbed into the front passenger seat. 'OK, get him up,' he said.

The two men in the rear reached down and grabbed the arms of a figure that had been lying on the floor beneath their feet. They wrenched their prisoner to his knees and one of them held a pistol to his head.

'Right, Simon,' said Eisener conversationally. 'Now it's your turn. Which way?'

Simon Henley had been taken prisoner ten hours earlier on his return from work. Two men had been waiting for him inside the flat where he lived alone. He had endured ten hours of stark terror, and had been reduced to a state where he would have done literally anything they demanded. Shaking, he began to give directions. 'T-Take that road round to the left . . . the one near the b-building,' he said. 'Look, I p-promise I won't try to trick you. I promise!'

'Shut up, Simon,' ordered Eisener quietly. 'Just give directions.'

The Range Rover drew up outside the rear door of the complex and the driver switched off the engine. Eisener climbed out; so did the other two rear-seat passengers, pulling Simon Henley with them. One of them opened the tailgate and grabbed a bulky holdall.

'Your card, Simon,' demanded Eisener. 'Then the code number.'

Henley took his security card out of his pocket, inserting it into the slot by the door. Then – hesitantly, for his hands were still trembling – he tapped in a five-figure number. There was a faint buzz from the computerised lock, and the door clicked open.

'Lead the way, Simon,' said Eisener.

Simon Henley pushed open the inner swing door, then turned left down a long corridor. It was dark inside; Eisener snapped on a pen-torch and handed it to Henley, and the others turned on their own torches. At the end of the corridor Henley turned right, stopping outside the first door on the left. 'This is the room,' he whispered, anxious to appear helpful. 'Number 137.'

'Unlock it,' said Eisener.

Henley used his security card again, this time with a different code; the door swung open and the men entered. There were small lights at desk level all round the room; a gentle humming noise could be heard.

'Blinds,' commanded Eisener.

The man with the holdall unzipped it and produced three large squares of heavy black cloth and a staple-gun. While Eisener kept his eye on Henley, the other two *Stasi* men covered the three windows in the room, stapling the cloth round the frames on top, sides and bottom. 'OK,' said the man with the staple-gun finally.

Eisener switched on the light. The fluorescent tubes flickered and then revealed a room full of computer equipment. There were cabinets, printers and monitors of all sizes on the benches and desks, and larger boxes on the floor beneath them. Eisener knew these boxes would be uninterruptible power supply units, containing banks of heavy, lead-acid batteries to guard against power failures or fluctuations. The monitors seemed dead, but the computers themselves were switched on. 'I thought you said only four of you worked in here?' he asked Henley.

'That's right, but each of the machines is for a different—'

'All right,' said Eisener, cutting him short. 'Which one is it?'

Henley led him over to one of the desks and patted

the top of a mini-tower cabinet. 'This one,' he said.

'Is it logged on to the network at the moment?' asked Eisener.

'It's always kept logged on at night, as a security measure. If anyone tries to interfere with it, the central alarm will go off.'

Eisener looked at his watch. It was twenty past three. 'Put the monitor on, enter your password and log it off. Make sure you do it right.'

'Done,' said Simon Henley a few moments later. 'No problem.' He attempted a weak smile.

'Switch it off and unplug all the cables.'

The sound of the cabinet's two internal cooling fans winding down to a stop was hardly audible. Henley began to disconnect the power supply, the monitor, the keyboard and the ethernet connector from the ports on the back of the cabinet. One of the *Stasi* men produced a blanket and wrapped the cabinet up, zipping it inside the holdall.

'OK, let's go,' said Eisener, turning towards the door.

'What do you want me to do?' asked Henley tentatively. 'I mean, in the morning?'

Idiot, thought Eisener, glancing over his shoulder at Henley. He pulled out his pistol and turned round.

There was another soft thud, and Simon Henley died before he realised what was happening. He fell back and lay sprawled untidily on the floor, staring at the ceiling, a small, neat, red hole in the centre of his forehead. His left hand twitched briefly, then he lay still.

Eisener bent down to retrieve the young programmer's security card. He straightened again. 'Nothing, Simon,' he said. 'You don't have to do anything. Just stay here for a while.'

The door clicked shut behind them as they left.

The raid on the compound was discovered seventy-five minutes later. A patrolling police car, cruising slowly through the industrial estate, drew into the cul-de-sac and approached the gate. Seeing nothing out of place the driver, Police Constable Vic Hughes, swung the car round to head back out. But his partner, PC Dave Cassell, held up his hand.

'Hang on just a mo', Vic.'

'What's up?' asked Hughes.

Cassell was frowning, looking at the yellow security cabin. 'Switch off, will you? I thought I heard something.'

Hughes killed the engine; Cassell wound his window fully down and listened. There was an insistent squawk-squawk-squawk noise, not very loud, coming from the cabin. Cassell got out and walked over to the gate, shining his powerful Maglite torch.

'What is it, Dave?' called Hughes.

'Buzzer, coming from the hut. Where's the guard?'

'Probably doing his rounds,' suggested Hughes. 'Gone to see what made the buzzer go off, I expect.'

Cassell lowered the beam of his torch and noticed a dark stain on the ground. Some of the congealing liquid had seeped under the gate. He bent down and gingerly dipped a finger into it, then shone his torch on the finger. 'Vic!' he shouted.

Cassell noticed that the gates were unlocked; careful to use just the tips of his gloved fingers to raise the bolts, he swung them open. The two policemen stepped round the large pool of blood and entered the compound.

Following the smeared trail of blood along the ground, they found the guard's body fifteen seconds later. Cassell spoke tersely into his radio, giving details of what he had discovered. The men were instructed to remain where they were, by the gate, until back-up arrived. It was 4.46 a.m.

The police sergeant who had taken the radio message quickly scanned through the register to check whether there were any special notification instructions for 5 Fairton Close. He didn't know much about the company – its anonymous name, AMS, provided no clues as to its business – but he had the feeling he had seen something about it before. He was right. When he read down the list of those to be notified in the event of an incident, he frowned. *Blimey*, he thought. This was a bad one.

'Trish,' he said pushing the list across to WPC Carey, 'start working through this lot. The list for AMS, in Fairton Close. Ring 'em all up and tell them there's been a murder and possible security breach there. I'll contact the Super and DCI Heywood. Eddie?'

'Yes, sarge?' said PC Gibbs.

'Take over the radio here. Send Hollingsworth and Tilley round there straightaway – urgent. Then blow for an ambulance.'

'Right, sarge,' said Gibbs.

Over the next forty minutes, a large number of different vehicles converged on the compound at 5 Fairton Close. Constables Hollingsworth and Tilley, on vehicle patrol on the A30 nearby, were the first to arrive, six minutes after Cassell's first radio message. Tilley stayed by the gate while Cassell, Hollingsworth and Hughes did a tour of the inner perimeter, examining the chain-link fence and checking the outside doors and windows of the complex. They found no obvious signs of illegal entry and returned to the gate, where Tilley had coned off the congealing pool of blood. They were soon joined by further police vehicles and by Detective Chief Inspector Andy Heywood, who looked tired and cross at having had his night's sleep interrupted. Cassell quickly briefed him on what had been found.

Heywood, grim-faced, began barking out orders, assigning tasks to the rapidly growing force of men. He was aware that for the time being there was not a great deal he could do. 'Where's that bloody key-holder?' he cursed in frustration, addressing his question to no one in particular.

'He's just arrived, sir,' announced a constable, propelling a pale, worried-looking man through the police cordon. 'This is Mr Bennington, sir.'

Francis Bennington, AMS's managing director, was in a state of shock. Heywood explained briefly what appeared to have happened and told him exactly what he wanted him to do. It appeared to Bennington that what was more important was what he must *not* do.

'So you don't touch anything yourself, OK?' concluded Heywood. 'Leave that to us. You just let us in and show us where everything is.' He saw Bennington nodding anxiously. 'By the way,' added Heywood, 'is there any particular reason for the room round the back being blacked out?'

'Blacked out?' echoed Bennington, nonplussed.

'Yes, sir,' said Heywood. 'Black curtains over the windows.'

'That can't be right,' said Bennington. 'All the windows have blinds, but they're white.'

'I see,' said Heywood grimly. 'Well, you'd better come and have a look at it, from the outside first. If it doesn't look right, we'll know where to start looking when we get in, won't we?'

Ten minutes later, Bennington's security card and personal over-ride code activated the lock on the door of room 137. Heywood carefully used the point of a pencil to flick on the light switch. Bennington pushed forward, his eyes staring at the body on the floor. He recognised Simon Henley. Recoiling in horror, he blundered back out of the door and was violently sick in the corridor.

'Good morning, Max,' said Gordon Scott, poking his head round the door of Goodale's office. 'Have you got a minute?'

'As much time as you want, Gordon,' said Max Goodale wryly. 'Come along in – take a seat. Things haven't exactly been buzzing with new developments recently.'

'Well,' said Scott thoughtfully, 'we may just have something now. Could be unconnected, but I don't think so.'

'Oh?' said Goodale with interest. 'Tell me more.' He leaned forward, his hands clasped together on the desk.

'I spent the whole day yesterday in Bracknell. There was an armed raid on a company there called AMS – Automated Monitoring Services. Two men were shot dead – one was a security guard, found dead at the gate, and the other was a computer programmer who worked there. His body was found in the room where he worked. We think he may have let the robbers in, probably under duress.

'There are two interesting aspects to this, apart from the fact that the job was obviously professionally planned and ruthlessly executed. The first thing is that only one item of equipment was stolen – a computer, and quite a special one. The main processor chip in the thing is apparently extremely powerful and it's not available on the open market. It's something called a Gamma chip, and the AMS people are very worried that it's been taken. The odd thing is that there was plenty of other far more punchy stuff there, some of it worth an absolute fortune. One is forced to the conclusion that this particular computer may have been stolen for the program that was loaded into it, not for its value as a piece of hardware. But I can't see what use this particular program might be to criminals or terrorists.

'The second thing we only found out later, when they did the post-mortems on the guard and the programmer. It looks as though both bullets were fired from a "*Stasi* special". Small-calibre, low-power, smooth-barrelled pistol, almost certainly silenced.'

'Were they, indeed?' muttered Goodale thoughtfully.

'Our ballistics people recognised the type straight

away. They compared the two bullets with the one that killed Sir Reginald Hislop's police protection officer. Same weight, same calibre, same metallurgical composition. With no barrel markings on them, they obviously can't tell whether it was the same actual pistol, but they are satisfied that it was the same *type*. Interesting, don't you think?'

Goodale frowned briefly, then shook his head. 'I don't think you'll find that this raid has anything to do with the abduction of Hislop. Even if the same people were involved, he won't have anything to do with this. This is something quite separate. But you mentioned a computer program,' he said, changing the subject. 'Tell me about it.'

Scott was surprised at Goodale's abrupt dismissal of any possibility of a connection between the raid and Hislop's disappearance. How could he be so sure? Did he know something no one else did? Scott cleared his throat. 'Well, Max,' he said, 'it's something known as a pattern recognition program. AMS are developing it for the Government. Apparently we'll be getting it eventually, and so will Customs. I don't really understand it, but I gather it is a refinement of the system our traffic people are now introducing on motorways. The idea is that a camera spots a car speeding, and the computer connected to it reads the number-plate automatically and flashes up a message on a big screen by the roadside telling the driver to slow down. Essentially, the computer recognises each letter on the registration plate and prints out the number. It's a fairly simple idea, but I gather that it takes a fairly complicated computer program to recognise even the simplest shapes.' Scott sighed. Francis Bennington, AMS's managing director, had bombarded him with scientific details, most of which had gone straight over his head. 'Anyway,' he continued, 'what they are working on now is a more advanced version of the program, one with greatly extended capabilities.'

Goodale cut in. 'Do you seriously expect me to believe,' he asked, 'that the *Stasi* have committed an armed robbery, during the course of which they murdered two people, just to get their hands on some device that can tell the difference between two car number-plates?'

'No, Max,' said Scott. 'Of course not. There's more to it than that. As I said, what was on this particular computer was a more advanced version of the number-plate program. Much more advanced, in fact. Mr Bennington at AMS was singing its praises – but then he would, wouldn't he? He's not worried, of course – he says back-up copies are kept centrally, so he hasn't really lost anything at all, apart from one computer that he can no doubt replace, even if it did have the latest whizz-bang chip in it. And, of course,' he added, 'one member of his staff who was working on the program . . . Anyway, this new version is a sort of proto-type. It's still at the development stage, but Bennington says trials have been encouraging and it's due to go into service some time next year. The program is called IRIS, which stands for . . .' Scott consulted his notes. 'Yes, here it is: "Image Recognition and Identification System". Apparently it can assimilate the features of different faces and compare them with mug-shots of known criminals held on a central database. Quite a useful aid to us and Customs for checking identities at airports, I suppose, but I can't see that it would be much use to anyone else.'

Max Goodale was frowning, his expression suddenly very serious indeed. 'So this thing can in effect recog-nise different people?'

'Bennington says so, yes.'

'And it works, according to him?'

'Well,' replied Scott, puzzled at Goodale's sudden concern, 'it's still in the development stages, as I told you – but yes, he says it's already worked pretty well in the trials they have done.'

For a moment, Goodale appeared almost stunned. Recovering, he looked up at Scott, his eyes icy. 'Gordon, I think we'd better get that bloody fool Bennington in here. He's got rather a lot of explaining to do. Quite apart from anything else, we'd better find out why security at those premises of his was so lamentably slack, bearing in mind what he was working on.'

Scott was now thoroughly perplexed. What on earth had suddenly bitten Max? This was a pretty strong reaction for an MI5 man to have to a crime, even one as serious as a robbery and double murder. He rose and left the room.

Two minutes later he was back. 'I've sent a car for Bennington,' he reported. 'He'll be here within the hour, even if he has to be trussed up and frog-marched in.' Scott stared curiously at Goodale, who was nodding distantly, a worried frown still on his face. 'Max?' he ventured finally. 'Would you mind telling me what you think this is all about?'

Goodale snapped out of his thoughts and waved Scott to the chair. 'I'm sorry, Gordon.' He managed a brief smile. 'Perhaps I had better explain.' He began to do so. He noticed the police commander's face turn pale with alarm as he voiced his fears. 'Do you now see what I mean, Gordon?' he said finally.

'Oh, God,' muttered Scott, horrified. 'I should have seen it. It's a bloody nightmare. Oh, my God.'

9

The girl was young, about eighteen. The man had seen her coming towards him along the street – something about her had caught his eye. About fifty yards before she reached him she started running, and he realised what it was: she was frightened of something. There was a blank, wide-eyed look on her face, and the man had seen that sort of expression before. She wasn't just frightened – she was terrified.

Suddenly the girl felt her left leg buckle under her as the high heel of her cheap shoe snapped. She saw the pavement rush up to meet her with awful inevitability – but before she hit the hard concrete, two powerful arms seized her and pulled her back to her feet. Half dazed and gulping for breath, she looked up uncomprehendingly into the man's face.

'Are you all right?' the man asked. 'What's upset you?'

The girl, still panting, said nothing, but glanced fearfully over her shoulder. Three young blacks in jeans and trainers were approaching them. As the man watched they slowed from a jog to a walk, their eyes on him.

He bent to the girl's right foot and with a quick twist snapped the heel off the second shoe. 'There,' he said. 'That will even you up a bit. You shouldn't try to run in these things, you know.' But his eyes never left the three youths who were still coming on, now only twenty yards away, sauntering confidently along the pavement. 'Listen,' the man said softly to the girl, 'do you know these three bozos? Have they been giving you any trouble?'

Her voice betrayed her fear. 'They've been following me! Let me . . .' She tried to break free of his grip and run, but could not. Staring up into his face, she saw his eyes narrow menacingly as he gazed at the three figures, coming ever nearer.

He glanced down at her briefly. 'Just go and stand in that doorway there,' he ordered quietly, indicating the locked entrance to a tobacconist's shop. 'Don't worry. I'll sort this out. But whatever you do, *don't run*! Understand?'

She nodded. For some reason she ignored all the

instincts that screamed at her to take flight again. Scuttling over to the shop doorway she shrank into the recess, making herself as small as possible.

The three youths had stopped a few feet away, and now he turned to face them. 'What do you want with the girl?' he asked evenly.

'None o' your fuckin' business, man,' answered the one on the left, rocking forward on to the balls of his feet. He was tall and athletically built, with expressionless eyes and an unmistakably aggressive posture. He spat on the pavement, then glared again. 'Get lost!'

'Yeah, fuck off, shitface,' said the one in the middle. 'She's ours.'

The third youth, shorter and stockier than the others, had been glancing around the dingy street. Satisfied that no one was watching, he reached into the back pocket of his jeans and drew a long knife. He flicked open the blade and held it threateningly in front of him. 'Get the picture, *shitface*?' he taunted, his voice full of venom. 'Take a hike – before you get cut!'

Cowering in the doorway, the girl watched in terror. The tall one on the left leered at her as he too brought out a knife and flicked it open. He raised it to his lips and kissed the blade, then held it before him. The horrified girl simply could not understand why the man who had stopped her falling was still standing there, daring to confront them. Yet he appeared entirely unmoved by their threats and started to speak, his voice only just audible.

'Three little snot-nosed babies,' he remarked contemptuously. 'Trying to pretend they're grown-ups. Can't open their mouths without using B-movie dialogue, and not even convincing in that. Pathetic. Go away, little babies – or suffer.'

The three faces clouded with fury. The tall one on the left lunged forward, the hand holding the switchblade scything through the air towards the man's stomach. The knife on the right followed, as the youth in the centre hung back slightly and shifted his weight on to his left leg, preparing to kick the man's groin with his right.

The girl had sunk to the ground in the dirty shop doorway, her eyes shut, her knees clasped to her chest and her whole body shaking. She heard an explosive grunt, followed by a strangled scream of agony which tailed off into a weak moan. There came a swift blurred noise of scuffing feet, a hard crunching sound, a horrible cough and four heavy blows in very rapid succession. There was a noise of a body collapsing to the ground. For perhaps half a second, all that was left was the low moan that had followed the scream. Then there was a further hideous noise of something very hard colliding with something soft. The moaning sound fell abruptly silent. The girl still shook with terror and her eyes were still clenched shut.

'Are you OK?' The man's voice was easy and unhurried. She jumped as she felt a hand on her shoulder. 'Hey! It's all right.' He squeezed the shoulder gently. 'It's over. There's no problem. Those idiots have been decommissioned.'

The girl opened her eyes, but for a moment she had trouble focusing on the face of the man bending over her. Then for the first time she took in the strong lines of his features, and his thick brown hair. He had an athletic build, but she noticed that he was moving somewhat awkwardly, with a slight limp. In any other circumstance she would have registered that he was good-looking, but she was beyond all such considerations and could scarcely even believe that she was still alive and unhurt.

'W-what happened?' she stammered. Her eyes took in the spectacle of the three motionless bodies on the pavement. He started walking her away, but her legs were weak and she would have collapsed but for his support. After about ten yards she glanced behind her, scarcely able to take in the events of the last minute.

Then she started to cry uncontrollably. 'Oh, God,' she sobbed, 'have you killed . . .?'

'No,' said the man simply. He volunteered nothing more for a few seconds as he helped her further away from the scene, then added, 'They'll survive, but they'll be at the menders for a while – if you see what I mean.' He paused again, then continued in a light, conversational tone. 'One has a very dislocated shoulder. I'm not a doctor, but I would be quite surprised if he ever regains full use of his right arm. Lots of torn muscles, you see? Nasty type, and he wouldn't stop moaning, so he suffered a bit of concussion, just to shut him up.'

The man smiled down at her, gauging her reaction to the details of the injuries. *Good*, he thought, seeing her return his look with a quick, nervous smile. *She's going to be OK. She doesn't mind hearing about it*. He went on: 'The second fellow has a broken right knee, concussion and a hernia. Actually,' he continued, 'I'm not one hundred per cent sure about the hernia, but when he wakes up it will certainly feel like one.' The man pulled out a packet of cigarettes. 'Want one?'

She took one gratefully, and when he lit it for her she nodded her thanks. 'OK,' she said, 'what about the third one?'

'Oh,' replied the man, smiling, 'he wasn't a problem really. He has a broken ankle, and for some reason he head-butted the pavement. Went out like a light, just like his two friends. He won't try to kick anyone again for quite a while. Now, listen,' he said, suddenly serious, 'this is important. Have you ever seen those three morons before? Do you know them, or do they know you?'

Her reply was instant and emphatic. 'No. I've never seen them before. They followed me from the underground. They were making a lot of noise on the train and for some reason they latched on to me. When I got off they followed, making foul suggestive remarks. Horrible remarks . . .' She shuddered tearfully. 'I tried to ignore them, but they turned nasty. I kept walking away faster and faster, and in the end I panicked.'

'Do you live near here?' asked the man.

'No,' she answered. 'I've been visiting a friend. I'm still four stops away from where I live.'

'Good,' said the man. 'I suggest you avoid this area for a while.'

'Don't worry,' said the girl with feeling, 'I won't be coming back to this part of London again.' She drew on the cigarette, temporarily lost in her own thoughts. Then she noticed again that the man was limping, and stopped in alarm. 'Oh!' she said, worried. 'I never thought . . . Are you hurt? Your leg . . .'

The man smiled. 'No,' he replied. 'I'm fine. That's an old injury. Over a year old, now . . . I go for a long walk most evenings to exercise it. In fact, that's what I was doing when I bumped into you.'

The girl smiled with relief. 'Look, I don't know how to thank you. You saved me from those animals – God knows what they would have done to me.' She shuddered again at the thought, her hand gripping his arm tightly. 'I really can't thank you enough.'

'No need to,' he said. 'I've come across low-life like those three before. Forget them. Now,' he said, decisively, 'I think I've had enough of a workout for this evening, and you certainly can't walk too far in those shoes. We'll grab a taxi. I'll drop you off at your place and then I must get home myself, or I'll be in even worse trouble than those three back there.'

Ten minutes later they were settled in the back of a black cab. She laid her head on his shoulder, physically and mentally drained but at last relaxing after her ordeal. She was pondering the significance of his last remark when her eyes fell to his left hand. For the first time she noticed the wedding ring on his finger, and she felt a sudden, surprisingly keen twinge of disappointment. She turned her head and gazed out of the window as they rattled their way through the streets.

It didn't seem long before they drew up outside her block. The man got out and held the door for her as the taxi waited, its engine clattering.

'Would you like to come up for coffee or something?' she asked, knowing what the answer would be.

'I don't think I'd better,' he replied, smiling. 'Look, are you sure you're going to be OK?'

'I'll be fine,' she said, looking up with what she hoped was a confident expression. 'By the way, I didn't tell you my name. I'm Lisa. Lisa James.' She shook his hand.

'Well, goodnight, Lisa. I'm sorry for what happened to you tonight. And I apologise,' he added, grinning, 'for wrecking your other shoe.'

She managed a smile. Fishing in her purse for her latch-key, she started up the steps. Then she suddenly turned and faced him again. 'What's yours?' she asked.

'Huh?' He was momentarily nonplussed; then he smiled. 'Oh, yes,' he said. 'Sorry. My name's Johnny. Johnny Bourne.'

'Thanks again for everything, Johnny,' she said.

'Take care, Lisa.' He watched her open the door; then, with a little wave, she was gone. Johnny Bourne climbed back into the taxi and, with a crunch of gears, the cab drove away.

Juliet heard the sound of the key in the door. She zapped the television remote control, killing *News at Ten*, and went through into the entrance hall to see her husband closing the door to the flat. Folding her arms, she gave him a cool, appraising glance from under arched eyebrows.

'OK, mister,' she said coldly, 'do you mind telling me just what you've been getting up to?'

Johnny Bourne turned to face her, astonished. He had not seen that expression on his wife's face for a long time. He spread his hands. 'How can you tell?' he asked simply.

'It doesn't take a genius,' she answered acidly. 'Well? Explain yourself!'

Johnny glanced down at his clothes, wondering whether one of the knives had . . . No. Not a scratch. Not even a scuffed shoe. He was so surprised by his wife's apparently uncanny perceptiveness that he couldn't think of anything to say.

Juliet Bourne's face darkened. *He is so transparent!* she thought. 'What are you checking for?' she asked angrily, her voice rising. 'Clues? Do you think I need physical evidence? You've got guilt written all over your face, you sap!'

Johnny frowned, and finally he asserted himself. 'What do you mean, *guilt*?' he fired back. 'I'm not guilty of anything!' He reflected for a moment, staring into her eyes. 'Well,' he conceded after a moment, 'I suppose I should have telephoned for an ambulance, but those idiots weren't in any terminal danger. God damn it, it was self-defence! They attacked me! And the girl . . .' His voice tailed off.

'You should have *telephoned*?' yelled Juliet, interrupting him and stabbing her finger towards him, ignoring most of what he had said. 'You want to know about the telephone? I'll tell you about the bloody telephone! I've had a call from someone neither you nor I will ever have any excuse to forget until such time as we're both in the final stages of senile dementia, and you start wittering about telephoning an ambulance?' She paused, suddenly recalling the rest of his words. 'What girl?' she yelled at him, her eyes flashing with fury.

'Don't you start yelling at me, Madam Inspector!' he retorted forcefully. 'Where the hell were your people when they were needed?' His anger rose and he advanced on her, his eyes suddenly as cold as hers. 'I told you, it was self-defence! She was in trouble – what was I supposed to do?' He was now a bare three feet from her, physically dwarfing her.

Juliet was now too furious to be fully aware of the way the angry exchange had developed. She screamed right back in her husband's face: 'Trouble? You've got a girl in trouble, and you give me some crap about not calling an *ambulance* in time? And then I get our favourite MI5 bigwig phoning with a cryptic message, saying he wants to see you urgently? Pull the other one, mister!' Her hands on her hips, she glared into his eyes.

'*What?*' Johnny Bourne's astonishment was now complete. 'Are you mad? MI5? What the hell are you talking about? How can MI5 possibly have anything to do with this? Bollocks,' he said finally, dismissing the idea.

He brushed past her and strode into the sitting room. 'Perhaps I should have reported it straight away,' he said, throwing a couple of ice cubes into a glass and adding a splash of whisky, 'but for God's sake, it only happened about half an hour ago! And what possible reason could MI5 have for homing in on something like that?' He looked at Juliet evenly, raising the glass to his mouth.

It was now Juliet's turn for anger to give way to puzzlement. 'Half an hour ago?' She frowned. 'But the message was left on the answering machine just before six this evening. That's more than four hours ago . . .' Her voice tailed off. 'Look, Johnny,' she went on, regaining her composure, 'I'm sorry. I lost my temper. But I was worried by that call. I told you I'd skin you alive if you ever got involved in anything shady again, and I meant it. Do you promise me you haven't?'

'Yes,' he said crossly, 'of course I bloody well haven't. Well . . . That is, apart from the nonsense this evening, and I told you that was self-defence. God, I'm beginning to wish I'd never clapped eyes on that girl. Do you interrogate all your suspects like this?'

She came towards him with the hint of a smile. 'I'm sorry, Johnny. We've obviously been talking at cross purposes,' she said. Then her expression turned serious again. 'But what exactly did happen tonight? I think you'd better tell me. It sounds as though it'll have to be reported. Maybe I can help.'

Johnny told her about the girl and his brief but conclusive encounter with the three would-be muggers. 'I wouldn't mind betting they were high on something,' he concluded. 'God knows what they would have done to her. Raped her, robbed her and left her for dead, I expect. I mean, what was I supposed to do? You're the policewoman – you tell me what I should have done!'

She smiled up at him. 'I'll think of something in a minute.'

'Yeah,' he said sarcastically. 'Forget your minute, Juliet. I didn't have more than a few seconds to react. No chance to think of nice, cosy solutions. And don't tell me I should have grabbed the girl and made a run for it. I can still hardly walk properly, let alone run, and those three shit-for-brains testosterone-freaks were about half my age.'

'OK, OK,' she conceded. 'But even so, it will have to be reported. I'd better do it now.'

'Oh, God,' he said. 'Can't it wait until morning?'

'No,' she said decisively. 'Otherwise my colleagues will be chasing round all night looking for whoever could have beaten up those three goons. The Met doesn't take kindly to having its time wasted on wild goose chases. But I'll see what I can do about getting them to interview you tomorrow, rather than straightaway.' She looked at her watch; it was 10.15 p.m. 'Yes,' she said finally. 'They'll have to wait, anyway. There's something more important on your schedule for tonight. I'll just give them a quick call.'

Detective Inspector Juliet Bourne of the Metropolitan Police turned and went out to the telephone in the hall. Johnny poured himself a second drink, sat down wearily on the sofa and listened with half an ear as his wife gave brief details of his recent affray. Five minutes later, she was back.

'OK,' she said. 'It's fixed. I've agreed that you'll be there at 9 a.m. sharp to make a statement. They sounded quite pleased, actually,' she added with a smile. 'I was given the firm impression that the trio you dealt with tonight have a long history of extremely anti-social behaviour. The DC I spoke to told me he reckons there'll be quite a lot of people on his patch who'll be anxious to buy you a large drink when they hear what you did – and he wants to put himself first in the queue. Off the record . . . nice work, Johnny.'

She went over to the sofa and sat down on his lap, wrapping her arms around his neck. 'Now,' she said, gazing fondly into his eyes, 'let's start tonight all over again. Our first effort was a bit of a flop.' She kissed him gently. 'Good evening, darling Johnny.'

'Good evening, darling Detective Inspector,' he responded, smiling. He pulled her to him and they kissed again, lovingly. A minute or so later, he pulled back gently. 'What was that you said about a call from MI5?' he asked her.

'I'll tell you later,' she murmured. 'Take me to bed, Johnny.'

He pulled her slowly to her feet, then picked her up and walked through to the bedroom. He stopped at the door. 'So,' he said in a low, teasing voice, 'this was what you had in mind when you said I had something more important to do tonight, was it?'

Her eyes were dark and smoky with desire, and there was an enigmatic smile on her face as she gazed up at him. 'Well . . .' she whispered mysteriously.

The door closed softly behind them.

'You know,' he said, some time later, stroking her naked back as she lay beside him, 'I'm not surprised you're a good policewoman. Talk about the hard-guy, soft-guy method of loosening up suspects. You're both, rolled into one. I've never seen such a contrast.' He kissed her gently, his hands caressing her.

'You're not much different yourself,' she replied dreamily. 'The way you glared at me out there was pretty scary . . . Johnny?'

'Yes, ma'am?'

'Johnny, do you *really* promise you're not in trouble with MI5?'

'Yes, of course I do,' he said with a slight touch of impatience. 'I told you, darling. Relax.'

'Good,' she said. 'Good.' She paused again, as if uncertain how to continue, then glanced quickly at the bedside clock. 'Johnny? You know that call I got from MI5?'

Johnny's eyes narrowed slightly. 'Well?' he asked carefully. 'What about it?'

'Well,' said Juliet, 'I returned the call. He did say it was urgent, after all.'

'So?' He looked at her curiously, trying to fathom what she was driving at. 'What did he say? Come on Juliet, what's eating you all of a sudden? Spit it out!'

'Colonel Goodale is coming to see you – here.'

Terrific, he thought impatiently. *That will save me a bus fare*. 'When?'

Juliet glanced again at the clock. Her dark eyes were suddenly dancing with mirth. 'If he's punctual, which in my experience he usually is, he'll be here in about three minutes.'

'*What!*' bellowed Johnny. Leaping out of bed as if he had been scalded, he began scrambling for his clothes. Then he stopped and turned to face her, pointing his finger in accusation. 'Juliet, are you pulling my leg . . .?'

Juliet's face finally cracked and she broke into helpless laughter. Tears of mirth poured down her face. 'No,' she managed eventually between fits of giggles, 'I'm not joking! You'd better get dressed!' There was another long peal of uncontrollable laughter as she watched her husband swearing and cursing, struggling with his jeans. He pulled on the right leg and began wrestling with the left. Then, turning sharply to give her a furious look, he lost his balance and fell heavily to the floor.

'*Ow! Fuck!*' he shouted. For a brief moment he lay still, his face squashed against the carpet, a further burst of piercing laughter from his wife ringing in his ears. The sheer, infectious sexiness of it suddenly hit him as he rolled over onto his back to pull on the left trouser leg. He peered over the end of the bed and saw her doubled up, screaming with mirth, clutching herself, her knees drawn up to her breasts. Unable to resist the sight, he leaned forward onto the bed and sank his teeth into her bare backside.

'*Yow!*' she yelled loudly, suddenly straightening, the movement knocking him back on to the floor.

Johnny got to his feet again, and for a moment there was silence as they glared at each other. Juliet rubbed her backside indignantly, while Johnny zipped up the jeans with an elaborately defiant gesture. Then both, simultaneously, burst into laughter. Johnny launched himself onto the bed and into her arms; there was an ominous twang from the bedsprings.

'Dammit, Bourne, that hurt,' she said accusingly, still rubbing her backside and at the same time kissing his neck. 'You're under arrest for biting a police officer. I'll have a mark tomorrow.'

'It didn't hurt at all,' he insisted, 'and even if it did, it served you right.' He moved his mouth downwards towards her breasts. 'And you won't have a mark. We've been through that before. You'll have me,' he murmured. 'Exclusively.'

'Not now, Johnny,' she moaned softly, feeling herself respond. 'I mean it! He'll be here any minute!'

'We've played this scene before, as I recall,' muttered Johnny, 'on our very first night. You're trying it on again, aren't you? You can't fool me again, you little minx.'

At that moment the doorbell rang.

'You see?' asked Juliet with a giggle.

'*Shit!*' yelled Johnny, leaping to his feet again. 'Dammit, Juliet, I swear I'll get even with you for this!'

Juliet rose quickly, gathering up her scattered clothes and retreating into the bathroom. I'll be a couple of minutes. Go and let the colonel in.' She smiled sweetly at his scowl and closed the door.

Muttering crossly to himself, but smiling when a further peal of laughter came from the bathroom, Johnny swiftly pulled on his shirt and buttoned it up, slipped into his shoes, ran a comb through his hair and went to answer the door.

Colonel Max Goodale politely declined Johnny Bourne's offer of tea, coffee or a drink, then relented and asked for a glass of plain water. He settled himself in an armchair, and the relaxed expression on his face gave no clue to the careful study he was making of the younger man's movements and demeanour. *Not bad*, he thought. *He's done quite well to get over that nasty wound. Touch and go, that leg . . .*

'Well, young Johnny?' Goodale asked affectionately, a hint of mischief in his bright blue eyes. 'How are you? Been behaving yourself?'

Bourne smiled. 'You bet, Colonel,' he answered. 'I'm under permanent surveillance by one of the Met's finest, aren't I?' He rolled his eyes. 'What do I mean, *one of*,' he mused. 'She's not *one of*. She's *the* finest. There's no contest.'

Hmm, thought Goodale appreciatively. *Nothing wrong there. Nothing at all.* His thoughts were interrupted as the door swung open and Juliet Bourne entered. Goodale immediately observed the fond look Johnny gave his wife – *Fond? Adoring would be more accurate.*

'I'm extremely sorry to bother you at this late hour,' Goodale began, 'and I'd like to reassure you at once – both of you,' he glanced at Juliet, 'that the circumstances are very different from those surrounding our last, ah . . . discussions. I'll be brief.'

Goodale paused, but Juliet, observing him, realised at once that this was purely for effect. Colonel Goodale, she knew well, had no need of pauses to collect his thoughts.

'I need your help.' Goodale smiled, his expression suddenly disarmingly open.

Johnny was instantly alert and leaned forward in his chair. 'How do you mean?' he asked carefully.

'I want to talk to a friend of yours.' Goodale's eyes were now fixed on Bourne's face. 'We need him,' he said simply. 'We need him badly. In fact, we need . . .' His voice tailed off deliberately.

Johnny Bourne's eyes were now bright with anticipation, and he looked poised to launch himself out of his chair. But glancing at his wife, Goodale saw no expression on her face at all – it had gone completely blank.

'No,' said Juliet in a small voice. 'No.'

'You want Ed,' said Johnny, ignoring her, his flat voice failing to conceal the fierce light of excitement suddenly in his eyes. 'You want to talk to Ed Howard. There's a job you want us to do.'

'Yes,' said Goodale.

10

'I have called this meeting, gentlemen,' said the Intelligence Co-ordinator in the tall-ceilinged room overlooking Whitehall, 'because Colonel Goodale says he has something of importance to report. It would appear that a new and potentially very grave threat to international security has emerged. Max, I am still in the dark about this, like everyone else. Perhaps you could explain to us what this threat is.'

Goodale cast his penetrating gaze around the figures seated at the long table – senior representatives of government departments, MI5, MI6, GCHQ, the police and others who needed to know. 'I will be as brief as I can, gentlemen,' he began. 'There are a number of apparently disparate and unconnected threads to the investigation I have been conducting, but I ask you nevertheless to bear with me while I go through them. By the time I have finished, I hope things will seem a little clearer. The story begins,' he said, 'on the 24th April, with the Bishopsgate bomb.'

Goodale swiftly ran through the details of the bomb-blast which had resulted in the scatter of paper all over the City of London, and the purely fortuitous discovery of the secret document. 'We were again lucky,' he continued, 'when a fourth page of this document was unearthed – due entirely, if I may say so, to the extremely prompt and efficient action of the Metropolitan Police.' Goodale nodded courteously at the Commissioner, who smiled back at him. 'Police officers searched through many tons of recovered paper and found this extra page. But due to the passage of time I am afraid we must assume that the remaining two pages have been lost or destroyed, and that there is little chance that we will get our hands on them.'

He explained to the gathering what MI5 and Special Branch had already discovered: that the document was a thoroughly professional assessment of organisations around the world whose services would now, in the 1990s, be available for hire for terrorist purposes. When he revealed who had been awarded the 'contract' he saw, as he had expected, expressions of surprise on some of the faces around the table.

'Yes,' he continued, 'the *Stasi* – perhaps the most dangerous of all these set-ups – still exists. In fact, it is very much alive and kicking.' Goodale paused, nodding for emphasis. 'But to return for a moment to the report. We are now satisfied that the writer is of Iranian nationality. We also know that the report was commissioned, and received and acted upon by the government of Iran.'

'Forgive me, Max,' interrupted the Intelligence Coordinator, 'but I think it would be helpful if you were to explain how you know that the Iranian government has actually received this report.'

'Of course,' said Goodale. 'The fact is, we had a stroke of luck. You see, the writer compiled his report in rather stilted and official English – perhaps due to training he had received at some stage. We think that when the time came for him to send it to his masters he had second thoughts about transmitting it in clear, uncoded form, despite the fact that it was written in English. He also, apparently, decided not to deliver it via his embassy. What he did was amend it. Curiously, though, he didn't retype the whole thing; instead, he changed it by first using correcting fluid, then overtyping various names and other details with apparently harmless code-words. Luckily for us, he made a mistake. Each of the original pages had been headed "MOST SECRET". He blotted this heading out on pages one, three and six, but for some reason failed to do so on page five.' Goodale paused and turned to a mild-looking man sitting on his left. 'George, perhaps you could explain how this mistake led to the report's destination being confirmed.'

George Seagrave nodded. 'Delighted to,' he said. He sat forward and launched into his explanation. 'Part of our brief at GCHQ is to monitor a large number of transmissions, of one sort or another, every day. Thousands and thousands of them, in fact. The point is, we obviously don't have enough people to sit around all day with headphones on, listening to absolutely everything that is said. Instead, we have specialised equipment which is programmed to listen out for key words, names or phrases. When one of these words or phrases is detected it triggers a response, and the conversation – or whatever other sort of transmission it may be – is then automatically recorded for later analysis. For example, the word "terrorist" or the name "Ahmed Jibril" might trigger the response. In this case it was the phrase "most secret" that did it. I am not saying that the detection of this particular phrase would always set things going. In fact, by itself, it would not usually do so. In this case, however, there was one other contributory factor – the telephone number involved.'

'What?' asked the Intelligence Co-ordinator. 'Do you mean the report was actually read out over the telephone?'

'No,' answered Seagrave. 'It was a fax transmission.'

'What was the fax number it was sent to?' asked the Intelligence Co-ordinator.

'It was that of the Ministry of Foreign Affairs,' said Seagrave, 'in Teheran.'

'I see,' said the Intelligence Co-ordinator. 'Thank you, George – that was most helpful. Max, perhaps you would continue.'

'At this stage,' said Goodale, resuming his briefing, 'I think it might be useful if I said something about the attitude of the Iranian government to its mounting of offensive operations overseas. Put simply, the Iranians are not squeamish about such matters. Usually they organise things themselves, using their embassy in the country concerned to cover the movement of agents and provide them with shelter and whatever equipment they need. The operations usually fall into the category of retributive action – to be precise, murder – of those individuals perceived to be enemies of Islam. Iranian terrorists have enjoyed a fair degree of success in the past, even with more complicated and risky ventures than the simple murder of individuals, but there's no shortage of evidence that they are not the world's most competent or subtle operators.

'Why, then, would the Iranian government go to all the trouble of commissioning an assessment of outside organisations, eventually selecting the *Stasi* and then hiring them to perform some task for them? It has to be because they don't feel their own operators can handle it. They are well aware of the limited skills and experience of their own people, and they are not at all averse to acquiring outside assistance when they realise that they need it.

'One is therefore forced to the conclusion that what is being planned is something likely to have major international repercussions. We do not yet know what this act might be, but I think we may safely assume one thing: that it will be fundamentally damaging to western interests.' Goodale studied his audience; there were nods of agreement all round. He continued. 'I would now,' he said, 'like to turn briefly to the case of Sir Reginald Hislop.

'I allude to Hislop's case here,' he began, 'only in order to demonstrate the sort of problems we face. I must emphasise that Hislop's abduction has no bearing on this matter at all, apart from the fact that we are almost certain that this abduction was carried out by *Stasi* personnel. We have evidence for this. At first the only real evidence we had was that of the bullet which killed the protection officer assigned by the police to guard Hislop. It is of a type we have seen before and which we know has frequently been used in the past by the *Stasi* for assassinations. Since Hislop's disappearance, there has been no trace of him; no ransom demands have been received, and no hard evidence of his whereabouts has emerged. He has simply vanished. The evidence of the bullet, by itself, is not a conclusive indication of *Stasi* involvement; weapons of the type used have on rare occasions surfaced in different circumstances. There is, however, one other pointer.

'I spent some time interviewing the principal witness to the abduction, a Mr Wiggins. Wiggins was scared, but he was anxious to be helpful. Ultimately, without realising it, he was. He mentioned that he had heard one of Hislop's abductors saying something to Hislop while manhandling him into the vehicle. I pressed him to remember what he had heard, and he eventually recalled that he had heard the word "come" – as in "come here". I asked him whether he had in fact heard the abductor say "come with me", or "come on", which would of course have been more idiomatic. Surprisingly, Wiggins was emphatic on this point – he had only heard the single word "come". There had however been something peculiar about the way the abductor had pronounced it. I then asked Wiggins if it had sounded more like "komm" than "come". He immediately confirmed that that was exactly what it had sounded like. The word "komm" is commonly used by itself in German to mean "come on".

'As I say,' continued Goodale, 'I offer this merely as an illustration of the diverse capabilities of the *Stasi* organisation. Because they are involved, a parallel investigation is being run by my department; but I am satisfied that the Hislop case has nothing to do with the Iranian connection.'

'Just a minute, Max,' interrupted the Intelligence Co-ordinator. 'Could you please explain how you can be sure of that? Could Hislop's abduction not be the very thing the Iranian government hired the *Stasi* to do?'

Goodale frowned briefly as he considered his reply. He glanced at George Seagrave on his left. 'No, it could not,' he said. 'The explanation is quite simple. The document recommending the services of the *Stasi* to the Iranians was found after the Bishopsgate bomb, which occurred on the same day that Hislop was abducted. We know that the document had been transmitted by fax to Teheran that Friday – just one day before the bomb and the abduction. It is therefore not possible that Teheran could have received and approved it in time to pass it on to the *Stasi* and give them sufficient time to set up Hislop's abduction. It therefore follows that kidnapping Hislop was not what the Iranians had in mind. They were planning something else. But of course George can confirm all this quite simply' – he glanced again to the GCHQ director on his left – 'from the records of the fax transmission date.' Goodale was looking meaningfully at George Seagrave on his left, and for the briefest of moments the two men's eyes met. There was a thoughtful look on Seagrave's face.

Opposite them, the Commissioner of the Metropolitan Police was the only one to spot the silent exchange between the two men. The most senior policeman in the country, he had not risen to the top of his profession by failing to observe even the smallest details of people's behaviour. He knew both George Seagrave and Max Goodale well. *Something interesting there*, he thought, looking at them keenly. *George is curious about something, maybe even a bit puzzled, while Max is confident, perhaps trying to reassure him. Very interesting . . .*

'Please continue, Max,' said the Intelligence Co-ordinator.

'Thank you,' said Goodale. 'If I may, I will now move on to the raid carried out two days ago on the AMS premises in Bracknell.' He gave a detailed account of the circumstances of the raid, and the almost total lack of evidence that had so far been uncovered. The members of the Joint Intelligence Committee appeared puzzled at first about the significance of the theft of the single computer, but as they listened to Goodale's analysis of the importance of the IRIS pattern-recognition program they immediately grasped his meaning and their expressions turned very grave indeed.

'I think, gentlemen,' said Goodale, eyeing the faces round the table, 'you now appreciate the seriousness of this matter. I think you will also probably agree that we must do everything in our power to recover the IRIS program before it can be put to ill use. We must track down the *Stasi* team responsible and put a stop to whatever they are planning to do. In the circumstances, the Special Air Service would be the obvious people to undertake this task. They have the necessary skills and capabilities. Unfortunately, however, in view of where the *Stasi* group responsible is located, and the extreme risks involved, I very much doubt that official authorisation would be given for the SAS to be tasked to do it. Instead, I —'

'Just a minute, Max,' the Intelligence Co-ordinator broke in. 'You're way ahead of me there. Why couldn't the SAS be used? Also,' he added, 'how on earth do you know where this *Stasi* base is? Where exactly is it?'

'We know where it is,' said Goodale, 'thanks again to George and his people at GCHQ. There was a recent transmission on a fairly open radio-telephone link, and it was intercepted. Perhaps George would like to explain how this was done.'

'As Max says,' Seagrave began, 'the transmission was intercepted. As I explained a few minutes ago, in the case of a fax transmission we are usually alerted by a combination of things: in this case the content of the transmission – in other words, what was said – and its geographical origin. This was a one-way conversation in German, giving a set of instructions, and we were initially alerted because of direct references to AMS and IRIS. We could not establish who the speaker was talking to as there was apparently no acknowledgement.

'At this point,' continued Seagrave, warming to his explanation, 'I should pay tribute to our opposite numbers in the USA, the National Security Agency. There's close co-operation between us. In this case they were able to provide us with a high-quality recording of the conversation, obtained from one of their satellite-borne COMINT monitoring facilities. With the NSA's help we were able to run a voice-match to identify the person transmitting the message. The voice was that of a man named Gerhardt Eisener. He was, until the collapse of the East German regime, a high-ranking officer in the *Stasi* – a colonel, I believe.

'The voice-match was of course not the only useful information to be gleaned. Again with the NSA's assistance, we were able to establish by triangulation methods the exact source of the transmission to within one hundred metres.' Seagrave referred to his notes. 'The transmitter was located at longitude 125 degrees, 57 minutes and 27 seconds east, latitude 39 degrees, 49 minutes and 12 seconds north.'

'Where exactly is that?' asked the Intelligence Co-ordinator.

It was Goodale who answered. 'It's about one kilometre north-east of a very heavily guarded nuclear facility in the heart of one of the most unpleasant and repressive regimes in the world. The place is called Yŏngbyŏn. For those of you who haven't yet heard of it,' he added, 'Yŏngbyŏn is in North Korea.'

'Hmm,' said the Intelligence Co-ordinator, muttering to himself. 'I see what you mean – that does make things rather difficult. I agree that the use of the SAS would probably be ruled out. Nightmare of a place, North Korea. Far too dangerous.'

I doubt the SAS themselves would take such a diffident and timid view, thought Goodale. But he knew that the Intelligence Co-ordinator was right in one sense: the government would never countenance it. 'Of course they wouldn't,' he said.

'What was that, Max?' asked the Intelligence Co-ordinator, surprised.

'My apologies,' said Goodale hurriedly. 'I was just thinking aloud. I'm of the same mind as you – the government would never agree to SAS involvement. Fortunately,' he continued, 'there's an alternative group that might be prepared to undertake such a mission. They're unconventional, but I happen to know they're very effective. They accomplished a quite remarkable feat in the Middle East in 1992. And they have the added advantage, of being, shall we say . . . freelance.' Goodale sat back in his chair, a bland and unreadable expression on his face.

'You mean *mercenaries*?' asked the astonished Intelligence Co-ordinator, his voice dripping with disdain.

'Not exactly,' replied Goodale evenly. 'Far from it, in many ways. But does it matter? They'd have as good a chance of success as anyone. They'd need some unofficial assistance, of course, but it need never be publicly acknowledged even if they fail. You see,' he added, leaning forward and looking straight into the Intelligence Co-ordinator's eyes, 'they would be *deniable*. Need I say more?'

The word 'deniable' had an instant effect on the Intelligence Co-ordinator – it was a word that he hugely appreciated. If anything went wrong, neither he nor the Joint Intelligence Committee would be held to account, because this group would be acting unofficially. If things went right, on the other hand, he and his committee would be able to claim all the credit for it. 'May I have your personal assurance on the matter of deniability, Max?' he asked, his voice silky.

Goodale raised his eyes and met the Intelligence Co-ordinator's satisfied gaze. 'Yes, you may,' he said softly. His blue eyes bored brightly into those of the Intelligence Co-ordinator. 'If my personal assurance is what you want, you may have it.'

The Intelligence Co-ordinator was briefly unsettled by Goodale's penetrating stare. The man had always had a disconcerting way of looking at people, he thought – it could be unnerving sometimes. Never mind, he decided, dismissing the thought. He had received the assurance he wanted.

'Well, gentlemen,' he announced to the room at large, 'I think that settles the matter. On your behalf, if I may, I would like to thank Max for his thorough and exhaustive report, alarming though its findings may be. I think we can now agree to leave the matter in his capable hands. Unless there are any dissenting views .. .?' The Intelligence Co-ordinator's smiling face swept round the table, conveying the unmistakable message that dissenting views would be highly unwelcome. 'Excellent,' he said smoothly. 'Thank you all for coming, gentlemen.'

The members of the Joint Intelligence Committee began to pack up their papers and leave. George Seagrave, the GCHQ director, was more thoughtful than most as he rose and headed for the door. Outside in the corridor, the Commissioner of the Metropolitan Police caught up with him and fell in at his side.

'A bad business, George,' said the Commissioner.

'Huh? Oh, yes,' replied Seagrave. 'Yes. Very bad.'

'Still, you and Max have done very well to bring it to light,' persisted the Commissioner.

'We've had some luck,' said the GCHQ director absently.

The Commissioner did not reply. Together the two men descended the stairs in silence. In the car park outside, he turned to Seagrave again. 'George?'

'Yes?'

'I hope you don't mind my saying so, but something seems to be bothering you. Is anything wrong?'

'No, no,' said Seagrave defensively, forcing a smile. 'Not at all. Well,' he said, after a pause, 'I suppose it's this *Stasi* thing. It is very worrying.'

The Commissioner studied Seagrave's face intently. 'Yes, of course. Well, keep up the good work. I'll see you again next week, I expect.'

'Yes,' replied Seagrave. He smiled weakly. 'Good day, Commissioner.' Seagrave turned on his heel and headed for his car, deep in thought.

The Commissioner of the Metropolitan Police was rubbing his chin thoughtfully as he watched Seagrave walk away. He was now sure he had been right. Seagrave had been seriously rattled by something Max Goodale had said or done. He wondered what it was. He resolved to make it his business to find out.

Seagrave reached his car, unlocked it and got in, closing the door. He sat immobile for a minute or so, baffled. *What the hell is Max up to?* he wondered. *Why did he say the fax was sent to Iran just one day before the Bishopsgate bomb? He knows perfectly well it was sent in early March, seven weeks before that – I told him the date. That means Sir Reginald Hislop could well have been kidnapped in connection with this Iranian business. Why is Max so keen to make out that there is no connection?* Seagrave shook his head. He wondered whether he should have spoken up at the meeting; but he had known Max Goodale for a long time, and had never had any reason to doubt his judgement. *Up to now, anyway*, he thought grimly. He decided to tackle Goodale about it, the next time they met. He started his car engine, engaged gear and drove away, heading out of the security gates and on to the main road.

The drive back to Cheltenham took Seagrave just over two hours. One question recurred in his mind over and over again during the journey, but he could not for the life of him think what the answer was.

Why did you lie to the Committee, Max? he kept asking himself. *Why?*

11

'Oh, come *on*, Ed. The least you could do is agree to meet him. I can't see what possible harm it could do.'

'Johnny, if you think I'm having anything to do with

that devious bastard, you can think again.'

Johnny Bourne sighed. He had anticipated Ed Howard's strong reaction to the suggestion of meeting Colonel Goodale. Howard was not a man to forgive and forget. He was a complex, solitary man who rarely showed his feelings but bore grudges as deep as his character. The year's self-imposed exile in Italy had not improved things, by the sound of it. Bourne had been careful to avoid the subject before, but he could tell he had struck a nerve. Even on the end of the telephone he could clearly feel Howard's cold anger coming through. He knew Howard resented the way he had been treated the previous year, but in his opinion enough was enough. Ed had no claim to a monopoly on the right to feel let down – it had been much the same for the rest of the team, Bourne himself included. If they could get over it, why couldn't Ed? His thoughts strayed back to that time.

Howard and he had assembled a team of ex-Special Forces men, whose experience included the Vietnam, Oman, Falklands and Gulf Wars, and in April 1992 Howard had masterminded their clandestine infiltration across the Saudi Arabian border into Iraq; his team's mission was to assassinate President Saddam Hussein. He had been acting on behalf of a private client who he had every reason to believe represented the British government. Bourne and the others had believed it too.

On April 28th that year at Saddam's birthplace, Tikrit, three shots were fired from a long-range sniper's rifle. Three men fell dead; one was believed to have been Saddam himself. In the ensuing turmoil the assassination team managed to escape, but two of their number were killed. Bourne had survived, although badly wounded. Others who made it to safety included Tony Ackford, Mel Harris, Mike Ziegler and Howard himself. A former major in the Special Boat Service, Howard had already begun to suspect that he had been deceived – the British government had not been behind the plan at all and were in fact actively working to thwart it. Only quick thinking and clever last-minute improvisation on Howard's part had ensured that they had made it safely out of the hornet's nest they had stirred up. The rest of his team had returned to England and the USA and resumed their previous existences, but Howard had been forced to adopt a low profile and had gone to live in Italy, from where he continued to keep an eye on his company, XF Securities, a firm of highly trained and skilled security consultants. Bourne ran the London office in his absence, but they had almost daily conversations on the telephone – usually early in the morning, as now.

Howard's one foray into the murky world of mercenary soldiering had backfired on him badly, and Bourne could understand how it still rankled with him. No doubt it was partly hurt pride at having been duped, but Bourne guessed there was more to it than just that. Whatever it was, he thought, it was time to put an end to it.

'Damn it, Ed,' he snapped, exasperated. 'Don't be so bloody obstinate. He just wants to *talk* to you, for Christ's sake. What the hell are you going to do? Sit on your arse in Italy for the rest of your life, brooding about the past? It's about bloody time you rejoined the human race.'

Bourne knew he was one of only two people who could talk to Howard in such a way; the other was Mike Ziegler. The three men had a deep respect for each other, and Bourne knew that Howard listened to their opinions. He felt he now owed it to his friend to point out that he felt he was making a mistake.

At the other end of the line Howard was silent for a minute. Johnny was on the point of losing his famous temper again, he thought wryly. But perhaps the younger man had a point. It did no good to dwell too much on the past . . . Yet it was one thing to say that and quite another to accept it fully and forget all about it. After what had happened, Goodale was the last man he wanted to have anything to do with.

'What does he want to see me about?' he asked Bourne.

'He wouldn't say. And even if he had, I don't think it would be a very good idea to tell you over the telephone, do you?'

'I suppose not,' Howard conceded.

At the other end of the line Bourne heard the familiar snap of Howard's steel cigarette-lighter and the sound of the older man inhaling. 'Look, Ed,' he said reasonably, 'the man must be in quite a hole. Why otherwise would he be coming to us? He must have some specific task in mind, and I doubt it's rattling collection boxes for the Red Cross. Look at it this way – we'd be doing him a favour. And by him, that also means you-know-who. Genuinely, this time.'

Howard knew who Bourne meant – the British Government. That cut no ice at all with him. He didn't owe the government any favours. Nevertheless, he could see there might be advantages in rehabilitating himself. *Him*self? Something had suddenly occurred to him. 'Johnny, you mentioned "we" and "us". Who exactly do you mean?'

'Hell, Ed, I don't know,' said Bourne. 'I assume it means all of us. Or some of us, at any rate. I'm just guessing, but if it's the sort of thing I'm thinking, it has to be a four-man job at least.'

'In that case, that probably means Mike, Tony and Mel too,' said Howard. 'I'd like to talk to them about it before I agree to any meeting.'

'They'll trust your judgement, just the same as I do. In any case, we don't even know yet what the proposition is.'

'I dare say,' said Howard. 'But I'd like to discuss the principle of it with them beforehand, and it's no good doing that over the phone. Can you round them up and the four of you get out here tomorrow? It'll have to be tomorrow. After that I'm due to be away for a few days.'

'Ed, I absolutely can't manage tomorrow,' said Bourne truthfully. 'I'm completely tied up here. And you know as well as I do that Mike couldn't get over from the USA that quickly. No chance. If he was in New York, maybe; but he's in LA, for heaven's sake.'

'How about Tony and Mel?' Howard decided not to voice his thoughts about Bourne's own participation in any active operation – it would be an extremely sore point. Despite his leg-wound having healed reasonably well, Johnny wasn't fit enough yet for hard activity – if that was what would be entailed.

'Tony and Mel? I don't know exactly what their schedules are,' Bourne was replying. 'I'll check.'

'Tomorrow's Saturday. They should be clear. Even if they aren't, get them to drop whatever else it is they're doing. I'll meet them here at the airport. Ring me with the flight number when you know it.'

'OK,' sighed Bourne. 'I'd better call them now.'

'Fine. I'll speak to you again later.'

The telephone went dead. Bourne sighed once more. It had been hard going, but at least he had made some progress. Ed was no longer giving a flat 'no' to the idea. He looked at his watch. It was still only seven in the morning. He should be able to catch Mel Harris and Tony Ackford at home.

Mel Harris replaced the telephone and frowned, torn between two conflicting commitments. His conversation with Johnny Bourne had been intriguing, and it seemed that he hadn't been left with much option. Tomorrow, Saturday, he had to be on that flight with big Tony, to go and see the boss. The problem was . . . He walked quickly through to the kitchen, where his wife and nine-year-old son were finishing breakfast.

The boy looked up at him, his eyes bright and alert. He noticed his father's troubled expression and his smile faded. 'Everything OK, Dad?' he asked, a note of anxiety in his voice.

Harris's heart sank at what he was about to do. 'Look, Ben,' he said slowly, 'it's about tomorrow. I'm afraid . . .'

'Aw, Dad!' The boy's face crumpled in disappointment. 'You promised!'

'I know, Ben, I know,' said Harris. He hated having to let his son down. 'It's just that . . .' His voice tailed off. Explanations were useless at times like this, he knew. *Dammit*, he thought angrily. Then his face cleared as he made a quick decision. 'Tell you what,' he said suddenly, 'I've got an idea! I can't take you tomorrow, so we'll go today instead!'

The boy's eyes widened in surprise, his face suddenly shining with excitement. 'You mean . . .?'

'Yeah! The hell with school!' Harris began pacing restlessly around the kitchen, speaking rapidly. 'Go and change out of your uniform, get your cricket gear and we'll leave right away. We won't see that one-day match against Leicestershire, but in a way this'll be even better. I'll make a couple of phone calls and fix it up so that you can get some practice in the nets, meet all the players and pick up a few tips from them. There's a couple of the lads still there who were with me in the county team. They'll fix it. Your mum can call the school and tell them you're ill or something. I'd better call the office, too – we'll both go AWOL for the day. How's that?'

'*GREAT*, Dad!' yelped Ben, leaping excitedly from his chair. He pelted out of the room and away up the stairs. Thumping and banging noises came from above as the boy raced about, tearing off his school clothes and gathering up his cricket gear.

Janet Harris remained seated, shaking her head slowly, a wry smile on her face. 'You're a terrible influence, Mel,' she said slowly. 'You really can't make a habit of this sort of thing, you know. Whatever will he grow up to think?'

'I know, love, I know,' he said softly. 'But what could I do? I *did* promise him, after all.' He put his hands affectionately on her shoulders.

She gazed up at him. 'Then you shouldn't have made the promise in the first place. Don't promise him things until you know for certain you can deliver them. Spring the occasional surprise on him instead – like you did just now.'

'Yeah,' he said thoughtfully. 'You're right. I'm sorry.'

Janet stood and put her arms round him. She was a strikingly pretty, slim blonde in her thirties, at five feet nine inches nearly as tall as her husband. 'Don't be sorry,' she said softly. 'And I didn't mean what I said – about you being a terrible influence. You're a wonderful influence on him. He worships you, you know.'

'That's just his age,' said Harris. 'He'll grow out of it soon enough.'

'No, he won't,' she replied. 'Any more than I will. I love you, Mel.'

'I love you too,' he said. He meant it. He adored his wife and son; they meant everything to him. He held her close for a minute or so, kissing her tenderly. Then, restless as ever, he broke away and began pacing again. 'What sort of a school is that, anyway? They don't even teach the boys cricket. I ask you! You know, Janet,' he said, suddenly changing the subject, 'I think we made a mistake. I don't like living in London. Nor does Ben. He hasn't said so, but I can tell. Do you like it here? I bet you don't, really.' He was talking rapid-fire, not waiting for answers. 'I miss the countryside. We only moved here to make my journey to the XF office easier. It was a mistake. Let's sell up and go back to Worcestershire!'

'Whoa, there!' she said, holding up a restraining hand. 'Not so fast! We need to think these things through properly. We haven't even been here six months, and the only reason we came here at all was because of one of those sudden whims of yours. If we're going to move again, I want to be sure it's for good.'

'You mean you agree? Good! Good!' Harris's eyes were bright with enthusiasm. 'Excellent! Tell you what. While Ben and I are away today, you ring round the estate agents and see what they've got. Somewhere nice, not too far from Worcester itself. A good-sized cottage, big garden with enough space for some cricket practice – you know the sort of thing. We can afford it. Then you can get the local agents round here and put this place on the market.' Glancing at his wife, he saw her standing with her arms folded, one eyebrow raised satirically. Her right foot was tapping on the floor. 'Er . . . unless you'd like to come with us today instead,' he added lamely.

'You know, Mel,' she said eventually, 'you're absolutely *impossible*. Sometimes you're just like a nine-year-old yourself. You never stop, do you? You're always rushing about, flat out. I've spent practically the whole of the last fifteen years out of breath, just trying to keep up with you. I thought things would quieten down a bit when you left the SAS, but if anything you've been even more on the go since then. No – you and Ben go off together and enjoy yourselves playing cricket. It looks like I have some work to do. You've just given me enough to last a month or more.'

There was a clattering noise on the stairs as Ben descended at full speed, carrying a bulky holdall. 'Ben!' shouted his mother in exasperation. 'How many times have I told you not to run on the stairs! You'll fall down and break your . . .'

'Sorry, Mum! Ready, Dad? Let's go! 'Bye, Mum!'

God give me strength, thought Janet fondly, shaking her head as the front door slammed shut a few seconds later, leaving her alone in the house. *He's just the same as his father.*

* * *

'So, how are things, Mel?' asked Tony Ackford as they drove out to the airport the following morning. 'Haven't seen you for a while. Family OK?'

'Couldn't be better,' said Harris happily. 'Janet's fine, and young Ben is shaping up really well. I took him out for some cricket practice yesterday, and he's showing a lot of promise. Good eye for a ball, and very quick. I'd love to see him play for his county one day. How about you, T? How's Kath?'

'Oh, she's fine,' rumbled Ackford, his deep, growling voice sounding slightly non-committal. 'She gave me a bit of stick about today, though. We were supposed to go and visit my bleeding in-laws. I had to get the boss to talk to her and tell her that this outing was on the level. He got a bit of an earful, too.' He scowled morosely. 'Me, I was glad to get away. I can't stand my in-laws,' he added.

Harris smiled. He had known Ackford for a long time, and it never ceased to amaze him that the big man was so completely dominated by his tiny wife. Kathleen Ackford was Irish, barely five feet tall; she was a sparky, quick-witted woman who never failed to liven up an evening out with the ladies, but many had commented on the apparent incongruity of her and her husband as a couple. 'Little and Large,' someone had once dubbed them, amused at the sight of the huge, weatherbeaten Ackford with such a tiny, fragile-looking woman at his side. To their amazement, however, Ackford's Royal Marine colleagues had soon discovered that Kath also had a volcanic temper when roused. Ackford's physical power was awesome and he had for many years been the Marine's heavyweight boxing champion, with a pair of fists that could fell an ox; but one night, when he had stayed out late drinking with some mates, Kath had turned up spitting fire. The other marines had watched dumbstruck as she laid into her husband with a stream of invective in a way none of them would ever have dreamed of doing. Ackford had not only stood there and taken it, but had hung his head and apologised abjectly to her. This had only seemed to goad her further. Finally, to everyone's utter astonishment, she had swung her handbag at his head so hard that the big man had been knocked off his feet and sent sprawling, stunned, to the floor. 'Right, you sorry lot!' she had yelled at the others, 'bring the big dozy ape out to the car! And be quick about it!' With that she turned and marched out. In dead silence, the other marines obeyed, dragging the semi-conscious Ackford outside.

'Fuckin' 'ell,' breathed one marine back in the bar five minutes later. 'And there was I thinking that poor old T had got that beat-up face in the boxing ring.' The bar had erupted in laughter.

Kath Ackford had from then on been treated with a very healthy respect, bordering on awe, by her husband's friends; but at the same time they had been careful not to repeat the story in Ackford's earshot or to snigger too loudly when recalling it.

Mel Harris was one of the few people who could get away with ribbing him. 'Still carrying that half-brick around in her handbag is she, T?' he asked lightly, his eyes bright with mirth.

'Fuck off, you crap-hat,' growled Ackford crossly. 'Just concentrate on your fucking driving.'

Four hours later, both men were seated in Howard's flat in Rome's city centre. Howard had finished outlining what he knew; he stood up. 'Another cold beer, Mel? Tony?'

'Good idea, boss,' said Harris. 'That'd go down well.'

'Cheers, boss. Me too,' rumbled Ackford.

Howard fetched three more cold beers from the refrigerator and returned. It was hot outside; in his sitting room a ceiling fan turned noiselessly and it was pleasantly cool. 'So,' he said. 'What do you think, Tony?'

'I dunno, boss,' said Ackford, frowning. 'It sounds a big dodgy to me. What the fuck do they want us for, that's what I want to know. I mean, if it's a starter and we know it's on the level, then maybe. But it sounds a bit iffy, like. Don't want another one to go pear-shaped on us, do we.'

'What about you, Mel?'

'I reckon we ought to go for it, boss,' said Harris positively.

Howard had been anticipating almost precisely these reactions from the two men. Big Tony Ackford erred on the side of caution, when he erred, but he was not often wrong. His many years of service had taught him the value of healthy scepticism for the enthusiasms of others. The quicksilver Mel Harris, on the other hand, was a more impulsive and instinctive decision-maker. His service record was not as extensive as that of Ackford, but by any standards he was a highly experienced and knowledgeable professional, and a veteran of many actions. His speed and skill had somehow always enabled him to survive.

'No one's going for it, you crap-hat,' growled Ackford, 'until we know what "it" is.'

'Of course we aren't, you big lummox,' Harris shot back. 'That's what I meant. But we must listen to this guy. Boss,' he said, turning to Howard, 'surely you can see there's no harm in that.'

'Maybe, but I'm not convinced we have anything to gain from it either,' said Howard evenly. 'You don't know these tricky bastards like I do, Mel. Sure, I could meet Colonel Goodale and talk to him like you say, but that wouldn't be any guarantee that he would be straight with me. He could say one thing, and I might agree, and before very long we could quite easily find ourselves snarled up in a completely different game – or let down and abandoned completely. And we wouldn't have anyone to complain to about it afterwards. As Tony says, we can do without another op going sour on us.'

'*Sour*, boss? How do you think things are as they stand already?' The vehemence of Harris's rejoinder momentarily startled Howard. 'Things are difficult enough right now. No one really wants to know us. I wouldn't say we've been completely frozen out, but there's far more bullshit and red tape about than there should be. It's as if the word's gone out that we've been naughty boys, and everyone should steer clear. All of us back home are getting hacked off about it. And look at your own situation – you're stuck on your lonesome over here. Not exactly ideal, is it? This job might put an end to all that. Isn't it at least worth a try?'

'Mel's got a point there, boss,' Ackford's low rumble broke in. 'We're getting a lot more crap from official channels than we should. Maybe if you talked to this bloke you could persuade him to smooth things out a bit. Put a stop to the aggravation, like.'

Howard suddenly realised that he had not appreciated the full extent of the problems his men had been facing over the last year. Mistakenly, he had thought that his own absence would take the heat off the others. Obviously, it hadn't. He nodded thoughtfully.

'OK,' he said slowly. 'I take your point. I'll meet Colonel Goodale. I'll listen to what he has to say.'

12

Sir Reginald Hislop very slowly began to regain consciousness. The full process took several hours; at first he just stirred in his deep drug-induced sleep, then drifted off again, not moving for another forty-five minutes. After two hours he rolled over, from the coma position in which he had been placed, on to his back; then he opened his eyes. The eyes were dull and uncomprehending, registering nothing. After a few seconds, they closed again and he began to snore. An hour later he woke once more; his eyes blinked a few times and began to flicker around the room. There was no more comprehension in his expression than before, but something was clearly agitating him. His mouth opened and shut, but no sound emerged.

There was in fact just one instinctive thought in his mind – that he was very thirsty. His mouth felt dreadfully dry. No other thought went through his head. His eyes fell on a small bedside table; on it he saw a carafe of what looked like orange squash, and a plastic cup. He reached out for them.

His arms felt like lead; he found he could hardly move. It took him several long minutes to pour some of the squash into the cup; he spilled nearly half of the first cupful, but when he did finally manage to bring it to his lips it tasted like nectar. He immediately felt better. He poured himself some more. He felt stronger now; still very tired, but stronger. Soon the carafe was empty. He slumped back onto the bed, and before it occurred to him to wonder where he was his eyes closed once more and he slept.

He woke for the final time forty minutes later. For a while he just lay where he was, his eyes open, savouring the feeling of relaxation that comes after a long sleep. It was, he thought, the best sleep he had had in years. Then, for the first time, a small frown crossed his brow. Where was he? He tried to sit up, and eventually managed to prop himself against the headboard of the bed. He looked around.

The room was a bare one, quite small, with no window – just a ventilation grille set high on one wall, in the far corner – and only one door. The walls and ceiling were painted white; there was a single large square panel light set into a recess in the ceiling. The furniture consisted of the bed he was lying in, which was small but reasonably comfortable, the bedside table, and in the corner of the room an armchair and a round coffee-table. On the coffee-table there was a bowl of fresh fruit, a small wooden box and a book. *Where am I?* he thought. He realised he was wearing pyjamas. They were clean, as was the bed-linen, but they were not his own pyjamas. He tried to remember what had happened, and came to the conclusion that he must have had an accident and was now in hospital. He hated hospitals, but oddly enough he now felt extremely calm and detached, and the thought did not bother him. What on earth could have happened? It couldn't have been much of an accident, he decided; he felt absolutely fine. Weak as a kitten, but otherwise fine. For several minutes he just sat where he was, in bed, trying to remember. Eventually he gave up. It didn't seem to matter. He swung his legs out of the bed, and saw a pair of carpet-slippers. He put them on and stood up, looking around the room.

It was a funny sort of hospital, he decided. There was none of the usual equipment – no radio headset or buzzer to call the nurse, no thermometer in its little holder, no blood pressure apparatus hanging on the wall, nothing. The bed wasn't even a proper hospital one. Hospital beds had wheels so they could be moved about, and they had pedals and handles, for lowering, raising and tilting them. This one was just a plain, ordinary metal bedstead. Still, he thought, nothing too serious could have happened to him, otherwise there would be nurses and doctors swarming all over the place. He didn't mind. He yawned, walked over to the coffee-table and picked a grape from the bunch in the fruit bowl. Delicious. A muscat grape – his favourite sort. He ate another.

He picked up the book. It was a heavy volume, beautifully bound in red Morocco leather. What was . . . Good Lord! It was a copy of his own political memoir, *My Years in Downing Street*, written since his resignation all those years ago. What a magnificently bound copy! He had never seen such an exquisitely produced version. He smiled in genuine delight and sat down in the armchair.

Reaching across to the fruit-bowl for another grape, his elbow nudged the wooden box on the coffee-table. He had forgotten all about it in his happiness on discovering the copy of his book. Now he opened the box, and received a second pleasant surprise. Inside were two ounces of his favourite tobacco, a box of matches and some cigarette papers. *Perfect!* A thought occurred to him, and he chuckled to himself – it was a funny sort of hospital where they not only didn't mind you smoking, but actually supplied you with your favourite tobacco!

Relaxed and entirely unperturbed by any suspicion that something might be amiss, Sir Reginald Hislop rolled himself a cigarette and contentedly began to re-read his own memoirs.

In a room on the floor above, two men were observing Hislop's actions closely on a video-monitor. The camera was positioned out of sight behind the ventilation-grille in Hislop's cell; the monitor now gave the two men a view of the top of his head. They noted with satisfaction the old man's apparent lack of concern. He seemed quite calm and not at all bothered by his unfamiliar surroundings.

'He seems to have recovered reasonably well, Gerhardt,' said General Reinholdt Erfurt.

'His condition appears satisfactory, comrade General,' Eisener agreed.

'It took longer than I expected for him to wake up.'

Eisener's face remained bland. 'He is an old man, comrade General,' he said. 'These things take longer with the elderly.' *Particularly if they have been over-sedated,* he thought. *He should have come round thirty-six hours ago, long before I got back here. That fool Anna Linden gave him too much during the journey.* But Eisener knew he couldn't really blame Anna; she must have been under constant pressure from Erfurt to make sure that Hislop stayed unconscious throughout.

'Do you think he has any idea how many days have passed since his abduction?'

'No, comrade General. In fact, he does not yet appear to have remembered even the abduction itself. When the drugs wear off completely, he may remember a bit more. But by then he will have other things on his mind.'

'Yes, of course,' said Erfurt. 'The bowl of fruit . . . ?'

'Exactly, comrade General.'

'It will be interesting to see his reaction,' said Erfurt, rising to his feet. 'All right, Gerhardt. Get comrade *doktor* Linden back in here to keep an eye on him, then come upstairs to my office. I have something to show you. It arrived this morning.'

Ten minutes later Eisener was seated in a hard, upright chair, facing his commanding officer across the large wooden desk in Erfurt's office. 'Some good news, I hope, comrade General?'

'Yes,' said the general. 'I have here a report from our people in the United States. It is an initial assessment of the IRIS program. The computer arrived safely, and our expert over there, Kramer, has stripped it down and analysed it. I think we can be fairly confident that it will perform adequately.'

'That is indeed excellent, comrade General,' replied Eisener. 'In fact, it is better than I had hoped. When I interrogated the English programmer, Henley, he indicated that IRIS was not yet ready for operational use.'

'In some ways, Gerhardt, that was right,' said General Erfurt, 'but there is one factor in this case which will make its task a great deal easier. Kramer makes oblique mention of it in his report. Here,' he said, pushing the report across to Eisener, 'have a look through it, and tell me what you think.'

Eisener leaned forward to pick up the report, concealing his irritation. The general was being secretive as usual – but in time he was sure he would find out the details. He began to read.

General Erfurt leaned back in his chair, allowing his mind to wander as his second-in-command leafed through the report. *The good, faithful Eisener,* he thought. He had never quite fathomed the man, and had come to the conclusion that, despite his undoubted brains and ability, Colonel Eisener was simply not a leader. The man seemed perfectly happy to play second fiddle, to stay in the background – perhaps he was just hoping to step into Erfurt's shoes when he retired, he speculated. At any rate, Eisener seemed hardly the type to stage a palace revolution in the meantime. The odd thing was that men of that type usually had little initiative and very few original ideas. In this respect, Eisener was different. Over the years some of his ideas had been excellent, and the general was not so vain that he had failed to recognise this truth.

'Well, Gerhardt, what do you think?'

Eisener looked up. 'It is most interesting, comrade General,' he answered calmly. 'Kramer is clearly as knowledgeable as we hoped. His years spent in California, and his current position in Baltimore, have obviously paid off. He seems to know exactly what he is talking about. By the sound of things, he is completely at home with this sort of technology and could even have designed such a program himself.'

'I agree,' said the General. 'I don't think he will have any trouble adapting IRIS to our needs.'

Eisener was silent for a moment. Surely his commanding officer must have spotted the problem, he thought. 'Unfortunately, comrade General,' began the colonel, 'there is one point that does concern me. Kramer seems to confirm exactly what Henley said about IRIS – that the program is still in the experimental stage and therefore in some respects incomplete. He predicts that the pattern-recognition will prove reasonably effective in ideal conditions, but feels that some work will have to be done before it will be one hundred per cent reliable. We will, after all, require it to make no mistakes in identifying a particular subject. From reading this report, it would seem that we may be expecting too much of it. Kramer doesn't say that in so many words, but it is fairly obvious that he has his doubts about it.'

The general considered his reply. 'I feel,' he said evasively, 'we can rely on Kramer to iron out these final few problems. As you said yourself, he is quite capable of making his own refinements, and he has even suggested ways in which this might be done. He has plenty of time in hand.'

Eisener took the hint; the subject was closed. He rose to his feet. 'Then . . . if there is nothing more, comrade General?'

'Thank you, Gerhardt. I just thought you would like to be kept informed.' He nodded, dismissing the colonel.

Closing the door behind him, Eisener shook his head slightly. *Keep me informed, indeed*, he thought. *I'm just as much in the dark as ever*. Thoughtfully, he walked back down the corridor to his own quarters.

General Erfurt now sat alone in his office. It was good to be back, he thought. The return journey from Britain had seemed interminable, but everything had gone according to plan. During the sea-voyage from Southampton to Tangier he had felt slightly sea-sick; the purpose-built accommodation module, concealed as it was beneath hundreds of tons of cargo in the hold of the ship, had seemed to amplify every motion of the ship. The long flight in the big cargo plane had been scarcely any better; the constant, throbbing roar of the engines had left him with a residual ache in his left ear. Never mind, he thought, he was back now. He felt safe here. He had felt uneasy in England; he had taken a big risk in going there, but he knew there had been no option. Here, on the other hand, he was immune from arrest or any of that nonsense. The place had its disadvantages, but it was secure. His choice five years before of a new base for the *Stasi*'s operations had been a good one. Yes, he told himself again; he was safe here, in North Korea . . .

He picked up Kramer's report on IRIS once again, turning to the conclusions on the last page. 'The IRIS computer program,' he read, 'is comprehensive, well-compiled and effective. It is still, however, in some respects crude and in need of further refinement. As it stands, there is no guarantee that it will perform flawlessly. In short, unless the subject to be recognised is distinctive in appearance, IRIS may be unreliable.'

Reading this comment, the general smiled to himself. He could afford to do so, for he – and only he – knew the full story. Eisener didn't; nor yet did Kramer.

The IRIS program would work. Crude though it might be, it would recognise its target. It would ignore everyone else. There would be no mistake.

The package to be assembled by Kramer would consist of a video camera, the IRIS program itself and a memory database containing reference images of the subject to be recognised. Using the reference images for comparison purposes, the video camera would centre itself on the subject with the help of servo motors.

Precisely aligned with the camera lens, there would be a short-barrelled rifle. Kramer had confirmed that the whole package, including computer components, back-up batteries, servo motors, camera and rifle, would take up no more space than an attaché case. It could be planted anywhere. It would wait with tireless and infinite patience, activating itself automatically many days – even weeks or months – later, only when it 'saw' its target subject. As soon as the image centred itself on the target's head, IRIS would fire the rifle, and the target would fall dead.

PART TWO

PART TWO

13

Colonel Max Goodale emerged from the arrivals hall of Rome's Fiumicino airport, expecting to see a large throng of people waiting to collect passengers. To his surprise, the airport was relatively quiet; he scanned a thin line of chauffeurs, tour operators and company representatives holding cards with passengers' names, but was not surprised to see no card bearing his own. His eyes flickered along the row of waiting relatives and friends, wondering whether he would recognise the man whom he had never met before and had now come to see.

The only photograph Goodale had seen of Ed Howard was more than twenty years old – an official photograph taken when Howard had been a young officer in the Royal Marines. It had been an interesting face even then, thought Goodale: dark, angular features, and a purposeful expression revealing the strength of character that had already emerged. It wasn't difficult to imagine the changes that the intervening years might have made.

But it would be Howard's height and build, thought Goodale, that would mark him out. A man six feet three inches tall rarely managed to remain inconspicuous for long, and at one hundred and eighty pounds he would be lean, even thin. He would also, Goodale knew, be fit and hard, and he would move with the economical, fluid precision that no ex-Special Forces soldier could ever wholly disguise.

Goodale reached the end of the line of waiting people without seeing anyone who fitted Howard's description. In front of him a voluble and happy Italian family reunion and a party of chattering Japanese tourists with laden luggage trolleys were causing a bottleneck. Unencumbered by a trolley of his own, Goodale sidestepped them and headed for the airport information desk. *Watching from one of those chairs?* he wondered, his eyes swiftly assessing each person. *No.*

'Colonel Goodale?' The voice behind him was quiet and even.

Goodale stopped and turned. 'Mr Howard.' He smiled and extended his hand. 'Very kind of you to meet me.'

For about a second the two men measured each other up. Howard's face gave absolutely no clue to his thoughts. The thick black hair was now flecked with grey at the temples, Goodale noticed, and the face bore the lines of the experience that Howard had packed into his life since that old photograph had been taken. But it was the eyes that held his attention. They were intense, dark and compelling, although at the moment there was no expression in them at all. Goodale had expected to see a trace of suspicion – certainly a degree of wariness – but there was nothing. Momentarily Goodale felt unsettled.

'My car's outside,' said Howard. 'Shall we go and have some lunch? I have a place in mind.'

'An excellent idea,' said Goodale.

Howard spoke little during the drive and seemed to give his whole attention to the road. One of those drivers who immediately inspire confidence, he drove the Alfa Romeo fast and expertly. Within a hundred yards or so of setting off Goodale instinctively knew he would be quite safe, even in the noisy anarchy of Italian traffic. He guessed that Howard's silence was partly due to his concentrating on his driving and partly because he was not a man who had a reputation for wasting time with small talk. Despite his adventurous past, Howard was by nature a cautious and guarded man, he knew; he would need careful handling. His assessment was largely accurate, but not wholly so.

Howard was in fact thinking quite hard; his concentration on the road was peripheral. He had spent the past thirty-six hours trying to analyse the possible reason for Goodale's visit, and wondering how he should deal with the man. The problem was, he had never met Goodale before, and one could never really decide how to handle someone until one met them face to face. The colonel wanted something badly – that was obvious. He was here cap in hand to ask him to perform some task, but Howard had no idea what it might be, or what pressure Goodale might try to exert on him to make him agree to undertake it.

He had wondered briefly how much Goodale actually knew about him, and had almost immediately decided that it would be safe to assume that his knowledge would be extensive. He would know about his service record, of course, but he would also have made a study of his character. Howard had made a brief and frank self-assessment, picking out the points of his own character which Goodale's enquiries would have revealed – that he was something of a loner, that he appeared cool, aloof and standoffish to those he did not know well, and that he did not lightly put his trust in anyone. Fair enough, he had decided; he would play it exactly that way, and no more. He would not reveal the true depth of the distrust of others that had grown in him over the last year. He would certainly remain cool towards Goodale, because that would be expected; but he would do his best to give the colonel no hint, at any rate for the time being, that the coolness concealed something far more fundamental. Howard was a lethally dangerous man, but over the last year he had also become a bitterly angry one. Beneath the outward mere coolness there now lurked a cold and implacable fury.

He had been betrayed. Perhaps not by this man, he acknowledged to himself, but certainly by people like him. He had acted in good faith when he had undertaken the mission to Iraq the year before, but men like this one beside him now had deceived and ultimately disowned him. He had resolved bitterly that he would never allow such a thing to happen again. *Trust this man?* he thought: *Not a chance in hell*. He realised his jaw was clenched tight, the muscles standing out with tension. His dark eyes glittered, but he knew they were giving nothing away. *Keep it under control. Stay calm and aloof*. With an effort, he forced himself to relax. He reached for his pack of cigarettes and lit one, drawing deeply. The cold fury he felt gradually retreated back beneath the surface. *Control*.

Goodale had relaxed in the passenger seat. He noticed that they were heading away from Rome itself, and soon they were well into the countryside. The traffic grew ever sparser as Howard took a series of turns on to smaller and increasingly narrow roads. Forty minutes after leaving the airport he turned into a roughly gravelled track leading to a rather scruffy and ramshackle little *ristorante* on the edge of a small village.

'Don't be put off by appearances,' said Howard, killing the engine. 'It's good, and we won't be disturbed.'

Goodale got out of the car, savouring the air. *Couldn't be better,* he thought. *Miles from anywhere. No tourist would ever find a place like this, and even if he did he'd drive straight past*. 'Perfect,' he said aloud.

They were shown to a small table in the garden, in the shade of a big old olive tree. Goodale took off his jacket and draped it over the back of his chair. The temperature was high, but made bearable by a pleasant breeze. He appeared relaxed and at ease, despite knowing that the matter he had to broach with Howard would require very careful handling. Howard had had his fingers burned before, and badly so. He would be no pushover.

'Well, Colonel,' said Howard, giving Goodale the same disconcertingly direct, level stare that his companion had observed at the airport, 'I have to say I'm intrigued. All Johnny would tell me on the phone was that you had some sort of proposition for me, and that I ought to listen to you. You have my full attention.'

Yes, I certainly do, thought Goodale. This man was someone who attended to one thing at a time, giving it his total concentration. Not a man to be distracted from anything, whether it be driving a car or planning and executing a mission to assassinate a foreign head of state. Everything that Goodale had so far observed about Howard confirmed what he had heard or expected.

A carafe of local red wine arrived, and when the waiter had left Goodale began to explain the reasons for his visit. Nearly an hour later, the two men were still deep in conversation. Goodale was leaning back in his chair, still apparently relaxed. In some ways, he was. Lunch had been simple but excellent, and the local wine a perfect accompaniment to it. The conversation had in fact been largely one-way, with Goodale doing almost all the talking. Howard, hunched forward in his chair, had hardly interrupted except to ask the occasional brief but pertinent question.

'So,' said Goodale finally. 'What do you think?'

There was a long pause. 'Well,' replied Howard finally, 'it's quite a tale. Before I answer, there are one or two things I'd like to get straight. Do you mind?'

'Go ahead,' nodded Goodale.

'OK. First: how sure are you that this IRIS machine is such a threat? How reliable is it?'

'Pretty reliable, I'm afraid. Not one hundred per cent – not yet, anyway – but it's dangerous enough for us to be obliged to take it very seriously indeed. It's a classic case of a scientific development designed for beneficial purposes – in this case, the maintenance of law and order – being all too easily adaptable for ill use. Nobody seems to have foreseen that it could be programmed to recognise an individual and be used to trigger a bomb as soon as that individual appears. The whole thing, I'm told, could be no bigger than an attaché case, depending on the size of the bomb. And as I explained, it could be planted and concealed anywhere and wait indefinitely for that individual to appear – rather like the Brighton bomb, which came within a whisker of wiping out the Thatcher Cabinet. But that depended on a timing device, of course, and this doesn't. It actually recognises the target, so it's entirely independent of any schedule or remote control. That's what makes it such a serious threat.'

'Hmm,' said Howard thoughtfully. 'I see. And you have no idea who the target is?'

'None at all,' replied Goodale. 'We've simply assumed, bearing in mind that we know the *Stasi* has been hired to do the job, that the target is someone important. Even knowing the Iranians are the paymasters doesn't help us much. It means that the target is someone of whom Iran does not approve – but of course Iran seems to disapprove of practically everybody these days.'

'What about this *Stasi* base in North Korea?' asked Howard. 'How much do you know about it?'

'For a start we know exactly where it is,' answered Goodale, 'and from satellite photographs obtained from the Americans, we know what it looks like. It's a single building, relatively isolated, inside a wire compound. Probably a military outpost of some sort, which they're using courtesy of the North Korean government. We don't know how many personnel they have there, but the satellite pictures have shown a maximum of three trucks and two jeep-type vehicles parked in the compound at any one time. The vehicles and the size of the building would suggest about twenty men.'

'And the location?' prompted Howard.

'Yes, that's interesting. It's less than a mile away from the outside perimeter of the Yŏngbyŏn nuclear base. I'd hazard a guess that the *Stasi* have some involvement there – possibly advising on security, or something of that sort.'

'And you know all this simply on the basis of one radio message which was intercepted by GCHQ?'

'Yes,' replied Goodale. 'I can show you the transcript. It didn't say much, but there was enough to indicate that the base is a fairly permanent one, not some transitory arrangement. The voice exactly matched that of a former *Stasi* staff officer called Gerhardt Eisener. He used to feature regularly in radio and telephone traffic picked up by the Teufelsberg station in Berlin.'

'Right. I'm getting the picture now,' said Howard. A note of sarcasm had crept into his voice. 'You want me to assemble a team of people to get into North Korea, find this *Stasi* base, take it out, whack this guy Eisener, nick the IRIS machine and bring it back to you? Just like that?'

'More or less,' replied Goodale levelly, ignoring Howard's tone. 'But I doubt if you'll find IRIS there. It's probably already being adapted for its new role in the country where they plan to assassinate this unknown victim. What we really need to know is the who and the where – once we know those two details, finding the IRIS bomb will be less difficult.'

'Well, Colonel,' said Howard, 'I'll tell you one thing straightaway. I'm very sceptical about whether it can be done. That doesn't mean I won't think about it though – but before I do so I want to get a couple of things clear.

One thing in particular,' he added, lighting a cigarette and drawing deeply on it. His eyes bored into Goodale's. 'Who exactly do you represent?'

Goodale had been expecting the question. 'I represent Her Majesty's Government,' he said simply.

Howard's left eyebrow rose fractionally. 'How do I know that?' he asked.

'I can understand your feelings, Mr Howard,' replied Goodale. 'You were led to believe the government was behind your last escapade – and of course it wasn't. You were misled. But I'm not here,' he continued after a moment's reflection, 'to dredge up that affair, or to use it in any way to pressurise you into participating in this one. As to proof of my credentials, I can offer you none today that would convince you. But should you agree to involve yourself, you will see plenty of evidence. Within reason, you will be able to obtain official assistance, even though this operation is supposed to be "deniable". You'll have a shopping list, of course. Hereford, for example, or Poole, will be prepared to help. The Queen's Messenger Service may be of assistance with the transportation of . . . awkward items of cargo. Do you see what I mean?'

Howard nodded slowly. Access to SAS and SBS weapons and equipment would make life far simpler, and using the diplomatic bag would be very helpful – he recalled the enormous difficulties and risks involved in operating as an "illegal". 'That will certainly make a difference,' he conceded. 'One thing puzzles me, though. You're retired. Also,' he said, 'you're ex-MI5. Not SIS, not SF, but Five. This isn't Five's province. Why you?'

'Perfectly fair question,' answered Goodale. 'I was asked back just to handle this business. There's sometimes more overlap in these matters than you might think. Responsibilities are seldom clear-cut, and a task is often given to whoever knows most about it, regardless of their usual job. You know that. But the principal reason for my being here, I suppose,' he continued, 'is because it was my idea. And I'm the only person outside your own circle who knows of you, your colleagues and your past. Some people still don't believe anything happened last year in Iraq, and they certainly don't know you were involved. But I do. And if you could pull that one off, then I believe you can do this too.'

'If I agree to look into this,' said Howard carefully, 'what would be the terms?'

'You would be well paid,' answered Goodale immediately. 'We can agree details later, when you've worked out what will be involved. But I assure you I'm fully aware of the dangers and difficulties, and no one could reasonably expect something like this to be done as a gesture of charity – or atonement,' he added with a smile.

'So that's it?' asked Howard.

'More or less,' replied Goodale. 'Except, now that you mention it . . .' He contrived to look slightly embarrassed as he saw Howard's eyes narrow again in suspicion.

'There's something else?'

'Well, you see . . .' Goodale now gave all the signs of appearing thoroughly awkward about what he was going to say. 'The fact is, I've been asked to enquire whether you would do one other thing while you are in the area of Yŏngbyŏn. Just a little thing, really.'

'Oh yes?' asked Howard facetiously. 'And just what is that? Blow up the nuclear reactor? Take a day-trip down to P'yŏngyang and assassinate old grapefruit-head himself? Come *on*, Colonel! You know perfectly well you don't give someone two missions to do at once.'

'Yes, yes, of course,' said Goodale hurriedly. 'But this really is a relatively simple thing, you see. All that's involved is the positioning of some monitoring equipment near the nuclear base – or possibly somewhere inside it. The full details haven't been worked out yet. But we badly need to know what's going on there, and so far no one has been able to find out much. I'm assured it will be a fairly simple matter.'

'Simple or not, I don't like it,' said Howard forcefully. 'And getting inside that base is likely to be anything but simple. But my main objection is that this will be a distraction, and an added complication.'

'I entirely understand,' said Goodale with a placatory gesture. 'All I'm asking is that you consider it when you hear exactly what would be involved.'

'I'll consider it, but I —'

'Good!' beamed Goodale. 'Excellent! That's all I ask – that you consider it.' He paused. 'Then that just leaves one other small matter.'

'*What*?' Howard's voice betrayed his irritation. 'You mean there's something *else*?'

'When you get to the *Stasi* base,' said Goodale, ignoring Howard's outburst, 'you may find an old man being held captive there.'

'An old man?' asked Howard incredulously. 'What old man?'

'I can't divulge his name,' said Goodale, 'but you may well recognise him when you see him. He was once quite well known.'

'So just what the hell am I supposed to do about this old man?' asked Howard angrily. 'And don't even *think* of telling me I'm supposed to rescue him and bring him back home. That just simply wouldn't be possible. Forget it, Colonel.' He lit another cigarette and glared impatiently at Goodale.

'I rather agree with you,' said Goodale calmly. 'I dare say you will have enough problems of your own, just getting out of North Korea, without having to drag an old man along with you.'

'So?' asked Howard. 'What *am* I supposed to do with him?'

Goodale's eyes were as cold as ice. 'You must kill him,' he said quietly.

14

The engine of the big Chrysler station wagon purred smoothly as Peter Kramer cruised down the pleasant, tree-lined suburban street on the northern outskirts of Baltimore. Kramer slowed as he reached number 126; there was a slight squeal from the rear tyres as he turned the car into the driveway of the two-storey house and drew up in front of the garage door.

Meg Berman heard the sound, and turned. Recognising the car, she put down her watering can, wiped her hands on her jeans and walked over. 'Hi, Peter!' she called.

Kramer switched off the engine and got out, grabbing a bulky briefcase from the passenger seat. A slightly built, fair-haired man of average height, he looked much younger than his thirty-two years: his youthful haircut and casual clothes gave him the appearance of a college graduate. He smiled. 'Hello, Meg,' he said. 'Carl tell you I was dropping round? I hope it's not inconvenient.'

'Not at all, Peter!' she replied. 'It's always nice to see you.'

Meg Berman was an attractive woman, much younger than her husband, but she had never given him any cause to be jealous. But then, Kramer thought, Carl probably wouldn't have minded too much even if she had. He would probably have regarded it as a compliment if other men flirted with his wife. It would have reassured him that he had made the right choice, that he had married a woman other men wanted.

The front door opened and the solid figure of Carl

Berman emerged, a broad beam on his face. 'Hi, Peter,' he called. 'Good to see you, fella. Come on in . . . Meg, Peter and I have business to discuss. Do you mind?'

'No,' said his wife. 'You two go ahead. I'll be busy out here in the garden, anyhow.'

Carl Berman smiled fondly and closed the door, shutting her outside. 'You want a beer, Peter?' he asked.

'A beer would be good. Thanks.'

Berman led the way into the kitchen. The two men opened a can of Budweiser each and then went through to the back of the house. Berman's heavy boots echoed on the hollow wooden floor; Kramer's sneakers made hardly a sound. *Those boots*, thought Kramer. *Why does Carl always wear those big, heavy boots, even during the summer? His feet must* . . . He sighed. Berman never changed. Always the same – open heavy-check shirt, jeans, boots. A dark grey nylon zipper jacket if it was cold; otherwise never any variation. But the clothes suited the man's character, in a way.

Berman produced a key from his pocket and unlocked the door to the room he called his den. From the outside the door appeared to be a normal wooden one, but as it opened its thick, insulated construction and heavy hinges were revealed. 'Mind the step, Peter,' Berman reminded Kramer. The two men stepped up into the room; Berman locked and bolted the heavy door shut behind them. Kramer headed for an easy chair and sat down. Berman perched on a stool next to the long workbench and took a pull from his beer can.

'She's a great girl, your Meg,' said Kramer finally, giving Berman a direct look. 'She's never asked?'

'Yeah,' replied Berman, grinning sheepishly. 'I mean, yeah, she's a fine girl,' he added hurriedly, 'but she's never asked about this. I could leave it unlocked, and she still wouldn't. She's not even curious. Thinks it's just a den. You know – books, fishing gear, a few topless pin-ups. Male preserve, anyway, and she's happy to leave it that way.'

The relationship between the two men had undergone a subtle change. At forty-five, Carl Berman was a far stronger, more purposeful-looking individual than Kramer. Berman owned and ran a successful gunshop and sports store in downtown Baltimore. He had proved himself to be a shrewd and tough businessman; his no-nonsense reputation and forthright manner ensured he was treated with respect.

Peter Kramer could have been Berman's nephew, or junior employee, or perhaps his brother-in-law – Meg's younger brother, maybe. Meg herself, if she had given any thought to it, would have described him as her husband's young buddy and business associate, which would have been only partly accurate. Now, in the privacy and seclusion of Carl Berman's den, it was quite clear that Kramer was Berman's boss – a fact that the older man readily acknowledged.

Kramer looked around the room. Anything less like the den of the average American male could hardly be imagined. The room was a compact but fully equipped workshop. Berman had adapted the room several years earlier, before he married Meg, and had done all the construction and insulation work himself. The single window was of heavy, triple-glazed, shatterproof mirror-glass, allowing light in but preventing anyone out in the back yard from seeing what was inside. The thick glass gave an oddly bluish cast to the daylight filtering through it. The extra blockwork and noise-insulation panels had made the room smaller internally, but the result was virtually soundproof.

Berman had been like a child with a new toy when he first showed the completed room to Kramer. He had given his boss a demonstration. Asking Kramer to wait outside and listen carefully, he had shut himself inside. Ninety seconds later, he had reappeared taking off a pair of ear-muffs. Beckoning Kramer inside, he had shut the door again. 'Did you hear anything?' he asked eagerly.

Kramer sniffed the air and saw the bucket of sand in the corner. Some of the sand lay scattered on the floor around the bucket. He realised what the demonstration had been. 'A gunshot,' he said immediately.

Berman's face had crumpled in disappointment, until Kramer had slapped him on the back and congratulated him. He only knew it was a gunshot from the smell, he assured him. He had only heard a very faint noise, which he had guessed was a book dropping onto the floor. Nothing else. And he had been listening hard. Smiling, he repeated his congratulations.

Berman was delighted and produced a heavy .41 Magnum revolver as evidence – but Kramer had hurriedly declined the offer of a further demonstration. He was pleased; Berman's workshop would be useful. The machine tools could whine, screech and clatter, but no one would ever hear them. No one would know what went on in here, as long as Berman stayed out of trouble.

Berman had indeed been scrupulously careful to stay out of trouble; but Kramer had been alarmed when he had announced his engagement. There had been girlfriends, of course. Berman had an eye for younger women – some of them not much more than half his age. They had come and gone, but the important thing from Kramer's point of view was that none had been live-in lovers. With Carl married, there would be a wife – possibly a nosy or house-proud one who would want to know what lay beyond that door, and whether it needed the attentions of a vacuum cleaner.

But Kramer soon saw that he needn't have worried. Meg was a happy-go-lucky, uncomplicated girl; not too bright – in fact, Carl couldn't have chosen better. She took life as it came, and never seemed particularly curious about her husband's business affairs.

'Right, Carl,' said Kramer, 'let's get down to business. Any further thoughts on the firearm?'

Berman nodded eagerly. 'Yeah. Bearing in mind what you told me, I think we ought to settle for the .221 Remington Fireball cartridge. It's a competition-grade long-range pistol calibre, with a very high muzzle velocity. It has the characteristics of a rifle bullet, but it was specifically designed for short barrels of ten inches or so. If you use a normal rifle cartridge with a short barrel, you lose a lot because the powder doesn't have time to burn completely. You can load calibres like .223 Remington for barrels down to about fourteen inches, using faster-burning powders, but that's about the limit unless you're prepared to sacrifice a lot in terms of velocity and trajectory. The .221 RF is ideal, in my opinion.'

'Is it easily obtainable?'

'That's the other thing,' replied Berman. 'You want something reasonably untraceable. This is – it's factory-made ammo. That's not to say I won't be able to fiddle with it and make up some special loads using factory components and different powders, but that's something any handloader could do. It wouldn't be traceable. Nor would the pistol. That's what really decided it for me.'

'What's the pistol?' asked Kramer.

Berman pulled open a drawer beneath the workbench and carefully lifted out a long, evil-looking weapon with a heavy sculpted grip. 'Here.' He handed it to Kramer. 'It's an old XP-100 I've been hanging on to for years. Officially, it doesn't exist. It was bankrupt stock from a dealer who was prosecuted for failing to keep a proper register. The cops handed all his stuff over to me for cataloguing. I got rid of most of it legitimately, on commission, but this was one of the pieces I kept.'

Kramer examined it doubtfully. He worked the bolt, then closed it again. 'It's much too long for what we want, Carl.'

'Sure – just over twenty-one inches. But don't worry. We can lose at least four and a half off the barrel, and if we only need one shot I can take about the same again off the bolt – maybe even more. The firing mechanism will need complete modification anyway. The finished article should be about twelve inches long.' Absent-mindedly he patted the weapon, as if it were a dog, then put it down and lit a cigarette. 'As you know,' he went on, 'I do a lot of custom jobs for people in the shop. I've got everything I need here to modify this piece, but I'd deliberately make the work look crude and poorly finished, as if a knowledgeable amateur had done it. Rough-cut metal, no blueing or finishing – that sort of thing. It'll still work OK.'

'That sounds fine,' said Kramer neutrally. 'What about the silencer?'

'No need for one,' replied Berman. 'This is a high-velocity bullet and you can't silence it – it makes a sharp crack because it's supersonic. Don't get me wrong – a silencer *can* be used with high-velocity ammo, just to silence the report made by the propellant gases and to make it harder to detect where the shot was fired from. But in this case I can't see that it'll matter too much. I doubt we'll be able to retrieve this device after it's done its job, so it doesn't really matter how quickly it's found after the shot is fired – by then it'll be too late.'

'Fair enough,' said Kramer, seeing the logic of Berman's explanation. 'We'll forget the silencer.' He reached for his briefcase. 'Let me show you where I've got to.'

Kramer pulled out three bubble-wrapped packages. Undoing them, he laid each piece of equipment on the bench. The first was a single integrated circuit board, about the size of a piece of A4 paper. It had a large black processor chip in the centre, about three inches by two. 'OK,' said Kramer. 'This is the brains of the thing. That big chip is the main processor – I'd heard about it, but never actually seen it before we got hold of this one. It's called a Gamma chip, and it's much, much faster and more powerful than anything you can get on the open market. For example, have you heard of something called a Pentium processor?'

'No,' Berman admitted. 'Guns are my specialty, remember? I'm a bit of a rookie when it comes to computers.'

'Well,' said Kramer, 'The Intel Pentium is the successor to their 80486 microprocessor. It runs a great deal faster than the 486, at 75 megahertz instead of the 486's current maximum of 66. And within a couple of years, say by 1995, there'll be Pentiums running at 120 megahertz or more. Believe me, that's *fast*!'

'So that's what this is?'

'No,' said Kramer. 'This Gamma chip is in a different league altogether. Can you envision about a hundred Pentiums, all running in parallel and all working on the same thing, sharing the task and swapping information between themselves? That's effectively what this one is capable of.'

Berman peered at it. He could not envision any such thing. 'I need my reading glasses,' he grunted. 'That looks a bit like a "y" painted on it. Japanese, I suppose.'

'No. Actually, it's American-manufactured. The "y" is the Greek letter gamma. That chip's worth one hell of a lot of money, even if it doesn't look like very much. Now, do you see these things here?' Kramer pointed to the upper left part of the board. There were four rows of smaller chips, eight in each row, mounted vertically. 'Each of those thirty-two little chips represents sixteen megabytes of random-access memory. That's a total of five hundred and twelve megabytes of RAM – and believe me, that is *a lot*. You're looking at more than twenty thousand dollars' worth of memory there.'

Berman's eyebrows shot up. The man might not have known much about *that* kind of hardware, thought Kramer, but he could certainly relate to money.

'But that's chickenfeed,' he went on, 'compared to

the value of the Gamma chip itself. Now, look down here.' He indicated four blocks of processors beneath the RAM chips. 'This is one of my own additions. This is PROM – programmable read-only memory. It does away with the need for a hard disk on the machine. There isn't a great deal of it – only sixteen megabytes – but the entire IRIS program, along with the reference images of our target and the program I've written myself to aim and move the rifle, will be stored in this PROM by the time I've finished with it. In fact, the IRIS program is already on it, along with a test picture.'

'What? Why does it need so little space?' demanded Berman, perplexed. 'What's all the extra, uh, RAM for? There seems to be a hell of a lot more of that, if you compare them.'

'Fair question,' said Kramer. 'It's like this. The program itself, and the images, are stored permanently in the PROM. They just sit there, being consulted by the Gamma chip. The RAM does all the actual work – or, rather, the Gamma does the work, with the RAM helping to feed it information quickly. The RAM has to store up to twenty-five new images each second, while the Gamma chip processes them and then discards them if they don't match the reference ones. The images themselves come in up here.' Kramer indicated the top left corner of the board. 'These three things are called ADCs – that stands for analog-to-digital converters. There's one for the blue spectrum, one for red and one for green. They convert the signal from the camera into digital information so that it can be processed. The original IRIS program was written for black-and-white pictures, which would only need one ADC. But for some reason colour is an important factor with the target we'll be going for, so I've had to add two more ADCs and change things around slightly. I must admit, I'm intrigued as to who our target might be. Maybe the guy has a yellow skin, rather than a white one.'

'Or maybe he's black,' interjected Berman.

'Quite possibly . . . Anyway, the signal is processed by the three analog-to-digital converters, then it goes into this bigger component next to them. This thing's called a frame-capture system. Think of it as similar to the freeze-frame facility on a video-recorder, except more sophisticated. The frame-capture system stores the information until the main chip has processed and discarded it, then it grabs the next frame. All of this happens twenty-five times a second.'

'So the whole thing's on one circuit board?'

'Yes,' said Kramer. 'Now,' he added, turning to the contents of his last package, 'these two other components are much more straightforward. This is a backup NiCad battery, and this is a mains adaptor. Very ordinary.' Kramer began to connect the components together. He plugged the mains adaptor into a power outlet, then flipped a microswitch on the circuit board. There was a tiny humming noise from the Gamma chip's miniature cooling fan, otherwise nothing. 'There,' said Kramer. 'IRIS is now loaded and running in memory, along with a standard reference image. It's just waiting for an input image for comparison. That's all there is to it.'

'What?' asked Berman incredulously. 'You mean there's no computer screen? No keyboard?'

'No,' replied Kramer calmly. 'They won't be needed when I've finished setting it up. After all, who's going to type things on a keyboard when it's running? And who's going to look at a screen? I've set the program to load automatically on power-up, so no key input is necessary. The comparisons are done electronically, so no screen is needed either.'

Berman looked dubious. 'How do you know it works?'

In answer, his boss extracted a further item from his briefcase. Berman's first guess was that it was an ordinary video-camera. 'Yes,' confirmed Kramer, 'it's just what it looks like. Top of the range, but obtainable anywhere. I've modified its output, but I haven't had time yet to break it down and remove the parts we don't need, such as the tape drive and the viewfinder. When I've finished, its bulk will be reduced by more than half. This cable,' he said, indicating a small plug on the end of a thin coax line protruding from the camera body, 'connects into the computer circuit board, next to the ADCs, like so.' He plugged in the connector and switched on the camera, setting it down on the workbench. Then he aligned it to point at the bare wall near the door.

The camera's automatic focusing mechanism made a vain attempt to adjust, but the wall was blank. Kramer set the focus manually at ten feet. 'Eventually, the camera will operate from the same power source as the computer. Now,' he said, pulling out a large, flat envelope. 'Here are some nice ten-by-eight colour photographs.' He got up and went over to the door, pinning a picture of a vintage car on the wall. 'Just a test card, so to speak.' Using the viewfinder, Kramer adjusted the camera's position so that the car was in the frame. The picture was sharp. 'OK,' he said. 'Just cover the lens with this blank card, would you?'

Berman held the card in front of the lens to blank out the picture, while Kramer replaced the photograph of the car with a full-page nude from a girlie magazine.

'Something a bit different,' remarked Kramer wryly, eyeing the obvious appreciation on Berman's face. 'OK, take the card away now and let's see if it blows a fuse.'

Berman removed the card, grinning. 'What's supposed to happen?'

'Nothing,' said Kramer. 'IRIS doesn't seem to think much of her.' Berman sniggered.

'OK,' instructed Kramer, 'put the card back.' He substituted a photograph of someone whom Berman did not recognise. 'Right – take the card away again.'

'Who is that guy?' asked Berman. IRIS had not reacted.

'John Doe,' answered Kramer. 'I have no idea who he is. Just a test. Card again.'

Kramer repeated the exercise eight more times with photographs of different people. On the ninth occasion he pinned up a picture of himself. 'I've always rather liked this particular shot of me,' he murmured lightly. 'Card away.'

'OK, Peter,' sighed Berman, who was growing rather bored with all this. 'I get the point. Nothing's happening. What does it do when it sees someone it recognises?'

'Patience, Carl,' said Kramer. 'You'll see. Cover the lens with the card again.' He pinned another picture to the wall.

'Hey, that's me!' said Berman, recognising a photograph that Meg had taken recently.

'Take the card away, Carl.'

Berman did as he was told. Almost instantly there was a loud beep from IRIS's circuit board and a red light-emitting diode lit up brightly. 'Hey!' he said, startled. 'What's it doing? It thinks *I'm* the one it's got to recognise? What *is* this? Has it gone crazy?'

Kramer laughed at Berman's sudden expression of alarm. 'It's all right, Carl. For this exercise, I programmed your photo into its memory. But don't worry,' he continued, 'that was just a demonstration.'

Berman was rattled. 'This thing's creepy,' he muttered. 'How the hell does it do that?'

'Actually,' said Kramer, now serious, 'that was a very easy test indeed for IRIS – it had that identical photo of you programmed into it. The problems start when there are different light levels, or the subject is at a slight angle, or has his head bowed or something. Or if there are things like shadows, when the light strikes at different angles – maybe his nose or eyebrows cast a deep shadow in sunlight, but none on a dull day. How does it deal with that? What happens if his hair is a different length from the reference picture? Or maybe he's wearing dark glasses? Or he's grown a moustache? Or if he's wearing a hat? Or if he's standing sideways on? Those are only a few of the headaches.'

Berman looked thoughtful. 'Yeah,' he said. 'I see. Can IRIS make allowances for all those things?'

'To some extent, yes,' answered Kramer. 'But it isn't perfect, yet. Fortunately, I've been told that our target won't present a problem. But as I said, I don't know who he or she is yet.' He sighed in frustration. 'But it doesn't matter. I know where the hit has to be made, so I've been able to work out how it can be set up. It means we can start putting all this stuff together, and then we can give it a field-test. OK,' he said finally, 'let's talk about the casing and the servo motors for adjusting the aim.'

The two men discussed the aiming mechanism for a further twenty minutes until they were both satisfied with the requirement. Then Kramer dismantled the computer equipment and wrapped it up in its protective layers before replacing each component in his briefcase. Berman unlocked the door to the den and let them out, carefully locking it again behind them.

'OK, see you soon, Peter,' said Berman when they had walked through to the open doorway at the front of the house.

'Goodbye, Carl,' replied Kramer. On the far side of the lawn, Meg Berman was weeding a flower-bed. ''Bye, Meg,' he called.

She straightened and glanced round. ''Bye, Peter,' she called back, waving.

'Hey, Peter,' said Carl, a sudden frown of anxiety on his face. 'You change the picture on that damn thing, you hear? Don't you forget, now.'

Kramer laughed grimly as he got back into the

big Chrysler. 'Don't worry, Carl,' he said, 'I'll change it.'

15

Tom Levy pushed his way imperiously through the throng of people in the entrance hall, heading for the main staircase leading to the first floor. He squared his shoulders as he reached the first step. *Errol Flynn*, he thought. *Errol Flynn always handled himself well on staircases. Charisma. Presence. Power!* He began to ascend the stairs. A brooding, purposeful look on his face, he strode past others waiting in line to be received.

'Hey, what — ?' a woman squeaked in protest as Levy pushed brusquely past her.

Just a nobody, he thought, dismissively. He reached the top of the stairs and moved quickly forward to the front of the line.

'Tom Levy,' he announced in a sonorous voice, his tall figure towering over the ambassador's aide. 'Special Counsel to the President of the United States.' He bent forward and spoke into the aide's ear. 'Just make sure you get that right, OK?'

'Of course, Mr Levy,' said the aide politely, turning to announce his name and appointment in a voice that wasn't as loud and show-stopping as Levy would have liked.

George Hamilton, thought Levy. Fixing his twenty-thousand-dollar, state-of-the-dentist's-art smile in place, he stepped forward to shake the hand of his host. 'Mr Ambassador!' he declaimed loudly. 'Good to see you again! What a truly wonderful party!' Levy's eyes searched the room for a second or two, alighting briefly on some youthful female figures. 'Such a delightful setting!'

'Thank you, Mr Levy,' said the Norwegian ambassador evenly. 'It is most kind of you to come. You know my wife, Eva, of course.'

Levy turned and flashed his smile at Eva Carlsson. 'Of course!' He took both her hands in his, inclining his head. 'Mrs Carlsson. Eva,' he said meaningfully. 'It's just *great* to see you again. I really mean that!'

'I am pleased you could come, Mr Levy,' she replied. 'I do hope you enjoy our party.'

'I am confident I will, ma'am,' Levy replied. These middle-aged matrons were always bowled over by his devastating charm, he knew. *Who was there, these days, as glamorous as the old Hollywood idols? No, what the ambassador's wife was falling for was style as it used to be.* He smiled again at her, then turned away. Taking a glass of champagne from a waiter with a tray, he strode importantly towards the crowd of chattering guests.

Eva Carlsson had turned to her husband. 'I can't stand men like that,' she whispered to him.

The ambassador gave his wife a fond, conspiratorial smile, then turned to greet his next guest.

Tom Levy was progressing magisterially through the assembled company, graciously acknowledging a few faces whom he recognised. 'Alan!' he called loudly, seeing the senior senator from the State of Wisconsin a few yards away. Alan Glassner was on his hit list for the evening, someone he could profitably talk to, but there was a crowd of guests in the way. *Charlton Heston*, thought Levy. *Like in 'El Cid', or . . . No. 'The Ten Commandments'*. Setting his jaw, he drove forward with renewed vigour. The crowd parted in front of him like the Red Sea. He reached Glassner. *George Hamilton again*. The smile flashed. 'How are you doing, Alan? Great to see you. Say, there's something I'd like to discuss with you.' Completely ignoring Glassner's wife, whose face darkened with indignation, Levy threw his arm round the unfortunate senator's shoulder and drew him to one side, talking earnestly.

Power! thought Tom Levy ten minutes later. Glassner would now fall into line on the gay rights issue. It had only taken a few minutes to talk him round.

Levy failed to notice the expression of annoyance and renewed determination on the senator's face as Glassner rejoined his wife. He was still congratulating himself when he heard a little cry of alarm and someone cannoned into his left side, jogging his elbow and causing him to spill champagne over his hand and jacket. The glass tumbled to the floor and shattered.

'Oh! I'm *so* sorry!' said a soft, musical voice before a furious Levy had a chance to give vent to his feelings. He turned and found himself looking into a concerned but beautiful face. She pulled out a small handkerchief and began dabbing delicately at his jacket. 'Your clothes!' she apologised. 'I *am* sorry!' she said again. 'Someone pushed me and I lost my balance. Can you ever forgive me?' Shaking her head, she continued to dab, concentrating on her task.

As she dabbed, a deliciously intoxicating wave of perfume wafted up to Levy's nostrils. No, he thought, this wasn't what your average Washington bimbo splashed on before going out to smart cocktails. This was . . . *refinement*. Fluffy shoulder-length blond hair above wide but vacant blue eyes was his usual choice; but here, expensively cut dark hair framed an intelligent, high-boned face. His eyes travelled to the merest hint of a promising cleavage above a classily understated couture black dress. At forty-five, he had grown used to nubile twenty-year-olds who were happy to be wined, dined and bedded by one of the capital's most ambitious, influential movers and shakers. *They* let it all hang out, but this lady . . . This lady was something else.

Finished with her handkerchief, she smoothed down his jacket, her long, elegant fingers running lightly down his chest. Then she reached up and straightened his bow tie with a smile. 'There,' she said brightly. 'All fixed!'

At that moment, she was pushed again from behind. Her fingers slipped from the bow tie, brushing against his neck, and Tom Levy felt the whole length of her body thrust against his. He was smitten. From that moment, he knew he had to have this woman.

'Don't I recognise you?' he asked finally. 'You aren't by any chance . . .?'

It was so instinctive – dozens of women had fallen for it before. But as he saw her face cloud over slightly he instantly regretted the cheap chat-up line.

'Actually,' she replied smoothly, 'my name's Joanna Stone. And I'm sure we haven't met before. But I think I *do* know who you are. Aren't you Tom Levy? *The* Tom Levy from the White House?'

'I have that honour, ma'am!'

They both burst out laughing at the triteness of his reply.

'Look,' he said, 'I'd really like to get to know you better. Unfortunately I can't stay much longer because I've got another engagement. It's at the White House, actually, and the President will be there. Much though I'd like to, I don't feel I can let him down!' *Curious*, he thought, *I've never said that kind of thing with a hint of irony before. Something must be happening to me.*

'No, indeed, Mr Levy – a man in your position can hardly shirk his social responsibilities!' she replied brightly. 'And in any case I really think I must rescue my companion tonight. He's a Canadian businessman, quite new to Washington, and I see he's been cornered by that rather good-looking but undeniably boring Irish diplomat. They're probably talking fishing quotas,' she added, turning down the corners of her mouth expressively.

It was a very full, very kissable mouth, thought Levy, and he longed to prove it to himself at that very moment. But with this kind of woman, he knew, he would have to be more subtle.

'I really would like to buy you dinner one evening,'

he persisted. 'That is, if the Canadian . . .' He left the question unfinished.

'But it's I who should be buying *you* dinner,' she objected mildly. 'After all, you'll be paying the cleaner's bill! Actually, I'd be delighted . . . and don't worry, there isn't anyone else at present. In fact my Canadian friend's, well . . .' She fluttered her hand slightly. 'Not interested, shall we say?'

'Maybe it's the Irishman who needs rescuing?' Levy ventured.

'Could be,' she replied, her hazel eyes twinkling. 'Anyway, shall I give you my number?'

'You bet.'

'Do you have a pen on you?'

'I don't need to write it down.'

'Sure you won't forget it?'

'I won't,' he answered truthfully. He never forgot telephone numbers.

Joanna recited the number. 'I'm really glad I met you, Tom. Call me soon.' She flashed him a brilliant smile, turned on her heel and disappeared through the throng of guests.

She didn't get that smile in any dentist's office, he thought admiringly. *Jesus, what a woman!*

'Excuse me . . . excuse me,' he heard himself saying as he wove a path between tuxedos and backless dresses to pay his respects to his hosts before leaving. *Excuse me?* Suddenly Tom Levy realised that for a full half-hour he hadn't been rude, domineering or dismissive to anyone.

16

Sir Reginald Hislop had dozed off again in his armchair, his book in his lap. When he awoke he did so with a start; he could not be sure how long he had slept. He had a crick in his neck, and he realised he was feeling uncomfortably hot. There was an itch on his left forearm; he scratched it through his pyjama jacket, and felt something unfamiliar. Rolling up the sleeve, he saw there was a large piece of sticking plaster. He couldn't remember it having been there before.

The heat irritated him; he frowned and rose to his feet, looking up at the ventilation grille. As well as being hot, the air in the room smelled stale. Was the ventilation system working, or not? He rolled himself another cigarette and lit it, inhaling deeply.

A rush of thoughts and questions came to him. He suddenly wondered where on earth he was. Then he noticed something strange. On the cabinet by the bed, the carafe which had contained orange squash had disappeared; in its place was a plastic bottle of mineral water with a screw top. Someone had been in the room while he slept! He turned to look at the door, and noticed something else that had not been there earlier. A notice of some sort had been taped to the door. Above it was a small hatch. Had the hatch been there before? He could not remember. He walked over to read what the notice said.

THIS HATCH WILL BE OPENED AT REGULAR
INTERVALS.
IF YOU REQUIRE FOOD OR WATER, YOU ARE TO
SAY
'I CAN'T REMEMBER ANYTHING.'

What! What sort of a place was this? How dare they treat him this way! Hislop began pacing around the room, examining it with a fresh eye. He noticed that the furniture was all bolted to the floor. Nothing could be moved. Why? Looking again at the bottle of water, Hislop suddenly realised that he needed to urinate. He walked over to the door.

Almost exactly on cue, before he could bang on the hatch for attention, it opened. Hislop blinked in surprise, then bent to peer through the narrow aperture. He could see nothing except another wall, about six feet away. 'I need the toilet,' he called out.

The hatch instantly slammed shut in his face.

'Hey!' he shouted indignantly, rapping his knuckles on the hatch. 'Did you hear me? I said I need the toilet!' The hatch remained shut; despite banging on it and calling out, there was no response at all. After five minutes he gave up and returned to the armchair, his thoughts in turmoil. For the first time, he realised that he was a prisoner; but for the life of him he could not remember how he had been abducted.

After a further half hour of increasing discomfort, the pressure on his bladder became intolerable. Finally, in desperation, he tipped the fruit in the plastic bowl on to the table. Setting the bowl on the floor, he knelt down and relieved himself into it. His discomfort now eased, he carefully picked up the bowl and moved it into a corner of the room so there would be no danger of his knocking it over. *By God*, he thought crossly, *I'll give these buggers a piece of my mind when I . . .*

Returning to the armchair, he reached for one of the oranges on the table and peeled it slowly. His feelings of indignation began to be replaced by anxiety as he ate. The orange was dry and tasted slightly bitter, but his mind was elsewhere. He started to worry about his plight. His hands were shaking slightly as he finished the orange and rolled himself another cigarette.

'So,' said General Erfurt. 'He has finally realised what has happened to him.'

The closed-circuit television monitor in the room above once again showed the top of the old man's head; the microphone clearly picked up the sounds of his muttering.

'The beta-blockers have worn off,' said Gerhardt

Eisener. 'He will obtain some relief from the tobacco, but it will not be long now before the laxatives in the fruit take effect.'

'Good,' said the general. 'Tell Gerber to turn the heat up two more degrees, to twenty-seven Celsius.'

17

The first passengers from the Los Angeles flight began to emerge from the customs hall. Howard stood a little way back from the waiting crowd, smoking a cigarette as he scanned the faces of the arrivals. After a few minutes he recognised a tall, rangy figure dressed in jeans and a checked shirt. He was carrying a briefcase and a large green rucksack that had seen better days. 'Mike! Long time no see!' he called out.

'How ya doin', Ed?' Mike Ziegler smiled broadly, pumping Howard's hand.

'I see you've still got that same old clapped-out bergen,' Howard chided him, grinning. 'Why don't you treat yourself to a new one, or get a suitcase like everyone else?'

'I brought it along for old times' sake,' said Ziegler. 'And there ain't nothin' wrong with it, anyhow. At least no one would think of stealin' it, would they? In any case, I guess this is like an action replay of last year. Which country are we invadin' this time?'

'I'll tell you in the car,' said Howard. 'Come on, let's go.' He led the way out of the airport terminal towards the short-term car-park.

Ziegler had first met Howard twenty-two years previously, when he had been a young officer in the US Navy SEALS, based at Coronado. Howard, an officer in the British Special Boat Service – the Royal Marines' equivalent of the SAS – had been sent on an exchange posting to the USA and Ziegler had been detailed to collect him from San Diego airport and look after him. He had discovered to his pleasant surprise that Howard was more than capable of looking after himself. The two men had hit it off straight away, and became firm friends. Neither Howard nor his SEALS hosts had expected they would have much to learn from the exchange, but they soon realised that they had underestimated each other and that each stood to profit from knowledge of their opposite numbers' equipment, training, techniques and procedures. Later, Ziegler had been sent on a reciprocal posting to Britain, to the SBS's base at Poole, in Dorset.

Prompted by his wife, who had later divorced him, Howard had left the Forces in 1977 and had been offered a well-paid job by Mike Ziegler's father, a successful New York businessman. For three years Howard had run old man Ziegler's London office but had hated the inaction and left to start up a private security company. Mike Ziegler had immediately joined him and together they recruited a team of ex-forces personnel, mostly from the SAS and SBS, to advise wealthy individuals and corporations at risk from such threats as kidnap and ransom demands. XF Securities had been a success and was still very much a going concern.

Ziegler knew Howard's character well – probably better than anyone else did. Although the two of them had not seen each other for over a year, they had exchanged frequent business telephone calls and Ziegler had been vaguely puzzled by something. Howard had kept the conversations brief and to the point, which in a way was fair enough, but there had been less of the usual friendly chat and banter than normal. Ziegler had an acute eye for detail, and despite the genuine warmth of Howard's greeting he was now sensing the same thing again – this time strongly. Howard was walking ahead of him, quite fast. His serious expression and the barely controlled urgency of his movements seemed somehow out of place in the circumstances. Ziegler suddenly realised what was wrong. The man was as tense and tight as a bow-string. *Why*? He frowned briefly and followed in silence.

Out in the car-park he slung his rucksack in the back of Howard's hire car and climbed into the front, jacking the seat back to accommodate his long, athletic frame. Howard jumped into the driver's seat.

'Ed,' said Ziegler lightly, 'before we set off, d'you mind tellin' me what's eatin' you up? You're as tense as hell.'

'Huh?' Howard glanced at him, startled by the unexpected question. He saw that Ziegler was giving him a calm, appraising look. He sighed deeply and shrugged, managing a weak smile. 'I suppose I am,' he admitted. 'Trust you to notice it.'

'Well? What's the problem?'

'Oh, hell, Mike, it's nothing really. It's just . . .' He sighed again, frowned and shook his head. 'Well, I suppose it's that business last year. It still rankles badly with me. We were stitched up, dammit. I just can't get that out of my mind.'

'You mean that's it? You're still sore about that? Now listen here, Ed. For a while I felt the same way as you. Hell, I guess all of us did. We lost two buddies, and we were all let down. But the rest of us have gotten over it. You should too. It's history, for Chrissake. Put it down to experience. You play rough games, you expect rough treatment – you know that as well as I do. Come on – forget it.'

'That's easier said than done,' muttered Howard.

'In your case, I bet I know why. You got a woman at the moment?'

'What? Oh. Well, as it happens, no, I haven't. Why?'

'Get one. You've been livin' too solitary a life, and with no one to talk to you've just been bottlin' things up. You're fit to explode. At the very least you're shapin' up for an ulcer, or maybe even a coronary. You need a woman. And I don't just mean the occasional one-night stand. Find someone you can relax with and talk to, who can be a good companion.'

'That's easier said than done, too. You know me – I always end up having rows with them.'

'Well, at least you've figured out where you're goin' wrong with them,' said Ziegler wryly. 'That's a start, you have to admit.'

'Maybe,' muttered Howard non-committally. He started the car and pulled out towards the exit. 'How's Jackie, by the way?'

'She's in great shape. She sends you her love. Can't imagine why, but there you are. I'm still tryin' to persuade her to marry me, but she says she prefers things the way they are. You know what she's like – independent, knows her own mind. Comin' up for five years, now, we've been together.'

Ziegler's lover, Jackie Kosinski, described herself simply as being 'in the movie business'. She bore a striking physical resemblance to a glamorous and highly paid film star, and for many years had been acting as a 'body-double' in difficult or dangerous scenes where any risk to her famous alter ego had to be minimised for insurance reasons. The actress herself had no complaints at all – she had little taste for physical exertion and danger, and was happy to leave such things to Jackie. A dynamic character, Jackie relished the life and the degree of risk that went with it; it was interesting, the work was not too repetitive, she was well-paid and there were long periods of time off between films.

Five years previously a series of very unpleasant threats had been made to the actress's life and at the insistence of their insurers the producers of the film she had been working on had called in XF Securities to advise them. Ziegler, as head of XF's Los Angeles office, had been sufficiently interested in the novelty of the project to have taken it on personally. The assignment had been a straightforward one, but it had given Ziegler an insight into the frenetic world of the movies – and he had met Jackie.

'Stunt-lady, huh?' had been his first words to her. The comment had not been well received, but the two of them had of necessity spent some time together – Ziegler had known that the threat to the actress could also mean danger for her double, even if only when filming. Jackie had been impressed by his calm, sensible advice and he, in turn, had been impressed too, watching her in action – particularly in one scene involving free-climbing an extremely severe rock-face. Typically, she had suggested the idea of climbing it free – without any ropes or safety-harness – herself. Ziegler knew he would have thought hard before attempting such a climb and he felt a surprisingly keen pang of protectiveness and anxiety for her safety as he watched. She was an accomplished athlete, and as the film progressed, Ziegler increasingly admired her spirit and professionalism.

Later, they had both been watching the filming of a scene where the double for the film's ageing male lead had the task of engaging a group of 'criminals' in a firefight in a warehouse and taking out all eight of them, the last three in hand-to-hand combat. After half a dozen takes, the director was still not satisfied with the double's performance. Nor was Ziegler. 'That stunt-man's a complete asshole,' he commented loudly during a break following the sixth take. 'Can't even fire that little popgun of his without blinkin', and he moves around like a three-legged ox with gut-ache. My old grandpa would be more convincin', and he's ninety-four and half-crippled with arthritis, poor old guy.'

The film's director overheard the remark. 'Think you can do better, wise guy?' he snarled.

'Anyone could do better than that turkey,' Ziegler

replied. He had seen the previous six attempts, and knew how the scene was supposed to go. 'You want me to have a shot at it?'

The director had glared at him for a long moment. Then, seeing the opportunity for a little light relief at Ziegler's expense, he had announced loudly that the 'gumshoe' was going to give them a demonstration.

'Gumshoe, my ass,' said Ziegler scornfully. Half an hour later, dressed and roughly made up for the part, he strode on to the set and began calling out instructions to the camera operators. 'You guys keep all those things rollin' from start to finish – no breaks this time. And you'll need to move them quite a lot quicker than before, or you'll miss the action. OK?'

The director, a man notorious for his autocratic behaviour and frequent rages, had been so astonished at Ziegler's usurpation of his authority that he had just gaped and allowed him to proceed.

The result had been electrifying. Ziegler's movements had been so fast and fluid, and his actions so frighteningly authentic, that there had been dead silence for a few seconds after the last of the 'criminals' had been flattened with a devastating flurry of blows.

'Cut!' croaked the astonished director eventually, recovering his wits.

'Did you get all that, you guys?' Ziegler called out to the cameramen, not even out of breath. 'Or do you want another run through?'

'No! Print it!' yelled the director who, despite his other shortcomings, could recognise a good take when he saw one.

Later, someone had respectfully pointed out to Ziegler that he wasn't actually supposed to disable the 'criminals' for real, but just pretend to; the director had offered him a full-time job, which he had immediately turned down; and he had taken Jackie out to dinner. Since then they had remained together as a couple, and he had accompanied her whenever possible on location.

To Ziegler, she was the only genuine part of any of the movies in which she appeared. But, he mused now, there would be no more risky stunts for her for a while . . .

He snapped out of his thoughts back to the present and turned to Howard. 'Hey – that reminds me. How does the idea of becomin' a godfather grab you?'

'What? Do you mean . . .?'

'Yeah. Due next February. Kind of unplanned, but we've got used to the idea and we're both lookin' forward to bein' first-time parents.'

'Mike, that's terrific! My congratulations to you both!' Howard's pleasure was evident as he glanced at his friend.

'Is that a yes, or what?'

'Of course. I'd be delighted and honoured.' He frowned briefly. 'Now she'll *have* to agree to marry you. Maybe I should have a word with her about it.'

'You keep your interferin' ass out of it,' drawled Ziegler. 'The last thing I need is a clumsy goddam Limey like you foulin' things up between us. Now, come on. What's the job this time? Give.'

'I'm not in the least surprised she won't marry you,' said Howard, deliberately ignoring Ziegler's question. 'I mean, just look at you. Anyone would think you were a vagrant. I'm amazed our immigration people let you into the country.'

'They recognise real class when they see it, even if you don't. Come on, give.'

'You could at least shave once in a while, you shag,' said Howard, grinning. 'You look like shit.'

'Up your *ass*,' drawled Ziegler equably. 'What you see is what you get, you bum. Now, quit stallin' and give.'

Ziegler remained silent for a while when Howard had finished outlining the mission. 'Ed,' he said eventually, 'I hope you won't mind me sayin' so, but this sounds like one hell of a tall order. I don't like this idea of rollin' two jobs into one. Just gettin' in and out of that place is goin' to be tough enough. But to be weighed down with extra goddam monitorin' equipment, let alone havin' to mess around installin' it in an enemy nuclear facility . . . No, I don't like it one little bit, Ed.'

'I know,' said Howard. 'I don't go for that nuclear part of it any more than you do. I haven't said a definite "yes" to it – just promised to consider it.'

'OK,' said Ziegler. 'I guess we know each other well enough – I'll go along with whatever you decide. So who else have you got on board? Have you talked to Johnny about it?'

'I've spoken to him, yes. But I've decided he's not coming with us. Hell, Mike, he can't. He's not fit – that leg wound he got in Iraq has really slowed him down.'

'He won't like bein' left out,' said Ziegler thoughtfully.

'He doesn't like it at all,' said Howard. 'But he knows I'm right. I told him I'd take him on two conditions: that he did the equivalent of the SAS selection Test Week again to show he was fit, and that he got written permission from Juliet saying he could go.'

Ziegler laughed. 'Well, I haven't seen him for a while, so I don't know about his fitness. But from what I know about Juliet, there's about as much chance of her agreein' to let him go as of seein' a squadron of saddle-back pigs flyin' overhead in box formation, loopin' the loop and trailin' blue smoke out of their asses.'

Howard grinned. 'Johnny knew he was beaten on that one. I don't think he even dared ask her. But I did offer him a small consolation – he'll be going out to Seoul, to set up our radio comms link. It's not much, but it's something. Colonel Goodale's going with him.'

'OK. So who's in the rest of the party?'

'Tony Ackford, Mel Harris, Angelo Zeccara and Pete Halliday.'

Ziegler knew Ackford and Harris well; both had been with him and Howard in Iraq the year before.

'And what does Kath say?' he inquired, his eyes twinkling with mirth. It was a standing joke that Ackford's diminutive, fiercely possessive Irish wife never allowed him to go on a job unless she had first received a note from Howard to confirm that he was telling the truth.

'I haven't asked permission yet,' responded Howard. 'I'd better get it in hand!'

The wiry, mercurial Harris was another long-time colleague. The former SAS sergeant had the fastest reactions that either Howard or Ziegler had ever seen. Those reactions had stood him in good stead on the cricket pitch and he had turned out for his county once or twice, but he had long since put soldiering before any thoughts of a career as a sportsman.

Halliday and the half-Italian Zeccara were less familiar names to Ziegler. 'I've talked to Pete Halliday on the phone a couple of times,' he said, 'but I don't know much about him. And I don't know Angelo at all.'

'They're both ex-22 SAS,' said Howard. 'Pete was a sergeant; he came out last year. He was with the Regiment for twelve years, and he served in all the usual places. Johnny first came across him in the Falklands. More recently he was in the Gulf War. Angelo's record is much the same, except he only left the Regiment recently – he and Pete have known each other for years. Mel Harris knew them both, too. In fact, he recruited them to XF. Pete's a good radio man, right up-to-date on the latest gear. He developed a particular interest in it after that balls-up in the Gulf when some of the guys were let down by duff kit and wrong frequencies. In the circs you would, wouldn't you?'

'Yeah,' responded Ziegler. 'What's Angelo's specialty?'

Howard said nothing but made a circular gesture above his head with one finger. 'We're all out of practice at it,' he said, 'and Angelo has had more experience than any of us.'

'Oh, shit!' said Ziegler, laughing. 'Hell, big Tony is not goin' to like that one little bit!'

'I know,' Howard chuckled. 'I haven't told him yet. I'm leaving it until the last minute.'

'So that's it? Six of us?'

'Seven,' said Howard. 'We'll need one extra man. The colonel's looking around for someone with the right qualifications.'

'What qualifications?'

'I thought you'd have guessed. We're going to need a Korean-speaking interpreter. A good one.'

'Oh,' sighed Ziegler. 'Yeah, I should have guessed. Goddam jet-lag must have got to me.' He paused. 'That could mean a civilian, unless we can find . . . Hey, I have an idea. There's more likely to be someone like that in the US forces than here in the UK. We have people servin' out in South Korea the whole time. D'you want me to ask around?'

'The colonel thought of that too. He says he's already got a short-list. Apparently all but one of them are Americans, with one or both parents of Korean origin. The colonel's handling all the security vetting, so I don't think we need to do any digging ourselves – although I've told him we'll need to approve the man he selects.'

'Yeah,' said Ziegler, frowning. 'Well, I just hope the colonel is real thorough with his vettin' procedures, if you get my meanin'.'

'I know exactly what you mean. That's what worries me too.'

18

Tom Levy's sense of excitement and anticipation mounted as he rode the elevator to Joanna Stone's seventh-floor apartment. He was bringing her flowers, and had booked a table at the right sort of restaurant – smart, elegant, yet not so fashionable as to be vulgar – for a sophisticated woman in her thirties. Maybe after that there would be some dancing, then . . . well, he would see how it went. He wasn't going to rush it.

It had been four days since their meeting at the Norwegian Embassy party, and he had been unable to get her off his mind. Nevertheless he had resisted the temptation to hurry things; he had had three late nights at the White House working with the President, and he waited until he knew he had a clear evening and could do things properly. She had sounded pleased to hear his voice on the telephone, and, yes, she would love to see him.

He had known instinctively that Joanna was something special. And he had decided that, apart from being quite obviously both highly intelligent and stunningly attractive, she was the sexiest woman he had ever encountered. Paradoxically, it was because she didn't show everything she'd got. He was going to take a great deal of trouble – and, if necessary, time – over this particular lady. *Cary Grant*, he thought. *Cary Grant always behaved like a gentleman. Perhaps too much . . . OK*, he thought, compromising, *Cary Grant, but with a strong hint of Warren Beatty*.

The elevator stopped. Levy took a deep breath and stepped out. A sign informed him that apartments 701–705 were to the left. He walked down the wide, thickly carpeted corridor and stopped outside number 703. He took another deep breath and pressed the bell. *Hell!* he thought wonderingly. *I haven't felt as nervous about a date since my Harvard days*.

He heard approaching footsteps; then the latch clicked and Joanna was standing in the doorway.

She seemed even more beautiful than when he had first met her. Her short, dark hair framed her face, accentuating her cheekbones and the line of her jaw. Those steady, strikingly hazel eyes – almost leonine eyes – held his in their gaze.

'Hello, Joanna,' he stammered, gulping. All the smart things he had planned to say had gone out the window and he stood there like a shy, spotty teenager, awkwardly twisting the bunch of flowers in his hands. 'You . . . I hope you don't mind if I say . . . hell, I can't help it anyway. You look stunning!'

She smiled, the hint of seriousness in her face gone. 'Thank you, Tom,' she replied, her voice pitched soft and low. Her eyes widened as she noticed the flowers. 'Oh, they're gorgeous! Are they for me?'

'Oh, yes, of course,' he said, remembering at last. 'Two dozen of the best red roses I could lay my hands on. But . . . they don't compare to you. No flowers in the world could do that.' Even as he said it the corniness of the compliment appalled him, but he could not help himself – that was the way she made him feel.

To save him further embarrassment she reached out and took the roses. 'Thank you,' she murmured. 'They're lovely. And please come in. We simply can't stand chatting in the doorway like this.'

He followed her through to a sitting room which, just as he had anticipated, was furnished in expensive but understated style. Tom Levy couldn't tell a French antique commode from a down-and-out's cardboard box, but somehow he knew that these pieces were the real thing. Frankly, though, he was more interested in Joanna than in his surroundings. He had been vaguely conscious that she was wearing something pale, and now his eyes ran down her. Her narrow white dress emphasised the perfect lines of her figure, and in the soft light of the room her limbs looked tanned and supple.

'Sit down, Tom,' she said over her shoulder, disappearing into what he assumed was the kitchen. 'I'll just pop these in water. And then a drink for us, I think.'

'Sounds great,' said Levy.

There was a sound of running water, and over it Joanna's voice called, 'I need a moment to finish getting ready, Tom. If you wander over to the bar you'll find a bottle of something sparkly. Could you open it for us?'

He looked round the room and saw a discreet bar in the corner. 'Sure thing,' he replied. *Something sparkly, indeed!* he thought as he saw what lay in the ice bucket. *Veuve Clicquot – one of the best non-vintages*. He untwisted the wire and gently prised out the cork. There was a soft pop; slowly he filled the two crystal champagne goblets standing ready beside the bucket.

Behind the bar there was a mirror, and, quite unconsciously, Levy found himself staring at his reflection. His customary self-confidence had now returned, and he knew he was looking good. *You deserve this,* he thought admiringly. *Cary Grant, eat your heart out – Tom Levy's time has come!*

Suddenly he caught sight of another figure behind his own reflection. Joanna was standing there with an amused expression on her face. He turned quickly and held out a glass of champagne for her, noting with approval that she was now wearing a long, creamy silk wrap that moved fluidly against her body as she walked, stroking the lines of her endlessly long, slim legs. They clinked glasses and drank. Her eyes never left his.

'It's no good – I just can't decide what to wear,' she murmured. 'But while I'm thinking, what about a hello kiss for me?'

He put his glass down and gently drew her to him. Her face lifted towards his, her eyes half-closed. Their mouths met, slowly at first, then more demandingly. The touch of her body in its silky covering felt electrically erotic. To Tom there was something wonderfully new, and yet at the same time completely familiar, about her. It was as if he had known her for a long time, and that this was the most natural thing in the world.

'I booked the table for eight-thirty,' he said quietly. 'But I don't suppose they'd mind if we were . . . a little late.'

'In that case,' she whispered, 'I think I know what I'll wear.' She wriggled her shoulders and he trembled with anticipation; the wrap slipped down her body and landed in a silken pool at their feet.

'I didn't think . . .' began Tom.

'. . . that this would happen so soon?' she finished for him. 'I'm not nineteen, Tom. I know what I want. And just now I want you very, very much . . . And you do want me, don't you?'

'Oh, yes! Yes, I do,' Levy answered huskily. His eyes glanced hurriedly around the room, searching for the right door.

'No, not the bedroom, Tom,' she murmured. 'Right here.'

He glanced down at the exquisitely patterned rug on which they were standing. 'Here?'

'It's Persian, Tom. It's very old, and very valuable. Let's make love just here. I'd find that much more exciting.'

Slowly Joanna Stone started to undress the President's Special Counsel.

19

The telephone rang. Howard lifted his eyes from the maps and photographs he had been studying, lit a cigarette and lifted the receiver. 'Hello?'

'Some news for you,' said a familiar voice. Max Goodale had no need to identify himself. 'I've just been to see the Director, and he's agreed. He said he'd make the necessary arrangements. You can go and kit yourselves out any time you want. All right?'

'Good,' said Howard. 'That'll save us a lot of bother. I'll give them a ring before we go – in fact, I'll do it right away. It would suit quite well if we went down there today.'

'Should be fine – whenever you like, the Director said.'

'There's something else I need to talk to you about,' said Howard. 'Are you free tomorrow night? Say around ten, here?'

'Hold on a minute,' Goodale paused to consult his diary. 'Yes. I'll see you then.' He rang off.

Howard leaned back in his chair, satisfied. The brief, cryptic conversation had contained welcome news, but it had not been unexpected. The Director of Special Forces would probably have raised his eyebrows at Goodale's request, he guessed, but his eventual agreement to give Howard the run of 22 SAS's weapons and equipment stores would save a great deal of time and trouble. Indeed, Howard had warned Goodale that it would be essential. Some of the items he required would be practically impossible to obtain anywhere else, and certainly not from any legitimate source.

He thought again about the matter he would be raising with Goodale, the following evening. That would be a far trickier thing to set up, but he didn't see why it couldn't be done. Goodale would have to go right to the top for that one. Stubbing out his cigarette, he reached for the telephone again and dialled the Hereford number he knew by heart.

'Hadn't we better take three cars, boss?' asked Angelo Zeccara an hour later as they all met up outside the XF Securities office in West London. 'We'll never get all the fucking kit into two. It wouldn't look too clever if we were eyeballed belting along the motorway with a pile of Gympies and M16s on Mel's roof-rack, and a bunch of 66s and a crate of grenades in mine.'

'We'll take my car as well,' said Howard. 'I've got

some blankets to cover any clobber we have to put on the back seats. Mike, Johnny – you two come with me. Mel, you take Tony. Pete, you go with Angelo. Right, let's go.'

During the drive Angelo Zeccara and Pete Halliday, two of XF's more recent recruits from the SAS, caught up on each other's news. Halliday had been abroad for the previous two months on a security assignment in Namibia, although he had no suntan to show for it. His pale, almost anaemic complexion and his slight figure – he was almost painfully thin – did not fit at all with the popular conception of a tough ex-SAS man. Nor did his eyes – they protruded alarmingly and made him look almost permanently surprised at what was going on around him.

Many people had made the mistake of judging Halliday solely by his appearance; when he had first volunteered for SAS selection ten years before, the training staff at Hereford had looked askance at him and mentally written him off as a no-hoper. To their surprise, he had proved to be one of the fittest and most determined men of his intake. The training sergeant-major had watched sceptically one day as Halliday had set off from the Storey Arms hostel up the steep track leading to the top of Pen-y-Fan, at 2,900 feet the highest peak in the Brecon Beacons, carrying that day's required load of a 55-pound bergen rucksack and rifle. A very fit man carrying such a weight could maintain a fast walk climbing a gradient that steep, but Halliday was one of the very few the sergeant-major had seen actually *run* most of the way up.

As Halliday approached the top the sergeant-major frowned, put down his binoculars and reached for his radio handset, calling the corporal who was manning the checkpoint at the trig point on the summit. 'Tosh? Listen,' he said. 'That little weedy-looking bloke with the goggle-eyes and big feet, you know the one?'

'You mean Halliday?'

'Yeah, that's him. He should be with you in a couple of minutes or so. Check his bergen when he gets there, will you? I bet he's only carrying about half the load, if that.' Five minutes later the corporal reported back that he had weighed Halliday's bergen and that if anything it was a shade heavier than the prescribed 55 pounds.

I'll be blowed, muttered the surprised sergeant-major to himself, rubbing his chin thoughtfully. *I'd never have thought the skinny little bugger had it in him.*

There were only two others on the selection course who regularly managed to turn in times to match or beat Halliday's; one of them was Angelo Zeccara. Zeccara, whose father was Italian and mother English, was a compact, well-built man and a fitness fanatic. The two men, opposites in so many ways, grew to like and respect each other. When Halliday had left the SAS after nine years' service to join XF Securities, Zeccara had followed not long afterwards. 'So, how was Namibia, Pete?' he asked Halliday. 'Been breaking all the ladies' hearts down there, have you?'

'You've got a bleeding nerve asking that, with your reputation,' replied Halliday.

Zeccara grinned. A talented and fearless rugby player, his dark good looks were marred only by one steel front tooth; he had lost the original in an over-enthusiastic rugby-tackle and had never bothered to have it properly replaced by a white ceramic one. The result gave him a slightly evil expression when he smiled, but he had never found this a drawback — certainly not as far as members of the opposite sex were concerned; in fact for some reason they seemed to find it attractive. Zeccara had been married briefly; his wife very soon became fed up with his seemingly compulsive unfaithfulness and divorced him.

'What do you mean, my reputation?' he asked Halliday. 'I can't help it if the ladies like me, can I?'

'Bollocks,' said Halliday. 'There's a word for what you are, mate, and it ain't nothing like Angelo.

Lothario, more like. You spend more time with your strides round your ankles than the whole of "B" Squadron put together. They ought to put a padlock on your zipper before you wear the bloody thing out. Fucking sex maniac, that's what you are.'

'Jealous.'

'Bullshit. I've seen you with some right ponking grimmies. Probably given most of them the clap, I expect. Statistically, you must have caught it yourself years ago. Me, I'm more particular. I want to know where they've been, and if it's anywhere near you, no thanks.'

'Then your luck's out, mate. I've been through the lot already. Some of them twice over. You'd better get used to a life of eternal celibacy.'

'Anything would be better than carbolic soap and a wire bottle-brush up your dick twice a week to clean you out.'

'Shows how little you know,' said Zeccara. 'You don't treat the clap like that. You . . .'

'Got you! By your own admission! If you know so much about treating it, you must have it.'

'Of course I know about it. I'm a trained medic, aren't I?'

'No, you fucking well aren't. I'm the trained medic around here. And you're heading for a nasty amputation, mate. Let me know when the pain gets too bad, and I'll do it myself.'

'You just keep your hands to yourself. Hey – has anyone told big Tony yet what else we're picking up from Hereford besides hardware?'

'You mean the HALO gear? I don't think so,' replied Halliday. 'We'd have heard all about it by now, wouldn't we?'

'Yeah, you're right. I can't wait to see his face when you give him the good news.'

'*Me?*' cried Halliday indignantly. 'Fuck *that*. You're supposed to be the expert at that game. You tell him.

Maybe he'll knock that lump of shrapnel out of your gums and you can get a proper yellow one to match the others.'

'Yellow? *Yellow?*' It was Zeccara's turn for mock-indignation. 'Don't you know gleaming white when you see it? If you want to see yellow teeth, don't look at me. Look in the fucking mirror and open your gob. On second thoughts, that won't do. Yours are more a sort of vomit-green colour.'

'You must be fucking colour-blind. How did you ever get into the Army? Jeez, they're letting all sorts in, these days.'

'Like you, for example. I saw your papers. You were supposed to be sent to the Army Waste Disposal Corps, not the SAS.'

'There's no such outfit.'

'You were to be the first. As a sample of the sort of crap they have to pick up and chuck in the bin, not as a soldier.'

'You obviously can't read. And if you want to talk about records, as the Air Troop medic I saw your medical file. The Army Medical Corps were pushing hard for you to be transferred to them as a terminal VD case for them to practise on.'

'There must have been a spelling mistake. They meant VC.'

'Victoria Cross? Don't make me laugh. The only reason you were ever shot at was because you were fast asleep on stag at the time. Your mouth was wide open and you were snoring like a beached hippo. We had a hard time afterwards trying to work out what gave us away – whether the opposition heard your snores or saw the moonlight glinting off that piece of ironmongery in your mouth. Probably both, most of us reckoned.'

Zeccara laughed, ignoring Halliday's gross distortion of the reason for one of the enemy contacts they had shared during the 1991 Gulf War. He had been far from asleep at the time. 'If I was snoring,' he countered, 'it was only because I was overcome by the noxious fumes you were giving off after eating all that shagging curry you had for tea that day. Four plates of it you had, you gannet. If anyone had struck a match, the explosion would have sent us into orbit.'

'That metal gnasher of yours must have gone rusty and caused a short-circuit in your brain. You're imagining things. As your doctor, I'm going to have to refer you to a good dentist to have it pulled out.'

'You must be joking. I'm not seeing any dentist.'

'You're sitting next to one.'

'You, a dentist? Pull the other one.'

'I'll pull them all, if you insist.'

'You wouldn't know how. You've never pulled a tooth in your life.'

'There's always a first time. Pull over to the side of the road and I'll do it right away. There must be a pair of pliers in the toolkit, and the car-jack should be strong enough to hold your mouth open.'

'I'm beginning to wish I'd brought along a G-clamp to keep *your* mouth *shut*.'

The good-natured ribbing continued all the way to Hereford. The three cars arrived there at 11.30 and each man signed in at the guardroom. Zeccara and Halliday were soon spotted as familiar faces. 'Well, fuck me if it isn't the Angel Gabriel,' said an SAS soldier as Zeccara climbed out of his car. 'Feet Halliday, too.' He grinned evilly at Halliday's well-known size twelves. 'What are you two skivers doing back here?'

'Hello, Steve,' said Zeccara. His steel tooth glinted as he smiled. 'We're on the scrounge. Going to empty your stores for you.'

'Sounds fair enough,' said Steve Donkin. 'I heard someone was coming down, and the RQMS was looking pretty hacked off about something when I saw him earlier on. Who are all these other lurkers?'

'Watch your fucking language, Donk,' said Harris, emerging from the second car.

'Jesus – Mel Harris,' exclaimed Donkin, instantly recognising the cat-like movements and light, athletic build of his ex-colleague. 'Talk about bad news. How are you, Mel?'

'Well choked at bumping into a see-you-next-Tuesday like you,' responded Harris, shaking Donkin's hand. 'I thought you'd have been RTU'd ages ago. Still swinging the lead as a trooper, yeah?'

'Bollocks,' said Donkin. 'I'm a fucking corporal now, and you're ancient history. Who are all these other relics?'

'None of your fucking business, mate. Jesus, they must be hard up these days to give a tosser like you even one stripe, let alone two. Now piss off before I smack you one.'

'Up yours. Hey, which one's Howard?'

'I am,' said a voice.

'Good to meet you, boss,' said Donkin. 'When you've got a moment, the CO said he'd like to see you.'

'OK. I'll be with you in a minute.' He addressed the others. 'Right, everyone over to the "G" Squadron armoury. Get yourselves kitted out. And forget about M16s, Minimis and the rest. AKMSs for everyone, and at least three silenced shorts. All Warsaw Pact stuff, got it? We're going to have to pass for East German renegades, and they'd hardly be wandering about with the latest Western kit.'

'Aw, boss,' groaned Halliday. 'Can't we take at least a couple of 203s?'

Howard thought for a moment. There was nothing he would have liked better. The 203 was a 40mm grenade launcher, a devastating weapon in skilled hands. With regret, he shook his head. 'No, Pete. The whole point is that the only firefight we want to get into is when we take out the *Stasi* base, and that shouldn't be much of a contest if we do it right. We'll take some L2 hand-grenades and claymores for emergencies, but that's it.' He turned to Harris and lowered his voice. 'What's the form on this guy Donkin? I like the look of him.'

'Great bloke, boss. We ought to snap him up for XF if he comes on the market.'

'Keep your feelers out, then. But don't forget my rule – no active recruitment, OK?'

'Right you are, boss.'

Howard turned back to Bourne. 'OK, Johnny, take them over to the armoury.'

'D'you think he'll be able to make it that far on that leg of his, boss?' grinned Halliday.

'I was just wonderin' about that myself,' said Ziegler. 'You sure you're up to it Johnny?'

'Oh, very droll,' said Bourne sarcastically. 'Ha ha, I don't think.'

'Tony can carry him,' said Zeccara.

'Bollocks,' rumbled Ackford. 'He can fucking hobble it.'

'Get the poor bugger a wheelbarrow,' chipped in Harris.

'Oh, piss off, you lot,' said Bourne crossly. 'I can outrun you buggers any day. OK, let's go.'

Howard followed Donkin into the big headquarters building, down the corridor past the orderly room to the second-in-command's office. The SAS major, whom Howard had never met before, offered him a cup of coffee. 'He's got someone in with him at the moment,' he apologised. 'Hope you don't mind waiting a minute or two.'

'No problem,' said Howard.

Five minutes later the door flew open to reveal a figure in an open-necked shirt and pale corduroys. His fair hair had thinned since Howard had last seen him. 'Ed, you bastard!'

Howard rose from his chair. 'Alex! Great to see you. How are things?'

'Couldn't be better,' said 22 SAS's commanding officer. 'Come in and have a chat. Can you stay for a pint over in the mess afterwards?'

'Love to,' said Howard, following Alex Warren through the door. His mind went back to the time many years before when he had encouraged a young Army captain to go for SAS selection. 'Why not give it a try?' he had said. 'You know you're not too keen on ordinary regimental soldiering. But you're exactly what the SAS want.' Now, fifteen years later, that captain was a lieutenant-colonel, a holder of the Military Cross for his bravery in the Falklands War, and commanding the finest and most experienced fighting unit in the world.

'So you're on the scrounge for some of our toys, are you?' asked Warren.

'Sorry to be a nuisance,' said Howard.

'No problem,' smiled Warren. 'You should have heard the QM's language, though, when I told him. I must admit I'm a bit jealous, myself. I wish we'd been given this one to do.'

'In a lot of ways, so do I,' said Howard darkly.

'Anything else I can help with? Do you want to spend some time in the killing house? Just say the word.'

'Well, there is one thing,' said Howard thoughtfully. 'We could use some practice in the wind-tunnel over the next week or two.'

'Oh, I see,' said Warren, understanding immediately. 'Yes, that can be fixed. Who have you got with you?'

Howard reeled off the list of names. Warren threw back his head and laughed when he came to Tony Ackford's. 'Oh, God!' he chuckled. 'Mr T? Bloody hell! I've heard all about him. He's going to love that. Have you told him?'

'Not yet.' Howard grinned. 'I was going to wait until we took him to that particular store, then watch his face. By the way, where is it? Everything's changed. No more spiders, nothing.'

'This is a completely new set-up. The store you want

is over near the aquatic centre. Come on, I'll take you there.'

Howard followed Alex Warren outside. 'I suppose I don't need to ask whether you're keeping yourself busy?'

'Non-stop,' said Warren. 'Busier than you'd believe. This Bosnia job is a pretty major one, as I expect you'll have guessed, and there are plenty of other things going on.'

'Are you enjoying the job?'

'It's all I ever wanted to do,' said Warren simply. 'It couldn't suit me better.'

'Well, you're exactly the right man for it. I hope you'll go on to be DSF.'

'No,' said Warren. 'I think I'll chuck it when my time's up here. I couldn't stand the idea of driving a desk – not after this.'

'Oh, come *on*, Alex! They *need* you. Grit your teeth, do your staff job, go on to command 5 Brigade or whatever, then after that you'll be Director. Guys with brains like you are thin on the ground.'

'I'll think about it . . . OK, here we are.' As Warren opened the door, the sound of raised voices came from inside. 'Sounds as if we've already missed some of the fun.'

A wild-eyed Tony Ackford whirled round, his arms flailing. 'Fuckit, boss!' he yelled at Howard. 'You know I bloody hate parachutes – why can't we go in off a submarine like any normal bastard would? I'm not fucking doing this, sod it!' he paused, glaring, then pointed his finger. 'And who the fuck's that geezer?'

Howard tried to keep a straight face. 'This is Lieutenant-Colonel Warren, the CO of the Regiment.'

'Oh, hello, boss,' said Ackford politely. 'Yeah. I've heard of you. Nice one,' he added. He shook Warren's hand, then immediately rounded on Zeccara again, jabbing his finger at him. 'And you can stop sniggering, you devious bastard,' he honked, 'or I'll give you a good kicking. There's no way you're getting me into that fucking kit, and that's that! Boss,' he turned to Howard in desperation, 'tell me the little pisspot's joking.'

'It's no joke, Tony,' said Howard.

'Then what does *he* think is so fucking funny, then?' yelled Ackford, pointing.

Howard turned his head. Beside him, rocking with laughter, was the commanding officer of the 22nd Special Air Service Regiment.

20

'Hi, Peter,' said Meg Berman sleepily as she opened the door. She stood there in a dressing-gown, hair tousled. 'Come along in. God, you guys are starting early today,' she yawned. 'It's still dark outside.'

'You'd be better off back in bed, Meg,' said Kramer. 'You're missing your beauty sleep.'

'I think maybe you're right,' she yawned again. 'Carl? Peter's here.'

Carl Berman's stocky figure appeared, an avuncular grin on his face. 'Hi, young Peter,' he said, slapping him jovially on the shoulder. 'I'm just fixing coffee. Want a cup?'

'That would be great,' said Kramer. He followed the older man into the kitchen.

'I'm gonna leave you guys to it,' said Meg.

'That's just fine, baby,' said Berman. 'We'll be leaving you in peace in a few minutes.' He looked at his watch; it was four-thirty. 'I doubt we'll be back much before midday. You get all the sleep you want.'

Meg disappeared, and they heard the bedroom door close behind her.

There was silence for a moment as Berman poured out two mugs of black coffee.

'We may not be back until after midday, Carl,' said Kramer calmly. 'We have to make sure it all works perfectly.'

'Oh,' said Berman, suddenly anxious. 'D'you think there could be a problem?'

'I hope not. But you never know. There could be.' Kramer took a sip of coffee. 'You have everything ready?'

'Everything,' Berman replied, eager to please. 'Checked it all off last night against the list. You want to double check?'

'I'm sure you've been thorough.'

As usual, now that Meg was no longer a witness, the two men's roles had subtly reversed. After a minute Kramer put down his mug, the coffee unfinished. 'OK, let's go,' he said.

Berman went to unlock his strongroom. They brought out the equipment and began loading it into Kramer's station wagon. There were a dozen thin plywood boards and four packing boxes bearing the name of a removals firm. Berman added a red Coleman cold-box with a white lid, brought from the kitchen.

'Those three boxes can go in the trunk,' he said. 'The other one with the black tape is our little baby. She'd better go on the rear seat – we don't want to jolt her. Fragile. Use no hooks or grabs.' He grinned. 'Maybe the cold-box, too. We don't want the beers all shook up, either.'

When Berman had strapped the fragile box into the rear passenger seat he opened the front passenger door and saw a bundle of twelve cardboard document tubes in the footwell. 'These what I think they are?'

'Yes,' said Kramer. 'Put them in the back and climb in.'

Kramer started the engine and pulled out of the driveway, then took a series of turns leading northwards out of Baltimore. He drove carefully, always keeping within the speed limit.

Berman appeared preoccupied. For the first ten minutes he remained silent; then he broached the subject that was worrying him. 'I think we've got a problem with the one-way glass, Peter,' he said.

'Really?' inquired Kramer calmly. 'Haven't you managed to find any?'

'No, no, it's not that.' Berman shook his head. 'It's easy enough to get. Even as thin as three-millimetre, which is *thin*. The problem is, I've done a number of tests, and it causes deflections. Got bits of shattered glass all over my workroom,' he added ruefully. 'Even at the close distances I've been able to try it, it causes very slight but measurable deflections. It depends on the angle the bullet hits it at, but it isn't at all predictable – even square on. At greater distances, any deflection would obviously be magnified.'

'I see,' Kramer commented, giving a slight frown. 'What do you think causes it?'

'I can't tell for sure,' Berman replied. 'I figured the muzzle blast would shatter the glass before the bullet actually reached it, so there wouldn't be a problem. But about one in four times there's a deflection for some reason. It could be air pressures, it could be the bullet hitting a small fragment of glass – could be a number of things. Anyway, it's a problem. Even one time in four's too often for comfort.'

'I agree,' said Kramer thoughtfully. 'We'll have to think of something else.'

'But we do need mirror-glass on the front,' persisted Berman. 'Otherwise, anyone looking at it closely will see there's something odd about it.'

Kramer thought for a while, his face impassive. 'Gelatine,' he remarked suddenly. 'That's the answer.'

'Jell-O?' Berman was uncomprehending.

'No, no. Gelatine. Thin, brittle, translucent material used for colour filters. You know, for photography, theatre spotlights – that sort of thing.'

Berman looked blank. His personal experience of

photography was confined to small snapshot cameras, and he had never been to the theatre in his life. 'Do they make one-way gelatine? You know, half-mirror?' he asked tentatively.

'I don't know,' Kramer answered. 'I rather doubt it – offhand, I can't see what call there would be for it. But I can find out. I have a friend in the movie business. He'll know.' He considered the problem briefly. 'Anyway, I don't think that matters. If they don't make one-way, dark grey will do.'

'Dark grey?'

'Yes,' said Kramer decisively. 'It's an old principle. Think of dark-tinted windows on a car. The guy in the car can see out, but you can't see in. Simple idea, but it works. It's to do with the difference in contrast. It's dark in the car, but light outside. The guy in the car doesn't really notice the difference – his eyes adjust to compensate.'

'Wouldn't mirror-effect be better?'

'Actually, tinting is half the principle of one-way mirrors. It isn't really one-way – it's just dark, with a bit of silvering. You know those mirror shades some people wear?'

'Yeah,' said Berman. 'The sort those Secret Service guys use. Secret, my ass,' he added.

'OK,' said Kramer. 'Next time you're in a shop, try a pair. You can see through them OK, but no one can see your eyes. Secret Servicemen aren't as dumb as they seem. They have to look around the whole time, and they don't want people to know who they're watching. As a result, *everyone* thinks they're being watched . . . But that's not the point. Try on a pair of those shades, and look in the mirror. You won't be able to see your eyes. Then take them off and hold them back to front, close to your eyes. You'll still be able to see through them to your reflection, but you won't really be able to make out your eyes. The silvering isn't heavy, and it isn't really one-way. See what I mean?'

'Yeah,' said Berman, beginning to get it. 'OK. I think I get the point. So dark grey gelatine . . .'

'Doubles the difficulty of seeing through it into a darker area,' said Kramer. 'Every component of IRIS will be matt black, except the camera lens. And that won't matter, because even if anyone does see it, it won't look out of place. And,' he added, 'the grey filter will make no difference to the camera itself. The exposure mechanism is automatic, so it will adjust to compensate.' Kramer smiled to himself. 'IRIS's iris will just open up a couple of stops.'

Berman fell silent. He didn't fully understand, but Kramer seemed to have come up with a simple solution to a problem that had been bugging him for days. He trusted Kramer's intelligence and judgement, and the confidence in the younger man's voice had convinced him. He relaxed and sat back in the passenger seat.

Forty minutes later, Kramer slowed the car. There had been thick forest on either side of the road for several miles. He checked his rear-view mirror; it was still early, and there was no traffic in sight. Kramer slowed the station wagon to a crawl, then pulled off on to a rough dirt track by a small white stone.

'This the place, huh?' asked Berman as the Chrysler started jolting over the rutted ground.

'About three miles further along the track,' Kramer replied. 'Nobody comes here, so far as I've been able to tell.'

Berman frowned. 'Those tyre-marks ahead look fresh,' he said, pointing.

'They are,' said Kramer. 'They're mine, from yesterday and two days ago.'

'Oh. Right.'

'I stayed three hours each time and there was no sign of anyone else – but we'll need to be careful, just in case.'

'Yeah,' said Berman darkly, patting the slight bulge beneath his left arm.

Kramer noticed. 'You have a carry permit for that?'

'I sure have.'

'What is it?'

'Walther P-38.'

A mile and a half further on, Kramer turned off on to another track. They were now deep within the dark and gloomy forest. Tree-branches overhung the track, and encroaching undergrowth brushed against the car as it lurched forward. The track itself was now damp and boggy; not enough sunlight or heat permeated the tree canopy to give it any chance of drying out. Kramer made another turn, then a third.

'I'm lost already,' confessed Berman. 'I see what you mean about this place. Who'd want to come here?'

'Oh, I don't know,' Kramer replied easily. 'I quite like it.'

The car emerged into a clearing in the forest. Kramer stopped and turned off the engine. Both men got out. Berman looked around. 'Yeah,' he said. 'This is perfect. How do you want to set up?'

'Over there.' Kramer led the way out along the edge of the clearing, stopping about thirty yards from the car. He pointed off to one side. 'Set out the frames down in that direction,' he said. 'Vary the distances, and don't put them all in line. I'll set up IRIS on this tree.' He patted the trunk of a tall pine.

'How far away do you want them?'

'Between forty and a hundred and fifty yards.'

Twenty minutes later, Berman had finished his work. The twelve swivel frames were firmly planted in the ground, the four-feet-high plywood boards mounted on them. From each one, a line of thin nylon cord led back to the pine tree that Kramer had selected. Kramer tightened the metal strap round the tree and checked that the mount was rigid.

'Want me to load her now?' Berman asked him.

'Not yet. We'll do the photos first.' They set off with the cardboard tubes and a staple-gun.

From the first tube Kramer extracted a life-size colour photograph of a man. He unrolled it and held it against the first plywood board. Berman fixed it in place with a staple at each corner and one halfway down each side. They moved on to the next frame, repeating the process.

'Who are these guys?' asked Berman.

'Nobody,' replied Kramer. 'I just shot a couple of rolls of film at random in the park. I had the sharpest pictures enlarged. I've no idea who any of them are.'

After eight of the twelve anonymous photographs had been attached to the boards, Berman was still curious. 'Which one have you programmed into IRIS?' he asked.

Kramer smiled secretively. 'Patience, Carl.' They reached the ninth target. 'How far's this one?'

'One hundred and five paces,' Berman replied.

'OK. It'll do.' Kramer left one of the cardboard tubes lying beside it. 'We'll come back and do it last.' He moved on.

Berman was now intensely curious, but he remained silent. Obediently, he followed Kramer. They finished stapling the other three photographs to their frames and returned to the tube they had left on the ground.

'OK,' said Kramer, pulling out the picture. He unrolled it. The face was instantly recognisable.

'Oh, him,' said Berman. 'Wait a minute! You mean he's the one who . . .?'

'Yes,' said Kramer. 'He's the one. I got the message ten days ago.'

Berman's face split in a wide smile. 'Wow!' he exclaimed 'Yeah! All *right!*'

They stapled the photograph to the frame. Walking back towards IRIS, Berman was rubbing his hands and chuckling with delight. 'I can't wait to see this. You want me to load up now and switch on?'

'Go ahead,' Kramer was looking back down the clearing. The photographs in their frames were all edgeways on, the thin plywood boards almost invisible.

Berman took out a box of .221 Remington Fireball ammunition and extracted one cartridge. Opening a hatch at the rear of the black box mounted on the tree, he worked the modified bolt of the XP-100, inserting the small, deadly-looking cartridge. Then he closed the bolt and the hatch on the housing. Finally he flipped a small, inconspicuous switch on the top of the unit. There was a barely perceptible, high-pitched whine as IRIS activated itself, then a brief and almost inaudible noise from the servo motors as the camera focused itself and began to search for its programmed target. 'All set,' announced Berman, moving aside.

Kramer waited for two minutes to ensure that IRIS was up and running. 'OK,' he said at length. 'Pull and hold target one.'

Berman pulled on the line he had marked '1'. The first anonymous photograph, fifty yards away, flipped round to face them. There was a tiny whirring sound from IRIS, then nothing.

'Release,' ordered Kramer. The spring on the rotating target frame flipped the picture back out of sight, edgeways on again. 'Right. Targets two and six together.'

Two different photographs appeared as Berman pulled the cords. Again IRIS whirred, very briefly, then fell silent.

'Release.' The photographs disappeared again. Kramer was pleased. It had taken the unit no time at all to analyse the two faces and decide that neither was the one it was seeking.

'Right,' said Kramer. 'Let's make it more difficult. Three, four, ten and twelve all at once.'

Four targets now appeared. IRIS took only the briefest of moments to reject the faces before falling silent. 'Release,' said Kramer again.

'Hi!' The voice came from behind them. Berman whirled round, his hand diving for the P-38 in his shoulder-holster. Just as quickly Kramer laid a hand on his arm to stop him.

Kramer turned slowly and casually. 'Good morning!' he called out pleasantly to the newcomer.

The man was young, in his early twenties. Blond and strong-looking, he wore jeans and hiking boots and carried a large backpack. He smiled at Kramer. 'What are you guys doing? I didn't expect to see anyone out here.'

'Nor did we,' Kramer laughed. 'You startled us. Sorry – I'm Peter Kramer, and this is my associate, Carl Berman.' Kramer stepped forward and shook the young backpacker's hand warmly. 'We're conducting an experiment.'

Berman stood rooted to the spot, wondering why Kramer had stopped him.

'Chuck Anderson,' responded the young man. 'What experiment? Do those photos I just saw over there have something to do with it?'

'Yes,' Kramer replied. 'Would you like to see what it's about?'

'Sure.'

'Fine!' said Kramer, visibly pleased. 'Oh, let me help you off with your pack.'

'Thanks,' said Chuck Anderson.

Kramer moved to help with the large backpack. 'Hell!' he exclaimed, as he took its weight from the young man's shoulders and quickly lowered it to the ground. 'What have you got in this thing? Rocks?'

Anderson laughed. 'No, just camping stuff. I've been out for three days. Heading home tomorrow.'

'By yourself?'

'Sure. I prefer it that way.'

'Well, Chuck, after hefting that around for three days you either must be very fit or very tired. Hey!' Kramer's face brightened. 'I bet you could do with a beer! We've got a cold-box in the car. What d'you say?'

Anderson grinned. 'Well, it's a little early, but . . .

hell, why not? Great idea! That's real kind of you!'

'Come on, then.' Kramer led the young man across to the car. 'Listen,' he said conspiratorially when they were out of Berman's earshot. 'Don't mind old Carl. He's a sourpuss, but he's OK really. He's just, well, not very sociable.'

'I know the type,' agreed Anderson.

Kramer pulled out the cold-box and opened it up. 'OK, here we go,' he said. 'One for you, and one for me.' They popped the cans and drank. 'Oh,' said Kramer suddenly, 'we'd better not forget Carl, or I'll never hear the end of it.' He raised his head and called over: 'Beer, Carl?'

Berman was wondering what on earth Kramer was up to, acting so buddy-buddy with this unwelcome stranger. 'Yeah,' he managed finally through gritted teeth. 'Thanks.' He saw Kramer and the young man walking back towards him, chatting amiably. Cautiously, he moved so as to block Chuck Anderson's view of IRIS.

'. . . share an apartment in town, huh?' Berman heard Kramer ask as they approached.

'Yeah,' the young man answered. 'It's chaos. People in and out all the while. I like to get away every now and then. I keep to myself.'

'No girlfriend?'

'No one special right now.'

'Oh, come *on!*' said Kramer. 'Good-looking young guy like you? Don't tell me you can't pull the babes!' He leaned across and whispered in Chuck's ear. 'I mean, just look at poor old Carl there. What chance does a dumb ape like him have?'

Chuck Anderson nearly choked on his beer. Swallowing it finally, he laughed. 'Peter, you're a real bad influence!'

Berman wondered what on earth the exchange had been about. What the hell was Kramer up to?

'Here you are, Carl,' said Kramer, handing him

the third can and ignoring the expression on his face.

'So,' said Anderson cheerfully. 'Tell me about your experiment.'

'OK,' said Kramer. 'You see that unit fixed to the tree . . . Hey, Carl? Would you mind?' Kramer gently ushered Berman to one side, out of the way, to let Anderson see.

Jesus! thought Berman, too surprised to resist. *Has Peter gone crazy?*

'Yeah,' said Anderson. He glanced at IRIS, not noticing anything particularly interesting about it.

'Right. Well, you can see a camera lens peeping out. It's hooked up to a computer inside the casing. In a nutshell, what it does is recognise faces. To be precise, it's trained to recognise one particular face. It ignores all others.'

Oh, Christ! Berman was thinking. *What the fuck does Peter think he's . . .*

'It can do that?' asked Anderson, showing more interest. 'I didn't know that was possible. That's pretty smart.' He took a long pull from his beer can.

'It's a very new development,' explained Kramer. 'In fact, this is our first field-test. Hey, why don't we show you?' He ushered the young man to one side. 'Carl, pull numbers five and eleven. Carl?'

Berman was by now thoroughly alarmed. His suspicion showed clearly on his face as he slowly moved to comply. With an eye fixed firmly on the intruder, he pulled the cords of the targets.

The two photographs flipped round. IRIS whirred briefly, then fell silent.

'OK, release.' The two targets flipped back out of sight.

'See?' asked Kramer, satisfied, lifting his can of beer to his mouth.

'Yeah,' replied Chuck. 'Uh, sort of. But nothing much happened.'

'Precisely!' said Kramer triumphantly. 'That's

because neither of those photographs was of the guy this unit is programmed to recognise!'

'Oh,' said Chuck blankly. 'Oh. Right.'

'We'll try two more,' said Kramer. 'Carl, pull numbers seven and eight.'

Berman frowned darkly but complied again. Targets seven and eight flipped round, face on. As before, apart from a slight whirr from IRIS, nothing happened.

To Chuck Anderson this didn't seem to be a very interesting experiment at all. His face expressed his disappointment. 'What happens when it *does* recognise the right guy?' he asked politely.

'Aha!' exclaimed Kramer excitedly. 'You're about to see! Right: there are twelve different photographs out there on those frames. The machine has ignored eleven so far, but it hasn't been shown number nine yet. That's about a hundred yards away. We'll give her a tough test.' He turned to Berman. 'Carl? Pull all twelve at once!'

Berman gave Kramer a despairing look, then bent to gather up the cords. He pulled hard, and the twelve photographic targets flipped round simultaneously. There was a brief whirr . . .

CRACK!

'*Shit!*' yelped Anderson, whirling round. 'What the hell . . .?' He saw a thin curl of grey-black smoke coming from something he hadn't noticed before, beside the camera lens. A gun-barrel . . . 'Hey, what *is* this?'

Kramer didn't answer. He was staring down the range towards the targets.

Anderson's eyes followed Kramer's down towards the twelve photographs. Suddenly, he recognised the face on number nine and went pale. 'Christ! I know who that is! You mean he's the one this thing . . .?'

'Yes,' said Kramer calmly. 'But of course I don't yet know whether we've scored a hit or not. Hey, let's take a closer look at the target and find out.'

Chuck Anderson was badly shaken, and his sudden

fear was all too obvious. He made a brave effort to stay calm, but failed. 'Hell, I really don't know about this,' he gulped, backing away slowly. 'I think maybe I'll just leave you guys to it.'

'Oh, c'mon, Chuck,' pleaded Kramer. 'At least come and see whether it worked!'

'Look, if it's all the same to you, I think I'd just better be on my way.' There was a sick smile of nervous terror on the young man's face as he continued to back away. 'It's been real nice meeting you guys. Thanks for the beer. So long now.' He turned and began walking away, fast. After a few paces, his nerve broke and he began to run.

Kramer shrugged resignedly. 'Oh, well. So long, Chuck.' He took another pull at his beer, then turned his back and began walking towards the target, throwing his empty can aside. 'All yours, Carl,' he called over his shoulder casually.

A second later Kramer heard the P-38 bark once, but his attention was concentrated on target nine as he approached it and he didn't bother to look round. He stopped at the target and examined it, no expression on his face. A few seconds later, he heard Berman's running footsteps.

'Got him,' panted Carl.

Kramer frowned at the distraction, then turned. 'Where?'

'In the back of the head. Fifty yards, running. Not bad, huh?'

'Is there an exit wound?'

'No.'

'Then we'll have to extract the bullet before we bury him,' said Kramer coolly. 'If his body's found, the bullet could eventually be traced to your gun.'

'Hmm,' said Berman, 'I guess you're right.'

'Start packing up all our gear now,' ordered Kramer, his voice cold. 'When you've finished, dig a grave. Over there in that thick scrub will do. I'll drag the body over there and chop his head open to find the bullet. Did you bring an axe or something I can use for that?'

'There's a Bowie knife I brought along in case we needed to hack away any undergrowth. It's in one of the boxes . . . But,' he added, gulping, 'I didn't think we'd need it for – anything like *that*.'

'Can't afford to be squeamish in our business, Carl,' snapped Kramer. 'I'll split his skull in half, then dig around inside until I find the bullet.'

'That Bowie should be, uh, up to the job,' said Berman. 'It's big and heavy. And very sharp,' he added.

'Good,' said Kramer. 'We'll ransack his backpack to make it look like robbery. In fact,' he added, 'I'll do that first. The bits of his head can go into the pack when I have finished. We'll bury the pack with him. That will make everything tidier. OK?'

'Yes,' said Berman, nodding. 'Hey!' he recalled suddenly, glad to change the subject. 'Did it work?' He moved closer to examine target nine.

'Oh, yes,' said Kramer calmly, his eyes pale and unemotional. 'It worked all right.' He smiled coldly, then turned and walked away.

Berman peered closely at the life-size photograph of the man whom IRIS was now inexorably programmed to kill. He gave a low whistle of approval and grinned. In the exact centre of the forehead, an inch above the bridge of the nose, was a neat .221-size hole.

21

The stench in Hislop's cell was now overpowering and vile. In the corner, the plastic fruit bowl had long since overflowed and the filth was gradually spreading out over the floor. The laxative compound injected into the fruit had had the desired effect.

Hislop sat listlessly in his armchair. His spirit had held out for nearly twenty-four hours, and he had refused to utter the humiliating sentence on the notice in order to obtain food. He had felt a small moment of triumph when he had first defecated into the bowl; he realised that he had no lavatory paper and had torn the notice off the door and used that. 'That's what I think of your bloody instructions,' he had muttered angrily. The moment had soon passed, and the feeling of utter hopelessness set in again.

Each time the hatch opened he had smelled the enticing odour of food. On the second occasion, he had defiantly tried to tip the evil-smelling contents of the fruit bowl through the hatch, but it had slammed shut and there was now a dark stain running down the door. On the third occasion he had shouted insults through the aperture, but the result was the same: the hatch simply slammed shut. He began to realise he was not going to win.

On the sixth occasion, by now desperately hungry and thirsty – the bottle of water and all the fruit had gone – he had caved in. Miserably, he had muttered the required words, 'I can't remember anything' and was instantly rewarded with a plastic plate of stew, a plastic spoon and another bottle of water. Ravenous, he gulped the food down and finished the water. He felt better. Then he realised he now had two empty plastic bottles; he brightened. That would help solve one problem, he thought; just keep the fruit bowl for the other. Before long, he had filled one of the plastic bottles.

The next time the hatch had opened, he had uttered the necessary words again, but initially nothing had happened. Then a small slip of paper was passed through. There was one line of type. 'Pass out empty plate and bottle', it read. Hislop scuttled across the room, collecting the plate and the bottle which now contained his urine. The plate was accepted; but the bottle was immediately pushed back through. It fell at his feet and burst. Hislop moaned in dismay; urine was splashed all over his feet.

The implication was clear; only empty bottles were acceptable for exchange. Hislop's face wrinkled in distaste and misery, and he retreated once more to his chair, reaching automatically for the tobacco-box and the cigarette papers. In the back of his mind, he realised that he was smoking a lot more than he usually did. It was a comfort to him; he could not remember any previous time when the simple act of lighting up had been more calming to the nerves. Drawing deeply, he tried to relax.

Gerhardt Eisener politely made his excuses to his commanding officer and left him watching the television monitor. Fetching his hat and coat, he called for Captain Jürgen Kessler, his aide, and pushed open the main entrance door of the *Stasi* building. Outside he stood for a moment, sniffing the air. It was a dull, overcast day and there was a heavy, dank smell in the atmosphere. It rather suited the surroundings, he thought.

Beyond the main gate leading out of the compound, two kilometres away to the north, rose the only natural feature of note, a hill mostly covered by trees and scrub. On its summit, just out of view behind the trees, was the main North Korean air-defence site; its SA–6 missiles provided anti-aircraft cover for the whole of the Yŏngbyŏn nuclear installation. Off to the north-west twin plumes of dirty-looking steam were visible, rising from the two cooling-towers of the 5-megawatt gas-graphite reactors four kilometres away. Eisener wrinkled his nose in distaste and climbed into his UAZ jeep.

'The research centre, comrade Colonel?' asked his aide.

'Later, Kessler,' Eisener replied. 'The reprocessing plant first, please.'

The UAZ's engine rattled into life and Captain Kessler drove forward to the main gate. The *Stasi* guard on duty unlocked it and saluted Eisener smartly, closing the gate again after them. Turning left out of the compound on to the main road, the UAZ headed west and then south, towards the heart of the sprawling nuclear facility.

Most of the newer installations at Yŏngbyŏn, including the reprocessing plant, were enclosed within a loop of the Kuryong river, which meandered round in a wide arc, some four kilometres in diameter, before heading away to join the larger Ch'ŏngch'ŏn river to the south. The massive 6-storey reprocessing building lay five kilometres away at the southern end of the facility, at the most distant point of the loop.

After less than a kilometre, Kessler drew the UAZ to a halt at the first of the North Korean military checkpoints. The *Stasi*'s contract with the North Koreans meant they could come and go relatively freely – they were responsible for overseeing and advising on all aspects of security. The North Korean soldiers manning the checkpoint looked thin and malnourished, but they were alert and disciplined and Eisener knew they would have no hesitation in shooting an intruder or anyone whose credentials were not in order. Their unsmiling commander checked Eisener's and Kessler's identities carefully and waved them through. Eisener acknowledged the commander's salute, his face bland and expressionless.

There was no particular reason for him to visit the reprocessing plant that day, but in his capacity as chief security adviser Eisener carried out spot checks from time to time and had decided that he might as well do one today. He had no particular enthusiasm for the tedious business of double-checking procedures, but today he was glad to get out of the ugly concrete blockhouse that was the *Stasi* base. He had grown bored with watching the on-screen humiliation of Hislop, even though he could tell that his commanding officer remained fascinated by it. It was a somewhat squalid spectacle, Eisener thought, not dissimilar to many he had witnessed before, and its outcome was not only predictable but inevitable. As such, it was not evenly remotely interesting. The old man would break, and soon.

General Erfurt had not confided in him why Hislop was so important to his plans, but it was now becoming quite clear that the matter was not a routine one – if, that was, the abduction and torture of someone of Hislop's status could ever be described as routine. No, thought Eisener; this was something personal between Erfurt and Hislop, something that he, Eisener, hadn't yet fathomed. Never mind, he thought; he would find out in due course. In the meantime, he would need to be patient.

Patience. As the jeep jolted along the potholed road, Eisener knew he had long since become tired of General Erfurt's obsession with secrecy. The man was living in the past, where all information had to be compartmentalised. He rigidly persisted with the 'comrade this' and 'comrade that' form of address, as he did with all the other relics of the stilted, obsolete dogma that still seemed to govern his life. The general's inflexible adherence to the old ways grated on Eisener's nerves, as did the stultifying drabness of day-to-day life in North Korea. It was a godforsaken, anachronistic hole of a place with nothing whatever, in Eisener's view, to commend it. He had seen few parts of the country less attractive than Yŏngbyŏn itself; and he had been here now for five long, grinding years, with scarcely a break from the monotony it afforded.

For much of that time Eisener had felt as if he was banging his head against a concrete wall, trying to talk the general into accepting any sort of profitable, commercial work. Finally Eisener had talked him round, but Erfurt still refused to consider any proposition which was not demonstrably compatible with his ideological principles.

The Iranian contract was a case in point, thought Eisener. Erfurt had refused to countenance the idea of doing business with 'those barbarians', as he referred to them, until Eisener had pointed out to him that the interests of the Iranians were invariably inimical to those of the capitalist West. It therefore followed, he had argued, that any act the Iranian government was contemplating must be damaging to western interests and automatically worthy of support. It would be a bonus, he had added carefully, that Teheran was prepared to pay handsomely. Erfurt had eventually agreed but then, typically, he had taken over the project himself and Eisener had heard little more.

It had begun to rain, a thin drizzle smearing the windscreen of the jeep. Kessler turned on the wipers but the blades were old, chewed by frost and grit, and they just made the problem worse. New wiper blades were unobtainable here, and Eisener realised that it was just one measure of his own apathetic attitude to this existence that he had not bothered to bring some replacements back from England. Through the bleary, misting windscreen he could see that the sky had darkened further. There would either be a downpour, thought Eisener, or more probably the rain would soon fizzle out and the glowering clouds and damp, smoky air would linger on.

Four more military checkpoints punctuated the journey before the UAZ finally drew up outside the reprocessing plant. Eisener got out, telling Kessler to wait. Armed North Korean security guards surrounded the huge building; Eisener knew they all recognised him but he had to show his pass three more times before finally being admitted. Inside, escorted by one of the guards, he made his way along the corridor leading to the ground-level office set aside for the *Stasi*'s use.

Franz Gerber, a nuclear scientist working for the North Koreans on a *Stasi*-arranged contract, was already on duty. He rose to his feet as Eisener entered.

'Good morning, comrade Colonel,' said the scientist politely.

'Good morning, Gerber,' replied Eisener, taking off his coat and hanging it up. 'No problems, I hope?'

'Everything is proceeding as normal, comrade Colonel.'

'Good. My schedule for today includes among other things an inspection of the Pu–239 fuel figures. We will start with the ones for the 50–megawatt reactor. Get them for me, would you?'

As he waited for Gerber to return, Eisener reflected once more on the Iranian contract. He knew that it was an assassination, of course, and an important one. The fact that it was important made it more of a challenge, but it also involved greater risk to the assassin. It had been Eisener's own idea to adapt the IRIS technology to do the job instead; that way a machine, rather than an individual, would shoulder all the risk.

Oddly enough, Gerber, although he didn't know it, had indirectly had something to do with the idea. Eisener had been idly leafing through one of Gerber's scientific journals when he had seen an article about IRIS and its projected capabilities. The possibility of using it as a device to trigger a weapon had occurred to him almost straight away. A device based on IRIS could be more inconspicuous and more reliable than any human, Eisener realised, and he had begun to research the idea in greater detail. General Erfurt had been doubtful at first, but Eisener had eventually convinced him. And now the project – Eisener's own project – was up and running. There was only one major drawback as far as he was concerned. Because Erfurt had adopted and taken over the project as his own, Eisener himself had never found out who the intended assassination victim was.

Yet, Eisener told himself. He didn't know *yet*. But he would find out soon. And when he did, it would be time for a change.

There was a knock on the door, and Gerber entered with the file containing the latest Plutonium reprocessing figures. Eisener thanked the scientist and dismissed him. Alone in the office, he leafed through the file until he found what he was looking for. He placed the first of the pages flat on the desk and pulled a tiny camera from his pocket. *Time for a change*, he repeated to himself. *And time now to make a few little additions to my insurance policy, too.*

22

Max Goodale walked briskly down the empty street and approached the black-painted front door. Although he had been to the house on numerous previous occasions, he had always arrived by the rear entrance. He felt somehow uncomfortable entering by the main door, but it was late and there was no one about at that time of night to show any interest in visitors.

The duty policeman checked his credentials and knocked. When the door opened Goodale gave his name and was asked to wait. He sat down with his briefcase beside him.

Soon a secretary appeared. 'Will you come this way, sir? The Prime Minister will see you now.'

Goodale had at one time or another met all the previous occupants of No. 10 Downing Street who were still alive, including Sir Reginald Hislop. He had found each of them impressive in their own particular way, and had only actively disliked two out of five of them. He had not, however, yet had occasion to meet John Major, and found himself wondering whether the reality would be any different from the image portrayed in the media. He hoped so.

'Colonel Goodale to see you, Prime Minister,' said the secretary, holding open the door of the study.

John Major looked up from his papers and rose from his chair, a warm smile on his face. He came forward to greet his visitor, and Goodale noticed that he was limping slightly. The Prime Minister held out his hand and a pair of steady, friendly eyes looked at Goodale. Major was slightly taller than he had expected, and appeared relaxed and confident.

'Colonel Goodale,' Major said quietly, 'it's kind of you to have come. I've not yet had the opportunity to thank you for agreeing to handle this difficult matter. But I'm glad you've taken it on – I've heard a great deal about you. Please, come and sit down. Can I get you a drink?'

'Well . . . thank you, Prime Minister,' said Goodale, pleasantly surprised by Major's manner. 'I must admit, a small whisky would be rather good.' *Thank God*, he thought. *Much better than I anticipated. He's got genuine charm, and at the same time a strength of character I didn't expect.* 'I do apologise for bothering you at this late hour. It's very good of you to see me.'

'The pleasure's all mine, I can assure you,' said Major, grinning over his shoulder. 'Quite apart from anything else, your visit gives me a bit of a break from all those papers.' He gestured towards his desk. 'Ice?'

Major finished pouring two drinks, then brought them across and lowered himself into his chair, wincing as he did so. 'I'm sorry,' he confided disarmingly. 'An old knee injury. After a long day on my feet it starts to ache a bit. Your good health, Colonel.' He raised his glass.

'And yours, Prime Minister. Nothing better than this for aches and pains, in my experience.'

John Major smiled broadly. 'Tell me,' he said, his expression turning more serious, 'do you have any further news about the disappearance of Sir Reginald?'

'I'm afraid not, Prime Minister,' Goodale replied, shaking his head. 'We still have practically nothing definite . . . I'm sorry. To be honest, we have *absolutely* nothing definite, to go on.'

'Hmm,' said Major thoughtfully. 'A bad business. Speaking personally, I'm sure it was right to withhold news of the abduction. I know it has often been done in kidnapping cases in the past, to protect the victim and the family. The trouble in this case is that there are two other factors I have to consider. The first is obvious – that this is no ordinary kidnapping. The abduction of a senior political figure, even one no longer active in political life, never could be. The second is that nothing has been heard from the abductors, so it cannot be claimed that we are under some sort of duress to keep quiet about it. I am not sure whether it is either morally or legally right to continue to suppress the news any longer. The Home Secretary, for one, has raised doubts. The Attorney General has taken a more robust view, but more recently I have noticed a softening of his position. It may not be long before I have to put the matter before the full Cabinet, and follow that up with a statement to the House of Commons. Do you see my difficulty?'

'I certainly do, Prime Minister,' said Goodale. 'And you must obviously do what you think is right. But if at all possible, could I ask for a little more time? Another month, say?'

The Prime Minister gave Goodale a searching look, then nodded. 'All right. I'll see what I can do. Now,' he said, visibly brightening as he changed the subject. 'This other matter. This North Korean business, and the *Stasi* link. I'm intrigued. Tell me all about it.'

'Are you sure you want to know *all* about it, Prime Minister?' asked Goodale carefully. 'The Joint Intelligence Committee was quite categoric in its wish to avoid any possibility of your being implicated – in the event of something going amiss.'

Major smiled broadly. 'Oh, I'm sure they were,' he said, his eyes bright with mirth. 'Bunch of old fusspots, some of them. Never mind them. Anyway, I gather there's something you want me to do. And if you want my help, you'll have to tell me what's going on.'

Goodale grinned. 'Very well, Prime Minister. You've asked, so I'll tell you. It's quite a story, but if you have half an hour to spare . . .?'

'Fire away, Colonel,' said Major, leaning forward, 'I'm all ears.'

As Goodale talked, he noticed the Prime Minister's expression change from humour to gravity, and then finally to surprise. Major was an excellent listener, he saw. His eyes never wavered, and his attention was absolute.

'So that's it,' Goodale concluded. 'The point is, if our men are going to have any hope of getting into North Korea and out again, they're going to need some assistance.'

'I can well imagine it,' said Major. 'But before you tell me what it is you want me to do, please satisfy my curiosity about this man Howard. Who is he? And why have you picked him for this job?'

Goodale knew the man had had a busy day. 'I hesitate to take up too much of your time, Prime Minister – but if you'd really like to hear about him I'll try to keep it brief.'

'Take all the time you want, Colonel,' said Major, smiling. 'I have a feeling I'm going to enjoy the story.'

As Goodale recounted the tale of Howard's deeds in Iraq in 1992, he saw the Prime Minister's face light up in sudden recognition. When he had finished, Major seemed delighted.

'Well, that explains a great deal!' exclaimed the Prime Minister, his eyes sparkling. 'You know, I had a couple of highly confusing conversations with President Bush at the time of that business. I couldn't really make out what he was on about, and at the time I think he suspected me of being behind it all. Well, well!' He laughed again.

Goodale found himself grinning in return. 'Naturally I warned Howard off after it was all over,' he said. 'I made it pretty clear he'd better behave himself in future. To be fair to him, he was under the impression that it was all official and above board. It was only afterwards that he realised he'd been duped. He's been keeping a commendably low profile ever since. Anyway, I think you can understand why I feel he and his men are right for this one.'

'I certainly can!' exclaimed Major, still chuckling. 'All right. What is it you want me to do to help?'

'Well, Prime Minister,' Goodale began hesitantly, 'first of all you should understand that what I'm about to say is Howard's idea, not mine. It may sound a little outrageous, and I have no idea whether or not it could work —'

'Let's hear it!'

Taking a deep breath, Goodale launched into the request he had been asked to make.

'Good God!' said Major when Goodale had finished. 'Are you quite sure he's serious about this?'

'Oh yes, Prime Minister,' replied Goodale quietly. 'He's serious, all right. He's worked it all out – planned everything down to the last detail.'

'I believe you,' muttered Major thoughtfully. Suddenly he laughed again, taken with the sheer audacity of it all. 'All right! I'll try. I can't guarantee it – you'll understand that. But I promise you, I'll do my best to arrange it. Now,' he said, getting to his feet, 'I'd better not detain you any longer.' The man suddenly looked tired, but Goodale could see that there was a quality of determination in the Prime Minister which would override thoughts of fatigue.

At the door Major turned. Once again, Goodale was struck by the strength of his gaze. 'In return for my help with this, Colonel,' said the Prime Minister quietly, 'I want you to promise me three things.'

'If it's within my power to do so, then I will,' replied Goodale, wondering what was coming.

'First, I want you to keep me fully informed about this. Personally. Come and see me here whenever you have something new to report. Will you do that?'

'I'd be glad to, Prime Minister.'

'Second,' said Major, 'I would like you to tell Howard and his men, from me, that I wish them the very best of luck. The *very* best. I shall be thinking of them. Please tell them that.'

'They'll be most grateful for your support, Prime Minister,' said Goodale sincerely. 'As indeed am I. It's very kind of you to give it.'

'It's the least I can do,' responded Major. 'It's they, and you, who are doing everyone a favour. I owe you my support – and you have it, without any qualification. Now,' he continued, 'the third thing. If they manage to pull this off and return safely, I want you to bring them here to Number 10. I'd very much like to meet them. They are brave men for even considering this undertaking. Will you do that?'

'I certainly will, Prime Minister,' said Goodale. The two shook hands.

You'll do, thought Goodale as he walked down the lamp-lit street in the direction of Whitehall. *Oh yes, you'll do*.

23

People had begun to notice a difference in Tom Levy. Those who came into daily contact with him at work were the first to pick up on it – in fact, they would have been extremely unobservant not to have done so. Almost overnight, Levy seemed to have lost some of his aggressive pomposity. He appeared more relaxed and at ease, and the frenetic belligerence which was his hallmark had softened to the point where junior White House staffers, all of whom heartily loathed him, had even begun to suspect that he might be human, after all.

Levy's secretary, Jane Margolyes, could pinpoint his personality change to exactly fifteen days previously. Normally her boss would arrive in the morning and immediately begin to pick holes in her work, barking out orders in the offensively overbearing, patronising manner that he always affected. Somehow he seemed to be particularly rude and unpleasant when he stalked self-importantly back to the office after his daily meeting with the President. Each time Jane would grit her teeth and bite back a retort.

She knew that her work was good: she was conscientious, painstaking and thorough. An enthusiastic Democratic Party supporter, she had arrived at the White House five months previously. But it had been the start of a nightmare, rather than the glamorous life she had imagined. After one particularly trying day she had confided in a friend whom she had made in the Attorney General's office. Levy had found fault with almost everything she had done that day, and she was feeling very unhappy.

'Don't worry, Jane,' Cathy Todd soothed her. 'We're all rooting for you. Everyone knows Levy's a prize jerk. If it's any comfort to you, he treats everyone the same way. Except for *his* boss, of course – he's so far up the President's ass, all you can see most of the time are his goddam toenails.'

Jane had managed a wan smile at Cathy's earthy humour. 'But he's so *nasty* all the time. I do a good job for him – I know I do. I don't deserve to be treated like this.'

'I know, Jane, I know.' Cathy put an arm round her friend's shoulder. *Poor Jane*, she thought. *So young and idealistic* . . . 'Listen – you've done pretty well, you know, putting up with him for so long.'

'But I've only been here two months.'

'Hey, that's already a record!' said Cathy. 'No one else has lasted longer than three weeks.'

'But what am I going to do? I just can't go on like this!'

Cathy could see that Jane was close to tears. 'There's all sorts of things you *could* do – but quite a lot of them are illegal and not many of them would make any difference anyway, in the long run. You want my advice? Just go cold.'

'What do you mean?'

'Freeze him,' said Cathy. 'Turn your brain to ice and freeze him solid – don't allow what he says to get to you. Exaggerate the politeness and overdo the apologies. Ice and saccharine. Not too much, but just enough for him to realise you know what his game is. He's just one big ham actor himself. I'll bet you can put on a better act.'

Jane had followed Cathy's advice, and had been amazed to see how well it had worked. Levy had noticed straight away, she knew. Not that it made much difference – after a couple of days of puzzled wariness on his part, he had simply carried on as before. But the great thing was, thought Jane, it no longer bothered her. She had risen above it.

Soon afterwards, Jane noticed the sudden change in Levy. He had come bouncing in much as usual, although she hadn't turned her head to look at him. 'Good morning, Jane,' he had said.

Jane? She thought, startled. *He's never called me Jane before. What happened to 'Ms Margolyes'?* She turned round in astonishment, but Levy was already through the door into his inner office. *And 'Good morning'? I've never heard him say that to anyone, especially me.*

'Er, good morning, Mr Levy,' she managed to reply, just before the door closed behind him. *Closed, not slammed*, she noticed. Shaking her head briefly, she returned to her work. *He must be in a good mood today.* Then she dismissed the thought. *It won't last long.*

A few minutes later, the intercom buzzed. *Here we go,* she thought. *Normal service has been resumed.* 'Yes, Mr Levy?' she asked politely.

'Jane, would you mind coming in for a moment?'

What? Not 'In here NOW, Ms Margolyes'? she wondered. 'Right away, Mr Levy.'

Entering his office, she noticed his expression. For once he looked reasonably civil and the smug, slightly cruel smile was missing.

'Please take a seat, Jane,' he said.

'Well . . . thank you, Mr Levy.' She had never been invited to sit before, even while taking dictation.

Levy smiled 'Jane . . . I'm conscious that I've been . . . quite tough on you in the past. I want you to know that I really do appreciate your work. And I'm sorry if I've given offence.'

Jane realised she was gaping at him. She swallowed, forcing herself to remain cool. 'Well, er . . . I don't know quite what to say, Mr Levy. You can sometimes be, er, quite demanding, but I understand the pressures of your job.'

'Tom,' said Levy. 'From now on it's Tom, OK? Now, I'd better leave you in peace for the rest of the morning. I know you have plenty to be getting on with.'

Jane returned to her office, her thoughts in a whirl. *What the hell is going on here?* she wondered. *Oh boy, just wait until I tell Cathy about this!*

In the canteen during the lunch break, her friend listened in astonishment as Jane described Levy's apparent personality change. 'You mean, he actually asked you to call him by his first name?' Cathy asked, amazed. 'What the hell have you *done* to the man?'

'That's just the point – I haven't done anything different at all. I really can't work it out!'

Understanding dawned. 'I've got it,' Cathy exclaimed, snapping her fingers. 'I'll bet it's a woman. He must have got himself a new woman!'

'He gets himself a new one of those practically daily,' commented Jane acidly, thinking of Levy's seemingly endless succession of young escorts.

'I know. But this one must be something special.' Cathy smiled wryly. 'And you'd better just pray she sticks around. As soon as she's out of the picture, he'll revert straight to type . . . Bet you anything you like it's a new woman!' she repeated triumphantly.

Tom Levy had never felt happier or more relaxed about life in general. His new geniality – even bonhomie – seemed if anything to increase as the days passed. It was Joanna, of course – he knew that. For the hundredth time, he told himself she was the most wonderful, most exciting, sexiest creature on earth. They were seeing each other almost daily now; he could hardly remember what life had been like before her. And it had only been two weeks since their first date. Strangely, he found that having Joanna almost constantly on his mind did not adversely affect his work. Instead, he had a new energy, a new confidence.

Ascending the elevator to her apartment he wondered what she would have in store tonight. Each time it had been sensational.

The elevator crept to a halt at the seventh floor and the doors opened with maddening slowness. Levy hurried out and along the corridor. As he rang Joanna's doorbell, he noticed a couple in their late fifties approaching from further along the corridor, arm in arm.

'Who is it?' Joanna's voice was muffled by the door.

'It's me,' called Levy. 'Tom.' He smiled self-consciously at the approaching man and woman; they nodded back politely.

There was a hurried rattle as the security chain was released, then the door opened and Joanna threw herself into his arms. As she kissed him hungrily, Levy was suddenly aware again of the older couple. They had stopped and were watching wide-eyed.

'Uh, Joanna,' Levy whispered in her ear.

'Oh, Tom!' she breathed, nuzzling his neck. 'It's so good to feel you again! I want you in bed right now!'

Levy cleared his throat. 'Joanna!' he insisted, pink with embarrassment, his eyes on the mesmerised audience.

Looking round in surprise, Joanna disengaged herself from Levy and turned round to face the couple. 'Oh, I'm *so* sorry, Mr and Mrs Garrett!' she exclaimed innocently. 'I had absolutely no idea you were . . . please forgive me . . .' She smiled sweetly, then turned towards the door of her apartment. 'I really didn't mean to embarrass you. I hope you have a good evening out. We're . . . staying in.'

Back inside the apartment the two of them collapsed on to the floor, crying with silent mirth. 'Joanna, you are *wicked*!' Levy whispered. 'Did you see that woman's face?'

'Did you see *his*?' cried Joanna. 'He nearly had a heart attack – I don't suppose he's had so much excitement in years!'

Her laughter died away as Levy lowered his mouth to hers and started to run his hands over her body. As she quickly began to respond he swept her up in his arms and carried her through to the bedroom.

Later, as their breathing slowly subsided, they lay together in the soft light of the room. Levy chuckled, thinking again of the Garretts. 'Who were those two?' he asked her.

'George and Bea?' she murmured. 'Oh, they're in 705, two doors down. He's in real estate or something. Listen, don't worry. I'll apologise again when I next see them. Why?' She suddenly sounded alarmed. 'Do you think they recognised you?'

'I very much doubt it,' laughed Levy. 'I don't think

they even glanced at me. You had all the best lines, shall we say? . . . Anyway, it doesn't matter. They'll get used to seeing me around here – I hope.'

Joanna fell quiet. Then she sat up, her back turned to him and her head bowed. 'Tom,' she began in a low, drained voice, 'there's something you need to know. I . . . I don't think we can go on seeing each other any more.' She turned to face him and there were tears in her eyes.

Startled, Levy sat up and anxiously pressed her to him. Her head dropped on to his shoulder and he could feel the wetness of her tears on his skin. 'Why?' he urged, his heart pounding with sudden dread. 'I love you, Joanna. More than anyone I've ever known. You must realise that. I *love* you!' A note of desperation crept into his voice. 'Why?' he repeated.

'I . . . I love you too, Tom,' she whispered, swallowing hard. 'That's why I . . .' She turned and clung to him fiercely.

A terrible feeling of emptiness assailed the uncomprehending Levy. He grabbed her shoulders, forcing her to look into his eyes. 'But why, Joanna? *Why?* If we love each other . . .'

Joanna gulped, determined to remain calm, but her words came in a rush. 'Because I'll damage you, Tom. Why do you think I've always refused to go out in public with you? Why have we spent every evening here on our own? The sex is great, but it isn't just that. It would damage your career if it became known that you and I . . .' Unable to explain further, she dissolved into tears again.

Levy's hands were tight on her shoulders and his eyes had narrowed. 'Spit it out, Joanna! *Why?*'

Fighting her emotions, she took a deep breath. 'You remember a couple of weeks back, when I told you I was a commercial consultant? I didn't elaborate, and I was pretty vague about exactly what I did. And you didn't press me. You remember that?'

'Yes,' replied Levy. 'I remember.'

'Well,' she went on, searching his face, 'I didn't tell you the whole story.' She kept her gazed fixed on his, fearful of his reaction. 'I lied to you about my job. I didn't think it would matter to start with, but now . . . it's gone too far.' Her voice sank, and her eyes filled with misery. 'I work at the Israeli Embassy, Tom. I'm the Commercial Attaché at the Israeli Embassy.' She lowered her head.

'I know that,' said Levy.

Her head shot up. 'You knew?'

'Of course I knew.' He smiled. 'Good old US government security regulations. Rule one for senior staff: report any personal liaisons, so they can be checked out. It's a routine matter. Sorry,' he shrugged with an exaggerated gesture, 'but you don't get away from me that easily. Or at least,' he added, 'I don't intend to let you.'

Joanna appeared dumbfounded. 'But your career, Tom!' she exclaimed. 'In your position, surely you can't be seen to be having an affair with a foreign diplomat? You have to think of that!'

'It's not a problem in this case,' replied Levy gently, stroking her shoulders. 'Do you have any other objections to seeing me again?'

'Oh, God, Tom,' she said melting against him. Then she pulled away and stared once again into his eyes. 'It's . . . not quite as simple as that. In an appointment like mine – well, from time to time, I am asked for my opinions and judgements on various matters. Usually by my ambassador, you understand, but occasionally – well, I report direct to an office in Tel Aviv . . .' Her voice had gone quiet.

'The Institute,' said Levy, nodding. 'Mossad.'

Joanna appeared dumbstruck. 'You knew that too?'

'Yes,' he said softly, 'I knew.' He pulled her close, enfolding her in his arms, and they sank back on the bed. At that moment he knew he would never love anyone as much as he now loved her. 'Oh, Joanna,' he whispered tenderly, playing with the damp tendrils of hair that clung to her cheek. 'My beautiful, adorable Joanna. If it comes to it – the hell with my career. But it won't. Don't worry, darling!' Cupping her face in his hands, he gazed reassuringly into her eyes. 'I'm sorry, but I had to tell them about you, and they checked you out. Truly, they don't mind. With a name like mine, dammit, how could they? I've been a card-carrying, up-front, pro-Israel activist my whole life. I'm on record for it. True, I've had to tone down my public statements of support for Israel since taking on this job at the White House – but I promise you our relationship is no problem!'

Joanna had gone very still in his arms as he spoke. Levy felt her warm breath against his neck. Then, very slowly, she raised herself and looked down into his face with a disbelieving expression. 'Do you really mean we can . . .'

'Yes, darling,' he said softly. 'There's absolutely no need for us to stop seeing each other. Unless . . .' there was a question in his eyes, '. . . unless you want to?'

Joanna stared at him for a moment, then threw herself on him in wild abandon and cried ecstatically over and over again, 'I love you, *I love you*, Tom Levy! Don't leave me, ever! Oh God, how I love you!' And then, her emotions now totally confused, she began to cry again. But this time they were tears of relief and joy.

Levy's happiness was complete. Suddenly he heard himself saying something he hadn't anticipated. 'Will you marry me, Joanna?' he whispered in her ear. 'You're part of my life now, and I just don't think I can go on living without you!'

She looked into his eyes again, then clutched him

tightly to her. 'Oh yes, yes,' she murmured. 'I love you, Tom Levy. I *need* you.'

24

Ed Howard glanced up from the papers in front of him and rose to his feet. 'I'll get it, Johnny.'

Johnny Bourne stood and flexed his stiff leg as Howard went to answer the doorbell. He regretted that he had missed his exercise that day, but he and Howard had been fully occupied with maps and plans.

Max Goodale breezed in, a glint of satisfaction in his eye. 'Good evening, Ed. Hello, Johnny.'

'Good evening, Colonel. Can I get you a drink?' asked Howard.

'Mmm, good idea. Small whisky, please.'

'You seem quite pleased about something,' said Howard, pouring the drink and handing it to him. 'Good news?'

'Yes, I think so,' Goodale replied, lowering himself into an armchair. 'I saw the PM again today, and he's quite optimistic he'll be able to arrange what you want. "Quietly confident" is the expression I think I would use in his case, and from what I've seen of him, that's a pretty good sign. There's something else, too. I think I've found you your Korean interpreter.'

'OK,' responded Howard carefully. 'Who is he? Is he in good physical shape? Does he have any special forces experience? You know it won't work otherwise.'

'Let me give you the background,' began Goodale. 'It's someone who defected from North Korea two years ago, via Russia. That's a fairly common route for people to take – there are lots of North Koreans working there, mostly in slave-labour conditions. There were plenty of *South* Koreans we could have chosen, but I'm told it would be impossible for any of them to pass themselves off as Northerners. The dialect has grown apart over the forty or so years since partition. So have the idioms and accents – and even the vocabulary.'

Howard shot a questioning glance at Bourne.

The younger man was nodding. 'I'll buy that bit about the two dialects having grown apart,' he said. 'It doesn't take long for idioms and expressions to change. Anyway,' he added, 'it sounds like the guy voted with his feet when he defected. More likely to be genuine than otherwise, I'd say.'

'All right, Colonel,' said Howard evenly. 'I'll take your word for it. What's he been doing since he defected?'

'Working for the CIA, mostly in Seoul,' said Goodale. 'Naturalised American, in recognition of valuable services rendered. Name of Kim Sumi.' He spelt out the unfamiliar name to Howard. 'Very able, so I'm told. Intelligent and resourceful. And certainly pretty fit, by the sound of it.'

'I'll have to meet him to make my own assessment,' Howard stated firmly.

'We can't take anyone on trust,' added Bourne. 'You have to understand that.'

'Of course,' said Goodale carefully, 'yes, of course. Actually, you'll get the opportunity to do that in a couple of days' time.'

'He's coming to London? Good.'

'Yes,' said Goodale cagily. 'I . . . look, I hope you won't judge on first appearances. A mistake, that.'

Howard's eyes had narrowed in suspicion. 'You're holding something back, Colonel. What's wrong with this man?'

'Well, ah . . . you see,' began Goodale awkwardly, 'the fact is . . . well, Kim Sumi is actually female.'

'A woman?' asked Howard, surprised. 'But I thought Kim was a man's name.' He frowned. 'For Koreans, anyway,' he added. 'You know, Kim Il

Sung, Kim Jong-Il, Kim Young Sam, all that lot.'

'A reasonable enough assumption,' said Goodale quickly. 'But incorrect. Koreans put the surname first. Kim actually means "gold" or "golden". It's a very common family name, like "Smith" is in English. Sumi is her given name – a popular one for girls, I'm told. It means "surpassing beauty", actually. I don't know exactly what *her* beauty surpasses,' he added lightly. 'I haven't seen a picture of her yet.'

'Oh,' said Howard, apparently satisfied with the explanation. 'I see.' He glanced again at Bourne. 'What d'you think, Johnny?'

Bourne shrugged. 'Your decision, Ed,' he said simply.

'All right, Colonel,' said Howard finally. 'I look forward to meeting her. Are you sure she understands what she could be letting herself in for?'

Goodale was amazed by Howard's mild reaction to the suggestion of including a woman in the team. He had expected caustic objections, or a flat refusal even to consider the idea. But, poker-faced, he answered Howard's question. 'Obviously she doesn't know any details yet, but she's been told the assignment will be both hard and dangerous. In view of her particular linguistic qualification, I imagine she'll have a pretty good idea of where she'll be going. Anyway, she didn't seem at all doubtful, other than to ask who else would be going. I imagine,' added Goodale drily, 'she will be taking as good a look at you as you will at her.'

Howard grinned. 'Fair enough. I hope she does. I'd think less of her if she didn't.'

Goodale had planned to leave the next subject for later, but Howard's completely unpredicted reaction emboldened him. 'There's one other matter,' he went on casually. 'You remember I mentioned taking some extra equipment with you?'

'I do,' replied Howard. 'Some gear to monitor the comings and goings at the Yŏngbyŏn nuclear installation. And you will remember I told you of my extreme reluctance to do so. It will simply complicate matters. Johnny agrees with me, and so do the others.'

'I know. But I can assure you that this is something of very great importance. It is probably almost as important as the primary mission, to find out about the *Stasi*'s plans for IRIS.'

'Well, I told you I would consider it. If it's a relatively simple matter, I may – *may* – say yes. If it isn't, I'll say no. What exactly is entailed?'

'The problem is,' Goodale explained, 'the equipment is apparently very specialised. It isn't large or heavy, but it will need very careful setting up and calibrating. These bloody scientists,' he muttered with feeling, 'seem incapable of making simple gadgets – but there we are.' He shrugged. 'The long and short of it is that there won't be sufficient time to train any of your people to operate it.'

'Well, that settles it, then,' said Howard lightly.

'Not quite,' said Goodale.

'What do you mean?' demanded Howard, glowering.

'The proposal is that you take along with you someone who *does* know how to work this box of tricks. Then you won't have to worry about it. You can leave it all to him.'

'What!' Bourne was incredulous. 'Colonel, are you joking? That's a crazy idea!'

'A passenger!' growled Howard. 'You want me to take a bloody *passenger*? On something like this? And what do you mean, we won't have to worry about it? We'll have to nursemaid him and make sure he gets to the right place, won't we? And then get him out again? Come off it, Colonel!'

'I know how you feel,' said Goodale. 'If it's any comfort, I rather agree with you. But I know just how vital this is. I urge you not to turn the idea down flat. We have a man in mind. He is a scientist, but not at all what you might expect. I've met him. He's tough and able-bodied, and he seems sensible. I think he'll do – but of course I'll leave the final decision up to you. Will you at least meet him?'

Howard's eyes glittered darkly as he studied Goodale's face. 'All right, Colonel,' he said. 'I'll meet him. But I make no promises.'

25

'You mustn't let it get you down, darling,' said Tom Levy, a concerned look on his face.

'You're right, Tom,' she gave him a little smile. 'It's just been a rough day at work, that's all. But I shouldn't bother you with it. Let's talk about us instead.'

Levy grinned. 'I'm not sure we ought to do that right now, in a public place. I won't be able to keep my hands off you.'

'I don't want you to,' she said, smiling seductively. 'The choice is yours, Levy. A fiancée with a long face, moaning about her problems at work, or something more exciting.' She reached for him under the table.

'Stop it, Joanna,' he laughed, 'or we'll be thrown out. Next time I'll have to book us a private room, or a booth with a curtain and a "Do Not Disturb" sign.'

'Just as long as the food's as good as it is here,' she answered. 'Thanks for bringing me, Tom.' The hazel eyes glowed at him, happy again.

Levy smiled. 'I'm glad you enjoyed it, darling.' He was relieved to see that her mood had now changed. Throughout dinner she had seemed uncharacteristically downhearted. It was his fault, he realised, for starting the discussion about her work. She had poured out a catalogue of the difficulties and obstructions that her department faced almost daily. It didn't seem that any trade deal ever came without strings attached. If Israel wanted to buy something, a political concession was invariably required as part of the deal – often one that was completely unacceptable to the Israeli government. At the same time, if Israel wanted to sell something overseas, even in the USA, there would be tariff barriers and overseas corporate interests – as well as political objections – to contend with. As she explained, Levy had begun to grasp just how difficult things were.

'You ought to let me help, you know,' he said as he refilled their glasses.

'What are you talking about, Tom?'

'You know what I mean. I could use my influence to help ease some of these restrictions you've been telling me about.'

'Stop it right there, Tom,' she said. 'We decided to change the subject, didn't we?' She gazed at him, open desire in her eyes.

'I mean it,' said Levy seriously. 'I'd like to help. I have a lot of influence, you know.'

'Cut it out, Tom,' she told him gently. 'You know you can't do that. Anyway, I won't let you,' she added, dismissing the matter. 'Hey, give me your foot.'

'What?'

'Your right foot.'

Obediently, he raised his foot. Beneath the table, he felt her slipping off his shoe, then his sock.

'What the hell . . . what are you doing, Joanna?' he kept his voice low. 'People will see . . .' He glanced around.

'No, they won't,' she breathed, stroking his foot. 'Floor-length tablecloth.'

Levy felt a shock of excitement as she gently pulled his foot between her legs. Her inner thighs felt soft and warm.

Joanna started to rock gently back and forward, her eyes glazing over with pleasure, her mouth slightly open.

With an effort Levy pulled his foot away and hauled himself back upright from where he had slid slightly forward in his chair. 'Damm it, Joanna,' he whispered with a grin, 'you are absolutely incorrigible. Now put my shoe back on!'

'Let's skip dessert,' she whispered. 'I'd like you to take me home, to bed. I don't think I can bear to wait any longer.'

Levy grinned. 'Now, how the hell did I get the impression you felt that way?'

Five minutes later they were settled in the back of the big Lincoln as Levy's driver, Ronald, sped them back towards Joanna's apartment. Ronald glanced in his rear-view mirror. He had witnessed similar scenes many times before, but usually it was the boss taking the initiative, rather than the other way round. *Oh, boy is this one hot*, he thought. *She's all over him. A nympho, if ever I saw one.* He averted his glance and tried to concentrate on the road. He didn't mind. At last he'd had the opportunity to meet the famous Miss Stone, presently the talk of the White House. Like everyone else, he hoped she would last. She had made a great difference to the boss.

Ten minutes later, Ronald pulled back the glass divider behind him and coughed tactfully without looking round. 'Nearly there, Mr Levy, sir,' he called over his shoulder through the opening. 'About another three minutes.' *Better give the guy a chance to get his pants back on*, he thought, closing the divider again.

Ronald pulled up smoothly at the apartment block and got out to hold open the rear door. He glimpsed a flash of bare thigh as the young woman climbed out, and wondered whether it was deliberate. 'Goodnight, miss,' he said, smiling at her.

'Goodnight, Ronald,' she said. 'Thank you very much.'

'Thanks, Ronald,' said Levy. 'Could you pick me up at seven-thirty in the morning?'

'Sure thing, Mr Levy, sir. Goodnight.'

Upstairs, just as the door clicked shut the telephone rang. 'Never mind,' she breathed, kissing him hungrily. 'The machine's switched on.'

The answering machine played through her recorded message, and then after the tone a man's voice said, 'Joanna, it's David.'

She gave a start of surprise.

'. . . I'm flying in to Washington on Monday,' continued the voice. 'Short notice, but it'd be great to see you – and I have something I'd like to discuss with you. Could you pick me up at Dulles International at midday, your time, on Monday? Call me here if there's a problem.' The voice rang off, and there was a faint whirring sound as the tape rewound for the next call.

'Well, well,' said Joanna, turning to face Levy with a wry expression. 'Long time, no hear from *him*. I wonder what he wants this time?'

'Who's David?' asked Levy, curious.

'My brother, the hot-shot banker.' She grimaced. 'Always on the make. Never calls me unless he wants something. Pick him up at the airport indeed!' she snorted crossly. 'Why can't he get a cab like everyone else?'

'Where was he calling from?' asked Levy.

'Tokyo, probably,' Joanna replied. 'He's with the Goldman Sachs office out there. Works in the international bond market.' She brightened. 'Now, come on, darling. Let's forget about him.'

She reached down and pulled her dress up over her head. 'I want you to kiss me all over,' she breathed, her fingers now unfastening his clothes. 'And I mean *all* over.'

'Just you try to stop me,' said Levy, completely dismissing Joanna's brother from his mind.

26

'Yeah, I've met her,' said Ziegler to Ackford and Harris. 'Last night, in fact. Ed's bringing her round here right now. Should be here in a few minutes.'

The huge lumbering figure of Ackford sat hunched over the table and leaning forward on his elbows, his small, dark eyes peering keenly into Ziegler's face as he shifted a wad of chewing gum from one cheek to the other. 'What's she like?' he asked.

'Well, Tony,' drawled Ziegler, 'for starters, she's about half your size. And maybe a quarter your density, you overweight slob.' He grinned as Ackford raised a gorilla-like fist in feigned anger. 'She doesn't say much, but what she does say makes sense. And of course she has one other major advantage going for her.'

'Oh?' Harris chipped in, interested. 'What's that?'

'She's American,' said Ziegler, draining his glass. 'Bound to have more sense than you guys. God, I hate this warm beer,' he added, grimacing.

'Stop your whingeing, Yank,' rumbled Ackford easily. 'Want another one?'

'Yeah,' said Ziegler. 'Thanks, Tony.'

'Cheers, Ack,' said Harris, 'Same again for me too.'

Ackford rose and went over to the bar, where his massive frame and glowering expression attracted instant attention from the barman.

Back at the corner table Harris frowned. 'American?' he asked Ziegler. 'Ed told us she was Korean.'

'Well, I suppose she is, in a manner of speakin',' conceded Ziegler. 'But she's a naturalised American, anyhow.'

Harris continued to look doubtful. He still had serious reservations about having a woman in the team.

Halliday and Zeccara turned up just as Tony Ackford returned clutching three pint glasses. Groaning in mock annoyance, he went back to the bar for two more.

'Are they on their way, Mike?' asked Halliday as he sat down.

'Yeah,' said Ziegler. 'Shouldn't be long.'

'What about this other bozo, Mike?' asked Zeccara. 'I mean, I can understand the girl – we've got to have someone who can speak the language. But a bloody egghead scientist! What the fuck do we need him for?'

'Ed will explain,' Ziegler replied. 'But in any case it's not definite yet that he's comin'.'

'Well, I bloody hope he doesn't,' grumbled Ackford, dumping down two more pints. He had caught the tail-end of their conversation and guessed who they were talking about. 'We don't know if he's fit enough. And even if he is, I don't reckon there'll be time to teach him even the basics of what he'll need to know.'

'At least the girl's had some operational experience,' chimed in Halliday. 'This guy hasn't had any. He could hold us up – or worse.'

'Exactly!' Ackford loudly informed the bar, thumping his fist on the table. 'He's going to be a cork in the arsehole of progress, that's what he's going to be!'

The others were smirking. Ackford looked slightly puzzled until a voice came from just behind him.

'Good evening, Tony,' said Ed Howard. 'In one of your usual sunny moods, I see.'

Ackford looked round, completely unperturbed. 'Oh, hello, boss,' he rumbled. 'Can I get you a pint?'

'Kind of you. But ladies first, I think.' He stood to one side. 'I'd like to introduce Kim Sumi.'

Ackford rose to his feet, dwarfing the young woman in front of him. She was tiny, barely five feet tall, and slightly built. Ackford's first impression was of solemn, dark eyes in an unsmiling, inscrutable face. 'Good evening, miss,' he said, shaking her hand gently. 'Can I get you a pint? It's still my round.'

'Thank you,' said Kim Sumi. 'A mineral water, please.'

'OK.' He started back for the bar, then turned as Howard spoke.

'Tony?' Howard indicated a tall, blond-haired man. 'This is Dr Richard Weatherill.'

'Yeah,' growled Ackford darkly, mashing Weatherill's hand. 'Mineral water for you too, doc?'

'Pint,' said Weatherill, returning Ackford's stare. 'Thanks.'

Howard had watched the brief exchange with interest. He could see that Weatherill's inclusion would face considerable opposition from Ackford; probably from the others, too. *Fine,* he thought. *I'm far from convinced myself.* To his credit, though, the young scientist had not seemed put out by Ackford's less than wholehearted welcome, nor had he buckled beneath the force of the big man's bone-crushing handshake.

Ziegler was already introducing the two newcomers to the rest of the team. Howard could see curiosity on his men's faces. Kim Sumi's flat, expressionless face and monosyllabic conversation was not winning her any friends. In Weatherill's case, the situation was if anything worse – he was being largely ignored.

Ackford returned with the drinks. There was a temporary silence, broken by Harris. 'Tell us a bit about yourself, Miss Sumi,' he said.

'Just Sumi will do,' she said. 'My surname's Kim – these things are different where I come from.' Anyone else explaining such cultural differences would have smiled to ease things. 'I speak Korean,' she went on, 'and I'm used to hard conditions. I'm told those are the two qualifications you require.'

Once again Howard was impressed by this woman. She had made no attempt to seem communicative or outgoing, but at the same time there had been no animosity or challenge in the way she had spoken. She had stated the bare minimum, aware that her abilities would be tested.

Zeccara was frowning. 'What do you weigh, Kim – I mean, Sumi?'

'One hundred and four pounds,' she answered immediately.

No surprise at the question, no 'Why do you want to know?' – nothing, thought Howard.

Zeccara looked pensive, then nodded at Howard. 'Shouldn't be a problem,' he said. 'But I think maybe we'll give her a seven-cell, rather than a nine.'

'You're the expert,' said Howard. 'I'll leave it up to you.' He glanced again at Kim Sumi, knowing that neither she nor Weatherill would have a clue that Zeccara was talking about parachutes. Her expression had not changed; she gave no sign of appearing curious.

'I weigh a hundred and ninety,' chipped in Weatherill helpfully. Unlike Sumi, he was clearly making an effort to be sociable.

Their heads turned to face him. Zeccara spoke first. 'I guessed you were about that. Your weight's not a problem.'

'Are you fit?' Harris asked the scientist coldly.

'Reasonably so, but probably not as fit as the rest of you. My main recreation's fell-running. You know – up and down hills, in competitions. You have to be in reasonable shape for that, and I can hold my own with most.'

Howard could see Harris nodding. Competitive fell-runners did indeed have to be in good physical condition.

'We'll have to try you out,' said Harris. He turned to Howard. 'What do you think, boss? A week's outing to the Beacons? Finish off with Endurance?'

'Something like that,' Howard replied. 'But I don't know if I can give you a whole week.'

'Endurance?' asked Weatherill. 'What does that entail?'

'Scenic tour of Wales – forty to fifty miles over the Brecon Beacons and Black Mountains in twenty hours or less, depending on the conditions. Carrying a seventy-pound pack and a rifle. And water – that's not included in the weight.'

'Wow!' commented Weatherill thoughtfully. 'That sounds hard. I'm not sure I'm up to it – but I'll try my best.'

'You'll have to,' Ackford interjected. 'But you won't be carrying a rifle, of course. Can't let you have one of those. Against the law, that.'

'I'm not expecting any preferential treatment,' said Weatherill flatly.

'You won't be getting any,' grated Ackford, glowering at the scientist. 'You can carry a fucking six-foot crowbar instead. Oh, sorry, miss,' he added, turning to Kim Sumi. 'Don't mind my language. Fucking terrible, isn't it?' He raised his glass and emptied it.

The others were studying Weatherill carefully. Despite Ackford's obvious hostility, the scientist had smiled at the mention of the crowbar. He appeared open and honest, and Howard could see that the previously suspicious expressions on the team's faces had eased a little.

'You'll want me to do this too.' Sumi's voice cut in, and it was a statement rather than a question.

'Well,' said Harris, glancing at Howard. 'It's not so . . . I mean, we wouldn't expect you to carry . . .'

Sumi reached into her jacket pocket and produced a photograph. She pushed it across the table to Harris. 'Please don't patronise me,' she said lightly. 'I'm stronger than I look. Admittedly the pack in that picture only weighed about fifty pounds. And I wasn't carrying a rifle or extra water. But I carried it all the way there myself.'

Harris raised his eyes from the photograph. He looked at Sumi with interest. 'Is that . . .?'

'Yes, Mount Everest. Two years ago . . . As to endurance,' she went on, 'there's also this.' She produced a second photograph.

The others crowded round to see. The picture showed Sumi in light running shorts and vest, crossing a finishing line, her face strained but wearing a look of absolute determination. Above the finishing line was a large digital clock.

Halliday let out a low whistle. 'Was that your time?'

'Yes. Two hours and thirty-five minutes. Last year's New York marathon.'

'Phew!' he said in amazement. 'That's within a couple of minutes of my own best time! Or perhaps I should say,' he added with a broad smile, 'my best is within a couple of minutes of yours. That's an international-class time for a . . .' his voiced tailed off suddenly.

'Yes, Mr Halliday,' she said, with irony in her voice and for the first time showing a trace of humour. 'I know exactly what you mean. For a woman.'

The others laughed loudly, Ackford banging his huge fist on the table with mirth. Only Harris remained silent, his eyes intense, fixed on Kim Sumi's face.

Not a bad start, thought Howard, smiling. *Better than I expected.*

27

Russian Air Force Colonel Yevgeny Mikhailovich Barushkin slowly replaced the receiver, expelled a long breath and leaned back in his chair, shaking his head in surprise. It was not every day that he received a telephone call from the Defence Minister himself.

Barushkin reflected that the world, and Russia in particular, seemed to have gone mad in the last year or two. Perhaps Grachev's call was simply another manifestation of that lunacy. He wondered about it, and considered what he had been ordered to do.

Top secret, Grachev had said. *You must tell no one else,* he had said. *Select your own aircrew, swear them to secrecy, but don't even tell them the destination until you have taken off.*

Barushkin had flown many secret missions before, and had been given many similar instructions beforehand, but none of them had concerned transporting cargo. *Cargo*, for God's sake! Booze, caviar and other goodies – luxury items. Tons of it. What was so bloody secret about that? Probably another of Grachev's little scams, he thought. Maybe that was why – if it came to public attention, there would certainly be one hell of a rumpus in the Duma. 'Shit,' he said aloud, disgusted. Had he been reduced to acting as a courier for Grachev's bribes?

Barushkin thought about his previous secret missions. One of the first had been the time when he had received sudden orders to transport an emergency medical team down to Tashkent. He remembered the date well: 2nd January 1980. His had been one of two aircraft, with himself in overall command of both. He couldn't understand what all the secrecy was about – but it was highly secret, that was for sure. The orders had been hurriedly signed by Yuri Vladimirovich himself: Andropov, at that time head of the KGB, later President of the USSR. The medical team had consisted of a clutch of high-ranking professors, doctors and surgeons from the renowned Sklifakovsky Institute in Moscow. Barushkin had recognised two of them – Professors Kovalenko and Kanshin, both regarded with awe for their surgical skills – and he wondered what sort of disaster must have occurred in the Uzbek capital for such specialists to be required. It was normally unheard of for them to leave Moscow itself.

Barushkin had soon found out. At Tashkent, the aircraft had been accorded the sort of status it might have received if it had been conveying a senior Politburo member. High-ranking Uzbek KGB officers had swarmed on board and escorted the distinguished doctors away in a large convoy, sirens screaming. Barushkin and his fellow officers had been treated like VIPs themselves; in the KGB's airport headquarters they were plied with refreshments and comforts, and given full opportunity to rest before their return flight. Waiting there on standby, Barushkin had fallen into conversation with another pilot, a weary-looking major who had arrived earlier.

'Have you come to pick them up and take them home, then?' the major had asked.

'Who?' asked Barushkin.

'The casualties,' replied the major.

Aha, thought Barushkin. *So that's what this is all about.* 'Yes,' he said casually. 'How bad are they?'

'I've never seen anything like it,' said the major. 'There must have been a full-scale massacre. Battle casualties. Two or three dozen of them, and practically all of them badly wounded. Four dead, I think. But I'll tell you something – they're the toughest-looking bastards I've ever seen. What's more,' he continued, 'they must wield some clout. Heaven and earth is being moved for them. I wish I knew what was going on. There are certainly plenty of rumours flying around down in Kabul, I can tell you. I'm in no hurry to get back there myself,' he added darkly.

Kabul – Afghanistan! Barushkin's mind raced. *But there's nothing going on in Kabul. Or is there?* 'It is extremely unwise to talk of rumours, comrade Major,' he said warningly. 'You will not speak of this further. To anyone. Do you understand?'

The major, cowed into sullen silence, had departed soon afterwards.

Barushkin had kept his thoughts to himself, both during the casevac flight back to Moscow two days later, and subsequently. He had, however, filed a report on Major Ivanenko and his loose tongue. For his pains, Barushkin had been summoned to the KGB's headquarters in Dzerzhinsky Square. With his heart thumping as he passed through the black door in the centre of the huge, granite building, he prayed that he was not about to be taken downstairs to the cells.

After what seemed like an interminable delay, to his astonishment he was shown into the office of the Head of the 7th Directorate. He stood rigidly to attention as the slightly built, white-haired man behind the desk finished leafing through a file – Barushkin's own, no doubt. *What have I done?* he wondered in trepidation.

'You have done well, Major Barushkin,' the general had said calmly, looking up from the papers. 'Your report on Major Ivanenko was timely and well-advised. The advice you gave him in Tashkent,' the KGB officer gave a wintry smile, 'was excellent. Steps have been taken to ensure that he follows it in future. I trust you have followed it yourself?'

'Yes, comrade General,' said Barushkin stiffly. 'I would never discuss operational matters with anyone.'

'Good,' said the general. 'I have noted your reliability in your file. You may go.'

Years later Barushkin realised that that episode had marked a curious upturn in his career. He had gained his second star as a lieutenant-colonel, and eventually a third as a full colonel; but somehow he seemed to have stalled at that point. His 'reliability' had marked him out for a number of sensitive or secret assignments, and in many cases he had flown similarly hard, tough-looking passengers on unspoken missions in a variety of aircraft. Yes, he was regarded as reliable, all right. But he had never attained the rank of major-general.

Barushkin sighed. It didn't really matter. A colonel's life was not a bad one. Or, at least, it hadn't been, until the world had started to go mad. The rank and the uniform didn't seem to count for much, these days. Democracy? Pah! What price democracy, when Pavel Grachev – Pasha Mercedes himself – gave him orders to fly cargoes of whisky and caviar from one place to another, doubtless with a view to expanding his personal monopoly on the German car concession?

Select your own aircrew, Barushkin repeated to himself. *Swear them to secrecy. Take on cargo at Vnukovo Airport. Fly to Vladivostok and wait there until ordered. Pick up one KGB passenger, who will accompany you and your cargo to your destination.*

Sod it, thought Barushkin disgustedly, thinking of his final destination. Moscow these days was bad enough, but of all the miserable, stinking shit-heaps in the world, P'yŏngyang, capital of North Korea, had to be the worst.

28

Shortly after eleven o'clock the following Monday morning, Joanna Stone left her apartment and took a taxi to Dulles International Airport. The twenty-six-mile drive west took fifty minutes, and by noon she was standing in line with the many others who were greeting arriving passengers. After she had waited for fifty-five minutes, her expression of impatience began to give way to one of anxiety. Finally, after glancing at her wristwatch for the twentieth time, she walked over to the public telephone booths. Choosing at random one of the booths that accepted credit cards, she pulled out a card and dialled a number from memory. It was a few seconds after 12.59 when it rang.

Joanna had not in fact been waiting for anyone to emerge from the arrivals hall. Her time there had given her the opportunity to see whether she was being tailed or watched. Even if any surveillance operation had been skilled enough to pass without her noticing it, her behaviour would have seemed entirely normal, and for her to appear worried enough to make a telephone call was perfectly natural in such circumstances. The phone booth was in a public place, but in the throng of travellers and relatives nobody gave her a second glance. The credit card she was using was not her own; it had been stolen two days previously.

The Tokyo number that Joanna had dialled answered on the first ring. The voice of her 'brother', David, was clear and uncluttered by static. His message of two days previously had given her a time – midday – to which she was to add one hour before making her telephone call.

'Hello?'

'Oh, David, is that you? I've been so worried!' she said loudly. 'What happened? Why aren't you here?'

'I'm very sorry, Joanna,' he replied. 'Something came up at the last minute. I couldn't make it. My trip's been cancelled.'

'What am I supposed to do?'

'Walter will explain. Here he is.'

The rehearsed preliminaries were over and a deeper, more powerful voice came on the line. It was her controller. 'Hello, Joanna. How have things been proceeding?'

Joanna lowered her voice. 'Very well, so far. As planned.'

'How co-operative is the man being?'

'I haven't yet put that to the test,' she said, glancing casually around to ensure that no one was taking any interest. 'But he's hooked. I think he'll do pretty well anything I ask. In fact, he's proposed marriage to me... What do you have in mind?'

At the other end of the line in Tokyo, Walter smiled. He wasn't surprised. Joanna was a good-looking woman. She had a talent for ensnaring men, and an utter ruthlessness when it came to using them. He suspected that she enjoyed sex even with someone whom she despised, although he could not be sure. She had certainly never jibbed at any order to seduce a man, but at the same time she had never shown the slightest reluctance to leave him high and dry once his usefulness was at an end. He ignored her question. 'He's proposed to you?' he asked, amused. 'What was your reply?'

'I accepted, of course. But that's beside the point. I can ditch him any time, whenever you say. What do you want me to get him to do?'

As Joanna's controller explained, her forehead creased in concentration. She took no notes but committed the instructions to memory. Finally she confirmed, 'That should be simple enough. Is there anything else?'

'That's all for now,' stated her controller. 'When you've made the arrangements call David here with full details, and he'll pass the information on to those who need to know.'

The line went dead, and Joanna hung up. She wiped her fingerprints from the stolen credit card and deliberately let it fall to the floor on her way out of the airport terminal. With luck, she reckoned, it would be picked up by an opportunist thief and used again, further muddying the waters. Outside, she hailed a cab and headed back into the city.

In Tokyo, her controller put down the telephone with a sigh of satisfaction. Joanna had sounded confident. He had come to Japan specifically to make that call, and his long journey had not been wasted. He chuckled to himself. 'David,' he said, 'from tomorrow, I want you to stay by this phone until she reports back. I'll leave it to you to arrange the details of the handover of the necessary documents. My only condition is the obvious one – that she must not meet the others at any stage. Is that clear?'

'Yes, Walter,' said David obediently.

'Good,' said the controller. He yawned; it was now

after 2 a.m. in Tokyo. 'What time is my return flight in the morning?'

'I've booked you on JL 781, leaving at ten o'clock. It arrives in Beijing at thirteen-forty. That will give you time to make the connection with flight JS 152, which leaves at fifteen hundred hours and arrives at Sunan at seventeen-thirty.' He handed over the itinerary and air ticket.

'Thank you,' said the controller, stuffing the documents into his jacket pocket. He yawned again. 'Well, I have a long day ahead of me, with a sixty-five-mile drive on a cart track of a road at the end of it. But at least there are no time-zone changes. I'm going to get some sleep. Wake me at six-thirty, will you?'

'Certainly, Walter. Goodnight.'

The controller walked through to the spare bedroom and began to undress. He glanced briefly in the mirror at his powerful physique, running a hand through his short, iron-grey hair. He would do half an hour's vigorous exercise on awakening, to keep himself in good trim. *Not bad for an old man of sixty-eight,* he thought. He chuckled to himself, thinking of Joanna. *It has been far too long,* he reflected, *since I last bedded that one. So compliant and uninhibited!* He sighed and climbed into bed, still chuckling quietly to himself. *Those Israelis would have a bloody fit if they knew she worked for me. One of my best assets . . .*

General Reinhold Erfurt, *Stasi* commander-in-chief, drifted off into an untroubled sleep.

29

Richard Weatherill was in the last stages of exhaustion. The huge weight on his back seemed to hammer him down into the ground with every step he took. His muscles howled at him to stop, to rest, to lie down. His shoulders felt raw from the straps of the bergen rucksack, his ribs pummelled by its jolting against them. With each pace forward, pain lanced up from his bruised and blistered feet.

He was not sure what had kept him going. It was not the knowledge that Kim Sumi was going through the same ordeal on a different route – though, in view of her slight build, she had been given a lighter weight. When it had still been daylight, he thought he had glimpsed her a couple of times in the distance, accompanied by Pete Halliday.

It wasn't pride, either. He had long since lost any sense of that. Something else had replaced it, about twenty kilometres back, when he had started to feel real pain. He had focused his hatred on Mel Harris, the tormentor who dogged his footsteps and monitored his progress. Harris would come and go, never saying a word, never far away. Weatherill was convinced that the man was mad. The super-fit Harris was doing all this voluntarily and carrying the same weight – seventy pounds. Occasionally he would disappear in a different direction, but Weatherill knew now that this was simply an attempt to disconcert him, to make him think he had chosen the wrong route. Just once the scientist had made the mistake of following him, only to see Harris a mile or so later take a dog-leg turn leading back to the correct route. Since then, Weatherill had trusted his own judgement, and his map and compass, as he plodded agonisingly from one checkpoint on the seventy-kilometre route to the next.

A feeling of sheer bloody-mindedness had taken over. There was nothing else left to drive him on. He had passed through one pain-barrier after another, and utter determination was now all that kept him going. *One step at a time,* he told himself. *Only four kilometres to go. Just over an hour, maybe.*

The knowledge that the ordeal was nearly over did not help. If anything, it made it worse. All he could think about now was the end, the Land Rover waiting, food, water, rest at last. He tried to force thoughts of comfort from his mind, but could not. The last kilometre, he knew, would be the worst.

At last, his strength failing, he saw the light in the distance. It had to be Tony Ackford and the Land Rover. No more than four hundred metres, down by the bend in the road. Downhill. He blinked, his mind almost numb. It was nearly over. He felt nothing but the pain from his feet, knees and shoulders. *Keep going . . .*

Four hundred metres. Three hundred. Two . . . Nearly there. *Just keep going!*

He heard the Land Rover's engine start. Ackford must have seen him coming – he was getting ready for him. The headlights came on. Yes, it was the Land Rover. *Thank God, nearly there. Keep going. Lift the head, finish in style.*

Weatherill heard a crunch of gears. Unbelievably the Land Rover gradually pulled away, driving off down the road. No! What was Ackford doing? He had got it all wrong. *Come back!* In a stumbling run now, Weatherill floundered the last short stretch to the final checkpoint and collapsed, his strength gone, tears of desolation streaming down his face, breathing hideous curses against Ackford, Harris and the whole world.

'That's a nuisance,' remarked Harris lightly from behind him. 'Tony seems to have gone a bit early. Must have got the time wrong. He's off to the alternate checkpoint, I suppose. We'd better get going, or we won't make that one either. You OK, doc?'

'Bastard, bastard, bastard,' rasped Weatherill with each breath, unable to inject any force into the words.

'It's up to you, doc,' Harris stood over him, showing no sign at all of his own fatigue. 'But here's the map reference if you're interested.' Harris passed him a small slip of paper with a six-figure number. 'I'll see you there. Don't be too long.'

'Get fucked!' Weatherill's attempt at a vicious snarl had no strength; Harris barely heard the muttered curse.

'Suit yourself, doc. I'll be off, then.'

Weatherill watched Harris's departing figure, which was soon lost in the dark. He gave another groan and sank back on the damp ground, oblivious to the cold. For a minute or so he lay there, his breathing gradually returning to normal.

He had been beaten. Beaten, within sight of success. The feeling of defeat swept over him, and he began to sob with fury and frustration. Ackford had done it deliberately . . .

Deliberately. A detached element of his mind suddenly cottoned on. It was all part of the plan, just to see how he would react!

Still lying on the ground, he wrenched his map from inside his smock and held the beta-light to it. Plotting the map reference that Harris had given him, he saw it was three kilometres away. He groaned, and tried to wrench himself up. His shoulder muscles screamed as the weight of the big bergen bit into them, and he fell back panting. He tried again, straining every muscle. He got to his hands and knees, then to his feet. His head felt light with pain and exhaustion as he set his compass and began to plod off on the bearing.

'I'm knackered,' said Harris to Ackford forty minutes later, sitting in the front passenger seat of the Land Rover, a mug of tea cupped in his hands. 'Haven't done that bugger for years.'

'Well, I'm bored waiting,' said Ackford, his jaws chewing gum as usual. 'Is he coming?'

'I think so. Usual sorry-for-himself crap when he thought he'd finished, and for a moment I thought I'd got a case of give-up-itis on my hands. But he pulled himself together after a minute or two – I watched him get back to his feet. I think he'll come.'

'Didn't think he had it in him,' said Ackford. 'More tea?'

'Thanks,' said Harris. 'Actually, he hasn't done badly. To be fair to him, we don't normally lob in a sickener on this one.'

'Well, it was only a little one,' said Ackford easily. 'And we won't have time for the real sickeners, will we? The boss wants us back tomorrow.'

'Tomorrow?'

'Yeah. I got the message today. Final packing, a few days' leave, then we're off.'

'How'd the girl do?' Harris asked.

'Didn't turn a hair. Pete was impressed.'

'Looks like we're on, then. Hang on, I think I heard something.' Harris quietly stepped out of the Land Rover and scanned the dark hillside above the track. A smile crossed his features briefly as he observed a figure stumble towards them, still three hundred metres away. 'Yeah,' he whispered to Ackford, 'he's coming.'

'Took his bleeding time,' muttered Ackford.

Two minutes later, Weatherill saw the dark shape of the Land Rover loom up in front of him. *It's just going to drive off again,* he thought despairingly. He staggered up to the vehicle, expecting it to pull away.

'Evening, doc,' said Ackford, shining his torch into Weatherill's face. The scientist hardly had the energy to wince in the glare.

'You sadistic fucker,' gasped Weatherill. 'Give me a bloody cigarette, would you?'

'Bad for your health, doc,' grated the big man. 'Anyway, I didn't think you smoked.'

'I don't,' said Weatherill in a strained voice. 'Not until now *anyway* . . .' His legs gave way and he collapsed onto the ground.

Ackford leaned down and felt the man's pulse. It was fast and steady, but he was out cold. 'He's flaked,' he remarked to Harris. 'Stupid egghead. Come on, Mel, give me a hand to sling him in the back. Then we'll be off.'

'He didn't do too badly,' said Harris a few minutes later as Ackford guided the Land Rover back down the rough track towards the road. Weatherill's inert body lay on a pile of old sacks in the back. 'He did finish it, after all.'

'Too slow,' said Ackford. 'Nineteen hours. Shouldn't take nineteen, not in nice weather like this, should it? The girl did it in seventeen and a half. Good effort, that,' he commented, a note of admiration in his voice. 'He shouldn't have let himself flake out, either,' he added.

'No,' Harris agreed, 'He shouldn't. Still, he didn't do too badly. Borderline, but I reckon he just about scrapes through.'

'Stupid bleeding egghead, flaking like that,' muttered Ackford.

They let Weatherill sleep for ten hours; he woke to the harsh clanging sound of a cooking pot being hit hard by a spoon. His eyes seemed gummed together, and when he tried to sit up he groaned at the effort imposed on his stiffened muscles. Slowly he unzipped his sleeping bag. It had been the deepest sleep he had ever known. He was still wearing the same filthy clothes; he hadn't even had the energy to change out of them. 'OK, OK,' he mumbled. 'I'm awake.'

'Get your daps on, doc, and grab a mug of tea – then it's twenty minutes' easy PT to loosen you up. After that, you can have a shower and some lunch.'

Weatherill reached obediently for his trainers, wincing painfully as he pulled them on to his swollen, throbbing feet. He felt about ninety years old. After he had crawled out of the tent Harris put him through a series of warming-up exercises. Soon protesting muscles began to respond, and he started to feel better. Then he took a shower, put on a clean tracksuit and made his way to the main tent in the small camp. His feet were still sore, but otherwise he felt almost human. As he caught the smell of hot food he suddenly realised he was also ravenously hungry. He pushed open the flap. Harris, Ackford and Halliday were there, seated at the bare table and already eating; so was Kim Sumi. She looked as relaxed and composed as she had when he first met her.

'Grab yourself a plate and some peelings, doc,' said Harris without looking up. 'Not that there's much left, since Pete's had seconds.' Halliday's gargantuan appetite was notorious, though his pale face and thin frame always belied it.

Weatherill tried to walk normally as he hobbled to the table, but he knew he was still limping

'What's up, doc?' asked Ackford in a silly voice. '*Har, har*,' he laughed coarsely. 'I've been waiting for the opportunity to get that one in. Got a blister, have you?'

'I've got about five hundred,' he replied with a weary smile, piling food on to his plate in a fair imitation of Halliday. 'It's all right for you lot – this is routine stuff for you. I've never felt so crocked in my life.' He began to eat, shovelling his food up rapidly.

'Yeah, well, you can relax now,' said Harris. 'It's over. Back to London this afternoon. The boss wants to see you. Looks like you've passed after all. Didn't think you would, but you have.'

Weatherill's 'Thanks' came filtered through a large mouthful of food.

'Just don't flake again, OK?' growled Ackford, pointing a fork at him. 'When you get to the end of a long march, you've still got to be able to think straight. And fight, too. That's the whole point of the training, see? Getting there's only half the job. No bloody use if you flake out as soon as you get there.'

'I'll try to remember that,' said Weatherill quietly.

30

'I don't trust you, Bourne.'

'Juliet, I'm telling you God's honest truth!' exclaimed Johnny Bourne, exasperated with his wife's suspicions. 'I swear – I'll be with the Colonel in Seoul the whole time. In the city, for heaven's sake, sitting on my backside in some hotel! I've got to be there to man a radio link to the others. I won't be with them – in fact I'll be nowhere near any excitement. Ask the Colonel, if you like!'

'I have. He wouldn't tell me much. I bet he's covering up for you.'

'He isn't! Dammit, Juliet, d'you really think he would do that?'

'Yes.'

'Oh, for goodness' sake.' Bourne got to his feet stiffly and began pacing the room, his limp pronounced. 'All right, let's get him on the phone. Ring him right now. You can talk to him again. Ask him whatever you like. Would that convince you?'

'No.'

Bourne threw up his hands. 'Then I give up. You're beyond hope. Ed's told you, Mike's told you, the Colonel's told you . . . What else do you need before you're convinced, for God's sake?'

'Those three can say what they like,' said Juliet stubbornly. 'And they may even mean it. But I know you. You'll use any excuse to get back into the action. I *know* you, Bourne.'

'Stop calling me Bourne,' he said crossly. 'I hate it

when you do that. Look, think about it. Be logical. My leg's crocked – I'd be no use in action. You know that as well as I do. I'd only hold everyone else up. My God,' he moaned, 'I wish things were different! I'd be with the others like a shot – I don't mind admitting it. But . . .'

'You see?' shrilled Juliet accusingly. 'You *do* admit it! You *would* go with them, given the chance!'

'Yes!' shouted Johnny. 'I would! If I could!' He stopped pacing and subsided into his chair again, suddenly deflated. 'But I *can't*!' He put his head in his hands. 'I'm just not up to it any more.'

Juliet was silent for a moment. 'Do you promise me, Johnny?' she asked, her voice pleading.

'Of course I do,' he muttered dully.

Juliet bit her lip. He probably even meant it, too, she thought. But it was one thing for him to mean it now; it would be quite another thing if . . .

'Please don't forget that promise, Johnny,' she said softly.

Kath Ackford stormed into her small sitting room brandishing a piece of paper. 'Tony! What's the meaning of this?' she demanded fiercely.

Tony Ackford looked up from the sports page of his newspaper and examined the letter, frowning. After a minute his face cleared. 'It's from the boss,' he announced helpfully.

'I can see that, you poor blithering fool!' snapped Kath scathingly. 'What's this nonsense about another business trip?'

'Well,' replied her husband lamely. 'We're going away, like. Look,' he said, pointing at the second paragraph of the letter. 'The boss says so.'

'Oh, good grief!' exclaimed Kath. 'Tony, are you being deliberately vague and stupid, or what? Now, you just tell me what the hell's going on, or else!'

'Well,' rumbled the big man awkwardly. 'I dunno,

really. Look, Kath, he explains it all here in the letter. He wants me to go, so I've got to go. I mean, that's my job, see? Got to do what the boss tells me. Orders, innit.'

'Well, I'll tell you what I think of you and your high and mighty boss, so I will. Him and his orders. Flaming cheek! The nerve of the man! How dare he . . .'

Kath Ackford launched into a diatribe which her husband knew would continue uninterrupted for a good ten minutes. He studied Howard's letter again as his wife showered him with invective, wagging her forefinger at him every few seconds to emphasise a point. His head bowed in a manner he hoped Kath would take to be genuine contrition, he let the sound of her voice wash over him. The boss had done well with this one, he decided admiringly. One of his better letters, this was. Kath would make a bit of a racket, maybe toss a few things about, then probably burst into tears and everything would be OK again. Terrific spirit, Kath had. A bit noisy sometimes, he admitted to himself, gave it a bit of stick every now and then, but everything would be fine afterwards. The boss's letter had done the trick.

'I've got another overseas trip coming up soon, love,' Mel Harris announced during a late supper. He had waited until his son had gone upstairs to bed before telling his wife.

'Oh? Where to this time?' asked Janet.

'Far East,' said Harris lightly. 'A new contract. I'll be leaving in about ten days' time.'

'Lucky devil,' said Janet, grimacing. 'When are you going to take me on one of these glamorous trips of yours? That's what I'd like to know.'

'You wouldn't enjoy it really,' said Harris truthfully, keeping his voice matter-of-fact. 'Hard work, no time for fun or relaxation.'

Harris hated deceiving his wife. He was normally open with her, but he certainly wasn't about to tell her any details of what he would be doing on this particular trip. It was kinder to tell her a few white lies, he told himself, but he would stay as near to the truth as he could. He had to tell her *something*, after all, to explain his forthcoming absence. He had decided to make it sound as routine as possible. He was frequently away on XF business, but usually only for two or three days at a time. Mostly it was to Europe, sometimes Africa, occasionally the Middle East; he made about a dozen such trips a year.

'Hmm,' said Janet severely, a jaundiced expression on her face. 'No relaxation, indeed. You expect me to believe that? You just make sure you behave yourself, you understand? If I get to hear you've been living it up, chatting up some little oriental number in a night-club or whatever, you won't know what hit you when you get home.'

'Oh, come off it, Janet,' said her husband, grinning. 'It won't be like that at all. I promise – I won't be going anywhere *near* any night-clubs. Honest. You can ask the others.' Harris had undoubtedly spoken the truth so far as night-clubs were concerned but he thought it would be unwise, to say the least, to make any mention at this stage of Kim Sumi. He smiled to himself at the incongruous thought of her being described as a 'little oriental number'. Little and oriental she might be, but she wasn't his type. There was something slightly creepy and mysterious about her, he had decided; he didn't like her at all. In any case, Angelo or Pete – Angelo, most likely – would be the ones making any moves there were to be made in that direction. As far as Harris was concerned he didn't mind them trying, as long as it didn't interfere with the operation, but Sumi seemed so cold and remote that he didn't think either of them would get anywhere.

'Others? What others?' Janet was asking him.

'Huh? Oh, yes. Well, big Tony's coming, and Pete, and Angelo . . . in fact, the office is going to be pretty stretched while we're away. Important new business contract, like I said. Johnny will be away too, in fact, but he won't be with the rest of us.'

'I hate you going away,' said Janet, her voice suddenly soft. 'You will be careful, won't you?'

Harris put his hand gently on his wife's. 'Of course I will, love,' he said quietly. 'Look, it's no big deal. It's not as if I haven't been away before, and I can look after myself – you know that. What could go wrong? Please don't worry. It just makes it harder for me, if I think you're going to worry when I'm gone.'

'I know. I'm sorry, Mel. I'm just being silly.'

Harris lowered his eyes to his plate and resumed eating, but his appetite had gone. His wife was being far from silly. Plenty could go wrong on this mission, he knew. A few years ago – hell, even last year – he would have welcomed the danger and the challenge, and nothing would have kept him away from the action; but things somehow seemed subtly different now.

He suddenly felt uneasy and apprehensive. A cold shiver of anxiety and foreboding crept into his thoughts. He wondered whether it was a sense of his own mortality sneaking up on him at last, after all these years. Perhaps a premonition . . .

Stop it, he told himself fiercely. *It's fatal to think like that.* He looked up again, a strange expression on his face. 'I hate going away and leaving you, Janet,' he said tenderly. 'I . . . Look, this is going to be my last trip. After this one, there won't be any more.'

Janet Harris gazed into her husband's intense blue eyes. Her heart melted, as it always did when he looked at her. Her voice was low and husky with emotion. 'Do you mean it, Mel?' she whispered.

He nodded slowly. 'Yes. I do. This will be my last

one.' He paused, forcing a smile. 'You . . . you'll look after young Ben when I'm gone, won't you, love?'

31

The inspection hatch on the metal-clad door banged open; the old man rose to his feet and shuffled over to stand in front of it. In a dull and lifeless voice he mumbled the required sentence. 'I can't remember anything.' He held out his hands.

The usual plate of sickly-smelling stew and a bottle of water were passed through to him and he took them without a word. He returned to the armchair, sat down and began eating. There was no flicker of expression on his face; his actions were those of an automaton, his movements almost robotic. His jaws moved slowly, and every few seconds he blinked, but that was all.

Conditions in Sir Reginald Hislop's cell were now foul in the extreme. A pool of filth now covered nearly half the concrete floor area. His hair was matted and dirty; he had a thin, straggly white beard and his pyjamas were stained with accumulated grime. He no longer noticed.

For the first week he had blubbered and whined to himself almost continuously. In the absence of paper he had been forced to tear pages out of the leather-bound copy of his memoirs, and it had been obvious that this had caused him anguish. Then the tobacco had run out, and for two days he had appeared restless and agitated. Gradually the blubbering had quietened and a blank look of uncomprehending resignation had taken over, with just occasional flashes of misery and self-awareness. Eventually even this had ceased. Nearly half the pages in the book had gone, and it no longer seemed to cause him any distress to mutilate it further.

Colonel Gerhardt Eisener was aware that there had been some muttering amongst the *Stasi* rank-and-file about the vile stench filtering upstairs from the cell. His aide, Kessler, had reported it to him, but not in so many words. He had merely enquired whether there were any repairs that needed to be made to the building's ventilation system, and Eisener had known exactly what he meant. Privately he agreed, although he said nothing. The smell was beginning to get on his nerves too. The only one apart from General Erfurt who appeared to be entirely immune to it, oddly enough, was Anna Linden. Perhaps, thought Eisener, that was partly to do with her medical training. Whatever the case, it was just as well she didn't seem to mind; she had to go in every night when the old man was asleep, to check him over and make sure that it was only his mind that was deteriorating.

The general would frequently accompany her into the cell, and he often demanded Eisener's presence too. He seemed to have more faith in Eisener's knowledge of drugs than he did in Anna's. To some extent, Eisener knew, the general was right in that respect. He did know more than Anna about the administration of mind-altering drugs, and had had more experience of it. He rather wished that he hadn't; he had no particular taste for the worsening squalor in the basement, although he could tolerate it and had seen similar conditions many times before. Now, though, it just seemed a chore, and a somewhat demeaning one at that. He was bored with having to dress in the overalls, boots and face-mask, and then undress again afterwards.

The entire basement smelled like a sewer. By Erfurt's order, someone had to be down there the whole time on watch. Eisener could not really see the point of it; the closed-circuit system provided a perfectly adequate view of the old man's cell, and if anything untoward had occurred someone could have been there in a matter of seconds to deal with it. Nevertheless, Eisener admitted to himself, the basement detail had become a useful form of punishment. He had swiftly realised that the men hated the hatch-duty, passing the food and water through; cleaning up after Anna, the general and Eisener himself was something they hated even more. The overalls invariably stank after emerging from the cell; discarded in a heap on the floor of the corridor outside, they would be left for whoever was on duty that night to wash and prepare for the next time.

In some ways, thought Eisener, it was useful to have an unpleasant duty to assign – it kept the men in line. It wasn't easy to maintain the old standards of discipline that were still insisted on by the general. A day or night spent down there, gagging from the vile smell, made them think twice about repeating any mistakes or showing any signs of slackness.

But enough was enough. It was hard to motivate these men after four grindingly boring years in North Korea, and to make their lives even more dreary and unpleasant was not really the answer. Besides, there would soon be no necessity for continuing Hislop's treatment in its current form. It was time to start cleaning the place up; Hislop wouldn't notice the difference. The next stage could begin, now that the combination of chlorpromazine and chlorpropamide had prepared the ground. The drugs had worked, as Eisener had known they would.

Despite the similarity in their names, the two medications were very different. Chlorpromazine was a sedative, prescribed for its calming effect; sometimes given to patients suffering from schizophrenia, it attenuated the more impulsive and sometimes violent nature of their behaviour. Chlorpropamide was prescribed for quite another purpose. It was a drug designed for diabetic patients to lower their blood-sugar level, thus facilitating the body's natural production of insulin. If taken by mistake by a non-diabetic person, it would lower their blood-sugar drastically; the resulting symptoms would include weakness, sweating, dizziness and a feeling of confusion.

In severe cases, a non-diabetic patient taking chlorpropamide could suffer a mini-stroke; there were some unfortunate cases on record of patients who had been prescribed chlorpromazine but who had in fact been issued with chlorpropamide, simply because the pharmacist had misread a doctor's handwritten prescription. Some patients had never fully recovered from the confused state induced by mistakenly taking chlorpropamide. Hislop, Eisener knew, was not a diabetic; it was precisely to induce such a state of confusion that chlorpropamide was being administered to him. His zombie-like demeanour attested its success.

'I think, comrade General, that the time has come for us to test his reactions,' said Eisener calmly.

'Are you sure?' asked Erfurt.

'Quite sure, comrade General. The drugs and the humiliation have broken him, as was intended. He doesn't know what is going on any more. His behaviour proves it.'

'Hmm,' muttered the general. 'What do you suggest?'

'Some simple tests,' replied Eisener. 'Basic things, such as general awareness, responses to questions and so forth. Some pain, perhaps, to induce a reaction, but I would suggest nothing too severe. He is in reasonable physical health, but he is old and it would be wise not to risk a mishap.'

'All right,' said Erfurt. 'When?'

'We might as well do it now, comrade General. He is awake, and he is not due to be fed for another couple of hours.'

The two men made their way down to the basement. In the corridor outside the cell they dressed in the usual overalls, face-masks and rubber boots; Eisener noticed that a dark stain had begun seeping out from under the cell door. The stench was almost overpowering, and he wrinkled his nose in distaste. He pushed open the door and stood to one side to allow his commanding officer to enter.

It was the first time anyone had been inside the cell while Hislop was awake. Despite this, Eisener noted with satisfaction, the old man showed no sign of awareness that anyone was even there. He stared vacantly at the blank wall above the bed.

'Sir Reginald,' said Eisener calmly in English, 'pay attention, please.'

There was no reaction from the old man. *Good*, thought Eisener; *this is just as I had hoped*. He stepped forward towards the seated figure and slapped him sharply across the face.

Hislop's head rolled slightly from the blow. He whimpered softly, a small animal sound, and put his hand up to his face where it stung. His eyes turned slowly to face Eisener, but they were blank and expressionless. After a brief moment Hislop looked away again and resumed staring at the wall; his hand fell back into his lap.

Eisener turned to Erfurt and spoke in German. 'There will be no point in asking him any questions after all, comrade General,' he said, pleased. 'His lack of awareness is complete. He will remember only the routine. It will not matter what we do to him now, as long as the routine is not interrupted for too long.'

Erfurt frowned beneath his face-mask. 'I don't think just one little slap proves anything. He will need a far bigger shock than that to make a proper test.' Taking a small pocket-knife from his overalls, he pulled off his face-mask and then bent down so that his face was a few inches in front of Hislop's. 'Look at me, idiot!' he bellowed.

Hislop continued gazing slackly in front of him, as if Erfurt was not even there.

The pocket knife snicked open and Erfurt grabbed

Hislop's left hand. Selecting the third finger, he gripped it hard and drove the small blade of the knife deep under the old man's fingernail.

The slack face contorted in agony and a thin nasal scream came from deep within Hislop's chest. His eyes closed tight, his teeth bared briefly and he thrashed and struggled weakly to pull his hand away as Erfurt twisted the knife-blade beneath the fingernail. Blood dribbled from the wound, running on to Erfurt's hand and Hislop's own clothes. Pulling out the knife, Erfurt stood up and shot a look of savage contempt at his prisoner.

The scream died to a whimpering, bubbling moan as Hislop clutched his left hand with his right and thrust the injured finger instinctively into his mouth, trying to suck the pain away. His eyes remained tightly closed and he continued moaning, rocking weakly back and forth in his chair. After a few minutes the moaning subsided to a soft whine; his eyes opened wetly and he stared once again at the wall, still sucking on his finger like a baby. His whole body was trembling with shock.

Erfurt bent down once more and stared the old man full in the face. 'Look at me!' he roared again.

There was no response at all. The old man's watery eyes registered nothing; he was still shivering from the pain in his finger.

'I think, comrade General,' said Eisener smoothly, 'that your test has provided a satisfactory and conclusive demonstration of his mental state. He does not know what is going on. He retains an instinctive response to pain, but he cannot connect it with its cause. He is aware of the discomfort, but of nothing else.'

Erfurt straightened again, glowering down at the figure of the old man in the chair. 'Disgusting,' he spat contemptuously. 'It is absurd that he has been so easily reduced to such a blubbering, useless wreck. Stupid, garrulous old fool!'

'He had the seeds of it in him already, comrade General,' said Eisener gently. 'He was always weak, and more recently his mental condition led to the indiscretions . . . But of course that was the very reason why he had to be dealt with. It was a simple matter, and perhaps we should not be too surprised that it didn't take much to push him over the edge.'

'I have seen enough,' said Erfurt, turning towards the door. 'Come. We might as well get this filth cleaned up. The smell is beginning to irritate me. Have the men see to it.'

'As you wish, comrade General,' said Eisener calmly, his voice betraying no sign of the satisfaction he felt about the instruction. 'I shall see to it straight away.'

The two men left the room. Outside in the corridor, they changed out of the overalls, boots and face-masks. General Erfurt stamped away up the narrow stone stairs while Eisener paused for a little while, adjusting his uniform. Then he too followed, emerging from the small, concealed door at the top of the steps into the ante-room just off the main hall.

'Kessler,' said Eisener to his aide, who was on duty at the front desk, 'I want you to organise a detail to get the basement cleaned up. Right away. Shovels, bins, disinfectant – whatever it takes. No trace is to remain of the mess or smell down there. Is that clear?'

'*Jawohl*, comrade Colonel!' said Kessler enthusiastically.

'The prisoner will be treated properly and carefully,' Eisener continued. 'Comrade *doktor* Linden's presence will be required – the prisoner has a minor wound in his left hand that needs treatment, and he will require sedation. Once he is sedated he is to be scrubbed down with soap and water and dressed in clean pyjamas, then put in the next-door cell until his own is once again fit for habitation. His diet and routine are otherwise to remain exactly as before. The same bowl will be provided for lavatory purposes, but it is to be emptied regularly from now on. Inform me when all this has been done. Report to me if he reacts in any way at all, either to the presence of the cleaning detail or to that of the comrade *doktor*.'

'I will see to it immediately, comrade Colonel!'

Eisener nodded and began to ascend the main stairs, heading for his room on the first floor. He was well satisfied. *The prospect of that mess being cleaned up should have a beneficial effect on the men's morale*, he was thinking. *For a little while it should, anyway.*

Below in the basement, the grimy figure of Sir Reginald Hislop rose from the chair in his cell, still whimpering and sucking on his injured finger. He began shuffling slowly across the filthy floor towards his bed, his face utterly devoid of expression.

32

The North Korean Air Force pilot rammed the throttle levers forward and felt the gigantic thrust in his back as the twin Tumanskii turbojets screamed into full life behind him, propelling the aircraft down the runway. The Mikoyan-Gurevich MiG-25 interceptor began to shudder and vibrate as it rapidly gathered speed; the banshee howl of the engines, delivering a maximum 20,500 lb of thrust, became a roar. Twenty seconds later, the pilot pulled back on the control column and the MiG was airborne. Clear of the end of the runway, he stood the aircraft on its tail and rocketed skywards, climbing steeply in a northerly direction, the massive thrust from the engines keeping him pinned back in his seat. The Sunan airbase, ten miles north of P'yŏngyang, fell away behind him, the altimeter on his instrument panel spinning rapidly as he gained height. At 2500 feet he engaged the afterburners and felt another giant kick in his back as the thrust increased to 27,000 lb. The MiG–25 was already travelling at Mach 1.2. Behind him, he knew, his wingman would be following the bright glare of his twin tailpipes into the night sky.

In just two and a half minutes from take-off, both aircraft had reached 36,000 feet. They levelled off and streaked northwards at Mach 2.0, heading for the intercept they had been given. Neither pilot spoke a word; as a team, they had performed similar missions many times before. The flight leader engaged his main Fox Fire radar, which automatically began sweeping forward, seeking a target. It registered the intruder almost immediately, twenty-five miles north and slightly east, flying as reported at 29,000 feet on a south-westerly bearing. *Already dead*, thought the pilot dispassionately as he switched the radar to CW guidance mode for the four AA-6 semi-active-radar-homing anti-aircraft missiles carried on his wing pylons. He armed the first missile and his thumb hovered briefly over the firing button, knowing he now had absolute power of life or death over the intruder.

But he had no clearance to fire just yet. His orders were to investigate why the intruder was off course, flying towards a maximum-security restricted area. He could shoot it down only if it had no satisfactory explanation for its presence there. His eyes flickered to his IFF indicator. *On*, he saw. The Kaech'on airbase SAM detachments would already be on full alert, and he had no wish to be mistaken for an intruder himself.

The pair of MiGs closed the twenty-five-mile gap in less than a minute. The lead pilot began circling in a wide banking turn, scanning the darkness below with one eye on his radar. He saw the intruder's lights almost immediately. *Fool*, he thought. *I will give him something to think about.*

He pushed his control column forward, and the

MiG-25 screamed downwards at Mach 2.4, diving straight towards the light of the uninvited guest.

33

The big aircraft cruised along through the clear night sky. At 29,000 feet it was high enough to be practically inaudible on the ground. Someone listening hard might have heard a very distant droning noise, but it would have seemed a very long way away.

Inside the huge cargo hold, the throbbing roar of the four engines would have made normal conversation difficult. What made it impossible on this occasion was the fact that those inside were wearing oxygen masks. The masks of the crew-members were connected by hoses to the aircraft's main console system, but the eight passengers had their own cylinders. Eighteen inches long and four inches in diameter, the cylinders were carried horizontally in pouches strapped at stomach level, below other equipment. Each cylinder contained sufficient oxygen for thirty minutes' normal consumption.

Twenty-seven minutes before, at P-hour minus thirty minutes, each person on board had begun breathing pure oxygen prior to depressurisation of the aircraft; at 29,000 feet ordinary air was too thin for normal breathing. During depressurisation they had felt their ears begin to pop; they equalised by pinching their noses and swallowing. Potential sinus problems had already been minimised by taking Sudafed tablets ninety minutes previously.

The hissing noise died away to a thin whistle, finally ceasing altogether; depressurisation was complete. The ninth man in the cargo bay, a member of the aircrew, went along the line of passengers, checking their equipment. In the centre of each passenger's chest, above the oxygen bottle, was an altimeter; the crewman checked the setting on each one to ensure that it tallied with the aircraft's radio-altimeter reading. Six of the eight wore second altimeters on their right wrists; they checked these themselves.

To the right of each chest altimeter was a small grey box, four inches by three, with a thumb-sized cylinder protruding from the bottom and a red knob on the top; it was known as a semi-automatic opening device. A thin sleeved wire led from the device, passing over the right shoulder to the passenger's backpack. Buckles were checked for tightness; each passenger confirmed with a thumbs-up sign that his oxygen supply was functioning properly. Just in time the largest passenger stopped himself from giving the thumb-and-forefinger circle, the equivalent sign given by sub-aqua divers; he had always felt far more at home underwater than he did airborne. Beneath his face mask he was glowering in disgust.

Twenty minutes later, at P minus ten, the partly spent oxygen cylinders were exchanged for full ones. Six of the eight passengers sat comfortably on their large bergens, their legs through the shoulder-straps with the rucksack's frame attached to a quick-release waist-belt; the other two, without rucksacks, sat on wooden crates. All had bulky packs strapped to their backs, attached by nylon webbing harnesses, with straps over their shoulders, round the top of each thigh and at chest and waist level.

The crew member, who was in contact with the pilot by intercom, signalled to the eight passengers that the time was P minus three minutes. They stood and waddled towards the rear ramp, the heavy bergens strapped behind their legs making movement cumbersome. There was a loud hydraulic whine and an increasing roar of air as a crack appeared in the section of floor sloping up towards the tail of the aircraft. The rearmost half swung slowly upwards on its hinge to the ceiling, while the nearer section, hinged where it met the flat part of the cargo bay deck, swung downwards until it was level.

The eight passengers stared out through the gaping void into the darkness. Despite their thick clothing they began to feel the piercing chill of the outside temperature: it was minus 70°F. They were at the same altitude as the summit of Mount Everest. The smallest of the eight, unrecognisable behind thick face mask and goggles, gave a wry smile; it would be a quicker descent from this altitude than the last time she had done it, Kim Sumi realised.

They moved forward on to the edge of the now horizontal ramp and formed up in the 'wedge' formation they had practised. On point, nearest to the edge, stood Pete Halliday and Kim Sumi, side by side. A pace behind them were Angelo Zeccara and Dr Richard Weatherill. In the third row were Harris, Ackford, Ziegler and Howard, in line abreast.

Richard Weatherill was struck once again, as he had been in practice jumps, at the lack of air turbulence. The whole of the rear of the aircraft was now gaping open and he was standing nearly on the edge of the ramp, but he could feel no significant buffeting movements from the air rushing past.

Sumi was momentarily distracted by Halliday's hands on the back of her helmet; she felt a brief twist and realised he had activated her cyalume stick. The thin plastic rod, when twisted, released two chemical components which combined to produce a yellow-green fluorescent light. The leader normally carried the cyalume stick so that the others could follow it and base their formation on him; but on this jump it had been decided that Sumi and Halliday, flying together, would act as the focus. The more experienced Zeccara, holding on to Weatherill and steering for both, would keep station on them and the others, flying by themselves, would follow. Sumi felt Halliday take her hand firmly again; she found his squeeze of reassurance comforting. All eyes were now concentrated on the light above the door, which showed red. The wait for it to turn green seemed eternal, and more than one of them felt a feeling of slight unreality.

Weatherill had surprised Zeccara. He had been a quick learner, and at no stage had he shown any sign of nervousness. He seemed calm even now; perhaps, thought Zeccara, he had a scientist's ability to analyse everything logically and force himself to function as a machine. If it worked, Weatherill had remarked to Zeccara on one occasion, then he had nothing to worry about, did he? It was simply a question of putting theory into practice and remembering the procedures he had been taught. Zeccara had detected no trace of bravado or over-confidence in the remark, and he hadn't argued; but he had quietly made the point to both Weatherill and Kim Sumi that there was the world of difference between practising in the vertical wind-tunnel, or even jumping from fifteen thousand feet – the highest the two novices had done in their six practice jumps – and a true HALO jump from twice that altitude.

High-altitude, low-opening parachuting techniques had evolved over many years as a method of inserting Special Forces groups clandestinely into hostile territory. A HALO drop demands skills completely different from those taught during regular parachute training. Conventional paratroops are dropped from low altitude and have little or no control over what happens once they leave the aircraft; their parachutes are opened straight away by static lines attached to the aircraft itself, so there is no freefalling. With the earliest circular parachute canopies no directional control was possible, but later refinements, such as vented canopies and steering toggles, gave more control to the individual. Despite these developments, conventionally dropped paratroops could never escape notice – their arrival was advertised by their low-flying aircraft. In modern warfare, the standard mass parachute drop is now all but obsolete – largely because of the vulnerability of the aircraft itself to ground-to-air weapons.

One of the key technological advances in parachuting was the invention of the nine-cell ram-air 'paravane' chute. The rectangular ram-air acts like a flying wing, with each tubular cell inflating into an aerodynamic shape as air rushes through it. The parachutist has a high degree of directional control; a forward speed of thirty miles per hour and a relatively slow rate of descent (typically fifteen feet per second, or ten miles per hour) make pinpoint landings – to within just feet of a target – possible for skilled flyers. With the ram-air chute, it became possible to achieve unprecedented accuracy in high-altitude, low-opening drops. For Special Forces units, and for the SAS in particular, this was an extraordinarily useful development. The night-time HALO drop remains to this day the least detectable method of inserting Special Forces troops deep into hostile territory.

The main problem, naturally, is that an aircraft is still required – and aircraft are detectable. They either have to fly high enough to be inaudible from the ground – in which case they are routinely tracked by civilian or military radar – or they have to fly low enough to avoid radar but are almost certain to be compromised by sightings from the ground. With sophisticated modern radar systems, only the smallest and most manoeuvrable aircraft can avoid detection, even if just a few feet above the ground; and parachuting at such low altitudes is in any case out of the question. The answer to the problem was straightforward: deception would be used. HALO drops, wherever possible, would use regular civil aircraft routes and flight paths, so as to blend in with normal commercial air traffic.

The logical extension of this argument, given that

absolute secrecy was essential, was to use actual civil aircraft rather than military ones – and indeed to use scheduled commercial flights, flight numbers and timings. There were, however, some drawbacks. Although most non-military aircraft have a minimum speed low enough for parachuting purposes – 130 knots or so – few have a suitable configuration.

The most common problem with commercial aircraft is the positioning of exits. Ideally there should be a doorway right in the tail; certainly there must be no risk of a departing parachutist colliding with the tailplane or an engine. Happily the Boeing 737 series has everything in the right place. Oddly enough, so does Concorde. On more than one occasion in recent years Concorde passengers have been told that their flight has been postponed or cancelled for some reason, and have remained unaware that their aircraft later took off with a small complement of purposeful-looking passengers, none of whom would complete his journey in the conventional way.

In addition to flying and navigating, the pilot and aircrew have to make a series of complicated calculations and judgements if the drop is to succeed. The judgements boil down to timing and windspeed. At a typical cruising altitude of 35,000–40,000 feet the windspeed is often one hundred miles per hour, and frequently greater, due to the high-altitude jet-stream. It is relatively simple for a pilot or navigator to calculate the windspeed at his own altitude, but he must be highly experienced and in possession of all the latest meteorological information to have any chance of calculating what the windspeed may be at various altitudes towards ground level, and how it might affect a freefalling parachutist. If a mistake was made the parachutist, freefalling at a terminal velocity of 125mph, could be blown perhaps five miles off course even before his parachute opened. Before the advent of the ram-air chute, the acceptable margin for error was less than half a mile – and even that was difficult to achieve. But with the ram-air's steering and forward flight capability, this margin was magnified fourfold. It no longer mattered if the calculations were out – they could be corrected.

At last the light turned to green. Halliday and Sumi, acting as one, threw themselves forward, diving off the end of the ramp and disappearing immediately from view. Zeccara counted one second, then he and Weatherill followed. Harris, Ackford and Ziegler piled off after them and dropped away.

Howard, also in the last row, should have gone with them; but he had turned his head to give the jumpmaster a brief wave of thanks. He saw the crewman gesturing forcefully and realised the others had already gone. Cursing himself for his inattention, Howard threw himself head-first into the void. There was a brief buffeting from the slipstream of the aircraft and he found himself swooping down; he spread his arms and legs out into the 'frog' position, his hands spread palm-down near his shoulders and his lower legs bent upwards behind his knees. He felt himself stabilising; then, as he reached the 125mph terminal velocity, swooping up again. He wasn't actually swooping up, but the sensation felt real. Still cursing himself, he searched for the light of the cyalume stick below. The noise of the cargo aircraft's engines quickly died away, to be replaced by the rough whistle of air rushing past his helmet. He could see no sign of the cyalume glow. The others must be well below him by now. Drawing his hands into his body he put himself into a head-first dive, his speed increasing to 150mph, to try to close on them.

Suddenly there was a deafening bang, followed instantly by a roar of sound and a scorching flash of light that disappeared almost immediately. Howard felt the air punched from his body as if by a giant fist. An immense shock-wave of turbulence threw him around the sky and for a few seconds he lost consciousness, tumbling out of control, his limbs flailing loosely.

Howard's senses returned. He felt dizzy and shaken, and his ears were still ringing from the explosion – or whatever it had been. Completely disorientated, he stabilised his fall by putting himself into the 'frog' position again and glanced around, his mind racing. He winced with pain as he spread his arms and legs. His left shoulder had been wrenched and he could move only with difficulty. He could see nothing at all.

He checked his altimeter. It read twenty-six thousand feet – he had fallen only three thousand since leaving the aircraft. There was a sensation of wetness inside his oxygen mask, and a salty taste on his lips and in his mouth; he realised he had a nose-bleed. Swallowing, he checked his compass, looking back and slightly up along the bearing towards where the cargo plane should have been. He saw nothing. *The plane must have exploded*, he thought anxiously. *Shit . . . A missile or something?* But there was no sign of a fireball, or of burning debris falling.

He thought he heard the screaming, roaring sound again, despite the shrill ringing in his ears. It sounded slightly different, and not nearly as loud. An echo? Then he saw it. Way off in the distance an intense, fast-moving tongue of blue-white flame was streaking up in an arc towards where the cargo plane ought to have been. A surface-to-air missile!

As he watched, it seemed to level off at an altitude that he estimated to be about four thousand feet above him and two miles distant, heading away from him. The blue-white flame softened to orange, and he could now see two distinct pinpricks of light. Two engines. Almost simultaneously he saw a second, similar pair of engine trails dropping down from a higher altitude and levelling out to follow close behind the first. Then, to his enormous relief, he caught sight of the cargo aircraft's flashing wingtip lights, very faint now, as the two fast-moving objects converged on it. *Thank God*, he thought, *it's still in one piece!*

Howard realised at last what had happened.

The sonic boom of the MiG-25 had shaken every rivet in the big cargo plane. The fighter had screamed past in an almost vertical dive no more than sixty feet away, creating a massive and deafening shock-wave. In the rear cargo compartment Alexander Plasnin, the crew member who had acted as jumpmaster, had been in the process of closing the rear cargo doors. He was tossed into the air as the plane lurched violently and was only saved by the safety-line that tethered him to the fuselage. Bruised and cursing, he picked himself up quickly, completed the closure of the cargo doors and opened a second valve to begin the repressurisation of the aircraft.

He was not the only one swearing. The aircraft's dazed pilot fought with the controls, shouting every foul curse he could think of. He knew straight away what had caused the crashing boom and the violent turbulence. He had been buzzed many times before by high-spirited fighter pilots, but never as fast or as dangerously as this. It was a bloody miracle, he thought, that none of the cockpit windows had been broken or blown out. He shuddered to think what sort of mayhem had been created in the cargo compartment; he was just about to press the intercom transmit button to find out when he was interrupted by a thin, high voice in his earphones.

'Unknown aircraft! You, with the headache! Turn left immediately and keep station on me! Comply at once or you will be shot down!'

Looking out of the cockpit window, the pilot saw the unmistakable shape of a North Korean Air Force MiG-25. It had throttled back and was now abreast of him, one hundred feet away. As he watched, the MiG drew slightly ahead and began to lead into the turn to port. The pilot resisted a powerful temptation to let the interceptor know exactly what he thought of him. 'Turning now,' he acknowledged through gritted teeth. He followed the MiG, banking his big aircraft hard round to port. When the turn was complete, the pilot glanced at his compass. It showed 160 degrees true; that meant his actual course was now 180 degrees – due south. That was about right; Sunan, the main airbase serving P'yŏngyang, would be due south by now.

'Another of the bastards on this side,' muttered his co-pilot over the intercom, glancing to starboard as the second MiG drew level.

'Identify yourself immediately!' barked the thin voice.

'Russian Air Force special flight 3248, out of Vladivostok, inbound to P'yŏngyang!' snapped Colonel Yevgeny Mikhailovich Barushkin angrily. 'Your people were notified of this flight! What is the meaning of this outrage?'

'You were off course, flying over a restricted area!' the thin voice continued. 'You will follow instructions and maintain radio silence. You will receive no further warning.'

Barushkin did not argue. Grimacing, he thought again of Alexander Plasnin in the rear and thumbed the intercom button. 'Sasha, are you still in one piece back there?'

'Speaking for myself, the answer is yes,' replied Plasnin. 'But some of the cargo straps snapped and the pallets have come loose. A lot of the bottles have been smashed. The floor back here is swimming in alcohol, so don't blame me if I'm half drunk from the fumes by the time we arrive. I'll try to secure the pallets as best I can, but don't make any sudden manoeuvres for a while. By the way,' he added, 'what the hell was that? An interceptor?'

'MiG-25,' Barushkin confirmed. 'Two of them. Little shit-faced NK bastards,' he added. 'Actually, I'm glad some of the bottles are broken. I'm going to report these two. Then the little sods can explain personally to their pig of a President why his personal luxury gifts from the Russian government aren't in one piece. I hope Kim Il Sung has the bastards nailed to a tree by their balls and then shot.'

'So do I,' Plasnin agreed. 'If you like, I'll check the rest and smash any that aren't broken. That should land the little shits in even more trouble.'

'Make sure you save a few for us,' said Barushkin, grinning. 'We'll need something to keep us going when we get down to that shit-hole. Incidentally,' he added, 'did our passengers get away all right?'

'No problem,' Plasnin replied. 'The last one jumped just before that MiG buzzed us.'

'Good,' said Barushkin with feeling. 'I don't know what their mission is, but I hope they're going to blow this dog's arse of a country to smithereens, along with all its miserable inhabitants.' He released the intercom button and fell silent.

'Start descent to Sunan! You will follow us down!' The thin voice screeched in the earphones.

About bloody time, thought Barushkin, throttling back the Antonov. Sunan Airport was now only about fifty miles distant. With any other city in the world, he knew, the blaze of lights would already be visible on a clear, moonless night like this. But P'yŏngyang was a soulless, gloomy dump, run by a corrupt, perverted megalomaniac and his undersized, platform-heeled, poncy little powder-puff of a son. Barushkin had visited the place before; the memory was a grim one. The fucking country was so broke, he reflected, that they couldn't even afford to turn the lights on most of the time except in the presidential palace, and the people were so brainwashed and malnourished that most of them were reduced to eating stray dogs and rats – if they could catch them. And here he was, Colonel Yevgeny Mikhailovich Barushkin, holder of the Order of the Red

Banner for gallant services rendered to his country, flying in with a cargo of luxury food and drink for the pox-ridden, lying leader of this filthy, festering latrine of a place. The last true bastion of socialism? *Pah!* Barushkin thought savagely. It would serve the bastards right if the entire cargo was ruined. The blame rested squarely with that moron of a MiG pilot and his mad aerobatics.

Well, Barushkin acknowledged to himself, perhaps not quite *all* the blame. He grinned into his oxygen mask. He *had* been off course, after all. *Deliberately* off course. He had a perfectly good explanation, naturally – a faulty compass. The instrument had been adjusted in Vladivostok to read twenty degrees below the true figure, which would account for his having veered well off course to the north, over the Yŏngbyŏn/Kaech'on complex. The NKs could check the compass if they liked – in fact, that was part of the plan.

Barushkin wondered for the twentieth time exactly whose plan this whole thing had been. It was certainly a first for him – he had never had any Westerners as passengers before, and although he had come across a few in his time, none of them had been quite like these. They reminded him a little of Sasha Plasnin and his outfit. He knew Sasha well; he had flown him and his comrades on plenty of special missions. Sasha was no ordinary crew member. If it came to that, Sasha and the men of Group 'A' were not ordinary *anything*. He was reminded once again of that early casevac mission to Tashkent, back in January 1980, when he had picked up those wounded in the first action of the war in Afghanistan. Those men, he had learned since then, had been Group 'A' members. Sasha himself had not yet joined them, but he had been there in 1982 when Barushkin had flown them down to Tbilisi, in Georgia, when they had sorted out another bit of unpleasantness. So was this mission now a Group 'A' plan too? No, thought Barushkin, that was unlikely. They had plenty of influence, he knew, but he didn't think it extended to eliciting personal instructions from General Pavel Grachev. And it wouldn't be Grachev's plan either, he felt sure. Grachev was too dim and clumsy to think of something as racy as this. Maybe Boris Yeltsin himself . . .? No, he thought sarcastically. Yeltsin wouldn't voluntarily part with all that booze, not if he had the chance to pour it down his own throat. So whose idea was it? And why were *Westerners* involved?

Westerners. To be precise, British. Yes, he thought; that must be it. The British government must be behind it. The Prime Minister must have offered Yeltsin an incentive – maybe political and financial support of some kind – in return for this favour. How else would the British be able to insert one of their own *Spetsnaz* groups into North Korea? Russian and Chinese aircraft were the only ones occasionally permitted overflying rights by the North Korean government, and due to their stupid and futile quarrel over Hong Kong the British and the Chinese were hardly even on speaking terms. Well, whatever the scenario, he would drink a large toast to them tonight in the hope that they would massacre as many as possible of those nasty, sub-human little NK bastards.

Unaware that his guess was spot on, Barushkin glanced at the cabin pressure gauge. Seeing that it had returned to normal, he removed his oxygen mask for the final descent into Sunan. Almost immediately, he gasped at the powerful reek of alcohol fumes being recirculated by the Antonov's air-conditioning system. He jammed the mask back on. Plasnin was right – the stuff must be sloshing around in the cargo bay about a foot deep. He would have to go easy on braking when he landed, or some ten thousand gallons of the finest cognac and whisky would come pouring through into the cockpit. What a way to go!

Behind him, through the thin bulkhead door,

Barushkin heard the sound of breaking glass. 'Hey, Sasha,' he called over the intercom indignantly. 'Don't forget to save some for us!'

Alexander Plasnin laughed. 'Don't worry,' he replied, smashing yet another bottle.

PART THREE

125°
126°
127°
128°
40°
39°
38°
Hŭich'on
Kwangsang-
dong
Mt Mudong
5781
Yaksuch'an
Kusong
Hajang
Kujang
Saengch'ŏn
Yŏngbyŏn
Kuryong River
Kaech'ŏn
Mt Pyŏngr'ung
5802
Ch'ŏngch'ŏn R.
Yŏnghung
Sea of Japan
N O R T H K O R E A
Sunchon
Un'gok
Ch'onnae
Hodo
Peninsula
Okp'yong
Sunan
Yangdŏk
Wonsan
P'YŎNGYANG
Poptong
Kudang
Songnim
Munam
Sep'o
Hyŏn
Hwangju
Imjin R.
Kimhwa
P'yŏnggang
Sinch'on
T'osan
Oeumhwa
(Kumhwa)
Demilitarized
zone
Kaesŏng
Panmunjŏm
Ch'unch'on
SEOUL
Yellow Sea
Kilometres
0 25 50 75 100
SOUTH KOREA

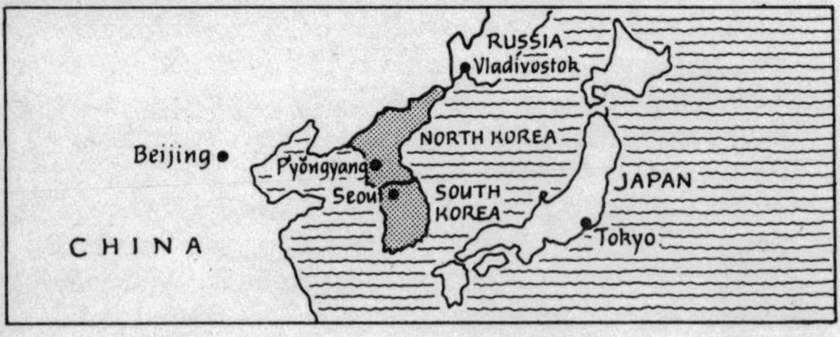
RUSSIA
Vladivostok
NORTH KOREA
Beijing
Pyŏngyang
Seoul
SOUTH
KOREA
JAPAN
Tokyo
CHINA

34

As he plummeted down through the night sky, Howard tried to put out of his mind the near-miss from the North Korean interceptor aircraft and the possible fate of the Russian Antonov and its crew. The aircraft, Colonel Barushkin and Sasha Plasnin were still integral to his plan and he hoped they would not be harmed in any way. They had been prepared for an ill-natured response to the aircraft's being off course, but the violent reaction they had received showed that the North Koreans were taking the matter very seriously indeed. He concluded that his Russian friends would probably be detained for a while and harangued at length by some humourless fanatic in the North Korean security forces, but it should not amount to much more than that. The NKs could ill afford to antagonise the might of neighbouring Russia, even though relations between the two countries were not what they once had been.

What worried Howard now, as he kept his eye on his altimeter, was the fate of the rest of the team, presumably still somewhere below him. It was very unlikely, he thought, that any of them had actually been hit by the interceptor – although it could not have missed *him* by very much – as the aircraft itself would not have survived such an impact at the sort of speed it must have been doing. But loss of consciousness, as Howard had briefly experienced himself, injury, damage to equipment, disorientation – these were all distinct possibilities. The disorientation and shock, especially for the two novices, Weatherill and Kim Sumi, could prove fatal. Weatherill was expendable, but the girl . . .

Still, there was nothing he could do about that for the time being, thought Howard grimly. In all likelihood, the shock-wave of the interceptor had dispersed the team and shattered the planned formation descent; each member would now have to navigate his own way to the drop zone. He just hoped that Halliday and Zeccara had managed to hold on to their two charges. Thank God, he thought, that he had selected a drop zone which everyone would be able to identify with relative ease.

Howard ran through the options in his mind and decided that he now had to concentrate on getting himself down in one piece and in the right place. His altimeter read fifteen thousand feet, which meant he had been freefalling for about one and a half minutes – he was about halfway down. He had already spotted the landmark he had been looking for. The distinctive bend in the Kuryong river was unmistakable; even in faint starlight, water reflected a glassy sheen that was clearly visible. He had spent a long time poring over old airphotographs and more up-to-date satellite ones, and the drop zone he had selected had filled all three of the criteria he had set: first, it was easily recognisable from the air; second, it was a sizeable area clear of trees; and third, it was nowhere near any road, track or building, so it was unlikely that anyone would be there to witness their descent and raise the alarm. Howard could not yet make out any of the ground features, but that particular bend in the river marked it out very clearly. He was sure the others would have spotted the DZ too – if they were still in one piece. Even if they were still unconscious, he thought, as he himself had briefly been, they would not plummet into the ground because their parachutes would have opened by themselves.

He resisted the urge to pat the small grey box on the right side of his chest. Even a slight movement of his hand might have destabilised his flight, but he silently thanked whoever it was who had invented the semi-automatic opening device, or SAOD. The 'Sod', he had always called it affectionately.

The SAOD was connected to the chest-worn altimeter. It was a relatively simple mechanical device. The silver-coloured, thumb-sized tube on its underside contained a spring, and the red knob on top was used for setting the opening altitude. Like all simple mechanical devices, it worked. Better still, the wearer could actually hear it working. It ticked and clicked and twanged reassuringly, reminding him that it had not gone to sleep; and even if the parachutist had lost consciousness, it continued to function. At the set height above ground level it would activate the spring, which would pull the sleeved wire leading over the right shoulder to the main chute; this in turn would release the feather-shaped clip to open the backpack and release the parachute. The lesson that all SAS-trained HALO parachutists learned, fairly early on in their training, was the importance of stable, face-down flight on opening. The slightest movement of just one hand from the 'frog' position could affect freefall and cause tumbling. With all the equipment carried on such occasions, coupled with the fact that drops were at night and into hostile territory, Special Forces parachutists had quite enough to think about without having to worry about watching altimeters every few seconds – although most did so.

The grey boxes had only been known to fail very rarely and in unusual circumstances; but it was always obvious, by a deafening silence, when it had happened. In such circumstances the parachutist simply moved his right hand to the D-ring positioned on the right of his ribcage and pulled the chute manually.

There were other built-in failsafe devices. Each person carried a reserve chute. If the main failed to open correctly or for some reason became tangled, the normal HALO opening height of 2500–3000 feet gave the parachutist sufficient time to jettison it and pull the reserve. The decision had to be a quick one; freefalling from a height of 3000 feet, in twenty seconds or less a human body will hit the ground with fatal results. For this reason, training is ruthlessly and repeatedly rammed home until the procedure becomes automatic: SAOD failure – right hand to the D-ring on the right ribcage and pull forward – manual release of the main chute – main chute failure – left hand to the 'three-ring circus' on the chest – release it, jettisoning the main chute – left hand to the D-ring below the left ribs – pull the reserve. And if that doesn't work, it's head-between-the-legs, kiss-your-arse-goodbye time.

On this occasion the height set for opening was the normal 3000 feet; the experienced flyers in the team would use their hands to track away from each other at the last minute, so as to avoid any risk of mid-air collision. The drop zone itself was less than two hundred feet above sea level. As Howard's altimeter indicated 4000 feet he listened for the noise of the semi-automatic opening device; a few seconds later, at 3000 feet, he heard the spring activate loudly. There was a rustling noise and a sharp crack as the nine-cell ram-air chute drew out above him and filled, and an oddly elastic jolt as his fall decelerated from one hundred and seventy feet per second to about one tenth of that speed. Then there was total silence, other than a very faint hum of air through the shroud lines and the ringing still in his ears from his close encounter with the North Korean jet. Grasping the two steering toggles, Howard turned the chute and began a slow, steady descent towards the DZ, the outline of the sky-blue canopy almost invisible above him.

Two minutes later, having checked the wind by making passes from different directions and observing his relative ground speed, Howard had lined up the paravane for his final descent to the DZ. The wind-speed, he reckoned, was about twenty knots; he would come in to land into the wind. By now, he hoped, the first members of the team should already be on the ground. He released the buckle holding the heavy rucksack and worked his legs out of the shoulder-straps until it was hanging on his feet; then he let it go. There was a jolt on his harness as it jerked on the end of the ten-foot line beneath him. Twenty-five feet above the ground he pulled down hard on both toggles. The parachute flared into a stall, the line went slack as the rucksack touched the ground, and then he was down. He landed agilely on his feet without the need for a parachute roll.

Quickly collapsing the chute and unfastening his harness, Howard pulled off his helmet, face-mask and goggles, unfolded the stock of his AKMS assault rifle and crouched down, screwing the silencer on to the end of the stubby barrel. He stayed immobile for a full minute, watching and listening. He could see nothing, and there was no sound. From a side-pocket of the rucksack he pulled out a lightweight nylon bag. Gathering up the parachute, he stuffed it hurriedly into the bag along with the harness, oxygen cylinder, helmet, mask and goggles. He strapped the bag to the bergen, then hefted the load on to his shoulders. The parachute equipment alone weighed sixty pounds, and the bergen another ninety – it was a massive load, making progress slow and difficult.

He did not need his GPS satellite navigation unit; on a bearing of 270 degrees, due west, he came to the river bank and followed it north-west to the distinctive sharp bend he had seen from the air. Two hundred metres due north of the bend, away from the bank, he quietly approached the RV he had designated, in a patch of thick scrub. He halted at the whispered challenge, relieved to hear it; whispering the password in return, he joined Ziegler and Ackford.

Five minutes later they were joined by Zeccara and Weatherill; they had heard Weatherill coming when he was still more than a hundred yards away. Howard scowled in the darkness. Despite the night training he had been given, the scientist had come nowhere near mastering the technique of moving noiselessly. Still, thought Howard, he hadn't done too badly.

Two minutes after that, the shadows of Halliday and Kim Sumi loomed up soundlessly, together. The team settled down to wait. For five minutes they made no sound. Finally, Howard turned to the others.

'Where's Mel?' he whispered anxiously. 'Has anyone seen him?'

No one had.

35

Mel Harris, like Howard, had been knocked unconscious by the concussive effect of the MiG-25, but he had not come round as quickly as Howard had. Tumbling out of control in unstable flight, he had drifted far away from the others. He dimly heard the twanging noise of his semi-automatic opening device and was jerked back to consciousness as his chute opened. Immediately he knew he was in bad trouble.

Harris found himself being whirled in a fast anti-clockwise downward spiral. The control toggles proved useless and he realised that his shroud lines had somehow become tangled, perhaps due to his not being in stable flight when the chute had opened. One of the shroud lines, he guessed, had somehow got itself looped over the canopy itself; there was nothing he could do about it.

He needed to make a very quick assessment of his rate of descent, then decide whether to jettison the main chute and use his reserve. For few vital seconds he searched desperately for some landmark that might give him an indication of how fast he was falling. Swirling out of control, he finally saw the river far off in the distance. After a few revolutions and a quick check of his altimeter he decided that his rate of descent was fast but manageable, and he decided not to resort to the reserve chute. He prepared himself for a hard landing.

Harris's decision was a courageous one. He did not want the main chute to be jettisoned – if he did it would float away freely, in all likelihood to be discovered fairly quickly by the North Koreans, who would immediately raise the alarm. But in strictly logical terms the decision was wrong. He did not have an accurate idea of his rate of fall, and it would be a far greater disaster, not only for himself but for the rest of the team, if he fell badly and was killed or incapacitated.

Once again he tried wrestling with the shroud lines on the left, but it was hopeless. His movements only made the situation worse. He released them. It would be no more than a few seconds before he hit the ground, and there was nothing more he could do. Then he saw something which in all probability saved his life. It was a small fire, not far away. He watched the fire as it appeared to spin round him, and he realised that he was falling faster then he had thought. He was very nearly down. Quickly he released his heavy bergen, kicking it free. As soon as he felt the jerk on the end of the ten-foot tether line he severed the line with his knife, hoping that this would slow his descent. The bergen dropped away, and two seconds later he heard the noise as it crashed into what sounded like a bush. Harris rapidly shoved the knife back into its sheath and braced himself for the impact.

When it came, it was totally unexpected. Instead of hard, stony, bone-breaking ground, he felt a sickening blow to his midriff. He had hit a large tree-branch. Winded, his body went limp; then, once again, he briefly felt himself falling. He landed on his back with a crash of splintering brushwood. He had been saved by the tree and the thick bushes beneath it.

For long seconds he lay fighting for breath, wondering whether he had broken anything. His ribs burned with pain from the impact with the branch. With an effort, he began to disentangle himself.

There was no time for niceties; he estimated the fire to be no more than three or four hundred metres away. Pulling out his knife again, he cut the parachute shroud lines and wriggled free. Finally clear of the bush, he did as Howard had done; he removed his parachute harness, helmet, mask and goggles and dropped to a crouch, unfolding his AKMS and looking around as he screwed the silencer on to the end of the barrel. He made another quick decision and pulled out a hard plastic case from inside his smock, opening it and taking out a pair of HNV-1 night vision goggles. The HNV-1 was a new, lightweight type utilising holographic optical elements, which meant that the user always had a see-through image and a large peripheral vision, irrespective of flares or flashes – in fact, whatever the conditions. Scarcely bulkier than a large pair of ski-goggles but protruding further from the face, they could be worn without a helmet.

Before putting them on, Harris ripped a two-inch-square piece of black masking tape from the fore-end of his AK and stuck it over his right eye as a patch. Then he put on the NVGs and flipped the 'on' switch. The scene in his left eye was transformed as the dim ambient light was intensified by a factor of fifty thousand, turning night into day in a grainy, monotone image of his surroundings. There was no one visible. He flipped a second switch on the goggles, activating a small infra-red light source. The IR light was invisible to the naked eye, but the image-intensification tube in the goggles was sensitive to it and it enhanced the light level. The IR had to be used sparingly, Harris knew, because anyone with similar equipment would see it clearly.

Now able to see, he gathered up the parachute,

pulling roughly to clear it from the undergrowth and the tree. The operation made a noise, but speed was now vital. After three minutes of tugging and hacking with his knife, he had it completely clear. He checked the tree carefully to ensure that no stray bits of cord or torn material had been left behind.

Harris paused to look around again; still there was nothing. The glow of the fire, the other side of some thick trees, showed up brightly in the goggles. He began to search for his bergen, knowing it could not be far away. Twenty metres from where he had fallen, he found it in a thorn-bush. He dragged it clear and carried it back to where he had left the parachute, then he switched off the infra-red light source. Pulling out a nylon stuff-bag as Howard had done, he stowed his torn parachute and harness, together with his oxygen cylinder, mask and helmet. He had just finished strapping the stuff-bag to his bergen when he heard the sound. He froze.

It was a dog barking. *Damn!* thought Harris. He had been heard, after all. And the dog meant bad news – it had to be military. There were virtually no domestic pets in this country, he knew – there wasn't enough food for them, and in fact North Korean dogs tended to end up being eaten themselves, mostly by their owners. The only ones left were Army patrol dogs. Shoving the bergen under the cover of the bush, he stared in the direction of the barking. There was a rough, single-track path about five metres off to one side, leading in the direction from which the sound was coming. He followed it for twenty metres, stopping by some more thick scrub. He heard voices and saw intermittently flickering lights approaching, about two hundred metres distant, still behind the trees. He counted three separate lights. Three torches, he realised – three men, possibly more. They were spread out, coming his way, clearly searching.

At last, when they were just over a hundred metres

away, he saw the figures themselves as they broke through the cover of the trees. There were four of them altogether. The one without a torch had the dog on a leash; it was a thin, rangy-looking brute – some sort of Alsation cross. All four men were carrying rifles slung over their shoulders.

Harris switched off the night vision goggles and stowed them away. The goggles had a wrap-around visor which meant that they emitted no light, but Harris did not want to risk them coming loose and giving his position away. Then he removed the piece of black tape covering his right eye. His left, now half-blind from the light of the NVGs, was temporarily almost useless; but his right eye, which had been shielded by the tape, now came into play. Already he could make out the approaching figures. Taking a deep breath, he filled his lungs and let out a low but audible groan, expelling the air by constricting his diaphragm. He knew the noise would sound further away than it actually was.

There was silence for half a second, except for the dog's renewed barking, and then he heard the voices. There was a briefly snapped command and the handler bent to unleash his dog. It began pelting up the track, yelping excitedly, heading unerringly in Harris's direction.

The dog stopped suddenly, five metres short of Harris. It had scented him. Growling menacingly at the man crouched in front of it, it leaped. Harris's hand moved with quicksilver precision. His knife struck the dog beneath the jawline, near the top of its throat. Angled upwards, the blade drove straight through the tongue and palate into its brain. It died instantly, without a sound.

Harris quickly dragged the animal's body well clear of the track, behind the bush. He knelt down to cut the dog's throat to bleed it, preventing any residual trembling spasms that might give away its position. But then he changed his mind. The blood would smell, and one of the North Koreans might notice it. The dog's movements had ceased anyway. He picked up a handful of sandy dirt and threw it over the path to conceal the marks of the brief struggle.

The first of the men was now only fifty metres away; all four had converged on the track, hurrying along in the direction the dog had taken. They had halted briefly as the barking ceased; one of the men said something in a puzzled tone and another issued a sharp order. They came on in single file, moving more warily, their weapons now off their shoulders and at the ready.

The first man passed only a couple of feet from where Harris was crouching in the scrub. His torch flashed briefly on the ground near Harris's feet, then he went on. The dog-handler, and then the third man, followed a few metres behind.

Finally, the last man approached. Harris waited until he was just past, then stepped soundlessly on to the track behind him. His left arm snaked rapidly round the North Korean soldier's throat and fastened on to his right shoulder; simultaneously his right clamped over the man's mouth and nose. Harris gave a sudden, wrenching pull on both hands. There was a crack as the man's neck snapped. Harris lifted the Korean's body clear of the track and set it down next to the corpse of the dog. The dead man's feet drummed briefly on the ground in a reflex death-spasm. Cautiously Harris poked out his head and looked up the track. The third man in the line had obviously heard something; he had stopped and turned round, hesitating.

'Sss, sss,' hissed Harris softly, giving an almost universal signal to attract someone's attention.

It worked. The third soldier retraced his steps, apparently convinced that his comrade had seen something and was discreetly signalling to him to come back. Three paces short of the hiding-place, seeing nothing, he stopped and urgently whispered something quite unintelligible to Harris.

Harris considered throwing the knife, but decided against it because of the degree of accuracy required to produce instant, noiseless death. Anywhere in the body, or even in the neck, would have resulted in a scream or at best a groan loud enough to alert the remaining two Koreans, now thirty metres away and still unaware of what had happened. Even an accurate hit in one eye, with the heavy blade driving through the thin bone of the eye-socket into the brain, would still result in the enemy soldier's weapon clattering to the ground. Harris could not risk it.

Instead, he carefully pitched a small stone a few paces down the track. The Korean heard it and moved towards the sound. The man was alert and suspicious, and his finger was on the trigger of his rifle. If Harris had moved to break his neck as he had done with the first man, a reflex action could well have caused the man to flinch and squeeze the trigger.

As the Korean drew level Harris drove the knife in up to its hilt, straight through the side of his head at the left temple. The man folded up soundlessly; Harris caught his rifle to prevent it making any noise which the other two might have heard. There was a soft, lifeless sigh of air from the man's lungs as Harris lowered his body to the ground and they emptied for the last time.

Harris pulled out the knife, leaving the soldier sprawled on the path. He picked up the man's torch, then moved off down the track to catch up with the other two. Running silently on his toes and the outsides of his feet, he rapidly gained on the dog-handler. Ten metres from the man he switched on the torch, pointing it to one side, and slowed down to a walking pace. He saw the dog-handler glance round briefly; seeing the light, the man assumed that all was well and kept moving.

'Augh!' coughed Harris softly, as if alarmed by something he had seen.

The dog-handler turned again, seeing the shape ten

metres behind him, the torch now still and shining to one side. Tentatively, he began to approach. Five metres from Harris he hissed what was obviously a question.

'Augh!' repeated Harris.

The dog-handler repeated the question, taking two more steps forward. It was enough. Harris leaped at him, driving the knife up beneath his chin into the brain, killing him in the same way that he had killed his dog. Once again he lowered the body to the ground. As he did so, he heard a sharp question from the lead soldier. The man had turned and his figure was silhouetted twenty metres away down the track.

There was nothing else for it. Harris spoke no Korean and could not even understand the question, let alone make a convincing reply. At any moment the leader would dive off the track and take cover. Harris was confident that he could stalk the soldier and kill him, but knew that he would be unlikely to be able to do so before the man began firing his rifle or screaming for assistance. He levelled his silenced AK and squeezed off a single shot.

The baffles and expansion chamber in a silencer kill the noise of the muzzle blast created by the propellant gases of the burning powder – the loudest component of the sound that a rifle makes when it is fired – but a silencer can do nothing about the crack of a supersonic bullet. The whiplash noise sounded shockingly loud to Harris, and he hoped there was no one nearby to hear it. The North Korean patrol leader collapsed without firing a shot of his own; Harris's single bullet had caught him square in the breastbone, shattering it and tearing through the chest cavity. The man gave a despairing groan as he fell, and his rifle and torch fell heavily to the ground. He lay still and made no further sound.

Harris put on his night vision goggles again. He bent to retrieve the single empty 7.62x39mm cartridge case and pocketed it. *OK*, he thought. *Now where to hide the bodies?* He began scouting around, moving easily with the aid of the NVGs.

Ten minutes later he found the hole, sixty metres off the narrow track in the scrub. It was the result of subsidence of some sort – possibly a collapsed entrance to an old tunnel. One by one he carried all four dead soldiers and the dog to the hole, burying the human bodies and their weapons first. With the folding shovel from his bergen he covered them with a few inches of earth, then threw the dog into the now shallow hole. A further layer of earth and some loose brushwood went on top. He knew it was only a rudimentary attempt at concealment, but it left a slight chance that if the dog was dug up by someone they might not think to investigate further.

Cutting a branch from a bush, Harris set about obliterating the tracks that he and the North Koreans had made, brushing over the footprints and bloodstains. Then he returned to his bergen again and finished packing it. He consulted his GPS satellite navigation unit and found he was nearly four kilometres from the drop zone, where the others would by now be waiting for him. It would take an hour, if he pushed it; but he would need to take care not to be seen, so it might take twice that long or more. Besides, he thought, there was something else he needed to do first. He lifted the heavy bergen on to his shoulders and moved off silently, keeping well off to the side of the track.

Five minutes later he had approached to within a hundred metres of the fire he had seen from the air. It was still burning. A small, boxy-looking, Russian-made UAZ jeep with a canvas canopy was parked ten metres from it. *Only a four-seater*, thought Harris. *Good*. He circled the area, holding a light switch of wood out in front of him to feel for any trip-wires. There were none, and he saw no sign of life. Satisfied, he walked up to the vehicle and looked inside. In the rear were some blankets, two large cans of water and six of fuel. Between the front seats was an old, bulky, vehicle-mounted VHF radio transceiver; Harris saw that it was not switched on. Its eight-foot whip antenna was mounted on the front left wing of the vehicle. Next to the radio were a battered tin box and a map-case. He flipped open the map-case and examined the map; no notes or markings had been made on it and so it was of no use to him. Then he opened the box. It contained some rough slices of hard, stale bread and pieces of greasy, rancid sausage wrapped in paper. Harris closed the box, pleased. The vehicle and provisions seemed to indicate that the four Korean soldiers had been alone on patrol, and that they were due to be away from their base for perhaps another twenty-four hours. He emptied one of the water-cans over the fire and scattered the embers; they hissed and smouldered, but would not ignite again.

Consulting his own map once again, he saw that less than a kilometre to the north was a small tributary of the Kuryong river. He slung his bergen in the rear of the vehicle and went round to the front to open the bonnet catch. A minute later he had hot-wired the engine, which fired with a clatter. He climbed into the driving seat, briefly flipped on his infra-red light to locate the crude controls, crunched into first gear and drove off.

Driving slowly and without lights over the rough ground, Harris stopped well short of the river. He killed the engine and got out, taking only his silenced AK. Heading north-west, he reached the river and began moving cautiously eastwards along its bank. He saw no sign of life. For three hundred metres he continued along the river-bank, after which he circled back to the vehicle, satisfied. Then he drove forward to a point he had selected on the bank, inched the front wheels forward until they were just over a steep point on the slope, applied the handbrake fully and switched off the engine.

After placing a large stone in front of each rear wheel in case the handbrake failed, Harris removed his bergen from the vehicle. He snapped off the radio antenna and threw it into the river. Then he went down to the water's edge and refilled the empty water can. Next he stripped the vehicle of its seat squabs, placing them on the floor in the rear with the map-case, the tin ration-box and the cans of fuel and water. He cut loose the canvas canopy and spread it over them, then began piling more heavy stones on to the tarpaulin to weigh the vehicle down. It would make a splash, he knew, but that couldn't be helped. When he had finished, he removed the two wheel-chocks and waited for a couple of minutes, listening and watching. Nothing moved; the only sound was the gentle lapping of water against the river-bank.

Reaching into the jeep, Harris released the hand-brake. The vehicle needed a shove from behind but, once moving, it gathered momentum and rolled the few feet down the bank into the water. The splash was not loud, and after a few seconds Harris was satisfied to see the jeep disappear completely beneath the water. Some air-bubbles rose to the surface, but nothing else. He unstrapped the parachute equipment stuff-bag from his bergen, weighed it with more stones, slashed some small holes in it with his knife and threw it in the river forty metres downstream from the vehicle. It too disappeared beneath the surface.

Harris brushed over the vehicle tracks on the bank, his own footprints and the cavities left by the stones he had lifted, then hefted his bergen on to his shoulders, wincing briefly from the pain in his ribs where he had hit the tree on landing. His head still ached fiercely from the concussive effect of being knocked out in mid-air, and he wondered again what exactly had happened. He followed the vehicle's tyre-marks for five hundred metres back towards the fire, brushing as he went. It was a crude and hurried method of camouflage – he knew that a trained tracker would not be fooled for long – but it might make a difference and would certainly delay anyone who came after him. When he reached a hard, rocky patch of ground that he had crossed in the vehicle no more tracks were visible. He threw aside the piece of brushwood. He had been on the ground just under an hour; it was now almost midnight.

Moving fast and silently, Harris struck out to the west on the route he had selected to the DZ. He knew he was cutting it fine if he was to make the rendezvous in time, but he was satisfied that all traces of his presence – and that of the North Korean patrol – had been obliterated.

36

Thirteen times zones behind in Washington, DC, Jane Margolyes rose from the chair in her employer's office and turned towards the door. Tom Levy had given her a mountain of work to be getting on with for the rest of the day, but she didn't mind. Over the past few weeks, since Levy's sudden change of character, she had at last begun to enjoy her job.

'Oh, there's one other item, Jane,' said Levy. 'I'm sorry – I forgot to mention it. I need you to arrange a temporary security pass for someone. Can I leave it to you to process the usual application?'

'Oh,' said Jane, deflated. She turned from the door. 'Sure, Tom. Who is it? Another researcher?'

'Maintenance technician,' said Levy.

Oh god, thought Jane. She hated processing those wretched security passes. The paperwork and all the telephone calls that had to be made were unbelievable. For researchers it wasn't too bad – it was relatively easy for the security people to keep an eye on them, so the procedure for getting a pass was relative straightforward; but the Secret Service were almost paranoid about technicians of any sort – they had to be cleared for access to some of the most sensitive systems in the White House. 'It could take a while, Tom,' she said, trying to keep her voice neutral. 'They're pretty thorough when it comes to issuing those.'

'Oh,' said Levy blankly. 'Yes. I suppose I should have guessed. What exactly is involved?'

A few weeks ago, Jane realised, Levy would never have bothered to ask such a question. He would simply have snarled at her to get on with it, and sworn at her if it wasn't ready within twenty-four hours. 'Well,' she began, 'first of all there are all the reports and references. That includes education, medical, police, FBI, military, CIA, FDA, ATF, IRS – you name it. What was the subject like at school? Has he done military service? Does he have an FBI file? What do the local cops say about him? If the guy has lived in more than one state, or even county, it almost doubles the number of inquiries. Does he have a clean driver's licence? Has he paid his taxes? Has he ever been referred to a shrink? We have to send all the relevant authorities a form to fill in and return, and most of them just sit on it and do nothing. Usually I have to call two or three times to remind them to get on with it. Some of them can be a major pain.'

Levy was frowning thoughtfully. 'I had no idea,' he said eventually. 'Look, would it help if I got involved personally?'

'Well,' said Jane, brightening, 'you know, I think it might. They'd pay a lot more attention to you than they ever would to me . . . but honestly, Tom, it really could mean a lot of phone calls. You're too busy. Let me handle it.'

'No,' said Levy decisively. 'We're going to cut through the crap, here. If you find out the phone and fax numbers of all the people we need to contact, we'll fax the requests through and I'll follow up straight away with phone calls to the people in charge. You put me through, and I'll kick their butts into action. How does that sound?'

'It could certainly save an enormous amount of time,' said Jane with feeling. 'But are you sure . . .'

'No problem,' said Levy expansively. 'Let's get moving on it. Here are the guy's details.' He pushed a sheet of paper towards her across his desk.

'I'll get on to it right away,' said Jane. 'Thanks, Tom. Your personal input will be a real help. It's very kind of you.'

'My pleasure,' said Levy, smiling.

Jane smiled back at him and left the office, glancing down at the application. Her eyes were drawn to the photograph clipped to the top of the form. It had obviously been taken in one of those passport-photo booths – the quality was poor and it could have been a picture of almost anybody. Nevertheless, it showed a pleasant, smiling face; a dark-haired man about her own age. *Quite a nice-looking guy*, she thought absently.

The name beneath the photograph meant nothing to Jane. But she had a feeling that, with the sort of personal pressure Levy would be able to bring to bear, the application would sail through. *Yes*, she thought confidently, *this guy George McKinley is going to get his pass issued in record time.*

It did not occur to her for one moment that the name was a false one, or that the friendly, good-looking man in the photograph had dyed his hair and was wearing tinted contact lenses. There was absolutely no reason for her to suspect that George McKinley's real name was Peter Kramer, or that the smiling face was in fact that of a ruthless *Stasi* assassin.

37

It was almost two o'clock in the morning when, to the enormous relief of Howard and the others, Harris finally arrived at the rendezvous. In a few brief sentences he reported to Howard what had happened, adding that he was as certain as he could be that no one had seen him other than the four-man North Korean patrol and their dog, all now dead. The first indication that the North Koreans might receive of something amiss, Harris said, would be whenever the patrol was next due to report in over the radio. But the VHF set had looked old and would probably be known to be unreliable in rough, wooded country.

Howard nodded silently. He could have done without the delay, and Harris's encounter with the patrol almost certainly meant trouble in due course. But Harris had done well in obscuring the trail and buying extra time. 'Are you OK yourself, Mel?' he whispered.

'A couple of sore ribs,' replied Harris. 'I may have cracked them. Apart from that and a splitting headache, I'm fine. No problem to keep going.'

'Good,' said Howard. 'OK. We'd better be off.'

While they were waiting, the others had ditched their parachute equipment in the river as Harris had done. Without further ado, Howard led off on the route he had planned. Ziegler brought up the rear.

They made steady progress. Howard set as fast a pace as he dared, but his over-riding priority was to avoid being detected. Weatherill's apparent inability to move quietly was one of his principal concerns. The scientist seemed to kick every stone, step on every twig and brush noisily against every bush they passed. But Howard reminded himself repeatedly that the man was a complete novice with only the most basic training. He and Kim Sumi were carrying no equipment; their loads had been split between the others, mainly to keep the parachute drop as uncomplicated as possible for them, but also – as Ziegler had observed – because a man is inevitably clumsier in his movements when carrying a heavy load. The scientist was quite clumsy enough anyway, and a bergen on his back would only make matters worse.

As well as being nervous, Weatherill was finding the experience baffling. Apart from feeling completely lost, he was convinced that Howard was leading them round in circles. He could not understand why their leader did not use the tracks and paths they saw, but chose instead to keep well away from them unless they had to be crossed. When at one stage Howard was about to lead them across what looked like a deep river, he tapped Harris on the shoulder to attract his attention and pointed upstream. Harris immediately shook his head and abruptly gestured to the scientist to follow. The river had been chest-deep – and ice-cold. Weatherill had gasped at the chill, but resisted the urge to protest. Why on earth, he wondered, had Howard not led them across the perfectly good bridge which was plainly visible less than four hundred yards away upstream? And why did Howard keep stopping for no apparent reason, when he knew time was short? Weatherill signed resignedly, and eventually gave up wondering. Instead he concentrated on Harris's back and did his best to follow in his exact footsteps.

The first hint of twilight was appearing in the sky as they finally crested the brow of a low ridge. Below them, stretching along a wide valley away into the distance, were the thousands of lights of a huge industrial complex. Weatherill recognised immediately where they were; he began to register the features of Yŏngbyŏn he had seen from the air-photographs and maps he had studied.

Without breaking his stride Howard led the way down the slope, finally stopping near a large, dense thicket of thorn bushes. Gesturing to the others to wait, he and Ziegler skirted the area, returning a few minutes later. With Howard leading, they began crawling in line into the thicket, flat on their stomachs and dragging their bergens after them. Weatherill's clothes kept snagging on the sharp thorns; progress was painful and difficult, and he was tired and cross. Thirty yards into the thicket they stopped. Harris gestured to Weatherill to lie where he was and rest.

Wearily, the scientist complied, wriggling into the least uncomfortable position he could find. Stones and roots were digging into him, and his skin was stinging from thorn scratches. Yet to his surprise and despite his discomfort he found himself drifting off to sleep, dimly aware of Halliday hunched over the radio set with Howard beside him, talking quietly.

At about the same time that Halliday began transmitting Howard's progress report to Johnny Bourne in Seoul, a very different radio transmission was being initiated from a point six miles to the north-east. A small olive-green plastic box, the size of a cigarette pack, was activated by a built-in electronic clock and began emitting a regular 'beep' every two seconds on a frequency of 120 megahertz. This frequency is reserved by international treaty for emergency civilian use by any ship or aircraft in distress; it is constantly monitored by orbiting Cospasat TIROS satellites, which calculate the exact source of a signal by triangulation. The location of the search and rescue beacon (SARBE) transmission is immediately passed to the authorities of the country concerned, so that a recovery operation can be mounted. The military version of such a transmitter is known as a tactical beacon; TACBEs are routinely carried by air force pilots for emergency use in the event of being shot down, and by Special Forces units operating behind enemy lines.

This particular transmission was also picked up by the North Korean radio monitoring station at Kaech'on airfield, near Yŏngbyŏn itself. The radio direction-finding system kicked in automatically and within five seconds, by the time of the third beep from the beacon, a North Korean Air Force radio technician had a precise bearing on the signal. He alerted the duty officer, who was puzzled since there had been no reports of any aircraft in distress, and certainly not of any civilian aircraft, over that particular area. He immediately ordered a subordinate to go and rouse the station commander from his sleep.

Simultaneously, twenty miles to the west, staff at a similar monitoring facility at Panghyon airfield had detected the beeping signal and reacted in much the same way. Within two minutes, the intersection of the two bearings had been plotted on a large-scale map at Kaech'on. The two radio operators were ordered to double-check their bearings; both reported that the signal was strong and regular, and the result was precisely the same.

The two station commanders, conferring by telephone, were confident that the location of the transmitter had been pinpointed to within about two hundred yards. The information was passed to the North Korean Army base at Kujang, the nearest one to the plotted location. A strong detachment of ninety men, led by a thin-faced major, was urgently despatched to investigate its source and report back. Within thirty minutes, just as dawn was breaking, they had surrounded the area. A radio operator with a portable DF set and headphones rapidly homed in on the signal; the major and a platoon of soldiers accompanied him, advancing cautiously, fully alert and with weapons cocked.

Sweeping his DF antenna right and left, the radio operator quartered the area, finally coming to a stop next to a small, stunted tree. He could see nothing, but he told the major he was confident he was standing on the exact spot from which the beeping signal was being transmitted. The major ordered one man to climb the tree and search it, and another to scrape away the earth around its base. The soldier who went up the tree found the olive-green box almost immediately, resting in a fork of a low branch. He jumped down and presented it to his commanding officer.

The major had not seen anything like it before. It was a uniform green plastic box with an eighteen-inch long whip antenna and a snap-on cover, which he prudently decided to leave for someone more knowledgeable to open; but on the underside of the box was taped a clear plastic waterproof envelope containing a folded sheet of paper. The major felt confident enough to open it, but he was unable to understand the hand-written message. However, he knew just enough to realise that it was written in English.

Barking instructions to his junior officers to search the entire area thoroughly in his absence and report immediately if anything else was found, the thin-faced major ran back towards his jeep. Squinting against the sun now rising over the low hills ahead, he and his escort raced along the road back to Kujang. The major had no idea what the box or the written message attached to it signified, but he was quite certain that something very odd indeed was afoot. Behind him, his junior officers were shouting shrill commands to their men as they began a thorough search of the area where Howard and his team had landed by parachute six hours earlier.

38

Gerhardt Eisener strode into the main hall, his expression cold. 'Is everything prepared as I ordered?' he demanded.

'Yes, comrade Colonel,' confirmed Captain Kessler. 'The stretcher, the restraints, the clothing, the list of drugs, the other equipment . . . And of course the travel authorisations and arrangements have all been made. The aircraft is ready and waiting. I saw to all the necessary details myself. In particular, I . . .'

'All right,' said Eisener, cutting him short. 'Have the vehicle loaded up now.' He paused, looking around. A frown crossed his face. 'Where is Major Steiner?'

'A few minutes ago he was still upstairs, comrade Colonel, clearing his desk prior to departure.'

'The hell with that,' snapped Eisener. 'Go and find him immediately and bring him here. I want to talk to both of you.'

Jürgen Kessler's face briefly betrayed his surprise. It was most uncharacteristic of the colonel, he thought, to appear impatient or irritable. Something must be bothering him. Fifteen minutes ago had come that telephone call from the North Korean military intelligence headquarters in P'yŏngyang. Since then, everything had been a flurry of activity, with Eisener barking out new instructions but at the same time insisting that General Erfurt should not be disturbed from his sleep. Normally, Kessler knew, Eisener hardly even moved a paperclip on his desk without first referring to the general. What the hell was going on? Puzzled, he hastened upstairs to find the major.

He reappeared three minutes later, followed by Major Steiner. Hans Steiner was a strong, serious-looking man in his thirties; in contrast to the younger Kessler, whose dutiful temperament and almost obsessive attention to detail had long before marked him out for administrative duties, Steiner was a tough, no-nonsense individual who, when given the opportunity, preferred to delegate desk-work to others. He was an experienced and highly capable field operative, trusted by his superiors and subordinates alike.

'Time to get going,' said Eisener quietly, his pale eyes staring into those of the stocky major. 'You can forget about your bloody paperwork for a little while. I don't expect that prospect will disappoint you too badly.'

'I follow my instructions, comrade Colonel,' said Steiner evenly.

'Of course you do,' replied Eisner. 'And now I am issuing you with some new ones.' He paused to light a cigarette. He rarely smoked, principally because of the difficulty of obtaining good tobacco in North Korea, but he still had a few packs remaining from his trip to England. He proffered the pack to Steiner. 'Smoke, Hans?'

'Not for me, thank you, comrade Colonel,' said Steiner.

'Jürgen?'

The younger man's eyes widened eagerly as he accepted the cigarette. 'Thank you very much indeed, comrade Colonel!' he said, lighting it hurriedly.

'All right, you two,' said Eisner quietly. 'For a start, you can cut out all that idiotic "comrade" nonsense – just for now, at any rate. You can save that stupid claptrap for the general, when he wakes up. But right now, you will listen to me – and you will listen carefully.' He glanced from one face to the other. Both men, he could see, had his full attention. Steiner's expression had hardly changed, but Kessler was gaping in astonishment at Eisner's heretical and openly voiced disrespect for General Erfurt.

'I am changing the plans,' Eisner continued sternly. 'Major Steiner, you will escort the prisoner on his journey, as already instructed. The difference will be that neither I nor General Erfurt will be accompanying you. You will be in sole charge. You will take Lieutenant Dorfmann as your assistant. Both of you speak good English. Dorfmann has an adequate knowledge of the administration of the necessary drugs, and you know exactly where to go and what to do.'

Steiner was nodding carefully.

'But . . . but comrade Colonel!' Kessler broke in, agitated. 'Comrade General Erfurt—'

Eisener interrupted, his voice icy. 'What did I just tell you, Kessler?'

'My apologies, com . . . I mean, Colonel—'

'Well? What is your problem?'

'Well, Colonel, sir, with respect, I distinctly recall the general giving explicit instructions to the effect that you and he would be accompanying the prisoner. The documents are all prepared, and . . .'

'Shut up, Kessler,' said Eisener, 'and just listen to me. Both of you. *Listen*, dammit, and learn something!' He drew on the cigarette again, his pale eyes flickering between the two men but settling coldly on Kessler. 'I have a feeling, you see,' he continued softly, 'a feeling that there's something odd going on. It's not anything I can put my finger on. As yet, I don't have sufficient information at my disposal. But . . . the North Koreans seem to be jumpy for some reason. You must have detected that, Kessler – you put the telephone call through from that senior North Korean Mil-Int officer in P'yŏngyang. Something's happened. I don't yet know what – Colonel Zang wouldn't tell me exactly. But I don't like the smell of it. And just in case I'm right, we're going to bring forward the transfer.'

Eisener paused, his pale eyes regarding each of his subordinates in turn. 'Kessler – get the travel papers amended immediately, to reflect the change in personnel. It won't take you more than five minutes. Steiner – get Dorfmann and the prisoner organised, and get going as soon as you can. There is some sort of security clampdown at Kaech'on, so the first part of the journey will probably take you longer than usual. I'll square it with the general later. He will soon be awake. I have no doubt that he will agree that in the circumstances it would be wrong for either of us to absent ourselves from here. Anyway, you have your instructions. Are they understood?'

Steiner and Kessler nodded.

Eisener's eyes flashed angrily. '*Understood?*'

'*Jahwohl, mein Colonel!*' they said hastily, in unison.

Gerhardt Eisener's eyes appraised each man. Kessler still appeared shocked, but Steiner had just the slightest hint of a grin on his face. *Good*, thought Eisener. Taking a last draw from his cigarette, he flicked it to the floor and ground the stub beneath his boot.

'Dismissed!' he barked. 'Get moving!'

39

Colonel Yevgeny Barushkin was still seething with anger and resentment on his arrival back in Vladivostok. The treatment he had received at the hands of that little rat of a North Korean political commissar had been nothing less than an outrage. He had been forcibly detained for twelve hours. He had been thrown into a tiny, airless, stinking cell and left there; then he had been frog-marched back along a corridor into an interrogation room, where he had been screamed at and insulted, in execrable Russian, by the commissar. He had received the sort of lecture no pilot might expect to get, even for the most flagrant breach of discipline or dereliction of duty.

Twelve hours, thought Barushkin savagely, as he banged the Antonov down hard on the Vladivostok tarmac. Well, he had given that little bastard of a commissar something to think about, too. A smashed nose, for a start. Barushkin's temper had snapped after about fifteen minutes. He had swatted aside the two scrawny guards and launched himself at the commissar, delivering a punch of which even Sasha Plasnin would have been proud. The little bastard had been knocked cold. Resisting the impulse to follow up by throttling the man, he had simply sat back in the chair again as the two guards picked themselves up from the floor.

'Go and get your colonel!' he had roared at them. He pointed to his own shoulder stars. 'Colonel! Understand? Now, get out!'

The menace and authority in Barushkin's voice were unmistakable, and the guards had scuttled off. Barushkin had used their absence to rifle through the unconscious commissar's pockets. Finding a pack of cigarettes and a box of matches, he lit up. There was a sound of running feet outside, and four more guards appeared at the door. They raised their weapons nervously, covering him. He glared at them contemptuously, blowing smoke.

Ten minutes later an older, grey-haired North Korean officer had arrived. He carried no badge or insignia of rank, but from the deference shown to him by the guards Barushkin judged him to be his own rank or even senior. The man glanced expressionlessly at the still unconscious commissar sprawled on the floor, then gave a sharp order. One of the guards dragged the limp body outside.

Barushkin studied the North Korean coolly before he spoke. 'Your subordinate showed insufficient respect. His conduct was inappropriate and he has been taught a lesson. I trust you will see to it that he is more respectful in future.'

The North Korean tapped his foot before speaking. 'You were lucky not to have been shot,' he replied calmly in passable Russian.

'It's even luckier for you that I was not,' Barushkin shot back. 'I dare say you have no wish to be responsible for precipitating a war between your country and the Russian Federation, which is undoubtedly what would have occurred if any harm had come to me. Or to any of my aircrew,' he added pointedly.

'You violated your flight plan. You were over a restricted area. You know perfectly well that in such circumstances you are obliged to explain yourself. Furthermore,' the North Korean added, 'you have assaulted one of my senior officers. A diplomatic protest will be made to your embassy about your conduct.'

'I would strongly advise you,' snapped Barushkin, 'to ensure that any communication your government makes with mine is couched in the friendliest and most conciliatory of terms. This was a goodwill flight, bearing gifts from our President to yours. You have a strange way of showing your gratitude. As to my being off course,' Barushkin waved his hand and shrugged, 'I can offer no immediate explanation. There must have been an instrument failure of some sort. I will have the aircraft thoroughly checked before departure.'

'We have already checked it, with the assistance of your flight engineer,' replied the North Korean. 'Your compass seems to be faulty. I suggest you have it replaced when you return to Vladivostok, and that your maintenance crew are severely punished for their neglect. You will be escorted to the border to ensure that there is no repetition of this violation.' He paused, staring unemotionally at Barushkin. 'Bearing in mind the condition of your cargo on arrival, your flight would appear to have been an entirely wasted one.'

'I am grateful for your offer of an escort,' replied Barushkin levelly, returning the stare, 'and I accept it – on condition,' he continued acidly, 'that it does not include the maniac MiG-25 pilot who intercepted my flight here. If you want to know why my cargo was largely destroyed, you should ask him. Being subjected to a near-miss from a MiG-25 travelling at Mach 2 is hardly conducive to a comfortable ride. He is entirely responsible for the damage caused. In fact, we were extremely lucky not to collide or crash.'

The North Korean frowned briefly. 'That will be investigated,' he said. 'But our pilots are authorised to use lethal force in such cases, as I am sure you are aware.'

'Not before they have attempted to establish communications, or at the very least before firing a warning shot,' said Barushkin angrily. 'I would suggest you review your procedures.' He drew on the remaining stub of the cigarette and threw it to the floor, grinding it beneath his boot. 'As to any use of lethal force,' he went on tersely, 'I would advise you to think extremely carefully about the consequences of any such action being taken against aircraft of the Russian Air Force.'

'I shall take note of the points you have made,' said the North Korean, 'as I trust you will take note of mine. You are now free to return to your aircraft.'

He barked a series of orders at the guards, turned on his heel and left. Barushkin was accompanied out of the building and back to the Antonov. His crew, with the exception of Alexander Plasnin, were waiting there.

'Sasha not back yet?' he asked his co-pilot.

'No. He's been gone for three hours now, ever since they released us. I'm worried about him. Mind you, I was getting worried about you, too. What happened?'

'Boxing practice,' said Barushkin, grinning savagely, 'but never mind that for now. Anyway, I don't think we need worry about Sasha. He can take care of himself.'

But an hour later, Barushkin was beginning to think he would be unable to delay any longer. The North Koreans were growing impatient; the excitable demands from the Sunan control tower to prepare to depart were getting on his nerves. *Fuck this place*, he thought. *Do these sods think I actually want to stay here for one moment longer than I have to?*

Then, to his relief, he heard the noise of the Antonov's small side-access door being closed. A few seconds later there was a crackle in his ear and he heard Plasnin's voice over the intercom.

'My apologies for keeping you waiting.'

Barushkin gestured to his co-pilot to take control and prepare for take-off. He relaxed back into the left-hand seat and thumbed the intercom button. 'Good to hear from you, Sasha,' he said. 'How did you get on?'

'Not good news, I'm afraid,' replied Plasnin, his voice serious. 'The security here is unbelievable. I don't know where that intelligence report originated, but it's way off beam. I've been all round the inside of the perimeter. There are guards by the hundred, arc-lights every fifty yards, and a twenty-foot-high chain-link and razor-wire fence. In fact, there are two more fences under construction right now, inner and outer, with four or five hundred men working on each one. Recently started, by the look of them. Sandbag machine-gun emplacements, too. The entrance gates are impossible – they're swarming with bloody guards. Even their own vehicles are being torn apart before they're allowed in. I saw one truck-load of people being strip-searched, right there in the open. I don't see how anyone at all could get in without authorisation – let alone anyone who looks European. I wouldn't like to try it myself, anyway.'

'Shit,' exclaimed Barushkin, his anger rising again. The four engines were now running, and there was a slight lurch as the co-pilot increased power and began taxiing the big aircraft towards the runway. Barushkin hardly noticed the movement. *The hell with these bloody North Koreans*, he thought. He thumbed the intercom button again. 'No weak point at all that we can report?'

'None that I saw.'

Barushkin looked perplexed. 'Look, Sasha, we both saw that intelligence report. The original report was only a month old and it was updated last week – it said no change. It was made by the *rezident* at our own fucking embassy here, for God's sake. He was ordered to travel home on both occasions for the sole purpose of taking an up-to-date look around this bloody airfield to make the assessment. On each occasion he said security was routine – no particular problem. He's a KGB major – he wouldn't have got things that wrong. Something must have changed . . . when did all this new activity start?'

'I didn't ask anyone,' commented Plasnin drily. 'But if you want my guess – today. Probably only hours ago, while we were being held for interrogation.'

Barushkin's frown of concern deepened. 'Have we slipped up somewhere?'

'No,' said Plasnin emphatically, 'we haven't. And in case you're wondering, I wasn't noticed by anyone when I did my survey of the perimeter. Besides, the extra security measure were already well underway by the time I began my rounds.'

'Well, something must have gone wrong somewhere. Maybe our English friends have been killed or captured. I hope not, for their sakes and ours.' Barushkin was thinking aloud, worried; but he realised there was nothing he could do about it at this stage, and he would find out what had happened sooner or later. He changed the subject. 'As a matter of interest, Sasha, just how did you manage to get around without being noticed?'

'I borrowed a jeep belonging to military security. It was parked in the hangar where we unloaded. You remember those four guys who came up to check the cargo manifest? It was their jeep. I gave them a big smile and a complimentary sample – a litre for each of them, in fact. Then I led them off behind that pile of crates of dried milk powder at the back of the hangar, where I showed them the manifest and encouraged them to satisfy themselves that the samples were up to standard. We drank a few toasts of eternal friendship, then I left them to it and came back to the plane. I was taken away for another lot of questioning – as you were. I acted like a dumb sergeant, and they let me go after a while. My four babies obviously drank themselves senseless in my absence. When I was released they were still where I'd left them – but flat out. I took their jeep and went for a little drive around. When I got back just now they still hadn't moved. I put the keys back in the driver's pocket. They'll probably sleep for a week, unless someone decides to shift that fucking milk powder and finds them. I hope they get a stinking hangover.'

'I hope they're shot,' said Barushkin fiercely. 'Fuck this place. Let's go home.'

As the big Antonov rose slowly off the Sunan runway and climbed away to join the waiting fighter escort, the grey-haired North Korean Intelligence colonel watched from the control tower, his face cold and impassive. He knew that Barushkin had lied to him. The report from Kaech'on had been categoric about it. *Clumsy Russian gorilla*, he thought.

He had adopted his favoured tactic: when pushed, concede some ground. Appear to back down. Then, when the enemy thinks he has won, strike – strike hard. The gorilla would be back with another cargo, thinking he had got away with his subterfuge. He would receive a rude shock. Would it be better to interrogate him and confront the Russian government with the evidence of their duplicity, or would a simple accident be the answer?

He would decide about that when the time came, he concluded. But either way, the eight British parachutists whom the gorilla had dropped near Yŏngbyŏn would not be going home in that aircraft. From the written message attached to the radio-beacon the colonel knew how many of them there were, and that they were planning to get out of his country again on the same Russian aircraft on its return trip to Sunan. His nose twitched with distaste as he contemplated the idea of the Russians, of all people, now apparently helping the despised Westerners. The message had been curiously uninformative about the parachutists' exact intentions in North Korea, but that didn't matter, he knew. He had taken steps to reinforce the Yŏngbyŏn complex, which was obviously where they were heading for. There would be no escape for them. The British parachutists would not be going home at all – not even in coffins.

40

'I can hardly hear you, Sasha,' Johnny Bourne bawled into the telephone receiver. 'Could you say that again, please?'

The line from Seoul to Vladivostok was, if anything, even worse than it had been less than twenty-four hours before, when Bourne had spoken to Howard just before his boarding the Antonov. The earpiece was crackling and spitting with static, and there was a hollow disembodied echo reverberating down the line. The South Korean telephone network was a good one and Bourne guessed that the fault lay at the other end, in the antiquated Russian system. But at least it worked, he acknowledged.

'I said, news not good,' yelled Sasha Plasnin in his halting, heavily accented English. 'Heavy activity at airfield. Penetration will be big difficulty for Ed and others. Maybe impossible, I think.'

The apparently clipped style of Plasnin's reporting was less to do with his previous KGB/military training than with the fact that in the Russian language there are no definite or indefinite articles, such as 'a' and 'the'.

Bourne's brow knotted with worry as Plasnin detailed his assessment of the increased security he had noticed at Sunan. The Russian avoided using place-names and specific details that would have revealed the precise subject of the conversation to an eavesdropper, but to Bourne the substance of what he was saying was only too clear. What most alarmed him was Plasnin's definite opinion that the new North Korean security activity was just that – new. It was as if they had got wind of something – that they had somehow discovered what was going on and were taking drastic steps to bolster their defences. Bourne's knuckles went white with tension as he gripped the telephone handset. For five minutes he listened as Plasnin made his report, interjecting a few questions and occasionally nodding his head, his frown deepening.

'Thank you, Sasha,' he said eventually. 'I'll pass this on to Ed, and I'll let you know what he says.'

'*Shto?*'

'I said, I'll let you know what Ed wants to do.'

'*Da. Prashchaytye*, Johnny.'

'*Da-svidanya*, Sasha.' Bourne quietly replaced the telephone receiver and looked up. Lines of worry were etched into his face.

Goodale had been watching him. He leaned forward in his chair. 'I think I got the rough gist of that,' he said quietly. 'Exactly how bad is it?'

'It's bloody awful,' muttered Bourne dully. 'Sunan's crawling with troops, new fences and God knows what else. Plasnin doesn't think Ed and the others have a chance in hell of getting in there to meet the plane on its return flight. And by the sound of it, I believe him.'

Goodale could see that Bourne was badly shaken by what he had learned. 'It could just be pure coincidence,' he said kindly, 'and of course it may be only a temporary measure. A routine exercise. Things will probably revert to normal in a day or two.'

'I'm sorry, Colonel,' said Bourne, shaking his head, 'but what's happening there sounds anything but temporary and I don't believe in coincidences of that sort. And neither does Ed, I can tell you. He didn't believe it was a coincidence when that warehouse blew up in Iraq last year, nearly killing us, and he was right. He won't believe this is a coincidence either.'

'Well, we'd better not delay in telling him,' sighed Goodale. 'I don't think our speculating about it at this stage will do any good. Do you want to write the message? You know all the details.'

Bourne nodded dejectedly, trying to imagine what effect the news would have on his friends. He reached for the signal pad and began to draft the radio message. *Marooned in North Korea*, he thought. *The operation has hardly even started, and already it looks as if the planned escape route has been cut off. How the hell did the North Koreans find out?*

41

Ed Howard sat hunched in thought as he digested the radio message he had received from Johnny Bourne. The message had been brief, but to the point. Bourne had expressed relief that the team had landed safely and were now in position about half a mile from the *Stasi* base, but he had gone on to report the gist of the telephone conversation he had had with Colonel Barushkin and, more importantly, Alexander Plasnin, following their return from P'yŏngyang to Vladivostok. Sunan airfield, it seemed, was being sealed off. Only a month before, the intelligence reports and satellite photographs had all indicated that the plan to rejoin the Antonov at Sunan would be fairly easy to carry out. A similar report, less than a week old, had repeated this view. Suddenly, everything seemed to have changed. Plasnin's first-hand account of new security measures at Sunan was gloomy in the extreme.

'Maybe he's wrong, Ed,' suggested Ziegler eventually. 'This could just be a temporary security exercise. A twenty-four-hour blitz, then things will return to normal. I mean, Plasnin seemed like a good guy, but you can't expect an Air Force sergeant to be an expert on security.'

'He's not wrong, Mike,' replied a worried-sounding Howard. 'You heard his report about the new fences and the rest of it – they didn't sound at all temporary to me. And Plasnin's not an Air Force sergeant, either. I didn't tell you that. He's highly qualified, and he knows what he's talking about.'

'Oh, yes? Who is he?'

'He works for an acquaintance of mine in Moscow. He's ex-Special Forces, like you and me – did ten years with them, and ended up as a major.'

'What?' Ziegler's eyebrows rose in surprise. 'You mean he was a major in the *Spetsnaz*?'

'Yes,' Howard replied, 'but the word "*Spetsnaz*" really only means special-purpose unit, and there are plenty of different ones. Some of them aren't particularly special, in fact. But Plasnin's unit is in a different league from the others. It's KGB – in fact, the best of the KGB units.'

'Shit,' said Ziegler, falling silent.

'We should have come by boat, boss,' growled Tony Ackford. 'You know, off a submarine. Low-profile boat, like you and I used to use in the SBS. We wouldn't have been seen, and we'd have had transport out. I hate fucking parachutes,' he added unnecessarily.

'We discussed all that before, Tony,' sighed Howard. 'Sure, we wouldn't have been seen. The latest low-profiles can run with less than two inches of freeboard, quite invisible and inaudible to anyone on the bank. You can even run them submerged if you have to. We could have gone all the way up the Ch'ŏngch'ŏn and Kuryong rivers without radar or anything spotting us. But there was one insuperable problem – the NK hydrophone arrays. They listen for engine or propeller noise, and we'd have been picked up before we'd got within a mile of the coastline – we'd have been blasted out of existence before we started.'

Harris sat up, wincing at the pain in his ribs. 'So what *are* we going to do, boss?' he asked quietly. 'Nick an aircraft from another airstrip, or an NK patrol boat, and make a run for it?'

'Maybe,' said Howard. 'But in the meantime we've got a job to do. Go and relieve Pete, would you? I want to hear the latest.'

Harris crawled off through the thicket, and a few

minutes later Halliday returned. Kim Sumi was with him. 'Mega traffic on the main road, boss,' reported Halliday wearily. 'All heading towards the nuclear base. Must be hundreds of vehicles gone past in the last couple of hours. They're still coming, too. Want to see the log?'

'Thanks,' said Howard. He studied the notebook anxiously. 'What about activity at the *Stasi* base?'

'That's the only good news,' replied Halliday. 'No change there. The traffic's going straight past it.'

'Nothing's stopped anywhere near? Are you sure of that?'

'Positive,' replied Halliday. 'Not since we've been here, anyway. The nearest NK unit is an anti-aircraft gun emplacement outside the main gate of the nuclear site, over a mile away. A couple of ZSU-23s and an SA-6 battery, with infantry guarding them.'

'Any other nasties?'

'Well, I've counted fourteen BMP-1s so far. Not exactly tanks, but I'd prefer not to argue the toss with a 73mm gun. And, er, there are five BM-21s, too.'

'Oh, dammit,' groaned Howard. 'Katyushas. I hate those bloody rockets. One's bad enough, but forty launcher tubes on one vehicle . . . damn, damn, damn.'

'Actually,' Kim Sumi added quietly, 'they're BM-11s, not BM-21s. You can relax a little. They only have thirty tubes each, not forty.'

Howard turned in surprise. 'BM-11s? I haven't heard of those.'

'Local model,' she explained. 'Different chassis – slightly lighter.'

'That's interesting,' said Howard slowly, giving Sumi a curious look. 'Did you spot anything else we might have missed?'

'Yes,' she replied. 'The soldiers aren't special units or paratroops. They're competent, but by no means the best. They won't really have any idea why they've been sent here – but they'll be alert, nevertheless.'

'I see,' said Howard. 'Anything else?'

'There'll be a problem with the road,' said Sumi.

'How do you mean?'

'There's a transport shortage. The vehicles that have brought the soldiers are already beginning to return to collect supplies for them. There'll be almost constant traffic for at least another twenty-four hours.'

'Damn,' said Howard, his consternation growing. 'I was hoping it would slacken. We need to cross that road tonight, and there's very little cover down there.'

'Then we'll have to use the tunnel,' said Sumi.

'Tunnel? What tunnel?' asked Halliday. 'I didn't see one.'

'Well, it's more . . .' Sumi searched for the right expression. 'A drainpipe? You know, under the road – to prevent flash floods.'

'A culvert?'

'Yes,' she said. 'But it starts well away from each side of the road. It's quite usual, in Korea, to make them like that. You can see them quite easily if you know what to look for. This one is about two hundred yards long. It comes out near the building Pete pointed out to me, the *Stasi* one.'

'I'd better come and take a squint at it with my binos,' said Howard. Sumi's local knowledge was proving useful.

'Bugger it,' muttered Ackford disgustedly as Howard and Sumi crawled off through the thicket towards the vantage point overlooking the road. 'If there's one thing I hate even more than bloody parachuting, it's crawling along fucking tunnels and drainpipes. I get that, er, whatever it is. You know – when you don't like confined spaces. They give me . . . bugger it, what *is* that word?'

'The shits,' said Ziegler helpfully.

'Yeah, that's it,' said Ackford.

42

Pete Halliday had no illusions about what he had volunteered for. As the smallest man in the party, he was the obvious choice to go first. Like Ackford, he had no particular taste for crawling through concrete drainpipes; but at least, he reflected, this one looked slightly larger in diameter than those he had had to tackle during his SAS selection course back in the mid-eighties. Crouched in the dark near the entrance, he estimated it at twenty-two inches. The only other thing he knew about it was its length – about two hundred yards. He had no idea whether he would encounter obstructions or flooding due to subsidence, which would make further progress impossible. The most likely place for problems, he reckoned, would be about halfway along, where the pipe passed beneath the road itself.

Putting his head closer to the entrance, Halliday sniffed the air inside. It smelled damp, musty and unpleasant, but it was a smell of rotting vegetation rather than sewage, which was at least something. He attached the end of a reel of twelve-hundred-pound breaking strain parachute cord to his belt with a bowline, gave Howard a brief nod and crawled in. As he disappeared the cord began to pay out, with Ziegler holding on to the spool.

It was utterly dark inside, as he had known it would be. Halliday had thought about using his night vision goggles, but had decided against it – because it was so dark he would have had to use the infra-red illumination beam, which might have been detectable at the far end. For the first few yards he found himself crawling on a thin layer of hard mud encrusted with stones. The air became damp and fetid, and it seemed to get worse as he inched his way forward. The layer of caked mud gradually thickened, and he was soon unable to use his knees at all. Using just his toes to push, and his elbows, hands and forearms to pull, each movement gained him four or five inches at most. Two hundred yards of this, he realised, would be the equivalent of about a thousand press-ups. Sweat was soon pouring down his face.

After what he estimated to be thirty yards, the mud lying in the pipe softened. It was glutinous and foul-smelling and it slowed him down, but he welcomed the relief it afforded his elbows and knees, which were already sore from rubbing against stones and grit. The feeling of claustrophobia was now powerful, but Halliday forced it from his mind and concentrated on each slow movement forward. *Forty-eight, forty-nine, fifty; rest. Count to twenty, breathing back to normal, pulse back down to about a hundred. Start again. One, two three . . .*

He lost track of time. His watch was on a nylon cord round his neck, buttoned inside his shirt. On night operations he always kept it there out of habit – a luminous watch face had too often given away its wearer's position. Nevertheless he felt a twinge of regret; he could have done with its feeble light as a contact with reality in this pitch-black, stinking pipe.

The rumbling noise from the nearby road had disappeared soon after he had entered the pipe. Now there was just the sound of his own laboured breathing and the scuffing noise of his boots and clothing as he dragged himself along. At least, he thought, he did not have to worry too much about making any noise himself – there was enough outside to drown it out.

Suddenly the air became really foul – a sickly stench that Halliday recognised with disgust. He clenched his jaw against the feeling of nausea. Some animal – he hoped it was only a small one – had obviously taken refuge inside the pipe and died, probably from drowning. It must be just ahead, he realised. He would have to crawl straight past it.

Something sharp stabbed into his face. Groping forward with his hands, he found that a small thorn bush was blocking his path. Halliday reached for his knife and began to slash and hack away at the bush with the blunt edge of the saw-blade. The wood was dead and brittle, and within two or three minutes he had broken up most of it into small pieces. He thrust the pieces behind him and was eventually left with just the main stem, about an inch thick. He pulled at it: it was being held by something. He pulled again.

There was a soft, hissing sigh as the stem pulled free; the stench of hideously rotten meat hit Halliday's throat like a blast of poison gas. He gagged uncontrollably, retching and vomiting. Dimly he recalled the only other time he had been completely unable to control this kind of reaction – when he had smelt gangrene. Desperate to get away, he pulled on the wooden bush-stem again. It came free; Halliday felt a piece of wire attached to it. At the same time there was a high-pitched squealing and screeching, accompanied by the scratching sound of rapid, pattering movements. *Oh God*, he thought. *Rats.*

Still gagging at the dreadful smell, he realised what the wire was; it was a snare. It had been anchored to the bush; but the wretched animal, whatever it was, had somehow managed to pull the bush free and had dragged itself away. It had taken refuge in the pipe, where it had died and was now being eaten by rats and maggots. Halliday guessed it had probably got a foreleg through the snare's wire loop, as well as its neck, which explained why it hadn't strangled to death quickly. Shutting his eyes and trying not to breathe, Halliday lunged forwards, desperate to get past the body of the animal and the terrible stench of death. There was a further shrill cacophony of squeaking; some rats scampered over his back and away, the noise echoing down the pipe. His left elbow dug into something squashy, lying on the surface of the mud; it was the body. A hare or wild cat, he thought, but he did not have any desire to find out. He lunged forward again, coughing and retching; then he was past it. The foul air did not improve. Forty-six, forty-seven . . . but no stopping for a rest at fifty this time, he decided – not until he was well clear. *What a place to die . . .*

At last, his lungs heaving and his hands trembling, Halliday stopped. His neck and shoulders were aching from the exertion, and he felt weak and dizzy from the uncontrollable vomiting.

There was a heavy rumbling sound now and the pipe seemed to vibrate slightly. He thought he was imagining it, but as his breathing slowed he heard and felt it again. He realised he must now be directly beneath the road. *Only halfway . . .*

Howard and the others had seen the line of para-cord slacken against the slight tension that Ziegler was maintaining on it. Knowing that Halliday must have encountered an obstruction they waited anxiously, wondering what it might be. When the spool began to turn again a little later, Ziegler noticed that the movement was jerkier and faster than before. He exchanged a glance with Howard, who had noticed it too, but said nothing. Gradually the movement became more regular; it settled into its previous pattern, with a pause after each thirty feet or so of progress.

Halliday was close to exhaustion. The pipe had dipped due to slight subsidence, and the section through which he was groping was more than half-full of stagnant water. Yet although it was an added effort to keep his head above the water-level, he welcomed the coolness. It was foul and dirty, he knew, but he could not smell it. He hoped it would wash away some of the traces of the dead animal. The water became deeper and deeper, until at one stage it was lying within just a few inches of the roof. He plunged on, movement becoming easier as the water took some of his weight, but he knew that if the level rose any further he would have to consider turning back. *Please,*

God, not now, he thought, *I must be nearly there* . . .

Dimly Halliday realised that the pipeline must have turned upwards again, as the water-level was beginning to drop. It gradually became shallower; after another twenty-five yards he found himself on a thin layer of damp mud again. Thirty-four, thirty-five . . .

Suddenly, his elbows encountered a void and he felt himself lurch forward. His chest jarred on to the edge of the pipe, his arms hanging loose. He heard the grinding noise of a lorry passing, and saw the shadows thrown by its headlights dancing across the rocky ground in front of him. He had reached the far end.

The reflexes of training and experience took over instantly and he tensed for action. Still lying in the pipe, he slowly reached inside his smock for the waterproof case containing his night vision goggles. Taking care not to smear the lenses with his filthy hands, he put them on, fastening the strap behind his head.

The landscape leaped brightly into view as he switched on the goggles. Halliday recognised the depression of the old stream-bed that he had seen with his binoculars from the ridge. He was in the gully itself but, on account of the bank on either side, could see no further than a few yards to the left or right. Because the gully was slightly deeper than he had expected, it would give plenty of cover. He slithered silently out of the pipe and moved to the right-hand bank, his AKMS ready. Pulling the weapon's silencer from a belt-pouch, he tipped it first one way and then the other, shaking it to empty out any remaining water, then screwed it on to the end of the AK's barrel.

Slowly, he raised his head clear of the bank and looked around. Three hundred yards away was the *Stasi* building. He immediately saw the guard on the gate, and . . . yes, there was the other one, on patrol as usual. Nothing else was moving, apart from the lorries still grinding along the road behind him. Halliday smiled to himself and returned to the mouth of the drainpipe. At last he looked at his watch. The crawl through the pipe had taken him nearly half an hour.

At the other end, Ziegler noticed the spool of para-cord suddenly pay out faster. He nodded at Howard. Halliday was obviously clear of the pipe and was moving around. Then the line went slack; Ziegler pulled it back in to maintain tension. Holding the line, he waited for the signal. There was one long pull; Halliday was confirming that he was through. Then there was a second long pull; difficult, but workable. *Please, not a third,* thought Ziegler; that would have meant a serious problem. A fourth would have meant 'abort'.

There was no third pull. Relieved, Ziegler made a loop in the line and attached it to Halliday's bergen, which he placed in the entrance to the pipe. He waited; after a two-minute pause he saw the line go tight and the bergen began to disappear as Halliday pulled from the far end. Without further ado, Howard climbed in after it. Ziegler continued to pay out more para-cord.

Half an hour later, Ziegler felt the signal pull as Halliday's bergen was untied at the far end. He began to reel the cord back in; his nose wrinkled in disgust as he smelled where it had scraped past the body of the dead animal. Attached to the loop was a brief written message from Howard: '2 at a time now on. 30-yard section near far end 70% flooded. 2nd in line pause at flood until first is clear'.

Ziegler nodded. This time he attached two bergens to the line. As they disappeared, Harris climbed into the pipe, followed by Sumi.

The cough of Ziegler's silenced automatic pistol was inaudible against the background clatter of a lorry two hundred yards away. The subsonic 9mm bullet struck the man high on his forehead and he spun round before collapsing. Even before the second man could turn towards the noise, there was a second cough and he too fell. Howard lowered his pistol and signalled to Halliday and Zeccara, who sprinted forward to the heavy chain-link fence.

With Zeccara pumping rapidly and Halliday holding the jaws, the light-weight hydraulic cutters made quick work of the steel ties holding the fence into the concrete at ground level. It took the two men less than a minute to cut through the ties along a fifteen-foot length between two main stanchions. Zeccara grasped the bottom strand of the fencing and heaved upwards until there was a two-foot gap; Halliday forced in a prop and Zeccara relaxed. The prop held; the others were already racing silently forwards.

Two hundred yards away, still lying in the gully, Ackford was watching through binoculars. 'They're through the fence,' he breathed to no one in particular. He turned to face Sumi, who was shivering hard from the chill of the night air on her soaking wet clothing. 'Not long now, miss,' he said reassuringly. 'We'll soon be inside. It'll be warmer in there.' He ignored Weatherill, who was crouched in a foetal position in the bottom of the gully, his teeth chattering and a haunted expression still on his face from his horrifying crawl down the pipe.

The five pairs of running feet made no sound on the concrete. Zeccara reached the door first and grasped the handle. At a nod from Ziegler he turned it smoothly and pulled, praying that there would not be a protesting squeak from the hinges. There wasn't. Ziegler moved swiftly into the open doorway and levelled his pistol; it coughed again, and a blond-haired man sitting twenty feet away crumpled forward soundlessly on to the desk in front of him. There was no one else in the entrance hall. The five men entered and spread out; Zeccara pulled the door closed behind him.

There proved to be only one other man awake, on duty in what appeared to be the communications centre. As Harris pulled open the door for Howard the man turned and instantly made a lunge for the pistol at his side. It was his last mistake; like the others, he died silently, slumping back in his chair. It had been the only room, apart from the hall and the stairwell to the first floor, showing any light. As well as radio and telecommunications equipment, Howard briefly noted a television monitor on the desk in front of where the man had been sitting; it was switched off. Leaving the body still slumped in the chair, Howard and Harris completed a swift search of the ground floor. All the rooms were empty.

Up on the first floor Ziegler, Halliday and Zeccara were working their way along the corridor, one room at a time. By the time Howard and Harris joined them they had already taken four prisoners. In each case, as the room light came on the man had woken abruptly to find himself staring into the barrel of Ziegler's pistol and ordered to silence by the sharply whispered command *'Ruho!'* Shocked and confused, the men were given no time to think. Within three seconds of waking they found themselves with their mouths taped shut, hands fastened behind their backs with self-locking plastic strips, and heavy black cloth bags over their heads to block out the light.

The sudden confrontation with a filthy, hard-eyed man brandishing a silenced pistol had robbed most of them of coherent thought. But one, a heavy-set bull of a man older than the others, tried to lash out with a kick. Something instantly hit him in the solar plexus with the force of a sledgehammer and he went down, gasping for air. The four men were herded together into one room and made to sit on the floor with black bags over their heads. Guarded by Halliday, a few seconds later they were joined by a fifth.

Harris was covering the stairway to the second floor. Ziegler, Howard and Zeccara completed their rapid search of the first, and found the remainder of the rooms empty. Then they silently began to climb the stairs to the next floor. Howard retained the mental picture he had formed of the interior layout of the building. Over the previous eighteen hours he had observed which lights had come on, and when; this suggested that there was a dormitory or common room of some sort at the top of the stairs on the right. He posted Harris and Ziegler outside it and took Zeccara with him to search the other rooms first. All were empty. Except for the large common room, the building was now clear.

The door swung open noiselessly, and all four men padded in. A line of beds was visible down each side of the room, and there were noises of breathing. The four spread out; Ziegler, nearest to the door, found the light switch. At a signal from Howard, he thumbed it on.

'*Aufwachen!*' bellowed Howard.

Only seven of the twelve beds were occupied; five figures instantly shot bolt upright, gazing uncomprehendingly at the intruders. A sixth rolled over, muttering a curse, while the seventh remained fast asleep.

'*Was ist . . .*' one man began.

'*Ruhe!*' snapped Howard menacingly. Faced with the four AKs levelled at them, the men raised their hands and stayed silent. Zeccara moved to the two who were still asleep. A sharp slap on the face of the first woke him. Staring at the rifle barrel inches from his face, then glancing at his companions, he too sat up. He rubbed his face, but said nothing. The last man received the same treatment; he had heard nothing as he had been wearing earplugs.

'*Aufstehen!*'

The seven prisoners obediently rose to their feet. Four of them were in their nightclothes; the other three were fully dressed apart from their boots, and Howard ordered them to undress to their underwear. All seven were then herded out of the room and downstairs to the first floor. 'Take them along to that big office at the end of the corridor, Mike,' ordered Howard. 'Have them all lie face down on the floor and put plasticuffs on them. Mel, you go with him. Angelo, you go and collect Tony and the others and give them a hand with the bergens. When everyone's inside the compound, take away the prop that's holding up the fence and push the wire back down into place so it looks normal.'

Howard rejoined Halliday downstairs; it was time to take a closer look at the first five prisoners. Since these men had separate bedrooms, they were likely to be more senior. One by one, Howard removed the black bags covering their heads, studying each face carefully before replacing the bag and moving on to the next.

The first man, sharp-eyed and middle-aged, wore an expression of defiance despite the alarm he was clearly feeling. Howard noticed that his left eyelid was trembling slightly with a nervous tic. He put the bag back. The second man was younger and thin-faced; plainly bewildered and fearful, his eyes flickered around the room. The third man was more interesting, thought Howard. Tall, blond and slightly built, he had pale, expressionless eyes and appeared completely calm. His eyes met Howard's steadily, giving no clue to his thoughts. The fourth man appeared sullen and anxious, and the fifth, the solid, older man whom Zeccara had flattened, looked plain murderous. The hood went back over his face.

Howard stood back and contemplated the five prisoners. 'Eeny, meeny, miny, mo,' he said aloud. He turned to Halliday and dropped his voice to a whisper inaudible to the captives. 'What do you think, Pete?'

'Number three,' Halliday whispered in Howard's ear. 'There's something about him. He's too controlled.'

'Yes,' whispered Howard. 'But number five seems to have a bit of spirit. I wonder.'

'Five's just hired muscle,' muttered Halliday, shaking his head contemptuously. 'A thug.'

'Well, we'll soon see,' said Howard aloud. 'Tony will be here in a minute. You stay here with them. Anyone moves, whack him.'

Howard made his way back down to the ground floor. The main door pushed open and Zeccara staggered in carrying two heavy bergens. Panting, he dropped them to the floor. Ackford followed with two more, then Sumi and Weatherill with one each. Zeccara disappeared to collect the last one.

'All OK, boss?' asked Ackford calmly, his jaw working on a stick of gum. 'How many have we got here?'

'Three dead including the two guards outside, and twelve prisoners upstairs. Go and bring in the two bodies, Tony.'

'No one downstairs?' asked Sumi. 'No,' she said. 'Probably not. Silly question – I'm sorry.'

'Downstairs?' Howard looked temporarily blank.

'In the basement.'

'Basement?'

'You haven't looked?'

Oh shit, thought Howard. His face betrayed his thoughts. *I didn't even think . . .*

'Tony! Belay that! Come with me!' He turned and raced off, Ackford following. He called over his shoulder. 'Sumi, you and Richard bring in those two bodies!'

Howard found the concealed door inside a small cupboard in a room off the main hall. He had looked inside the cupboard earlier himself, during his search of the ground floor; he mentally kicked himself for having missed the door. Carefully, he opened it; there were steps leading down. There seemed to be a strong smell of disinfectant wafting up from below; but with his own clothes still stinking from the drain-pipe he wondered whether he was imagining it. No light was showing at the bottom the the steps.

'Stay here, Tony,' he said. 'This was my mistake.'

Levelling his pistol, he slowly descended the steps. At the bottom was a light switch; he flicked it on and slowly poked his head round the corner.

There was the deafening noise of a single shot, and Howard felt a burning sting to his cheek. He rolled to the ground, facing down a long, dimly lit corridor, his pistol lined up and ready to fire. There was no one in view.

Ackford saw Howard flinch and dive to the ground, but he could just make out from the way Howard was lying, ready to fire, that he was not incapacitated. 'Are you OK, boss?' he called loudly. 'Boss? Hey – boss?' Ackford began to descend the steps. Twelve, thirteen . . .

On the fourteenth of the sixteen steps Ackford stopped, instead marking time with heavy feet to simulate the two remaining steps.

Howard's eyes glittered in the dim light. Tony was acting exactly correctly. The anxiety in his voice might just fool whoever had fired the shot into thinking that he had scored a hit. He waited, his heart thumping. *There!*

It was the slight movement of a shadow. Howard aligned his pistol, and a second later a figure moved smoothly from the recess of a doorway, firing a fast double-tap from a pistol at where Ackford's footsteps ought to have placed him. Howard's bullet struck home and the figure collapsed.

Howard lay still for a few seconds, listening for movement. He heard nothing, and wondered briefly about his next move. The normal procedure, which he knew would be as instinctive to Ackford as it was to him, would be for the two of them to clear the remainder of the basement together, working as a two-man team. He could see five doors along the left of the corridor, each presumably leading into a different room. He made a decision. 'OK, Tony,' he whispered. 'You go back up and join the others. I'll finish off down here.'

'But, boss . . .' Ackford was taken aback that Howard

was even talking. He knew as well as Howard did that clearing the remainder of the rooms would normally be carried out without any need for words – almost a routine matter, with only the occasional hand-signal or nod required.

'No buts, Tony,' hissed Howard. 'This was my fault. Stupid mistake for me to make, not thinking about a basement. I must be slipping. But it won't happen again. Off you go.'

Blind obedience to orders was not a natural part of Ackford's character. He was too experienced, and he knew the standard operating procedures as well as anyone. But he respected Howard, and now he was too surprised to argue further. Shaking his head in puzzlement, he disappeared back up the stairs.

Howard listened to him go, then rose silently to his feet. *Five doors,* he thought. *Handles on the left; five light-switches – one for each door – also on the left, at chest-height. Good.* He switched off the main corridor light.

In the dark, he moved soundlessly to the first door, feeling for its handle and light-switch. *Throw the door open, light on, inside fast, into the crouch.* The procedure took less than a second and was almost noiseless.

A boiler-room. A large stove, a pile of coal, an ashbin and a couple of shovels. A coal-chute, with a steel cover above it giving access from the outside. Nothing else. Light-switch off again. *One room down, four to go.*

The next door was heavier, clad with steel. Again, Howard was inside in less than a second, too quick for anyone inside to react effectively; but the room was empty. It seemed to have been constructed as a windowless cell, but it had been converted into a rudimentary laundry-room. It contained an old-fashioned washing-machine and some wooden clothes-racks with overalls and other garments draped over them. Otherwise, nothing. *Two down, three to go.*

The next two rooms also proved to be empty. *These cells will be useful for the prisoners,* thought Howard.

He approached the last door. *Are you in there, old man? Who are you, and will I kill you?* He paused, uncertain of the answers but aware that in a few seconds he might have to face up to them. He took a deep breath, pausing outside the door. Whether or not to kill the occupant of the cell would have to be a snap decision, or he knew he would not be able to do it. *You devious bastard, Goodale,* he thought savagely. *You've even got me going, deceiving my own men – sending Tony away so that he won't see me decide about whether or not to murder some anonymous old man.*

Howard banged the door open and snapped the light on, rolling inside, a filthy, nightmarish figure still reeking of death from the crawl through the drain-pipe.

Slowly, he lowered his pistol and stood up straight. *Thank God,* he thought. The last cell was empty too. *Thank God.*

As he turned to leave the cell the light illuminated the body lying outside in the corridor. Howard stared down at the face. 'Oh, damn,' he said, feeling suddenly empty. He knelt down.

The dead woman had short blond hair. She was slimly built, in her late thirties, he guessed. She was wearing dull-coloured overalls. His bullet had caught Dr Anna Linden just above the left eye, and she had died at once. 'Damn,' he repeated dully. Switching off the lights, he made his way back upstairs.

'Hey, boss, you're bleeding,' said Ackford a few minutes later. 'You OK?'

Howard put his hand to his cheek. 'Just a stone-chip, I think. From her bullet.'

'Her? It was a woman?'

'Yes. First one I've ever shot. Never thought I'd have to do that, somehow.'

'Not something you really expect, is it?' said Ackford awkwardly. 'Er . . . Is it any different?'

'No,' said Howard, his mind only half concentrating. 'Hard-looking bitch, anyway. OK, Tony, let's go. We'd better get on with finding out which of these jokers is in charge.'

Despite the shock they had received, eleven of the prisoners held their nerve and remained silent, refusing to answer any questions. The one exception was a squat, unintelligent-looking man who had volunteered the information that his name was Josef Kleinhoff. He was, Howard realised, unlikely to be of particular consequence since he had been one of those sharing the large dormitory on the second floor. There wouldn't be much point in talking to an obvious underling like Josef Kleinhoff. Or would there? Howard had a sudden idea.

'Mike – get Kleinhoff again. Bring him along to that big office at the end of the corridor on the first floor.'

'Sure.'

A few minutes later Kleinhoff was bundled into the office, looking bewildered and frightened. His sense of confusion increased as Howard cut off the plasticuffs binding his wrists.

'All right, Josef,' he said in German, 'go over and sit in that big chair behind the desk.'

Kleinhoff rubbed the red weals on his wrists. His perplexity was obvious, but he complied. He looked ill at ease as he lowered himself into the chair.

'Relax, Josef,' said Howard. 'Lean back in the chair. Come on, relax.' He gave an encouraging smile, and Kleinhoff leaned back as ordered. But the man looked far from relaxed; in fact he appeared thoroughly uncomfortable.

'Put your feet up on the desk, Josef.'

'*Aber* . . .'

'Do it!' barked Howard menacingly.

Slowly, the *Stasi* man did as he was told. Howard nodded and turned to Ziegler. 'OK, Mike,' he whispered, reverting to English, 'bring up the other six from the dormitory, one by one. Wheel each one in and then out again as soon as he and our friend here have had the chance to eyeball each other.'

Ziegler grinned in understanding. Two minutes later, the first of Kleinhoff's companions was bundled through the door. To his credit, the man gave only the slightest sign of surprise at seeing Kleinhoff lolling in the big chair with his feet up. Kleinhoff himself gave a weak smile of embarrassment and shrugged; then the man was led out again. The process was repeated for the other five men from the dormitory. It was obvious that Kleinhoff was utterly bemused; he could not see the point of it at all, but he was beginning to relax.

'Now the others,' said Howard. 'Same procedure.'

Kleinhoff stiffened as the first of the more senior *Stasi* men was brought into the room. The embarrassed smile froze into an expression of unease, and he moved his feet as if to take them off the desk. 'Leave your feet there, Josef,' snapped Howard as the officer was taken out again. 'Relax, remember?'

Kleinhoff was beginning to sweat. His increasing discomfiture was plain as the next man was brought in, and when the tall blond officer appeared he snatched his feet from the desk and sat bolt upright in the chair. Howard had been watching the tall officer's face; there was no expression on it at all. Ziegler marched him back out.

Howard gestured threateningly at Kleinhoff with his pistol. 'Feet up, Josef,' he growled. Reluctantly, the *Stasi* man obeyed.

The next man was brought in. Howard could see Kleinhoff's knuckles whiten as he gripped the arms of the chair; sweating freely, he now looked as tense and uncomfortable as anyone Howard had ever seen.

'Last one comin' up,' whispered Ziegler. 'Mr Muscles.'

As the older, bull-necked man appeared in the door, Kleinhoff could restrain himself no longer. He snatched his feet from the desk and leaped up as though he had received an electric shock, and stood stiffly to attention. 'My heartfelt apologies, comrade Gen—' His voice tailed off abruptly as he realised what he had said, and his jaw gaped open when he saw the murderous look on his commanding officer's face.

'OK, Mike,' said Howard with a smile, 'I think you can take Josef back downstairs. Better not put him with the others, though, or he'll be lynched when they find out what he's done. And send Tony up, would you? He and I are going to have a little word with the general.'

'Sure thing, Ed,' said Ziegler happily. He hauled the hapless Kleinhoff to his feet and fastened his hands again. Then he frogmarched him towards the door, pausing near the general. The older man's expression was one of implacable defiance. 'Pity, ain't it, General?' remarked Ziegler conversationally. 'You can't get good help these days, can you? Never mind – we'll look after old Kleinhoff here. Well,' – he looked at his watch – 'three-thirty in the mornin'. You have a nice day now, comrade!'

43

George McKinley had been dead for exactly forty-eight hours. It was a pity, really, thought Peter Kramer, that George had to die; he had cultivated his friendship for years for just such a purpose, but really he had quite liked the man. They had first met when they had both been programmers, working for the computer giant IBM. McKinley had straight away struck Kramer as a decent, friendly type; a little dull, perhaps, but assiduous and hard-working – in fact, in many ways the ideal employee.

In due course Kramer had left IBM, but he had kept tabs on McKinley and had been pleased when his former colleague had moved to a Washington computer consultancy firm. He had been even more pleased to learn that some of McKinley's consultancy work was with US government departments; it signified that his police record had to be a clean one, with nothing worse than the occasional traffic violation. There was only one potential problem – McKinley was homosexual. Kramer had nothing against gays; in fact he couldn't have cared less one way or the other. Fortunately, he had managed to dissuade McKinley from taking an active part in the gay rights movement. It hadn't been difficult. McKinley had seen the logic of keeping a low profile not only for the sake of his job, but also because he acknowledged that the more vocal and militant activists often did their cause more harm than good, alienating the rest of the population. In a sense, McKinley's homosexuality was actually an advantage – there was no wife or family cluttering up the scene. Certainly nowadays, with the Clinton administration taking a more liberal line on such matters, being homosexual was no longer the bar to some branches of public service that it once had been.

Yes, Kramer had decided: of all his acquaintances, George was the best choice for this job. He had known it immediately on being told where IRIS had to be planted. It was so much easier, if you wanted a false identity, to use someone else's real one. So, when he had heard that the *Stasi*'s unwitting agent in the White House was ready to act and facilitate the security pass, he had gone round to visit George McKinley and strangled him.

Kramer had briefly pondered the question of what to do with the body, and eventually decided to undress it and leave it in the chest-freezer in the basement of McKinley's house, along with one or two tell-tale clues to his homosexual lifestyle. The body would be found eventually, but the date of death would be impossible to determine and with luck the murder would be put down to a jealous lover. In any case, by then it wouldn't matter any more; Washington – and the world – would have been rocked to their foundations by an infinitely more important killing. Satisfied, Kramer filled in the application form in McKinley's name and signed it as instructed, then sent it off with a disguised photo of himself to the address he had been given. He had no idea who the White House contact was, but it must have been someone with a lot of influence. McKinley's details would have checked out squeaky-clean, Kramer knew, but these passes usually took some time to be processed. This one, and the job authorisation he needed, had arrived in less than thirty-six hours.

Kramer drew up in front of the heavy gates and waited for them to open. The marks left by the latest attempt to ram them were still clearly visible – twenty or more such attempts were made every year. In the 1980s the gates had been heavily reinforced; when they were closed, massive steel posts now rose from the ground to hold them in place. The gates were capable of withstanding an impact from a heavy truck travelling at speed; so too was the remainder of the White House perimeter which was protected by closely spaced reinforced-concrete posts and an eight-foot-high wire fence.

'First time here, Mr McKinley? OK,' said the security guard, 'just pull in over there, please, and we'll take a look in the back.'

'Sure,' said Kramer brightly, flashing an inane smile. He swung the van into the inspection bay, switched off the engine and climbed out. 'All yours,' he told the guard, smiling again as he opened the rear doors and stood aside. 'Careful what you touch, though – some of that stuff's real fragile.'

The guard was a member of the Uniformed Division of the Secret Service. Kramer was aware that the man would be well trained and would know his job, but he would not be of the same calibre as the hundred men assigned to the exclusive Secret Service presidential security detail – the men who provided round-the-clock close protection for the President, the Vice-President and their families. This man would be bored and stale with the routine, but he would be far from sloppy. Kramer had reasoned that success depended on presenting him with a series of irritatingly time-consuming minor breaches of procedure; that way, the major breach of security right under his nose would be overlooked.

The guard looked into the back of the van and rolled his eyes; it was packed almost to the roof with electrical and electronic equipment. Most of it was stacked neatly in racks, but there was a profusion of tools and cables strewn about the floor. He couldn't even guess what half the items were, and it would be impossible to search through them all. Why couldn't these maintenance guys ever turn up with just the gear they needed, he wondered crossly. 'Did you have to bring all that goddam stuff?' he snapped.

'You bet!' Kramer replied with annoying cheerfulness. 'You never know what you're going to need when you get a call-out – could find a whole lotta things need fixing!'

'Well, what exactly is it you've been sent to fix here?'

'One of these,' said Kramer, patting a large cardboard carton. 'New unit, to replace a faulty one. See? It's on the job sheet here.' He brandished the paper again.

'OK, let's have it opened up for inspection.'

'Sure!' said Kramer. He cut the seal on the carton and gently extracted the top piece of styrofoam packing. The black unit nestled in the box on the lower piece of packing. 'There she is!' he said proudly.

The guard bent forward to look. 'Oh, one of those,' he said, recognising immediately what it was. 'I'll need to look inside the casing. Open it up, please.'

'Sorry,' replied Kramer cheerfully. 'Can't be opened,

I'm afraid. Factory-sealed unit. Filled with inert gas. New model, see? You've already got one installed here, according to our records. All the old ones will be replaced eventually. Personally,' he confided, 'I'm not in favour of these new ones. Before, we used to get to service them ourselves – it isn't too complicated. Now, we aren't allowed to touch them – they have to go straight back to the manufacturer. I mean, look at it from my point of view. I'm a qualified technician on these things, and all I get to do now is replace a new unit and take the old one back for repair. That takes maybe a quarter of the time it used to, and pretty well anyone can do it. Sooner or later, once all these new units are standard, that's going to do guys like me out of a job, right?'

'Yeah, I suppose so,' said the guard disinterestedly. The idea of McKinley's impending unemployment was a matter of supreme indifference to him. 'OK. Park the van over there, in bay number 12. I'll have to get a dog over to check this out, and you'll need an escort.'

'Dog?' asked Kramer.

'Yeah. To check for explosives. Go park up over there in bay 12 and wait.'

'Sure,' said Kramer brightly.

He moved the van to bay 12, parked and sat waiting for the sniffer dog and its handler. He knew what would happen. Dogs weren't really all that smart, and it wasn't difficult to fool them. Or at any rate, it wasn't difficult to fool the combination of dog and handler. The carton containing the disguised IRIS unit had been placed right next to the spare wheel in the rear. Kramer had carefully placed a single 12-gauge shotgun cartridge – a spent one, naturally – in the recess beneath the wheel. The dog would go mad, because Kramer had smeared a tiny amount of commercial blasting gelignite inside the rim of the empty shotshell. He had prepared the cartridge a week before, wearing gloves, to ensure that by now no trace of the explosive remained on his hands, and he had used a pair of long-handled tongs to drop it into position in the van two hours ago. To the dog, the smell of the gelignite would be overpowering; it would mask the infinitely fainter scent of the single, sealed .221 cartridge in IRIS's gun-barrel. So the dog would find the shotshell and look pleased with itself, Kramer would look apologetic and say what an amazing dog, the security guard would give Kramer a standard dumb-ass reprimand about security and the dog-handler would drag the dog away. End of problem.

Ten minutes later, Kramer was congratulating himself on the accuracy of his prediction. The German shepherd dog had gone ape in the rear of the van and extra guards had come running, their weapons unslung. Kramer had been hard put to keep a straight face as the single empty shotshell was found to be the source of the dog's excitement. Observing the scathing looks on the guards' faces at his series of asinine remarks and questions, he knew the ploy had worked.

What idiots, thought Kramer as he waited for the guard who would escort him on foot into the grounds. He had expected rather better security procedures at the White House, of all places. In fact, he felt disappointed. He and Carl had gone to a lot of trouble to prepare the van and its contents for a thorough search, and yet no extra precautions had been taken after the discovery of the empty shotshell.

An X-ray inspection would have been interesting, thought Kramer; it would have proved his point that technology was only as good as the people who used it. Kramer had made a study of people trained to operate X-ray detection machines, and had expounded on his theory to Carl. Most operators were usually keen enough when they started out, and maybe they were even reasonably competent by the time they finished their training. But within a few weeks, what did you have? Just take one look at the average X-ray machine operator at an airport, he had said to Carl. Bored, overweight, half asleep, pissed off about the antisocial hours, wife-trouble as like as not, and couldn't really give a blind shit about the contents of yet another brightly-coloured kiddie's tote-bag with its teddy-bear, Game-boy, crayons, pop-up books and other cute 'junior-flyer' items which would be dropped on the floor of the plane for some poor slob of a cleaner to sweep up afterwards along with the paper towels, cellophane biscuit-wrappers, empty plastic drink-glasses and the rest. Or yet another woman's holdall, weighing maybe thirty pounds and large enough to hold everything a family of five might need for a week, crammed with enough leaking bottles of toiletries and chemical cosmetic crap to pollute an entire city block or induce major airframe corrosion. Or, for that matter, yet another executive's briefcase stuffed with mobile phones and all the other latest electronic shit, such as the dinky little computer the executive pretended he was going to use on the airplane and never actually did – either because he was too self-conscious about the guy in the next seat peeking and seeing that he was using a games program rather than the spreadsheet, or because he was already bleary-eyed from the free drinks in the business-class lounge, or because the air-stewardess wouldn't allow him to use it anyhow because it would fuck up the airplane's avionic systems, but she wouldn't put it quite like that, even though she wanted to.

It was simple, thought Kramer. IRIS's gun-barrel would have shown up on an X-ray picture, despite the other items packed around it – even despite the lead-lined casing – but it would be almost unrecognisable for what it was, and in any case the operator would not see it *because he would not be expecting to see it*.

Kramer sighed. It was a pity, he thought, that life wasn't more of a challenge sometimes. Why, he wondered, was it so easy to second-guess people? Why, just once in a while, didn't he encounter a really worthy adversary? It was so *boring*, coming up against half-wits and incompetents the whole time. Kramer realised that boredom was a major problem for him, and he knew that was the reason he liked to take risks.

There was an interesting paradox there, too, thought Kramer. People who liked to take risks were more likely to pull off a job than those who were over-cautious. Carl Berman was one of the most cautious men Kramer knew. If Carl had been here, he would have been sweating hard and paralysed with anxiety. It would have been quite hopeless to bring him along on a job like this – he would have had guilt written all over his face. Kramer recalled how Carl had behaved in the forest, when they had test-fired IRIS and that young backpacker had suddenly appeared from nowhere. Kramer had known what the outcome would be, just as Carl had. But what had Carl done? He had acted as suspicious and shifty as it was possible for anyone to be. If Carl had had his way, he would have shot the guy right away. Instead, Kramer had been friendly and talked to him, and had found out quite a lot of useful information – such as the fact that he would not be missed for a while and nobody knew where he had taken himself off to on his backpacking expedition.

Kramer had later bawled Berman out. Give the man an ordinary job, such as a straightforward killing, and there was no problem at all. But the minute you threw in a complication or anything unexpected, he started to twitch – it was in his nature. There wasn't much he could do about that, he reflected with a sigh.

In truth, Kramer realised, his mind had been elsewhere when he had chewed Carl out about his dumb behaviour. He had been thinking about the even dumber behaviour of young Chuck Anderson. The kid must have known, as soon as IRIS fired that shot, that he was going to die. It was inescapable. Anyone would have realised it, even someone really, terminally stupid. But young Chuck had seemed quite bright. So why had he panicked and run? He must have known there would be no point in it – the result would be the same in the end. Kramer had given him a unique opportunity – to see something really important, for the first and last time in his life, before he died. He had offered him the opportunity to look into the future, and see what was going to happen – to see the inevitability of the death of a major world figure, and to reflect briefly on the seismic international upheaval that would ensue. Did young Chuck really have no curiosity? Good grief – it was like being given a preview of Sarajevo 1914, or Dallas 1963, or . . . well, some pretty punchy political killing, anyway. Maybe not in the Golgotha AD34 league, but important, nevertheless. And what had young Chuck done, when given the chance of seeing a preview of history? He had turned and run, before he could see it. *Asshole*, thought Kramer dispassionately.

'Mr McKinley?' Another uniformed Secret Service guard had appeared next to the van, interrupting Kramer's thoughts.

'Oh, hi!' exclaimed Kramer chirpily. 'Yeah! George McKinley, at your service!' He climbed out of the van and patted the roof. 'My van. Parking bay 12, as instructed. Are you the security escort?'

'Your pass,' requested the guard imperturbably from behind his mirror-shades.

'Sure!' exclaimed Kramer, flourishing the brand-new pass. 'I got the job order here, too. By my reckoning, this replacement unit needs to go—'

'Unload just what you'll need from the van, please,' said the guard, ignoring him.

'You got it!' replied Kramer enthusiastically. Fastening a small tool-belt round his waist, he reached up and unstrapped an extending ladder from the roof of the van. 'Nice day, huh?' he said to the expressionless Secret Serviceman. The man did not reply. 'OK, tools, ladder, new boxed unit – that's it. Let's go, huh?'

The Secret Serviceman was studying the job order. He examined the accompanying diagram that showed the position of the faulty unit, then looked out across the grounds in front of the White House, frowning. 'Funny,' he said, 'I haven't seen mention in any report that one of these has gone down.'

'Well, someone must have reported it, right?' remarked Kramer, laughing inanely. 'I mean, these reports forms don't just fill out themselves, right? Hey, that's a good one!'

Moron, thought the Secret Serviceman, shooting Kramer a glance of contempt. 'Can the wisecracks, buddy,' he snapped.

'Sure,' said Kramer hastily, forcing a nervous smile on to his face. 'Sorry. Just trying to be friendly. Sorry.'

'Yeah, well, just shut the fuck up and follow me.' The Secret Serviceman led the way out across the open area.

Arrogant ape, thought Kramer as he lifted the ladder on to his left shoulder and picked up the carton containing IRIS. *Don't bother to lend a hand, will you?* He was grateful that he had fitted a carrying strap to the carton, which was heavy and would otherwise have been awkward to lift.

It seemed a long way across the grass to Kramer. The carton got heavier and heavier, and its carrying strap bit into his right hand. *Mustn't let it look as heavy as it really is*, he told himself, gritting his teeth.

Eventually the Secret Serviceman stopped beneath a tall tree and pointed upwards. 'That's the one on the order,' he said.

Kramer set down the carton gratefully, then the ladder. 'Right,' he said, looking up. About twelve feet above him was a black-painted casing almost identical in appearance to the one containing IRIS. He studied it thoughtfully, relieved to see that the mounting on the tree appeared sturdy and secure. A thick cable led down the tree-trunk and disappeared into the ground; it would run back, buried, to the main control point. 'Cable looks OK from here,' he said. 'Want to bet it's corrosion in the terminal? The shielding in the terminals on these old units isn't too great. Water gets in, and after a while you get corrosion, see?' He raised the ladder and extended it up towards the black box above. 'I'll go take a look.'

'You do that,' said the Secret Serviceman acidly.

At the top of the ladder, Kramer reached round behind the casing and unplugged the cable, leaving it hanging loose from the mounting; then he began to unfasten the casing itself. The first bolt came free; he pocketed it, then loosened the second. He swung the casing out on the loose second bolt and made a show of peering into the cable connector socket on the back. From a pouch on his tool-belt he extracted a small glass phial containing some blue crystals and a sticky liquid. Careful to shield his movements from the Secret Serviceman, he used a small spatula to smear some of the blue mixture into the socket; then he quickly replaced the glass phial and spatula in his tool-belt. 'I was right!' he called down. 'Corrosion! Just wait until you see it!' He finished unbolting the casing and lowered it gently to the ground on a length of nylon line, then came down the ladder himself. 'See!' he exclaimed triumphantly, pointing to the connection socket. 'Corrosion!'

The Secret Serviceman examined it apathetically. The socket looked a mess, he could see.

'Copper terminals and poor shielding, like I said,' the garrulous Kramer was saying. 'You don't want to touch that stuff. It's a mixture of copper sulphate and sulphuric acid. Eats away the terminals eventually. Caused by acid rain, over a period of time. Just compare that lousy shielding with what they have on these new units, and you'll see how it can happen.'

'I'll take your word for it,' said the Secret Serviceman. 'How about the cable? Does it need replacing too?'

'Nope,' asserted Kramer confidently. 'I just need to clean it up a little, is all. OK – now for the new unit.'

He carefully unpacked IRIS and fastened the nylon cord to a bracket on its side. 'Say, could you give me a hand with this?' he asked. 'I don't want it to bang against the tree on the way up. If you could just hold it like this, until I'm up there and can take the strain?' *Maximum danger time*, he was thinking. *If this guy takes a good look at it from this close up, he won't fail to see . . .*

The Secret Serviceman reluctantly obliged, holding IRIS steady on the ground and not showing any particular interest in it. He watched Kramer climb the ladder again.

As Kramer pulled on the rope, he realised he should have brought a pulley system to lift the device. IRIS seemed incredibly heavy, and his knuckles whitened with the strain of hauling it up. But with considerable effort, he managed to make it appear easy. Finally he grasped the bracket and hooked it over the top of the ladder.

Kramer saw that the Secret Serviceman had lost interest and was watching with only half an eye. He made a show of wire-brushing the cable connector clean, then he lifted IRIS into position on the tree clamp, inserted the bolts and tightened them. Reaching round the back, he inserted the cable into the connection socket; then he opened a small hatch on the side of the unit and flipped the microswitch inside. As he closed the little hatch he briefly heard the tiny humming noise as IRIS powered up; then he was climbing down the ladder again with a clatter, masking the noise. IRIS's built-in batteries would keep it going until mains power next came on. Then it would be recharged and the cycle would begin again the next day . . .

'All done!' he beamed at the Secret Serviceman as he reached the ground. He lowered the ladder. 'You're in business again! Eternal vigilance, huh?'

The Secret Serviceman gave Kramer a sharp look, but saw only an incurable babbler. 'Come on,' he said abruptly, leading the way back to Kramer's van.

Ten minutes later Kramer was driving away, whistling quietly to himself, his face otherwise expressionless. Behind him, high in the tree, IRIS had begun its endless, infinitely patient search for the target programmed into its memory. Its unblinking gaze scanned the grounds of the White House, waiting for its victim to make the appearance that would be his final one.

44

'Your name, please?'

'*Ich verstehe nicht.*' The general spat back the words contemptuously, appearing at once angry and unconcerned. In truth, he still felt slightly groggy from the punch. He had fought hard when Ackford grabbed him and started tying him down, but he was no match for the big man's sheer strength, and in any case his hands had already been bound by the plastic strip. Ackford had quickly tired of the general's kicking and struggling and had punched him just once, above the left eye. The fight had gone out of him at that point and he had put up no further resistance. He was now strapped into a heavy wooden chair that they had found in one of the basement rooms. His left eye was swollen and almost closed.

'That's no problem,' replied Howard, switching to fluent German. 'If you prefer to talk in your own language, that's perfectly all right as far as I'm concerned. I asked you for your name.'

The general let fly with a stream of angry abuse, his one good eye fixed on Howard's face.

'Did you say "arse fucker"?' asked Howard lightly. 'That's an odd name. I'm surprised you made it to general with an idiotic name like that. But actually,' he continued, 'I don't believe you. Let's not waste time any more, shall we? Your name is Reinholdt Erfurt, and you are now going to tell me all about your plans for the IRIS computer program.'

Shock was momentarily visible on the general's face. His jaw slackened slightly, then clenched again as he recovered. His thoughts raced. How had this Englishman discovered his name, and how had he known about the *Stasi* connection with the theft of IRIS? He collected his thoughts and spoke defiantly. 'You will learn nothing from me, Englishman.'

Howard's dark eyes glittered as he appraised the general's reaction. *That hit home*, he thought, as he pulled out a packet of cigarettes and a box of matches. *It won't take long before he realises we found his passport and got his name from that, but the mention of IRIS rattled him.* He lit the cigarette and drew deeply. 'Tony,' he said in English, his eyes remaining on the general, 'pass me that torch, please.' He slowly stood up. 'Hold his head and open his mouth, would you?'

Erfurt felt his head grasped from behind and pain shot through his jaw as Ackford forced his mouth wide open. He gave a strangulated roar of protest, but found himself unable to move at all. The Englishman's face was now only inches away from his and the torch snapped on as he peered into the general's mouth. *What on earth . . .?*

'Nice teeth, General,' said Howard calmly. 'You've taken good care of them. OK, Tony, you can let him close his mouth. But keep hold of his head, would you?'

Now what? wondered the general frantically. *The man is now feeling under my jawbone, like a doctor . . .*

'Tut tut, General,' said Howard, drawing again on his cigarette. 'You've got a swollen gland on the left side, just there. Can you feel it?'

The general could. He hadn't been aware of it until the Englishman's fingers had found it. It felt mildly uncomfortable, but that was all. He did not reply to the question. He saw Howard move round to the left, and felt the slight heat of the torch near that ear.

'Aha!' exclaimed Howard, satisfied. 'That's the cause of it. You've got an ear infection. Looks quite nasty. Are you taking antibiotics for it? You should be, you know.'

The general was thoroughly bemused. What on earth was all this nonsense? All right, so he had an ear infection. He had half-suspected it – the ear had been feeling sore ever since the long flight from Tangier with Hislop. It was probably just blocked with wax. He never took medicines unless he had to. But what the hell was the Englishman playing at?

Howard snapped off the torch and moved round to face the general directly again. The German saw that his calm, appraising expression had been replaced by a hard, menacing stare. 'Tell me about IRIS, General.'

Erfurt said nothing, staring back defiantly.

'Very well,' said Howard. 'But you'll soon change your mind. Keep his head still, Tony.' He moved round to the side again and took another match from the box. Holding it between his forefinger and thumb, he inserted it gently into the general's ear. Then he pushed, though not very hard.

Excruciating pain suddenly shot straight through the general's head. He was dimly aware of the sound of his screaming. Every muscle in his body fought to twist away from the hideous pressure in his ear, but he could not move. Then, suddenly, the terrible pain eased, to be replaced by a fierce, throbbing ache. After a few seconds he opened his eyes to see Howard seated in front of him.

'You see what I mean, General? Earache can be very painful, can't it? I had a bad case of it once myself, so I know what it can be like. Now tell me about IRIS, please, and you won't have to go through that again.'

'I don't know anything about it,' gasped the general. 'I don't know what you're talking about.'

'Suit yourself.' Howard moved round to the side

again.

The pain was if anything even worse than before, like a fireball inside his head – a deep red, burning, shrieking fireball . . .

'Save yourself some discomfort, General,' said Howard when the screaming had stopped again. 'We know you have IRIS, or that one of your *Stasi* groups overseas has it. Your organisation is being paid by the Iranian government to kill someone. The IRIS machine will recognise that person and set off a bomb when he is nearby. All I want to know is who that intended victim is, and where the device will be planted.'

'Please,' gasped the general weakly, desperately trying to think, to play for time. The assault on his ear had sapped him of all his strength and he was pouring with sweat. *One can force oneself to ignore pain from a leg, or an arm*, the general realised, *but when it is right inside your head* . . . 'Wait!'

'Take your time, General.'

The general had seized on one small hope. It was not much, but it was something. His mind forced itself to concentrate. He knew, if this went on, that he would soon crack completely unless he passed out first. No one could withstand that sort of pain for very long, and he had so far only suffered a few seconds of it. But the Englishman had made a mistake – a fatal mistake. It gave the general some courage, and his thoughts whirled as he wondered how he might exploit it. He exaggerated his panting and moaning as he realised how he would have to play it. Dully, he opened his one good eye, and looked at Howard. 'All right. I'll tell you what I know,' he muttered finally.

Howard's expression did not change. *Easy questions first*, he thought. *Once someone has started to give information, even minor details, the floodgates open.* 'Your name and rank?'

'Reinhold Erfurt, Lieutenant-General.'

'You command this *Stasi* group?'

'Yes.'

'Why are you based in North Korea?'

'It is a secure – we thought it was a secure base for our operations. Also, we have a security contract with the North Korean government at the Yŏngbyŏn complex.'

'Where are your other cells?'

'We have four or five in every major European country. More in the Americas and the Far East.' The general knew that a key question would come soon. The Englishman was clearly not an expert interrogator, but even he would be able to see that his prisoner was recovering his wits. *I must lie only when necessary,* thought Erfurt, *and I must not hesitate. That must wait for when I have to tell an obvious lie . . .*

'We'll come on to precise details of the cells later,' said Howard.

'It will do no good,' said the general immediately. 'I don't know exactly where they all are. Surely you must know that. We have a system of cut-outs. If I want something done I contact one of the cut-outs, or he contacts me.'

Howard nodded slowly. To debrief this man fully, he knew, would take a long time – time he did not have. He was keenly aware that knowledge of the details of *Stasi* cells worldwide would be of immense importance to the West, but he had to concentrate on what he had been sent specifically to find out. 'Who stole the IRIS computer program?'

'One of the cells based in England,' said the general immediately. *My first lie,* he told himself. *A simple enough one, and this Englishman should swallow it.*

'What did they do with it?'

The general hesitated, aware of what would follow. He steeled himself, telling himself that under torture he could let go with this one – it was not vital. It was a test. 'It was sent abroad to another cell. I don't know exactly where.'

The matchstick ground into the general's eardrum like a giant, white-hot tongue of vivid poisonous flame. Through his screams he heard himself repeat the name over and over again. The pain subsided; the general thought he had passed out.

'Did you say the USA, General?' asked Howard implacably.

'Yes,' croaked the general. He did not think he had the strength to endure any more torture, but knew that this time it had been necessary. The Englishman would think it important because he had resisted, but it was not as important as the things he *really* had to conceal. 'The USA,' he repeated.

'Give me details of your people who are working on this,' snapped Howard.

'I know . . . of them, of course,' answered the general weakly, 'but I don't know exactly where they are, nor the aliases they are using. I told you, there are cut-outs. We are organised that way!' *Second lie,* thought the general. *Dear God, let him believe it.* 'Please, some water!'

Howard was unsure. Was the man lying? He did not know, but thought he probably was. His hand went to the pulse beneath the general's jaw. It was racing dangerously fast, and the general was no youngster. Howard exchanged a glance with Tony Ackford, who was still bracing the general's head against movement. He saw Ackford shrug, reading his thoughts. *I dunno either, boss,* the big man seemed to be saying.

'You may have some water when you have finished answering my questions,' said Howard. 'Next question: who is the target to be killed?'

'We don't know that yet,' groaned the general. *Please, God, make him believe that lie, the third one.* 'We have not yet been told. All we know is that a VIP will be visiting the USA soon, that he will be easy to recognise, and that he must be killed. We will be told nearer the time who it is. It is easy, I am told, to program IRIS with any picture.' *Half-truth, half-lie. Get the agony of the truth over with, so I can lie again . . .*

Howard regarded the general closely. The man was almost done for. There were three more questions he had to ask, but the third was peripheral and could wait. 'Where will the device be placed?' he asked.

'I don't know that,' answered the general immediately, his voice almost inaudible. *The fourth lie. Thank God, the third lie, about the identity of the victim, seemed to have worked.* 'How can I know it, when I don't even yet know who the target is, or where he will be travelling? These details will be left to the discretion of the cell concerned, when I am in a position to pass on the person's identity to them nearer the time.' *Oh, God*, thought the general. *Even if he believes that, I will now have to lie again in a manner which will be obvious, and then tell another lie, the fifth, under torture, which must sound like the truth.* He slumped in the chair, his head still held in Ackford's rock-like grip. His jaw hung open.

'How will the IRIS device operate in practice, General?'

Erfurt mustered sufficient strength to close his slackened jaw. He opened his good eye and fixed it blearily on the implacable face of the Englishman in front of him. He licked his lips in an attempt to moisten his mouth. 'It will alert our assassination team,' he said. 'They will need notice of the target's arrival. IRIS is not competent to do any more than that.' He swallowed, knowing what would now happen. *Oh, God*, he thought, *give me strength, just once more. Lie.*

Howard's eyes had narrowed. He disappeared from the general's blurred field of vision.

A gigantic, hideous, slow-burning napalm fire seemed to light up in the general's head as the matchstick pressed hard into his infected left eardrum. Through his agony he faintly heard himself scream one phrase over and over again. *I have won,* he thought, just before he passed out. *The Englishman made a mistake and he still doesn't know it. I have won.*

'He's flaked out, boss,' stated Ackford unnecessarily as the general's body went limp. 'What was that he was shouting? Something like "automatic bomb", was it?'

'Yes,' said Howard in a low voice. 'What he told us previously – about IRIS alerting an assassination team – was nonsense. IRIS will recognise the target itself, and will automatically set off a bomb.'

Ackford's jaw worked slowly on his wad of chewing gum as he looked curiously at Howard, whose face seemed to have turned a little pale. 'Are you OK, boss?'

'Not really,' replied Howard, turning towards the door. 'I don't think I was cut out for doing this,' he muttered weakly. 'Come on, Tony. Leave the bastard strapped into the chair for the time being. We'd better go and keep the radio schedule.'

45

Colonel Yevgeny Barushkin was not anticipating any trouble this time. There was no point, after all, in baiting the North Koreans and making life any more difficult than necessary. This time he was sticking firmly to the flight plan and course that had been filed and cleared with P'yŏngyang. Naturally, the compass was giving a correct reading – it had been recalibrated and double-checked before leaving Vladivostok with the replacement cargo of gifts for the lying filth who ran this vile country.

Barushkin was looking forward to hearing what had happened to the MiG-25 pilot who had buzzed him on the first occasion, but he didn't really hold out much hope that he would be told. He would ask, though – he would make a point of it. He might even make a snide inquiry about the state of health of the unpleasant political commissar whom he had felled with that magnificent punch. After all, thought Barushkin, he was bound to come across that grey-haired North Korean Intelligence colonel again. And when he did, he had something up his sleeve, something that would startle the man – or, at any rate, unsettle him. He knew his name.

Yes, Colonel Zang, Barushkin said to himself. *I know who you are. I looked you up. Or, at least, my friend Sasha Plasnin did, as soon as I identified you from an old photograph. You have a big, fat file in the KGB's archives. I've read it.* He smiled to himself in the dark of the Antonov's cockpit as he prepared to make his turn to starboard and in towards the North Korean coastline.

Instead of flying in a straight line from Vladivostok to P'yŏngyang, the course that had been agreed for this trip was a dog-leg. The first leg went further to the south than before, roughly parallel to the coastline, out over the Sea of Japan; then there was a turn to starboard into Tongjosŏn Bay, making landfall over the Hodo peninsula and the Yŏnghŭng Delta; and finally westwards to Sunan. The lights of Wŏnsan, Okp'yong, Ch'ŏnnae and Yŏnghŭng itself were hardly impressive, but they were now clearly visible as Barushkin piloted the big Antonov in towards the coast.

He was five miles from the coast when he saw the flash of light on the ground dead ahead. It came from Panggumi, on the Hodo peninsula itself. As he watched, the light source began climbing into the sky, gathering speed at an incredible rate. For about half a second he groaned to himself, *Oh God, not another of those fucking MiGs* . . .

Then his blood froze. There was no airbase on the Hodo peninsula!

'*Missile!*' screamed Barushkin into the intercom, ramming the control column forward and putting the Antonov into a sudden, steep dive. He hoped to God that Sasha, in the rear, would realise what had to be done: open the rear doors and jettison the cargo when he pulled out of the dive. But even as he watched, he knew there would be no time. The white-hot pencil of flame had already reached twenty thousand feet and had turned, now heading straight for the Antonov . . .

The missile was an RK-SD-type surface-to-air weapon, nineteen feet long and just over thirteen inches in diameter, weighing 1276 pounds. It had a range of up to fifteen miles and an altitude ceiling of just over 47,000 feet. The RK-SD was not a smart missile of the 'fire-and-forget' type which locked on to a target and did everything for itself; it relied instead on a ground-base fire-control radar system. Nevertheless, it had proved itself highly effective since its introduction into service with the Soviet armed forces almost thirty years before. The missile had made its first appearance in the November 1967 parade in Red Square, and the apprehensive NATO authorities had immediately given it the designation 'SA-6 Gainful'. Guided by the ground-based SSNR G/H/I-band fire-control radar, it now homed in on the Antonov at a speed which the lumbering cargo plane could never hope to outrun.

The Antonov was diving almost vertically downwards, its engines screaming. Barushkin craned forward in his seat, the veins in his neck bulging in fury and desperation, and looked upwards through the top cockpit window. He saw his nemesis arrowing down towards him at more than two thousand miles per hour. In a final, all-or-nothing manoeuvre he used all his strength to yank the control column back and to the left.

There was a cracking, splintering sound from the Antonov's air-frame, clearly audible even above the howling engines. Barushkin, pressed heavily down into his seat by a G-force that the Antonov was never designed to withstand, felt himself blacking out. There was a roaring sound in his ears, but over it he heard a dull crash and brief scream, abruptly cut off, from somewhere behind him. The Antonov lurched heavily with an unexpected and violent twisting motion which flung Barushkin sideways in his seat, crashing his helmet into the left-hand cockpit window.

A sudden, white-hot flash of light and a violent explosion punched into the tortured aircraft. The right-hand side of the cockpit seemed to disintegrate and Barushkin saw his co-pilot's head explode in a shower of blood. Dimly aware that he was still alive himself, Barushkin fought the controls as the Antonov began to spin downwards.

The missile had been fitted with a proximity-fused fragmentation warhead containing 176 pounds of high explosive. Barushkin did not know it, but he had managed to achieve something which only a very select few pilots, and certainly no pilot of any cargo aircraft, had ever managed to do without employing electronic counter-measures: he had thrown an SA-6's guidance system into confusion. When he had lurched the Antonov to the left, the straps holding the cargo pallets in place in the rear had snapped under the enormous strain and the heavy pallets, now loose, had slammed violently against the starboard side of the cavernous cargo bay. The plane, now massively unbalanced, immediately adopted the aerodynamic characteristics of a lump of concrete, spinning briefly on its lateral axis and slowing momentarily as the air resistance buffeted violently against its no longer aerodynamic surfaces. One of the main starboard-side wing spars snapped, but the remainder, astonishingly, held. The SA-6's radar proximity-fuse had already acquired the target and had taken over from the ground-based guidance system, but the missile was fractionally slow in compensating for the sudden lurch of the Antonov. It overshot the target, exploding three hundred feet beyond it.

Somehow, Barushkin realised, he had survived. The explosive decompression of the cabin was the least of his problems as he wrestled with the now mushy controls, fighting the lumbering, wallowing Antonov. As he slowly regained control and put the aircraft into a gentle dive, turning back out to sea, he was keenly aware of only one thing – it had all happened so fast that there had not even been time to transmit a 'mayday' message.

As he groped blindly for the radio transmit switch, Barushkin was unaware that he was the only man left alive on the Antonov. Alexander Plasnin had been killed instantly by a two-ton pallet which had squashed him against the side of the cargo bay. The aircraft's navigator and flight engineer, like the co-pilot, had been killed by fragments of the missile warhead.

Barushkin found the transmit switch, but as he pressed it he was unaware that a second SA-6 missile was streaking up towards him. The plane, in a gentle dive, made a simple target and this time there was no mistake. Before Barushkin could utter a word over the radio he and the shattered pieces of his Antonov were flaming down towards the sea, ten thousand feet below.

Two minutes later and one hundred miles away to the west in P'yŏngyang, a telephone shrilled. A small, grey-haired man picked it up and listened to the brief report he had been expecting; then he replaced the receiver without a word and allowed himself a thin smile. *The noose is tightening round your necks, Englishmen,* mused Colonel Zang. *Your Russian escape route has just been closed – permanently.*

46

Howard was aware that his radio transmission to Bourne had been extremely uninformative. He imagined Bourne and Goodale sitting in their Seoul hotel room, groaning in frustration. *Well*, he thought, *too bad*. He was feeling frustrated himself. He was fairly sure that General Erfurt had been holding back some information – it would be in the man's nature, however desperate he would have been for the pain in his ear to cease. In a way, he admired the general's stubborn resistance; it had just been a damned nuisance that the man had passed out when he had. Tony Ackford had thrown a bucket of water over him, but it had made no difference – he was out for the count. They would just have to wait until he came round of his own accord. Then, if he still refused to divulge the name of the assassination target, they would have to interrogate his second-in-command, Colonel Eisner.

Howard had a slightly uneasy feeling about Eisner, who seemed a cooler, much more analytical character than the hot-tempered general. In some ways, thought Howard, he was probably the more formidable of the two. It was difficult to tell what Eisner was thinking. That bland, expressionless face gave absolutely nothing away – not even surprise. Well, thought Howard savagely, one of them would bloody well have to give something away. He had no intention of leaving this place empty-handed.

He thought again about the scant information that they had so far gleaned from the general. He had been able to pass on to Bourne the knowledge that IRIS was in the United States, for what that was worth; that the assassination was due to take place soon; and that the victim was distinctive in appearance. The last piece of information was possibly the most interesting, he decided; but what did it mean? Was the victim an albino, or totally bald, or hugely fat? Or did he have a large scar on his face? Whatever the distinguishing characteristic was, it made the puzzle an interesting one. But in the meantime it was also frustrating, just sitting and waiting for Bourne's reply.

The radio blinked briefly to life. Howard waited as Pete Halliday donned his earphones and replayed the high-speed burst transmission at normal speed. He watched over Halliday's shoulder as he began to transcribe the message onto a signal pad, writing rapidly in pencil.

DTG1ØØØ355N SEPT ⊙ JB TO EH ⊙ ONE ⊙ TKS YR MSG ⊙ KEEP TRYING ⊙ IF UNOBTAIN VICTIM ID CMM DATE AND LOC OF ATTEMPT WD HELP ⊙ TWO ⊙ COL G REMINDS ASK ABOUT OLD MAN ⊙ THREE ⊙ REGRET TO INFO THAT YR RUSS TPT DELIB DESTR IN FLT BY NKAF MISSILES CMM PROB TWO SA6 ⊙ AWACS CONFIRMS ⊙ IN CIRCS NO POSS REPLACE ⊙ FOUR ⊙ MUST THERFOR BE POSS NKS NOW AWARE YR MISSION ⊙ FIVE ⊙ WE ARE INVESTIG POSS ALTERNATE ROUTES OUT BUT PSE INFO ME YR IDEAS ASAP ⊙ ENDS ⊙

Halliday finished writing. He and Howard looked at each other, aghast. The news of the destruction of the Antonov, and the deaths of its crew who had become friends, was numbing.

Halliday was the first to break the silence. 'How could they have known, boss?' he asked, horrified. 'How the hell could the NKs have known about the Antonov? Is their Intelligence that good?'

'I don't know, Pete,' Howard replied slowly. 'But I can tell you one thing for certain. If it's the very last thing I ever do, I'm going to find out.' He rose slowly to his feet, his expression dark and murderous.

The door banged open. Tony Ackford entered, his expression grim. 'Boss, you'd better come,' he said.

'What is it?' asked Howard.

'It's the general,' replied Ackford. 'I went back up to check him. He's still strapped in that chair.'

'Well? Hasn't he come round yet?'

'No. And he won't, either. He's fucking dead.'

47

Ziegler, Ackford and Halliday received the news of the shooting down of the Antonov in sombre silence. As Ziegler caught Howard's eye, the obvious question was written on his face.

'So,' said Howard, 'we'll just have to think of another way out, once we're finished here. In theory we can get out by air, sea or land. Let's take air first.' He paused to light a cigarette and inhaled deeply. 'It might be possible to steal an aircraft – preferably an AN/2, a slow-flying type with a very small radar signature – and fly it out. Probably the best route would be westwards across the sea. There are some outlying islands about twenty-five miles away which are under UN control. In theory, once we reached there we would be OK.'

'And in practice, boss?' prompted Halliday.

'In practice there are problems. The first is that we'd have to find an unguarded aircraft. The second, which the NKs have so convincingly demonstrated, is that their air defences are pretty tight. The third is that they aren't squeamish about using them. If they're prepared to shoot down a Russian Air Force plane, I imagine they'd be quite happy to have a go at us even if we managed to make it to UN territory. But the fourth factor is the conclusive one, I think.' Howard drew again on his cigarette and shrugged. 'Unfortunately, none of us can fly a plane.'

'Yeah, well, that sort of decides it, doesn't it?' commented Ackford caustically. 'Unless we can find ourselves a spare Nik-Nok pilot and ask him nicely if he'll help us out.'

Howard smiled wryly. 'I know how persuasive you can be, Tony. But I really don't think it's a starter. Now for the option of getting out by sea.' He ground the butt of the cigarette beneath his boot. 'I know I decided against this as a way into the country, but in these circumstances we've got to consider it again. One of the Navy's ultra-quiet Upholder-class submarines might – I say might – have a chance of nosing into the coastline, and maybe – just maybe – an SBS team might get a boat party ashore to pick us up. All I can say is that the chance of their remaining undetected by the NK hydrophone arrays would be small – perhaps twenty-five per cent. The chance of getting away again afterwards would be even smaller.'

'Hell, Ed,' interjected Ziegler. 'We're not accountable. That's the whole point, isn't it? Your government guys are never goin' to commit their forces to helpin' us!'

'True,' said Howard. 'And that's not all. There are two other problems with the sea option. First, it would take a long time to set up – I don't think it would be possible to get a submarine on station for another week or more. You might think we could simply sit here until we get the word to move, but that's not on. These *Stasi* people have some sort of security contract with the North Koreans, and when they don't show up the NKs are going to wonder why. As soon as they do, they'll come looking for them to see what's gone wrong. And you can forget about leaving here and disappearing off to some hideout for a week. As soon as these *Stasi* guys get free they're going to raise a squawk, and the country will be turned upside down until we're found.' Howard frowned suddenly. 'In fact, I think they may be doing that already. I don't know how, but I think that somehow the North Koreans have already got wind of the fact that we're in the country. Pete,' he said, turning to Halliday, 'are you quite sure there's no possibility that our radio signals are being monitored?'

'No chance at all,' replied Halliday. 'I know they're good, but they'd never have got us with this LPI technology. I know that only stands for *low* probability of intercept, but it really should be ZPI – for zero probability. First of all, it's EHF, not HF, with a frequency band measured in gigahertz. The dish antenna shoots it straight up in a narrow beam to a polar-orbit Comsat. That's why it's simplex only, and why there's a delay of up to ninety minutes, while it waits for the satellite pass, before it transmits or receives. An aircraft directly overhead at the moment of transmission might pick something up if it was carrying the right equipment, but nothing else could. Also, the burst transmissions are incredibly fast. And as if that isn't enough, the frequency-hopping facility works every tenth of a second. There's no kit in the world that can follow that on EHF, let alone get a DF on it.'

'OK,' said Howard, happy to leave the details to the expert. 'They certainly can't have got a DF on us, anyway. They obviously don't know exactly where we are, or they'd already have come for us. But they do know something's up. Think of the evidence. There was Sasha Plasnin's report that security at Sunan airfield was increased. There's the evidence of our own eyes of all the military activity we've seen around here. And then the Antonov was shot down. Even if the NKs found the four grunts Mel skewered, plus their dog and their jeep, that wouldn't explain it. And we didn't leave any evidence behind at the DZ.' Howard shook his head, 'The more I think about it, the more I reckon we've got to get out of here – and fast. Within twenty-four hours. And the only way we have any chance of doing that is to do the thing the NKs would least expect – go overland.'

'Which direction?' asked Halliday. 'North or south?'

'North means either China or Russia,' answered Howard. 'China would be easier – it's nearer, and there's a long border. But the Chinese would hand us straight back – that is, if they didn't lock us up or shoot us first. As for Russia, there's only a very short stretch of border between it and North Korea. Also, it's more than five hundred miles away from here, right up in the north-east – not far from Vladivostok, in fact. Now Vladivostok's the home of the Russian Pacific Fleet, so not surprisingly it's one of the country's most sensitive and closely guarded areas. Worse than that, the border itself runs down the middle of a very large river – the T'umen. It's heavily patrolled and very exposed. After what's happened to the Antonov, I don't think the Russian border guards will be taking chances with incursions from North Korea. We're just as likely to get shot by them as invaders as by the NKs themselves for attempting to escape. No, I think we can forget the north,' he said finally.

Ziegler rolled his eyes. 'I knew it,' he said drily. 'We're goin' south. Terrific. Ed?' he yawned, 'just how many NK troops did you say there were between here and the demilitarised zone on the border?'

'Well,' answered Howard with a wry smile, 'at the last reported estimate there were about three-quarters of a million of them.'

'Great odds,' said Ziegler. 'One of us for every hundred thousand of them. I can understand your thinkin' when you say they won't be expectin' us to go that way. Didn't you say somethin' about barbed wire? Minefields? Artillery, too? Little details like that?'

'Yes, I did,' said Howard. 'The NKs have all of those things on their side of the border. But don't forget,' he added with a grin, 'the South Koreans have minefields and other defences on their side, too.'

'Well, it sure as hell is reassurin' to hear that,' drawled Ziegler. 'Yeah, that takes a big weight off my mind. If the eight of us somehow manage to make a journey of a hundred and fifty miles, sneak past three-quarters of a million hostile soldiers, dodge an Army corps-sized barrage of artillery shells and tiptoe across the DMZ avoidin' all those North Korean mines, it's real comfortin' to know that we'll wind up being zapped by South Korean ones instead. I'm sure their mines are much more user-friendly. I bet they've got little notices on them in three languages sayin' somethin' like "This here mine was made in South Korea. Sorry about your foot, but have a nice day."'

The door opened as if on cue, and Zeccara entered. 'What are you buggers grinning about?' he asked lightly. 'Mel's just told me. Doesn't sound good, does it?'

'No,' Howard replied. 'Any more bad news?'

'Road traffic's as heavy as ever – in both directions,' answered Zeccara. 'Mel's keeping an eye on it.'

'What are the others doing?'

'Sumi and the doc went to clean themselves up. I wouldn't mind doing the same – I'm beginning to wonder whether I'll ever get the stench of that dead cat or whatever it was out of my nostrils.'

'What about the prisoners?'

'All locked up in the cellars,' said Zeccara. 'I've just checked them.'

'Any luck with the files? Found anything interesting?' Zeccara, as one of the team's German-speakers, had been helping with this task.

'Not yet,' he replied. 'They all seem pretty routine to me. You know what I think, boss?'

'What?' asked Howard.

'Well,' said Zeccara, 'I may be wrong, but it's almost as if someone knew we were coming. I mean, we achieved surprise when we took this place, but there really isn't anything of interest in the files I've seen. And we've torn this bloody place apart. I reckon the important papers are hidden somewhere else.'

For a few minutes Howard remained silent, deep in thought. 'That's an interesting idea, Angelo,' he muttered finally, 'but I can't really see how anyone here could have been forewarned of our arrival, unless . . .' He frowned, then dismissed the thought. 'In the meantime, we've got a job still to do. All we know so far is that the assassination is due to take place in the USA, in Washington, DC.' He turned to Halliday. 'By the way, Pete,' he asked, 'did that signal go off OK?'

'Without a hitch, boss,' Halliday confirmed. 'In fact, Johnny acknowledged it from Seoul a few minutes ago. He's passed the info on to the Americans already.'

'Good,' said Howard. 'It's not much, but it's something. Even so, we're going to have to find out more than that.' He paused to light another cigarette, then turned to Ackford. 'OK, Tony,' he said. 'Let's get Colonel Eisener up here. I think it's time we had a word with him.'

48

Marvin Jefferson was forty-seven years old and overweight. He was a big man, standing six feet three inches tall and weighing two hundred and thirty pounds. His weight had increased by fifteen pounds in the months following his wife's untimely death five years previously, and he had never been able to lose it again. He was resigned to the fact that he would never lose those extra pounds, but in truth he didn't really mind. In a way, his heavyweight appearance suited him. The extra pounds hadn't all gone into a beer-gut, jowls and flab; it was evenly distributed – his arms, chest and legs were heavier too. In many ways, Marvin just looked well-muscled, in rather the way a night-club doorman did, and he did not consider that to be any disadvantage. In Marvin's job, it was sometimes a positive asset to possess an impressive physique. He had a square, pugnacious face with a powerful jaw, flattened nose and deep-set, grey eyes; his wavy blond hair, greying at the temples, was cut short. He looked business-like and authoritative; people usually thought twice about arguing with him, and that suited Marvin just fine.

Besides, Marvin told himself, if he lost weight, he

would just have to buy himself seven new suits in a smaller size, and there was plenty of wear still left in the ones he had, especially the dark blue one he wore on Sundays.

Marvin's other six suits were dark grey; they were all identical, and he wore a different one every day. Each suit had a label inside it with the day of the week on it, so he would know which one to put on in the morning. The same went for his seven shirts, which were all white; his ties, which were all dark blue; his socks, which were black; and his highly polished shoes, which were also black.

J. Edgar Hoover would have approved of Marvin Jefferson. In fact, J. Edgar Hoover once had approved of him, in 1970, when Marvin had passed out of the FBI National Academy and graduated as an FBI Special Agent. The final test for all new Special Agents was an interview with the Director himself, and the procedure hadn't altered for decades. Marvin had lined up with his other classmates and one by one they had filed past, shaking the great man's hand, having first taken care to wipe their palms to ensure they were dry. 'Hello, Mr Hoover, my name is Marvin Jefferson,' he had said, just as he had been briefed to do. Hoover had not uttered a word, but each man had felt the Director's eyes drilling into him. It had all been over in less than five minutes, and Marvin had only seen Hoover once more before his death two years later.

Since then the strict FBI dress code had relaxed somewhat, but Marvin had never bothered to change his ways. He had enough to think about, he told himself, without having to decide what outfit to wear each day.

Marvin Jefferson's twenty-three-year record with the FBI had been one of solid, steady achievement, punctuated with occasional flashes of intuitive brilliance which had resulted in some outstanding successes. His superiors gradually came to realise that Marvin was someone whom they appreciated having around. He could always be relied on to do a good job, and every now and then he would come up with something which turned a good job into a great one. He wasn't flashy, he wasn't showy, he wasn't pushy, he got on well with his colleagues, and he was uncontroversial. He could be obstinate and outspoken, but usually only when he was convinced he was right about something – and then he usually *was* right about it. The rest of the time, Marvin just got on with the job.

Today, wearing his Sunday dark blue suit, Marvin Jefferson was seated across the desk from Louis J. Freeh, the recently appointed Director of the FBI. Jefferson and Freeh had known each other since 1980, when Freeh had moved from New York to Washington to supervise the organised crime unit. Freeh had left the FBI the following year, moving back to New York to become an assistant US attorney, but he had continued to work closely with the Bureau. In 1991 he had been appointed a federal judge in New York.

Following his dismissal of FBI Director William S. Sessions, President Clinton had appointed Freeh to the post on 20th July. Jefferson liked Freeh and greatly admired his ability; he had been quietly delighted when the appointment had been made, but now he listened to what Freeh was telling him with a mounting sense of dismay.

Jefferson had always been one to keep in the background and had never wanted a high-profile role. Now he was effectively being told that he was being put in charge of what could amount to an exceptionally high-profile case – especially if something went wrong. 'Sir, this sounds more like a job for the Secret Service,' he protested eventually. 'They're supposed to deal with security for visiting VIPs, aren't they?'

'Well, yes and no,' said Freeh. 'Broadly speaking, that's correct. But the FBI does have a responsibility too. It's a federal matter, after all. In any case, that's beside the point. The President has decided he wants the FBI to assume overall control.'

'I bet the Secret Service are just going to love that,' muttered Marvin. 'But why me? Why not that guy Saunders – you know, the one who runs the FBI liaison office in the old Executive Office building? He handles all contact with the Secret Service and the White House. Shouldn't this be his job?'

'No,' said the director. 'He's not a serving FBI officer. He's retired. His responsibility is security checks on White House employees.'

'But why me?' persisted Jefferson. 'With respect, sir . . . I mean, OK, you and I worked together before, but this is a job for someone with more seniority. There must be someone else you know . . .'

'I hardly know anyone yet,' said Freeh sharply. 'I've been in this job for less than two months, for Chrissake. But I've talked to people about this, and they all agree you're the right man for the job. You get on well with people, and that's important – as you said yourself, the Secret Service aren't likely to be too delighted to have the FBI trampling all over their territory and their egos. If I assigned an ADIC or SAC who went blasting in there and kicked their butts around, that would only make things worse. But I know that if there's something that needs doing, you'll realise what it is and find a way of getting it done. As to seniority, you've been around for nearly twenty-five years, and it's only because you've consistently turned down promotion that you don't have the technical seniority of rank. But above all I'm assigning you because you're a good investigator, a good detective. You use your brains. And on this, you're going to need to use them. Anyway,' he concluded, 'that's an end to it. You're assigned, and that's that. Now, come on. You and I have an appointment in the Oval Office in half an hour.'

'Yes, sir,' said Jefferson glumly, rising to his feet and following Freeh out of his office. He looked at his watch; it was two in the afternoon. 'Sir, do you mind telling me when the notification was first received?'

'Only about half an hour ago, I think. It was flashed direct from Seoul.'

'And they don't even know yet exactly whose life it is that's being threatened?'

'Not yet,' said Freeh.

'Jesus,' muttered Jefferson. 'Well, I hope the CIA or whoever it is don't waste too much time finding out.'

'Actually,' said Freeh, 'I'm told the information came from the British, not from the CIA.'

'The British?' Jefferson was startled. 'How on earth did they get involved?'

'I've no idea,' said the director, punching the button of the elevator to take them to the ground floor. 'But I hope they're right about this.' There was a silence as they waited. 'On second thoughts,' said Freeh as the elevator arrived. 'I hope they're one hundred per cent wrong, and this whole thing turns out to be a wild goose chase. The last thing we need right now is a major political assassination. Have you ever had any dealings with the Brits before?'

'No, sir,' said Jefferson as they exited the elevator and headed for the director's car. Freeh's driver held open the rear door and the two men climbed in. The car set off through the light Sunday afternoon traffic.

'The White House seems to be taking this pretty seriously,' mused Jefferson as they sped along.

'It would seem so,' agreed the director. 'But a threat like this is hardly something they could ignore.'

'What have they done so far, other than ask for FBI assistance?' asked Jefferson.

'God knows,' said Freeh. 'They've probably just been running around in circles. The Secret Service are pretty good, when they're allowed to get on with their job, but the goddam White House staff doesn't seem to know which way is up. There are about half a dozen guys in the whole place who know what they're supposed to be doing. The rest are a bunch of obstructive, self-important assholes who just get in the way and foul things up. Fortunately there's a guy called David Gergen who does some useful work. He's only been there about three months, but he seems pretty sensible and competent, even if he is principally a policy-presentation specialist. But don't tell anyone I said any of this.'

'No, sir,' said Jefferson hastily, shaking his head.

Unusually, the President was on time. Jefferson learned only later that an important meeting with the Senate majority leader had been rescheduled at short notice, much to the senator's annoyance.

As Jefferson followed Freeh into the Oval Office, President Clinton rose from his chair and came forward, smiling.

'Lou,' he said, 'good of you to come.'

'Thank you, Mr President,' said Freeh. 'I'd like you to meet Special Agent Marvin Jefferson, who's been assigned to this case.'

'Good to meet you, Marv,' said Clinton, shaking his hand. 'Glad to have you on board. Come and sit down and have a cup of coffee.'

'Thank you, Mr President,' said Jefferson. He glanced curiously around the Oval Office and remained standing.

'Ever been in here before, Marv?' asked Clinton.

'No, Mr President,' replied Jefferson slowly, 'but my great-great-great-great-uncle—'

'Your great-great-great-uncle?' He worked in the White House?'

'That's four greats,' said Jefferson. 'Yes, sir. Thomas Jefferson. Third President of the United States, 1801 to 1809.'

'Hey, that's great!' said the President. 'How about that? Thomas Jefferson . . . Hey, did you know my second name was Jefferson? Bill Jefferson Clinton. Maybe you and I are related!' Clinton laughed. He put his hand on Jefferson's shoulder and ushered him round behind the large oak desk. 'Take a seat, Marv! Go on, sit down! Tell me what it feels like to be sitting at the same desk, in the same office as your forebear!'

Jefferson sat down slowly. 'Well, thank you, Mr President – it's a real privilege, and I appreciate it.' He frowned momentarily and looked up at Clinton. 'But I expect you know the original White House burned down in 1814, so of course it isn't quite the same as in Thomas Jefferson's time. In any case, the Oval Office wasn't even built then. If you recall, it was added on in 1909, exactly a hundred years after old TJ left office.' Jefferson pushed his legs under the desk with difficulty and leaned back in the big chair. 'They must have lowered the desk again, though,' he said.

'Huh?'

'Yes, sir. They had to raise it for President Reagan. Someone noticed he always sat sideways because he couldn't get his knees under it, so they had it raised a few inches for him. Kind of nice, that, huh? That he didn't complain himself? Most people would probably have hollered like hell at someone that it was too low.' Jefferson pushed himself back, stood up and walked round the desk again. 'Anyway, Mr President, I guess you want to talk about this assassination threat.'

'Yes, of course,' said Clinton. 'Sure. Let's talk about that.'

'Well, sir, I'll need to know who else I'll be working with on this, what authority I have, who I report to and so forth.'

'That's easy, Marv,' said the President. 'You'll be working principally with the Secret Service, I guess, but if there's anyone else you want on your team, all you have to do is ask. As to authority, I'm placing you in overall charge. And you report direct to me, here in the Oval Office. This is a matter of national security of the highest priority. Does that sound OK to you?'

Jefferson thought for a moment. 'May I make a

couple of suggestions, Mr President?' he asked. 'Rather than being given overall charge of this, could I be given joint charge, along with the head of the Secret Service? I think I'll be likely to get more co-operation if it's done that way. Also, could I suggest that I report to Mr Gergen, unless it becomes absolutely necessary for me to talk to you personally?'

'Fine, Marv, if that's what you want.'

'Perhaps you could ask them both to come in here right now, Mr President, so I can meet them. It would be nice if you explained that it was being done this way at my suggestion, despite your proposal that I should bypass them.'

Clinton grinned in understanding. 'I see what you mean, Marv. Yes. Good idea. Very diplomatic of you. I can see you're going to get along fine here.'

'Thank you, Mr President,' said Jefferson.

Twenty minutes later, Freeh took his leave of Jefferson at the north-west gate. 'Nice work, Marvin,' he said. 'I think the Secret Service will be on your side as a result of that.'

'I hope so, sir,' said Jefferson. 'I'm not going to get anywhere if they aren't.'

'You've got some goddam nerve, sitting at the President's desk and giving him a history lesson,' chuckled Freeh. 'But I never knew Thomas Jefferson was a forebear of yours.'

'Well, sir,' said Jefferson, 'I'll let you in on a little secret.' He grinned. 'As a matter of fact, we aren't related at all.'

49

Howard's radio signal arrived in Seoul forty minutes later. Bourne could read between its terse lines.

Howard, he knew, was an intensely single-minded individual who would concentrate on one thing at a time. In Bourne's view, it was not a good sign that Howard had so far said nothing about escape – it meant that he hadn't yet given the matter his full consideration. Certainly he would have thought about it, but Bourne could tell what was really on his friend's mind. It was the mission. His signal spoke of nothing else.

Neither Bourne nor Goodale mourned the death of the *Stasi* general, Reinhold Erfurt. Goodale's eyes had gone cold when he had heard about it, but he had said nothing. Bourne wondered what he was thinking. *The hell with the damned general, Ed!* thought Bourne. *Good riddance to him! Now just wring whatever information you can out of his deputy, that Colonel Eisener. Then get the hell out of there. And tell me which way you'll be going, so I can get something organised to help you.*

Bourne stood up and began pacing the room. Frustration was visible on his face, and it also showed in his movements. Reaching the large plate-glass window, he stopped and ran a glance over it. 'There isn't even a handle on this stupid window to open it,' he said angrily, banging his fist on it. 'Typical. I *hate* stuffy hotel rooms. Threadbare, smelly carpets, tacky and badly-made furniture, yellowing paintwork, shoddy fittings, a minuscule bath the size of a washbasin . . . The same cheap and nasty rooms you find everywhere nowadays. I can put up with all that, but what really gets me with these bloody places is that you can never get any fresh air – nothing except the recycled muck that the buggers downstairs choose to feed you through some filthy pipe.' He banged the metal window-frame again, hard. One corner of the frame seemed to spring slightly loose, and a sizeable piece of mortar outside fell away towards the street, four storeys below. 'Shit!' he muttered to himself. 'What the hell's this flop-house built of, anyway? Cardboard and chewing-gum? It's falling to bits!'

'Easy, Johnny,' said Goodale, who had risen and was now standing at Bourne's shoulder. 'Don't start breaking the place up. Her Majesty's Government can't afford to put us up in a first-class hotel, and they will certainly take a dim view of it if they receive a bill for completely rebuilding a third-class one.' The tone of his voice was light, but his eyes were serious.

'Why the hell couldn't we have stayed at the embassy? I feel completely cut off, here.'

'We're here unofficially, remember? We can make use of some of the embassy facilities, in the same way that all visiting businessmen can, but our staying there would have been awkward for the authorities if they ever had to explain our presence. I'm sure you understand that.'

Bourne fell silent, but his expression remained moody. Goodale could see that the younger man was still inwardly seething with frustration.

Together, they gazed out on the scene below. The streets of Seoul were awash with bright lights, honking cars and scuttling pedestrians. The frenetic activity was reminiscent to Goodale of Hong Kong, or perhaps Tokyo as he had known it many years before – teeming with life, energy and the pollution that accompanied them, but places which held little attraction for him any more.

It had begun to rain. Streaks of water appeared on the glass of the window, and the view below was temporarily obscured by a sudden squall. There was a whistling rattle of air through the new crack in the loose corner of the frame; for a few seconds it blotted out the hooting of horns and dull rumble of traffic filtering up from the street.

'I don't like being cooped up in this place any more than you do,' said Goodale eventually, glancing at Bourne's scowling face. 'Give me the wide-open countryside any day, preferably in the Scottish Highlands, and a window that won't shut rather than one that won't open. But look on the bright side, Johnny. At least we're better off up here with the air-conditioning than down there in that grimy street without it.'

'We certainly won't be better off if the building falls down while we're still inside it,' muttered Bourne darkly. He remained standing at the window for a few minutes, then glanced back towards his companion. Max Goodale had returned to his armchair and was once again sitting deep in thought, a small glass of neat whisky near his elbow. He had hardly touched it since pouring it out half an hour before. Goodale's eyes were still bright and intense, but it seemed to Bourne that they were slightly out of focus, concentrated on something a very long way away. 'Colonel?' he asked finally.

Goodale snapped back to the present. The bright blue eyes settled steadily on Bourne, unwavering. He smiled. 'Yes, Johnny?'

Not for the first time, Bourne found the intensity of Goodale's gaze slightly unsettling. *The man smiles with his face,* he thought, *but not very often with his eyes. And his eyes are not smiling now, despite his face. Well, stuff it. I'm going to ask him anyway.* 'Colonel,' he ventured, leaning forward in his own chair, 'do you mind telling me something? What the hell is all this emphasis on an old man, the one you expected Ed to find at the *Stasi* base?'

Goodale was no longer smiling. His eyes bore into those of the younger man, briefly revealing an anger he immediately regretted. It was a lapse, Goodale realised. He had given himself away. He hadn't done that for years. Stupid, *stupid!* Goodale knew that Bourne was not someone who could easily be written off. He saw the younger man had not flinched. In fact, he realised, Bourne was even staring him down.

Goodale smiled, genuinely this time. 'I'm sorry, Johnny,' he began. 'I was miles away. My apologies.' He reached for his glass and drank. 'You asked about the old man,' he said genially. 'Didn't Ed Howard tell you anything about him?'

'No,' said Bourne curtly, 'he didn't. And Ed's not here. I'm asking you.'

Dangerous, thought Goodale. *Frustration, anger, concern for his friends' safety – it's all there, written on his face.* 'Well,' he said calmly, 'he knows you much better than I do. And if he didn't tell you, there must have been some reason for it.'

'Don't bullshit me, Colonel!' shouted Bourne, his temper boiling over. 'You've pitched my friends into this bloody mess, and all you can do is ask them about some old man? What about this so-called assassination victim, and this IRIS thing? Is that all bullshit too? What the hell do you think you're doing, playing with people's lives like that?'

'Control yourself, please,' said Goodale quietly. His eyes fixed on Bourne's. For a moment there was a conflict of fury versus calm. The calm won, and Bourne's temper subsided as quickly as it had arisen.

'I am not going to tell you about the old man,' began Goodale. 'In many respects, his importance is secondary. It is a matter, I suppose, of opinion.' He drained his glass suddenly. 'But that rather depends on one's perspective. I can, however, satisfy you on one matter, I think.' Goodale stood and walked across the room to pour himself another drink. 'It is this. In terms of current events, there can be little question about the relative importance of the two issues. Even though we don't yet know who IRIS's intended victim is, that is the matter which must take priority. The scale of the operation that has been set up to kill him makes it plain that he's someone of great significance.

'The issue of the old man,' continued Goodale, 'is of importance in a rather more historical sense. It is not entirely without relevance today – otherwise the *Stasi* would not have bothered to kidnap him – but it concerns matters that are to some extent behind us, in the past. My concern is simply that these matters do not return to haunt us again at some stage in the future.

They are not inconsequential, and I am sure you will forgive me for directing some of my attention to them.'

'Well, Colonel,' said Bourne, 'I'm obviously in no position to judge, as I have no idea what it's about. But it seems to me that you and I should be concentrating on just two things here, and not allowing ourselves to be side-tracked. You said yourself that the IRIS affair must take priority. Fine. Then that's what we should be thinking about. Maybe even the little information we do have can tell us something. For example, we know that the assassination attempt will be made in the USA, and that it's due to take place soon. Let's start with an assumption – that the victim will be a visiting VIP. Let's get hold of the US Embassy and ask them for a list of all VIPs due to visit the States over the next few weeks. One or two names may stand out as likely targets. Then we can warn the Americans and leave it up to them. It's not too difficult to search for bombs, or to change a VIP's scheduled route to avoid places where a bomb could be planted.'

'I've already asked for that information,' said Goodale. 'The US State Department is putting a list together. I've been told it will take two or three days – apparently the list is surprisingly long . . . But what was your second point – the other thing you feel we ought to be concentrating on?'

Bourne groaned. 'I don't think we have two or three days,' he muttered, almost to himself. 'Colonel, the other thing is simple. We ought to be concentrating our thoughts on how to get Ed and the others out of there.'

'I agree,' said Goodale. 'We must do everything we can. The problem is, until we know what Ed's plans are – and he's in the best position to judge what to do next – there's not a great deal we *can* do. If he asks for something – a submarine, a diversion of some sort, or whatever – of course I shall do my level best to arrange it.'

'So in the meantime we just sit here and wait?' asked Bourne gloomily.

'We sit here and think,' said Goodale. 'It's extremely frustrating, but for the time being it's all we can do.'

The wind was now whistling shrilly through the crack in the loosened window-frame; a thin trickle of water from the rainstorm outside had began seeping through the aperture. It dribbled down the wall and began soaking into the carpet.

50

Gerhardt Eisener showed no sign of nervousness as he was led into the room by Ackford. His eyes went immediately to the body lying on the floor in the corner, but his expression did not flicker.

Howard was watching him closely. *This is a very dangerous individual,* he told himself. *He's completely in control of himself. A lesser man would have been unnerved by the sight of his commanding officer's corpse, but this one didn't even blink.*

Without a word, Ackford led Eisener over to the chair and began strapping him in, as he had earlier done with the general.

'The restraints will not be necessary,' said Eisener calmly, in good English.

The two men ignored him and Ackford went on tying him into the chair. When Ackford had finished he pulled out of his smock something that looked like a large screwdriver. A length of flex, with an electric plug on one end, protruded from its handle. He went to a wall-socket and plugged it in. For a minute or two he stood there as a faint smell of burning began to fill the room.

Neither Howard nor Ackford had said a word, but Ackford now moved to the chair and loomed threateningly in front of Eisener. There was a cold, vicious expression on his face as he held the hot implement in front of the German's face. He spoke. 'Electric soldering-iron,' he said. 'I found it downstairs in your radio room. As soon as it gets really hot, I'm going to shove it right up your arse.'

Eisener frowned briefly. Ignoring Ackford and the soldering-iron, he turned to face Howard. 'I repeat, this will not be necessary,' he said. 'My name, as you will know, is Eisener. My rank is colonel. Would you mind telling me yours?'

Howard regarded him coldly. He said nothing.

Eisener still appeared calm. There was no sign of panic or anxiety on his face as he continued to address Howard. 'You are a captain, I think, or . . . no, a major. May I call you Major? A civilised discussion would be in both our interests, as I am sure you will agree. I detest unnecessary violence and suffering. Why don't you ask me what it is you want to know? I will do my best to help.'

Howard drew up a chair and sat down facing their prisoner, a few feet away. He leaned forward, his dark eyes glittering. 'OK, Colonel,' he began. 'We'll try to keep this civilised. But be in no doubt. If I feel you're holding out on anything, I'll let this man loose on you. You can see what happened to your general.'

'Yes, I can,' replied Eisener hurriedly. 'I heard his screams. I have no wish to suffer a similar fate, Major.' His eyes settled palely on Howard's face.

His interrogator nodded slowly. 'Good. In that case, you can start by telling me what you know about IRIS.'

'It's a computer program which is able to recognise individual faces,' answered Eisener immediately. 'It was stolen and shipped to the USA, where it has been modified. One of our US-based groups is constructing a machine that will use the IRIS technology to recognise a particular individual and kill him by firing a single rifle shot. We are being paid to do this by the Iranian government.'

Howard was startled. Nevertheless he managed to keep his voice even as he asked, 'Why a rifle shot? Could it not be used to set off a bomb?'

'We considered that, Major,' said Eisener calmly. 'The problem with a bomb is that it needs to be close to the victim to be certain of killing him. Either that, or it needs to be a very large bomb, which is difficult to conceal. Also, because of its explosive content, a bomb is relatively easy to detect. To line up a rifle using the IRIS technology is obviously more complicated, but our experts confirmed that it could be done. The machine can therefore be kept to a reasonable size and can still remain lethal to its designated target, even if he is a hundred metres away or more. In fact, I understand that a short-barrelled rifle, or perhaps even a pistol, will be used. It isn't hard to see that the whole package could be kept to the size of, say, a briefcase.'

Howard's face remained expressionless, but he was thinking hard. This piece of information changed everything. If what Eisener said was true, the IRIS machine was far deadlier than he and Goodale had assumed. The logic of using a rifle, if it could be done, was inescapable. He stared at Eisener, appraising him again. The man had volunteered the information quite willingly.... *Yes, it must be true.* 'OK, Colonel,' he said. 'Now tell me who the intended victim is.'

'I do not know that,' replied Eisener. He shot a glance at the general's body. '*He* knew, of course. But he never told me. He was like that. He kept many things back from me. He did let slip the fact that the killing would occur in Washington, DC, so I assumed for a while that it would be an attempt on the life of President Clinton. This may be the case, but I cannot see any obvious reason why the Iranians would want to kill Clinton. I don't even know who is running the operation over there. General Erfurt was almost obsessive about secrecy. Every now and then he would make a remark about it, but he always spoke in riddles.'

Some resentment there, thought Howard. *Interesting*.

'Where did the general keep his papers?'

'Hah!' replied Eisner, his antipathy now very apparent. 'Wherever he kept them, it wasn't here. My guess is that he kept them in Tokyo. Maybe there is a safe-deposit box or something there. He used to fly there regularly – once a month or so. Do you think he would leave his secret papers here, for me to find? Not him. That's what he was like . . . Look, Major,' continued Eisner reasonably, 'have you yet had a look through the files downstairs? I'll tell you what you'll find. Low-grade, unimportant details, that's all. Security rosters for the Yŏngbyŏn security job we do. Procurement orders, with most of the names encrypted. Everything of importance or interest is encrypted, and the general had the only key to decyphering any of it. If he kept his code-pad here, I was certainly never able to find it. Do you think I didn't try? He would go away for days on end, leaving us here in this dump. I'm sure he must have kept files of his own, but he certainly didn't keep them here. God knows, I looked for them.'

'Did he ever refer to a file on IRIS?'

'He never referred to *any* of his files. In fact he never admitted to keeping any – but I knew he did. Actually . . .' Eisner frowned briefly. 'I will correct myself. He *did* refer to a file on this matter. Just once. He let it slip, about two weeks ago, when he seemed to be in a good mood. I pretended not to notice.'

'What did he say?' asked Howard carefully.

'It was really just a reference to paperwork. But it was a clear indication that a file existed.'

'What exactly did he say to you?'

Eisner's brow furrowed again for a second or two. 'Well, let me think . . . Yes, we were discussing IRIS. We had received the initial brief from our technician in the USA, reporting his assessment of the IRIS computer program. The report said that it was good, but still in the development stage. The technician was not sure it would be sufficiently reliable to give a guarantee that it would function correctly and identify the right person.'

'What did the general say?' persisted Howard.

'He seemed to know . . . something the technician did not. He seemed confident that IRIS *would* work. If I remember correctly, he said, "I know it will work. It's all in black-and-white." Yes,' said Eisner, frowning in concentration, 'those were his words. Obviously he had a file somewhere, containing another assessment of IRIS.'

'Is there a copy of that technician's report?'

'No,' said Eisner. 'He let me read it, which was unusual. That was where I learned that a rifle or pistol would be used. Later he took the report downstairs to the boiler room and incinerated it.' Eisner paused, then smiled at Howard. 'Do you mind if I have a cigarette?'

Howard lit up for both of them. 'Tony,' he said to Ackford, 'Untie the colonel's left hand, would you?'

Ackford produced a long, sharp knife and slashed the plastic strip. He glowered at Eisner, then moved aside again.

'Thank you, Major. You know,' he said expansively, gesturing with his free hand towards the corpse in the corner, 'General Erfurt was a very unusual man. Many people underestimated him. He appeared to be a crude, physical type, but he also had an almost perfect photographic memory. He could quote whole pages of documents he had read only once. It is a very rare ability, you know.' Eisner drew on his cigarette, then continued. 'For a long time I assumed that that was why he kept no files of his own – because he had no need to. He could recall with absolute precision the contents of anything, even many years after he had last read it. It is a pity, really, when a brain like that has to die.'

Howard rose from his chair and began to pace the room. His initial assessment of Eisner, he realised, had been correct. The man was exceptionally intelligent, complicated and dangerous. He wished that Goodale had been there to conduct the interrogation; he himself, he knew, was being tied in knots by Eisner. How much of what he was saying was the truth, and how much false? Probably ninety-nine per cent was the truth. That would be the way of a clever man like Eisner.

The problem, Howard realised, lay in identifying that crucial one per cent. The most obviously important fact must be the identity of IRIS's intended assassination victim. Or was it? Eisner's explanation, along with the information he *had* divulged, was utterly plausible. Eisner's picture of the obsessively secretive general had been completely convincing, and everything that Howard had discovered so far tallied with it. Eisner obviously resented the lack of trust placed in him by his superior.

Eisner would know that IRIS was the principal reason that Howard and his team were here; and he would know that the identity of the person to be assassinated was the one piece of information, above all others, that they needed to find out. If he had known who the target was, Eisner could safely have given him the name, but at the same time withheld the equally important information that IRIS was to trigger a rifle bullet rather than a bomb-blast. If he had done that, reasoned Howard, the police and FBI would have torn Washington apart in their search for a bomb – and the victim would still have died because all the time they would have been looking for the wrong thing. That way, Eisner would have appeared to have been co-operating, and he would not face the risk of being pressed further about the identity of the target VIP – which he must surely know would now happen. Why, Howard asked himself, if Eisner *did* know who the target was, had he done it the other way round and put himself at risk?

What Eisner knew would keep a team of skilled

interrogators busy for weeks. But with limited time, all Howard could do was concentrate on the essentials. There were two other things he needed to ask about. He decided to leave the subject of IRIS for the time being.

'Tell me, Colonel,' he said. 'What was done with the old man who was kidnapped in Oxford on April 24th?'

Eisener's expression did not flicker and he answered at once. 'I don't know,' he said. 'I heard something about it, though. General Erfurt said he arranged a kidnapping to test our people in England. Personally, I didn't believe that. Our teams have been used regularly, and they do not need stupid tests of that sort. It only puts them at added risk. In my view, this is something Erfurt organised on his own initiative. Certainly we had no request for such a job to be done – I would have heard about it. I do know that a man was kidnapped, but I don't know who he was or what was done with him. As you will have seen, he is not here. Actually, I would be curious to know about him. Perhaps if you tell me who he was, I might be able to throw some light on why General Erfurt wanted him kidnapped.'

'I don't know who he was,' admitted Howard. 'All I know is that it happened, and that your people were responsible.'

Eisener grinned. 'Now do you see, Major?' he chuckled. 'You and I are in the same position. Your controller and mine – they both agree to keep us in the dark, and on the same issues, too! I wonder what connection they had with each other!'

Eisener could see that his jibe had struck a nerve with his interrogator. He had managed to turn the conversation on its head, as he had intended, and he knew that by doing so he had successfully distracted Howard from the outright lie he had told in denying all knowledge of the abduction and captivity of Hislop. His face remained completely calm and impassive, betraying none of his thoughts.

Howard had already changed the subject. 'Tell me about your work here at Yŏngbyŏn, Colonel.'

'Ah,' said Eisener. 'Now, there I *can* help you.' For the next ten minutes, as Howard took notes, Eisener poured out a wealth of details about the North Korean nuclear installation. The *Stasi*, it appeared, had been active in procuring nuclear technology and expertise from former Eastern Bloc states, and now had a major role in the security set-up at the plant. Eisener and his men had almost unrestricted access, and control over many of the scientists who worked there. Howard asked if it would be possible for Eisener to get him and three others inside the plant.

Eisener considered the question for a moment. 'Normally,' he said, 'I don't think there would be a problem with that. What makes it more difficult is that there appears to be a sudden increase in troop movements here. I don't know why this is, and I wasn't consulted about it. But the fact remains that the North Koreans are obviously agitated about something, and security at the plant will be more than usually tight. It couldn't be that they have some idea of your presence, could it?'

Dammit, thought Howard angrily. *This man is running rings round me.* He returned to the chair and stared hard into Eisener's face. 'I am going to repeat one of my earlier questions, Colonel,' he said softly but with unmistakable menace. 'This time, I want a straight answer to it. If I don't get one, I will leave you to the tender mercies of my friend here and his red-hot soldering iron. Personally, I don't share his taste for inflicting pain, so I shall leave the room while he attends to you. Once I have gone, your screams will be to no avail. So you had better think very hard indeed when you give me your answer.' Howard lit a cigarette and inhaled; his eyes had gone dark as he stared into Eisener's face. 'Tell me the identity of the man to be assassinated by IRIS.'

'Major,' answered Eisener slowly, 'I am unfortunately cursed with a very low pain threshold. It is not something of which I am proud, but there is nothing I can do to change it. Your colleague would only have to touch me briefly with that hot iron and my will to resist would be gone. I have therefore co-operated with you, in the hope of saving myself . . . severe discomfort. At the same time, I have spared you the indignity of resorting to such crude methods of extracting information. There is nothing more I can do, other than to implore you not to proceed. It would achieve nothing. At the first touch of that iron I would scream out any likely names I could think of. Some of them might even be convincing. But that would get neither of us anywhere. It would be unbearable agony for me, and you would only receive inaccurate information. Instead, I can only repeat that I do not know who the victim is. You have to believe me.'

Howard stared long and hard into Eisener's face. He saw that the colonel had begun to sweat, and observed the first trace of real fear in the man's expression. Then he looked at his watch and frowned. 'I shall consider your answer, Colonel, but I am afraid that as things stand I just don't believe you. Right now I have a radio schedule to keep, so I'll be leaving you for a few minutes. When I return, I shall give you one last chance to tell me the victim's name.' He rose from the chair. 'Keep that iron nice and hot, Tony – but don't use it until I get back.'

In the main hall on the ground floor Howard found Ziegler, Harris and Zeccara. Harris was twiddling idly with the settings on the tiny short-wave radio that he took everywhere with him to keep abreast of the news. The other two, who both read German, were sifting through a large pile of files and papers.

Howard drew Ziegler to one side. 'I think Eisener's holding out on me, Mike,' he said wearily. 'He's calling my bluff. Tony looks pretty convincing, but he'd be no more prepared to use that soldering-iron than I would. Hey, Mel,' he snapped, suddenly irritated by the hissing static coming from the portable radio, 'turn that bloody thing off, would you?'

'Just a minute, boss,' said Harris. 'OK, I've got it now. Yeah, there it is. Good old nine-four-one-zero.' The static hissing from the little radio ceased, and the familiar strains of *Lillibulero* echoed thinly round the hall, followed by the hourly time-signal pips.

As the last pip sounded, Howard glanced automatically at his watch; it was ten seconds fast. He turned to his old friend Ziegler again. 'What do we do?' he asked.

'Someone's goin' to have to tweak the bastard, Ed. One of us is goin' to have to hurt him.'

'Who? You?'

'We've come too far and got ourselves too deep into this shit for me not to feel committed enough to consider it,' said Ziegler. 'But . . . no. It's not my style, any more than it's yours or Tony's.'

They stood in silence for a few minutes, thinking, with half an ear on the BBC World Service news. Then Howard turned away. 'Well, I suppose I'd better go and send Johnny the latest news – not that there's much to tell. Oh, by the way,' he added, 'Eisener says you won't find anything interesting in those files. On that point at least, I'm inclined to believe him.'

'Well, that's just great,' moaned Ziegler disgustedly. 'Somehow I just knew I'd been wastin' my time with that stuff.'

Howard started up the staircase again, his mind working more slowly than he would have liked. He was tired, he knew; but something was suddenly puzzling him as he recalled Eisener's words about the general's obsession with secrecy and riddles. What was it? Something about 'black and white' – a reference to paperwork. That was it. Then, dimly, he recalled an item of news he had just heard on Harris's little short-wave radio set . . .

Ziegler had sunk back into his chair and was watching Howard making his way up to the first floor. He frowned slightly. Howard had frozen halfway up the stairs. He watched, curious. Then he saw Howard suddenly whirl round, his eyes ablaze.

'Mike! Come on!'

Ziegler leaped to his feet and pelted up the stairs after him. Harris and Zeccara exchanged glances.

'What's got into them?' asked Zeccara.

'Dunno, mate,' grinned Harris. 'But at a guess, I'd say the boss just worked out the answer to something that had been bothering him.'

Howard and Ziegler raced along the corridor and burst into the bedroom where Halliday had set up the radio. Halliday looked round, surprised. He had a towel round his waist.

'Hello, boss,' he said cheerfully. 'Just about time for our radio schedule. Hope you don't mind, but I just took a shower. I think I've got rid of the stink of that dead animal.' He bent to switch on the LPI set.

'OK, Ed,' said Ziegler. 'So you've figured somethin' out. Give!'

Howard's eyes were glittering. 'I know who IRIS's target is,' he said. 'Pete, are you sure this radio's on properly?'

Halliday finished towelling himself dry and bent over the radio. He scowled and flicked the on/off switch. 'Sod it,' he said. 'Sorry. Battery.' He rummaged in his bergen for a fresh one, muttering to himself. 'Bloody well shouldn't be dead. Should be plenty more life in it yet . . .' Deftly he changed the battery and then flicked the switch again. Nothing happened. He glanced at Howard, his expression serious. 'Sorry, boss. Something's wrong. I'll have to have a look at it.'

'Quick as you can, Pete,' said Howard, trying to remain calm. 'Mike, let's go and have a chat while Pete fixes the radio.' He led Ziegler outside. In the corridor, he spoke rapidly in a low voice. Ziegler grinned and smacked his fist into his other hand.

Halliday's head appeared round the door. 'Boss? In here.'

Howard saw that Halliday had removed the rear panel of the LPI radio. The interior was exposed, its intricate printed circuit boards clearly visible. He bent over it. 'Well?' he asked.

'Completely burned out,' said Halliday. 'Look at those circuits just there. They've had it. History.'

Howard and Ziegler peered into the interior of the radio. There appeared to be some discoloration and bubbling around a number of the components. Howard glanced sharply at Halliday. 'Can you fix it?'

'I dunno, boss,' Halliday's thin, pale face peered into the radio's interior, his protruding eyes for once registering anger rather than the more habitual expression of surprise. 'Those burned-out bits are power supply components. You know, voltage converters and what-have-you. If it was anything else that had blown, I'd have said there was no chance of fixing it, but I may be able to rig something up. I won't be able to use the radio's own batteries, though – the voltage is too high.' He thought for a moment. 'A twelve-volt cell might do,' he muttered, rubbing his chin thoughtfully. 'Maybe a vehicle battery. Do those *Stasi* trucks outside have twelve-volt electrics?'

'I don't know,' Howard replied. 'I'll ask Tony. Are you sure you'll be able to get it going?'

'I won't know until I try, boss,' said Halliday. 'It's worth a shot, though.'

'Do what you can, Pete. Let me know if you need any help.' Howard turned to leave, then paused at the door. 'How did it happen?' he asked. 'Could it be water damage from the soaking it got in that tunnel?'

'It might be,' replied Halliday heatedly, 'if it wasn't completely jungle-proof. Also, it has its own waterproof case. No. This is a big electrical overload. And that can't happen, either – it's protected.'

'So?' asked Howard quietly.

Halliday shrugged, a mixture of fury and frustration in the gesture. 'I can't explain it, boss,' he said. 'It's a freak. A one-off. It's as if . . . well, the only thing I can think of that might have this effect would be if someone deliberately bypassed the circuit-breaker system and plugged the bloody thing into the mains.'

Howard's eyes had narrowed. He turned to Ziegler. 'Mike, get Mel and Angelo in here, and tell them to bring the two medical bags.'

Thirty seconds later Howard opened the two bags and examined their contents. 'OK,' he breathed, his eyes black with anger. 'Angelo, go and help Tony escort Colonel Eisener back down to his cell, on the double. Then I want the six of us back up here in the general's office. Two minutes, OK?'

Zeccara ran out of the room. A few seconds later, they heard hurrying feet as the *Stasi* colonel was manhandled back downstairs.

'Do you want the girl and Weatherill here too, boss?' asked Harris.

'No!' snapped Howard. He led the way along the corridor into the big office where the general's body still lay unattended in the corner. 'Strip him, Mike,' said Howard. 'Mel, you help. Pete, go and get some water and a cloth.'

Ziegler and Harris tore off Erfurt's clothes while Halliday, still clad only in his towel, went to fetch water. The involuntary relaxation of the corpse's muscles had led to the usual urinary and bowel discharges that followed quickly after death. After Halliday had swabbed the mess away Howard bent over to examine the body.

'OK,' he said finally when all six of them were assembled again. 'Here it is. This vein on top of the left foot. Pretty bloody obvious, when you know what to look for. Anyone want to see?'

No one needed to; they were convinced. First there

had been Alexander Plasnin's report of unprecedented extra security at Sunan. Next had been the massively increased troop movements around Yŏngbyŏn. Then the Antonov had been shot down. Now the radio, their one contact with the outside world, had inexplicably suffered a power surge which might prove impossible to repair. Finally, there were two items missing from one of the medical bags – a 10ml syringe and a hypodermic needle. The puncture mark on the general's foot was just confirmation, if any were needed.

Ziegler was the first to speak. 'What do you think it was, Ed?'

'I don't know,' said Howard, suddenly tired again. 'Potassium chloride, maybe. That would have been quickest and most effective. But a lot of things could have done it. Battery acid, a large squirt of air into the vein . . . it could have been almost anything. Tony and I just assumed it was a heart attack.'

'But it wasn't,' said Harris, his eyes burning with intensity.

'No,' said Howard. 'He was murdered. I can only assume it was done to stop him telling me something he knew. He was still tied up when he was found, so it wasn't self-administered. And none of the other *Stasi* prisoners had the opportunity.'

'That's *all* we needed,' said Ziegler.

'Which one?' asked Harris fiercely.

'The girl,' muttered Zeccara.

'No,' said Halliday.

'The doc,' growled Ackford.

'It's either one or the other,' said Howard. 'Kim Sumi or Richard Weatherill. One of the two is a traitor.'

PART FOUR

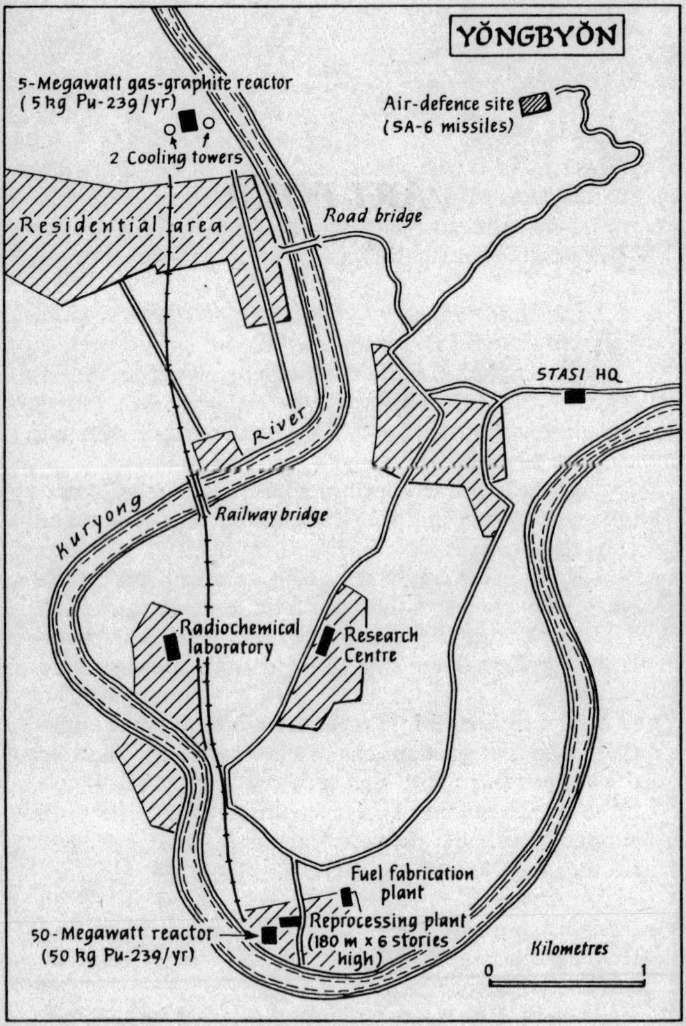
YŎNGBYŎN
5-Megawatt gas-graphite reactor
(5 kg Pu-239/yr)
2 Cooling towers
Air-defence site
(SA-6 missiles)
Residential area
Road bridge
STASI HQ
River
Kuryong
Railway bridge
Radiochemical
laboratory
Research
Centre
Fuel fabrication
plant
Reprocessing plant
(180 m x 6 stories
high)
50-Megawatt reactor
(50 kg Pu-239/yr)
Kilometres
0
1

51

Howard's face was white with anger as he talked the matter over with Ziegler. In front of the others he had been controlled and calm, but alone now with his oldest friend and colleague he was showing his fury and frustration.

'I should have seen it, Mike,' he said. 'God damn it, I should have tumbled to it earlier!'

'None of us did, Ed,' said Ziegler resignedly. 'But at least now we know what we're dealin' with. And I think it was a smart move to tell the boys not to let on to either of those two what we suspect.'

'I'm not giving either of them any more rope, Mike. One more lapse, and we'll have had it. We're in a bad enough bind as it is.'

'OK, let's find out which one it is,' said Ziegler. 'We can't leave here without first findin' out.'

Howard nodded. 'I agree,' he said. 'But I'd like to do it in a way that doesn't make either of them suspicious. Any ideas?'

Ziegler sighed. 'Me, I'd get them both up here, strap them into that goddam chair one at time, and then set to work on them with that solderin'-iron, when Pete's finished with it. One of them would start squeakin' soon enough. But,' he paused, frowning, 'maybe there's another way.'

'Let's hear it.'

At that moment there was a knock on the door and Halliday entered. 'I think I've fixed the radio, boss,' he announced cheerfully.

'Brilliant, Pete!' Howard jumped to his feet, elated.

'OK, get this signal off to Johnny right away.' He handed Halliday a coded message he had prepared for Bourne. 'There'll be a reply, then we'll need to send him another one in an hour or two's time.'

'No problem, boss,' said Halliday. 'There is one thing, though. The radio won't be portable any more. I've had to open the whole thing up and mess about with it, if you see what I mean. I've got wires everywhere, and components spread about the floor like a madwoman's shit. We'll have to leave the bugger here.'

'We'll chuck it in the furnace downstairs before we go,' said Howard. 'It doesn't matter, just as long as we can get this message and one more off, confirming things with Johnny.'

Halliday nodded. 'I'll send this one right away.' He disappeared.

Howard expelled a sigh of relief and turned to Ziegler again. 'Well, that's one thing to be thankful for, at least,' he said. 'I wouldn't have wanted to send anything in clear over that old *Stasi* set down in the radio room. The NKs would have got a DF on it straight away, and then we'd have had half their army round our necks.'

'Suicide,' agreed Ziegler. 'Listen, Ed, while we're waitin' for Johnny's reply, this business about whether it's Sumi or the doc . . .'

'Yes. Let's hear your idea.'

Ziegler spoke quietly, outlining his plan. Howard listened, nodding occasionally and adding some suggestions of his own.

'I like it,' said Howard eventually. 'OK. Where are they now?'

'Both still asleep, last I heard.'

'OK, I think I know how I'm going to handle this. Let's deal with Weatherill first. Tell him I want to see him up in the general's office to talk about where he needs to put his monitoring gear. Give me a minute or two to cover the body – I don't want to make it obvious that we've been examining it.'

'Sure.'

A few minutes later Weatherill joined Howard in the big office on the first floor, where he was standing in front of the large-scale map of Yŏngbyŏn on one wall.

'Richard, come over here and point out some of the features of this place for me,' requested Howard. 'Our friend the colonel seems to be very co-operative, but he says it's going to be difficult to get us anywhere near any of the important installations so that we can get your monitoring equipment into place. Frankly,' Howard shook his head, 'I don't know whether I can trust him. What I *do* know is that I'm certainly not going to rely on him to tell me what all these various buildings are, or where your equipment might best be placed. You're the expert – fill me in.'

Weatherill began to explain in detail what all the installations were. He tapped at the map. 'OK. We're here, just south of the road and about a quarter of a mile north of the Kuryong. The road curves off to the south, leading into this wide loop of the river. Inside the loop, which is about a mile and a half across, are all the newer installations. Right down in the south, following the river round, the North Koreans have built a massive dyke to stop the river flooding the place. It stretches for over two miles and it's well over a hundred feet high.'

'If the place is so easily flooded,' asked Howard, 'why did they risk putting this plant here?'

'Simple – they need the water for cooling the reactors,' answered Weatherill.

'Oh yes – I suppose they would. And where exactly are the reactors?'

'There's a small one up here in the north, on the far side of the river. It's a five-megawatt gas-graphite one, rather like the British installation at Calder Hall. It's been in operation since about 1985. You can see the two cooling towers, one on either side. We estimate that it produces about five kilograms of Plutonium-239 per year.'

'Is that a lot? I know nothing about these things.'

'Not compared to what the other reactor can produce – the one down here in the south.' Weatherill indicated a large building near the southernmost curve of the river. 'This one's a fifty-megawatt reactor. As you'd expect, it can produce about ten times as much – say fifty kilos a year. We don't think it's fully operational yet, but it's certainly working up to it. Anyway, with both these two reactors, the North Koreans have probably produced sufficient Pu–239 to manufacture about five or six nuclear weapons.'

'Hmm,' muttered Howard, looking serious. 'Even so, that doesn't seem to be very many. Why only five or six?'

'Well, in theory you only need a couple of kilograms of Pu–239 to make a bomb. But you have to refine it – reprocess it – and that takes time. Also, it's only about ten per cent efficient. Hence the waste.'

'Where do they do this reprocessing?' asked Howard.

'Here,' replied Weatherill, indicating a large structure near the fifty-megawatt reactor. 'This building is over five hundred feet long and the equivalent of six storeys high.'

Howard's eyes opened in amazement. 'That big? Just to reprocess a few kilograms of plutonium?'

'Yes. Pu–239 has to be stored and handled with extreme care, and the centrifuges and other equipment you need to refine it are massive.'

'I see,' said Howard. 'What about all the other buildings nearby?'

'This one here's interesting,' said Weatherill, pointing. 'It's a fuel fabrication plant for the reactors. The others in this complex are admin blocks, liquid waste storage tanks, that sort of thing.'

'OK,' said Howard. 'You've mentioned the two complexes where the actual reactors are. What are all these other groups of buildings?'

'They're all tied in to it, one way or another. For

example, this complex here –' Weatherill indicated a large group of buildings in the centre of the loop formed by the river '– is a research centre. To the west there are mostly radiochemical labs. Up here, just south-west of the smaller reactor, is a residential area for people working at the installation. This facility up on the hill in the north-east is an air-defence emplacement, and the town of Yŏngbyŏn itself is a couple of miles further off to the north-east.'

'OK, I get the general picture ... So what are we most interested in?' asked Howard. 'Where do I tell the colonel we need to gain access in order to plant your monitoring equipment?'

'Down here, definitely,' replied Weatherill, indicating a precise point on the southernmost complex. 'We need to put it right here to monitor temperature emissions. You've seen the equipment – it's small and unobtrusive. It beams its information directly up to a satellite called Skynet–4, which relays it back to Oakhangar so that we can interpret it. It will tell us precisely what is going on at this new fifty-megawatt reactor, and what the North Koreans are really up to.'

'Right,' said Howard, nodding. 'But tell me something ... This may sound a stupid question, but how does the West know for certain that this isn't just a perfectly normal power plant? I know the NKs have a bad reputation, but they need electricity just like the rest of us. How do we know this isn't all perfectly legitimate?'

'That's not a stupid question at all,' exclaimed Weatherill enthusiastically. 'It's actually quite a good one. But the answer's simple. There are no electricity-generating plants, no transmission yards or other infrastructure, no pylons and no power lines whatever leading out of this place. Yŏngbyŏn's entire output is being directed into producing Pu–239 – it has no other purpose. And the North Koreans haven't accounted for any of the plutonium they've produced to date – it's all been concealed from the IAEA. The only possible explanation is that it's being produced and refined for the express purpose of building up an offensive nuclear capability.'

'All right, Richard,' said Howard slowly, 'you've convinced me. That's really very helpful – thanks a lot for explaining it. At least I now know what we have to deal with. You go and get your equipment ready, and I'll haul that colonel up here again. If I simply tell him where we need to get to, he can't argue, can he?'

When Weatherill had gone Howard told Ackford to fetch Eisener. Two minutes later the *Stasi* colonel was seated once again in the chair. He appeared mildly surprised that this time Ackford did not strap him in.

'I'm not going to press you on the matter of the IRIS assassination for now, Colonel,' Howard began. 'First, I'd just like to clear up one small matter.' Producing a folder of photographs Zeccara had found downstairs among all the other files, he opened it at a place which he had flagged and held it in front of Eisener. 'Who is this man?'

Eisener's face showed immediate recognition. 'Oh, yes, poor Peter,' he said. 'That was a pity.' Outwardly he remained calm, but inwardly his mind was racing. What the devil was Kramer's photograph doing here among these others? He silently cursed the lapse in security.

'What do you mean?' asked Howard.

Eisener waved a hand. 'He was quite talented – a very capable young man. There was an aircraft accident. China Airways, flying from P'yŏngyang to Beijing. A very unreliable airline with an atrocious record, but of course nothing is ever reported – rather as was the case with Aeroflot in the Soviet Union, as I expect you will know, Major. The general had sent Peter to collect a package.' Eisener frowned. 'He should have sent an ordinary courier – even someone like that fool Kleinhoff would have been capable of handling such a routine matter. Anyway, the plane came down in the sea near Zhanhua, in the Yellow River delta, and everyone on board was killed. It was obviously way off course to the south, but we were never told why. The Chinese suppressed the details.'

Howard nodded. 'There's something else I'd like to clear up,' he said. 'Earlier you pointed out one or two features of the Yŏngbyŏn complex for me. Could you refresh my memory, please?'

'Certainly, Major,' said Eisner. 'What do you wish to know?'

'Just point out to me where the new fifty-megawatt reactor is, will you?'

Eisner walked across to the map and tapped his finger on the spot. 'Here,' he said.

'And the reprocessing plant?'

'Here,' said Eisner, tapping again.

Howard asked the colonel to indicate the other installations that Weatherill had pointed out, then waved him back to his chair. 'Thank you, Colonel,' he said. Then he nodded to Ackford, who seized Eisner and began tying him into the chair.

'Major, this is unnecessary,' protested Eisner. 'I will not try anything. You have my word.'

'Unfortunately, Colonel, I think it *is* necessary. You have lied to me. Those are not the correct locations.'

Will he now change his tack? wondered Howard. *Or will he stick to his guns?*

'I have told you the truth,' asserted Eisner indignantly. 'I can prove it.'

'Just how do you propose to do that, Colonel?'

'If you send for Dr Erich Gerber, he will confirm what I have said. He is one of the men you are holding downstairs.'

'Describe him, please.'

Eisner did so. Howard nodded to Ackford, who disappeared downstairs to fetch the man. Gerber was pale and thin, and appeared extremely nervous when he was roughly bundled into the room. When he saw Eisner tied into the chair he gulped, wondering fearfully what was about to happen.

'Tell him, Colonel,' said Howard.

Eisner spoke calmly in German. 'Gerber, I am about to give you a direct order. You will obey it at once. On the map, point out to the *Herr Major* where the new fifty-megawatt reactor is. Do it now.'

Gerber hesitated briefly. 'Are you certain . . .?'

'Do it!' snapped Eisner.

Gerber went to the map and pointed.

'Now point out the reprocessing plant,' ordered Eisner.

Gerber did so. Prompted by Eisner, he then indicated the other features.

Howard addressed the man in German. 'How do you know which these buildings are?'

Gerber looked at Eisner, uncertain whether or not he should reply.

Eisner nodded. 'You may tell him.'

'Well, *Herr Major*,' Gerber began hesitantly. 'I certainly should know. I am a nuclear physicist by training. My job here is to oversee aspects of the Yŏngbyŏn nuclear programme. But you can easily check the truth of what I say. All you have to do is ask your Dr Richard Weatherill.'

Howard was taken aback. 'How do you know Dr Weatherill?'

'I don't actually know him,' said Gerber, 'but I know *of* him. I have read his papers on nuclear physics, and I have seen his photograph in scientific journals, so naturally I recognised him when I saw him just now in the corridor. I must say I am extremely surprised to see that he is with your team of *kommandos*. He is a distinguished British scientist.'

The man was telling the truth, Howard realised. Who but another physicist would know Weatherill's background? 'Thank you,' he told Gerber. 'You may go. Tony, take him back downstairs.'

Howard walked across and began to untie Eisner from the chair. 'Please forgive me, Colonel,' he said: 'It was perhaps a clumsy test to subject you to, but I had to know. I have of course already checked the locations of the various facilities with Dr Weatherill, so I knew you were telling the truth. But I'm still rather curious about one thing?'

'Yes, Major?'

'Why is it that you are being so co-operative?'

For the first time since Howard had started questioning him, Gerhardt Eisner seemed genuinely taken by surprise. 'But, Major, I thought that should have been obvious to you from the start – I thought you would have understood. The answer is simple. It is because I am hoping it will be in my best interests. And I don't just mean that I want to avoid physical suffering.' He glanced towards the corner. 'General Erfurt's body seemed sufficient evidence of your determination to find out what you came for, and I meant what I said earlier about my inability to tolerate pain. But even if I doubted your determination, I would still now be co-operating with you.'

Howard's expression did not change. He was relieved to hear that Eisner had been convinced of his risk of torture, and made a mental note to have the general's body dressed again before they left. 'Please tell me why, Colonel.'

Eisner sighed. 'I thought you would have guessed. It's simple. I am what you might call a . . . mercenary. Not all my colleagues feel the same way, but the majority do. Why otherwise would we be here, working for the North Koreans, whom we dislike? It is partly, of course, because we are to some extent no longer welcome in our own country. But the principal reason, from my point of view, is that we are being well paid. For General Erfurt it was always a matter of ideology, of dogma. I never had any time for ideology myself, and of course the old Communist ideas, which we were formerly obliged to promote, are now discredited. I never shared the general's views, although of course I did not tell him that.'

'So how did the General take to the idea of hiring out the *Stasi*'s services, if he was so faithful to the principles of the Party?'

'Oh, it wasn't difficult to persuade him, provided that one could dress it up as being against Western interests. For example . . . I'm afraid that accepting the IRIS assignment was actually my idea. I was personally contacted by the Iranians, who had been using a scout in London to find a suitable organisation to work for them. I was asked whether we would undertake a major assassination for them, for which we would be well remunerated. I had to clear it with the general, of course. Normally he wouldn't have had anything to do with such an idea, but I pointed out that the Iranians too were by definition opposed to all Western interests – there was, after all, plenty of evidence! I told him that it could therefore do no harm, and possibly some good, to co-operate with them – and at the same time to be paid well. He accepted the argument, but as usual he took over the running of the operation and I heard little more about it. You see, for the general it had to be a matter of ideological correctness. I, on the other hand, saw it simply as a profitable business arrangement. Do you see my point?'

'I do,' said Howard, studying Eisner's face keenly. 'Tell me, Colonel, would you yourself work for anyone who paid you? Anyone at all?'

'Yes,' said Eisner simply.

'Would you work for us?'

'I was hoping you would ask that,' replied Eisner, grinning. 'Yes, I would. If I was paid well, of course I would . . . Look, Major, I have an idea – maybe the same one that you have in mind. I assume from some of your questions that part of your mission is to find out more about the Yŏngbyŏn complex?'

'Correct,' said Howard.

'Good. I am relieved to hear that you do not have some act of sabotage in mind. The place is so large that it would be almost impossible to cause anything other than minor damage, and anyway such an act would gain little. There are seven other nuclear installations in North Korea, although admittedly this is the most important one. The answer is simple. Instead of trying to get into the place yourself, why don't I provide you with the information you need? For a price, of course.'

Howard looked pleased. 'Colonel, you will understand that I am not authorised to discuss finances, but I think I can safely say that the British government would be extremely interested in doing business with you – if the information you provided was good.'

'Excellent!' said Eisner. 'For me this would be very satisfactory. I must of course continue to work for the North Koreans too – you will understand that if I cease my involvement here I shall no longer have access to the sort of information you require. I take it your government would not object to my being paid by both sides?'

'We wouldn't have it any other way, Colonel.'

'Good! Then I think we have an agreement in principle. If you don't mind, I shall keep this to myself for the time being, and I would be grateful if you would do the same. Perhaps you would continue to treat me like a prisoner until you leave here?'

'Certainly,' said Howard. 'The fewer people who know about this, the better.'

'It is a pleasure to do business with you, Major. And now I would like to demonstrate my good faith to you. I take it that you have searched my room?'

'We searched all the rooms here, including yours. Why?'

'I suggest you search mine again,' said Eisner. 'There's an old typewriter there.'

'Yes?' said Howard, intrigued.

'The roller lifts out of the carriage when you release the clips on both sides,' said Eisener. 'The right-hand knob of the roller pulls off quite easily. The roller itself is hollow.'

'And?'

'Inside, you will find some microfilm – my own copies of some two hundred and forty documents, plans, procurement orders and the like, all relating to Yŏngbyŏn. The originals are kept in a secure facility in Yŏngbyŏn itself, which is partly why you have found little of interest in this building. Take the rolls of film with you – they give a comprehensive and up-to-date picture of what is going on there, and I think your government will find them quite interesting.'

Howard's expression did not change, but he immediately realised the immense potential value of what he had just been offered. If, that was, the material was what Eisener claimed it to be. 'All on microfilm, you say?'

'A somewhat outmoded technique, I know,' said Eisener. 'But it still has its uses.'

'Did any of your colleagues know you kept copies of these things?'

'No, certainly not,' answered Eisener with alacrity. 'I kept them . . . for a rainy day, as you say in England. In the hope that one day I might profit from them. That day would appear to have arrived.'

'Colonel, you have surprised me from start to finish. You know, you are really quite something. Look,' Howard appeared suddenly uncomfortable. 'I . . . I would like to apologise for the way you have been treated by us, and for the deaths of your colleagues. I hope you understand.'

'There's no need for any apology, Major,' Eisener smiled. 'I quite understand, and I would have expected nothing else. We are professional people, you and I. Those who died when you took this building . . . well, they knew the risks. In a way, they would have understood too. As for General Erfurt . . . well, he was living in the past. His political convictions and prejudices were an obstacle to commercial progress. A new approach is now required.'

Howard nodded, saying nothing. He sat for a minute, thinking. In some ways he admired Eisener, but he didn't feel he would ever completely come to terms with the utter ruthlessness – and apparent amorality – of the man. But then, he realised, he did not have a background in Intelligence, as Eisener had. Howard was ex-Special Forces and, although the distinction sometimes became blurred, there was still a difference.

'Colonel,' he said at last, 'there is one more thing I would like you to do, if you can manage it. It may sound as though I'm asking a favour, but in fact it will help you as much as it will help me.'

'I'm listening, Major,' replied Eisener. 'Please explain.'

Ten minutes later, Howard called Ackford to escort Eisener back down to the cellar. Howard watched him go. He doubted whether he would ever see the *Stasi* colonel again, but he knew he would not easily forget him. Then he walked swiftly along the corridor and went into Eisener's room. After bolting the door shut behind him he began to dismantle the old typewriter.

52

In an average year, nearly four thousand direct threats are made against the life of the President of the United States. These are assessed by the Secret Service and classified in order of seriousness. Typically, fewer than one hundred fall into category three, the most serious; however, every one of the four thousand threats will result in the individual being visited, almost always by a grim-faced Secret Serviceman, and 'warned off'. Most people are stupid enough to telephone the threat from their homes; the calls are traced instantaneously by the White House switchboard, which makes the Secret Service's job easier. Individuals are reminded in stark terms of the fact that to threaten the life of the President, even if the threat is not acted upon, is a specific crime under federal law. Most are sufficiently cowed and cause no further trouble, but their names are nevertheless entered in the Secret Service's computer database. The database now contains in excess of fifty thousand names. Persistently threatening or dangerous individuals receive closer attention. Each of these requires a major investigation, often including round-the-clock surveillance of the individual concerned.

The White House itself is classified as a national museum. It is open to the public, and receives over a million visitors each year. The security of the buildings, which include the old Executive Office building and the White House itself, is the responsibility of what used to be called the White House Police. During Richard Nixon's presidency this force was renamed the Executive Protective Service; then a few years later, in 1977, it became the Secret Service Uniformed Division. Although the Uniformed Division likes to think of itself as part of the Secret Service, it is not – the qualifications, skills and training required are less rigorous. Nevertheless it has a major role to play in the security apparatus surrounding the President.

The Uniformed Division comprises more than one thousand officers. The division controls the White House motor pool, which is housed in two garage complexes, one on L Street and the other at the Anacostia Naval Air Station; it also maintains a canine unit, with a training base in Maryland, for the sniffer dogs that are used to detect explosives in all vehicles entering the White House premises. More visibly, Uniformed Division officers are responsible for screening all visitors, using metal detectors to find weapons and Geiger counters to detect radioactive material.

Uniformed officers maintain a number of emergency systems in the event of sabotage or failure; these include air and water purifiers, back-up power generators and a back-up water supply. They also monitor the White House and grounds with a comprehensive range of electronic systems designed to warn against intruders. There are cameras, ground sensors, infra-red and audio detectors, and closed-circuit television coverage of every angle of the house and grounds, monitored and recorded twenty-four hours a day.

An added complication is that the grounds of the White House are designated as a National Park. As a result any maintenance required is the responsibility of the National Park Service, and crimes committed in the grounds fall within the technical jurisdiction of the US Park Police. By virtue of the location, however, any crime committed there is highly likely to be a federal offence, which is where the FBI can become involved.

By any standards, the problem of maintaining a good level of security for the White House, its occupants and all its employees and visitors is a very major one. The blurring and overlapping of responsibilities among the various agencies charged with maintaining this security makes the task no easier.

Marvin Jefferson had been listening patiently as he was briefed on the subject. He was just about to cut in with a question when the door flew open and a harassed-looking Secret Serviceman flew in.

'Sir!' the man blurted out. 'It's Flagman! He's the target! We've just heard!'

'What!' George Reynolds, the head of the Secret Service, leapt to his feet. 'Oh, *shit!*' He looked at his watch and turned to Jefferson. 'Come on, Marvin, let's go. We haven't got much time.' He made swiftly for the door, barking at his subordinate to call for his helicopter immediately.

Jefferson, equally startled, was already on his feet. For a brief moment he searched his memory for the real identity of the person codenamed 'Flagman' by the Secret Service. *Oh, God*, he thought, suddenly remembering who it was. He followed Reynolds out of the door at a run and caught up. 'Where are we going, George?'

'Airport,' said Reynolds briefly. 'Flagman's plane is due to land in about an hour's time. Shit!' he muttered anxiously.

'Why are we going there?'

Reynolds did not break his stride. 'Damn it, Marvin,' he snapped impatiently. 'Do I have to spell it out? Because that IRIS thing could have been planted there, that's why. Shit,' he muttered again. 'It could be there, it could be on his route into town, it could be where he's staying overnight – in fact, it could be any goddamn place. *Shit!*'

Jefferson frowned. 'I don't think so,' he said.

'*What?*' Reynolds turned.

'I don't think so,' repeated Jefferson calmly. 'George – just hold on a second, will you?'

Reynolds stopped. He eyed Jefferson suspiciously. 'What's on your mind, Marvin? Quick – make it snappy, huh? We've got to go.'

'No,' said Jefferson firmly. 'We're not going anywhere. Just listen for a minute, for Chrissake.'

The authority in the big FBI man's voice had the required effect.

'OK, Marvin,' said Reynolds, now curious. 'I'm listening.'

'I don't think the IRIS weapon will be at the airport,' said Jefferson.

'How the hell do you figure that?' demanded Reynolds.

'Logic,' Jefferson replied. 'Think about it. Let's forget about timings for a moment. They're not important. The whole point of IRIS, as I understand it, is that it will be ready to fire automatically, whatever time its victim shows up. Fine – we've just this minute learned that it's programmed to kill Flagman. Obviously whoever planted IRIS knew that some while ago, and they've had plenty of time to select the best place to put it. What's important is the location. It will have been planted to cover a specific spot – somewhere the assassins know Flagman will definitely be at some stage. The *when* is not important. The where *is*. Do you see my point?'

'Sure I do,' said Reynolds scathingly. 'That's why the goddam airport's an ideal place. The assassin knows that Flagman has got to pass through there at some stage.'

'Do you have a large-scale plan of the airport in your office? And street maps of the city?'

'Yes, I do, but why—'

'Let's go back and take a look at them. Come on.' Jefferson turned and led Reynolds back the way they had come.

Reynolds followed, puzzled. So far, he had found Jefferson easy and amenable to work with. He had nearly hit the roof when he heard that an FBI man was to be placed in charge, but he had been pleasantly surprised and mollified by Jefferson's own suggestion of joint responsibility. The big man in the blue suit had given him no trouble at all – until now. Suddenly, Jefferson seemed to be asserting himself.

Back in his office, Reynolds closed the door and helped Jefferson unroll the map of the airport and spread it on the desk. 'Marvin, do you mind telling me—'

'OK,' Jefferson cut in. 'What area are we talking about on this map?'

Reynolds pointed. 'Well, after landing, the aircraft taxis up to this point right here, and then the motorcade—'

'Flagman rates a motorcade?'

'Goddam right, he does,' said Reynolds. 'He gets the full treatment. There'll be—'

'Could any of the cars in the motorcade have been got at?'

'No chance,' said Reynolds. 'In any case, the cars to be used were only decided on this morning. But what—'

'So that just leaves airport vehicles, buildings or other permanent fixtures that possibly *could* have been tampered with, right?'

'Yes, I suppose so, but –'

'Bear with me a moment,' Jefferson went on. 'Let's assume that IRIS has a maximum effective range of four hundred yards. My guess is it will be less – possibly one hundred yards.'

'I don't think we can assume that,' said Reynolds, puzzled.

'I do,' said Jefferson firmly. 'Here's why. At four hundred yards, even if IRIS is that accurate, the time of flight of a rifle bullet will be, uh, just over half a second, right? That's actually quite a long time. If Flagman moves *at all* during that half second – even if he turns his head or something – the bullet could miss him. But at one hundred yards the bullet's almost instantaneous. A tenth of a second or thereabouts. My point is this. The assassin hasn't gone to all this trouble just to miss. He'll have placed IRIS somewhere he knows it will guarantee a hit. So all we have to do is move everything Flagman does at least four hundred yards away from where he might normally be expected to do it. For example, we park the airplane here' – he pointed to a spot on the map – 'instead of there. See?'

'Yes,' answered Reynolds thoughtfully. 'So all we have to do is move the airplane reception . . .'

'Correct,' said Jefferson. 'We'll do that anyway, as a precaution. But it won't make any difference.'

'You've lost me there,' said Reynolds. 'Why won't it make any difference?'

'Because IRIS won't have been planted at the airport,' said Jefferson.

'What? How do you know that?'

'Because the assassin who planted it is a professional. He will know that planned positions, routes and entrances can be changed easily. He won't have taken the risk that a change like that could wreck his plans. As I said, he needs a guaranteed hit. He'll know we have the latitude to change things in pretty well every place Flagman will be visiting. There are alternate routes, alternate entrances to buildings – almost everywhere has an alternate. And that's why IRIS won't have been planted at any of them.'

'So where does that leave us?'

'It's simple enough,' replied Jefferson. 'The assassin has planted IRIS to cover the one place that can't be changed. The *only* place.'

'But you can't mean . . .'

'Yes,' said Jefferson. 'I do. I mean here. IRIS has been planted right here, somewhere in the White House.'

The suggestion was an affront to everything that George Reynolds stood for. It was impossible, he told himself. Impossible. Security at the White House was the tightest in the world. No one, but *no one*, got into the White House with a gun unless they were specifically authorised to bring it in, and the weapon had to be the exact one they were authorised to carry – no modifications, no specials, no bolt-on extras. The security checks, the sniffer dogs, the metal-detectors . . . Everyone was subject to the checks, however important they were. High-ranking aides, senators, visitors – *everyone*. Hell, one congressman had been stopped and his car turned inside out because a sniffer dog had indicated a positive trace. It had turned out to be fertiliser for his garden . . . 'Impossible,' he muttered finally. 'It can't be done.'

'Someone has done it,' said Jefferson softly. 'I don't

know how yet, but we're going to find out. We're going to have to turn the place upside down until we find this IRIS thing. Some clever bastard has found a way.'

53

Howard finished towelling himself dry and rapidly dressed himself in one of Eisner's uniform suits. It fitted reasonably well and it was a relief to be out of his own clothes, which still stank from the crawl through the long, fetid concrete pipe. There was a knock at the door; it was Halliday.

'Johnny's reply to your signal, boss,' he said, handing Howard the message.

Howard read it rapidly and looked up. 'Thanks, Pete,' he said, satisfied. 'I'll need a few minutes to check the map, then I'll be ready to send our last message confirming everything. Is everyone ready to go?'

'I think so, but Tony's still outside, checking the vehicles over. I haven't told the woman or Weatherill anything yet. He thinks we're off to install his monitoring gear in the nuclear plant.'

'Good. Are you clear about what to say for their benefit?'

'Yeah.'

'OK. Ask Tony to come up when he's got a moment, would you? Then get ready to send my reply to Johnny.'

Halliday disappeared and Howard bent over the map, plotting the set of co-ordinates he had received in Bourne's radio message. He frowned and thought hard for a few minutes, then came to a decision. He began writing out his final message and instructions to Bourne.

There was another knock on the door; this time it was Ackford. 'You wanted to see me, boss?' he asked.

'What's the verdict, Tony? Any of them any use?'

'There's a truck out there that will do. Piece of crappy old Nik-Nok junk, of course, but it's in quite good order. These *Stasi* people have been looking after their vehicles. Not quite *Vorsprung durch Technik*, but it'll do OK.'

'Fine,' said Howard. 'Fuel?'

'I've loaded it up. Plenty of spare jerricans. More than enough.'

'OK. I'll see you downstairs in a minute.'

Howard made one last check to make sure he had forgotten nothing and left the room. He dropped in on Halliday to hand him the message, then made his way down to the main entrance hall, where the others were already gathered. Pretending to be surprised at Halliday's absence, he launched into the act he had carefully prepared.

'Mel, go and ask Pete if he's had any luck fixing that radio, will you?'

Harris nodded and left. Two minutes later he reappeared with Halliday.

'Any luck, Pete?' asked Howard, injecting an anxious tone into his voice.'

'Sorry, boss,' Halliday lied, feigning anger and frustration. 'Effing thing's completely knackered.'

'Damn,' Howard cursed aloud, continuing the act. 'Sod it. Well, that's that. OK: listen, everyone,' he announced. 'I'll be brief. The radio's had it, so our overriding priority is to get ourselves out of here with the information we have about IRIS. Everything else has to take a back seat. There won't be time to get into the nuclear facility and install the monitoring equipment, and I daren't risk it.'

Weatherill looked both shocked and disappointed. Harris, standing next to him, saw his expression. 'Never mind, doc,' he said kindly. 'Things sometimes just don't work out. It isn't your fault.'

The scientist nodded miserably. 'Thanks, Mel,' he

said. 'It just – well, it seems I've wasted my time coming here, and I've risked all this for nothing.'

Howard was watching Kim Sumi's face. She seemed to have accepted his decision without demur; her face was its normal impassive mask. 'I suggest we don't hang about,' he continued. 'Make sure you've got all your kit, and sling it on the truck. Tony will drive, and Sumi will travel in front with me for when we run into NK roadblocks. Has everyone got a *Stasi* ID card and travel pass that fits their description reasonably well?'

They all nodded. Kim Sumi was the exception; she had brought with her the uniform of a North Korean Army captain, and false identity documents prepared for her by the American Central Intelligence Agency. She was the only one of them, thought Howard, who would not look completely out of place. He hoped to God this *Stasi* unit was held in high regard in North Korea; the presence of Westerners of any description was sufficiently unusual that they were quite likely to be shot on sight.

'What about that lot downstairs, boss?' asked Zeccara. 'Are we just going to leave the *Stasi* there?'

'Yes,' said Howard. 'They're securely locked in. They'll be able to break out eventually, but it will take them a few hours. And when they do, I don't think they'll be in any hurry to admit to the NK security people that we made fools of them. Do you think they would keep their security contract here for long if they did? No, my guess is that they'll cover it up, if they can.'

The others smiled at Howard's perceptiveness. One by one they followed him outside and began to load the vehicle and climb on. Ackford started the engine; it rattled, but sounded healthy enough. Sumi was about to climb into the cab when she stopped and turned to Howard. 'Oh,' she said. 'I'm sorry. I've forgotten my uniform cap.'

'OK. Quick – go and get it,' Howard told her.

'What was that she said?' asked Ackford impatiently.

'She's forgotten her cap,' said Howard, rolling his eyes. 'Dinky little number with a red star on the front.'

'Women,' muttered Ackford.

Kim Sumi hurried back inside the *Stasi* building. She looked around; the hall was empty. Quickly and silently, she made her way to the basement stairs and began to descend them. Alone in the end cell, Colonel Eisener heard the faint clicking of the key in the lock. He stood up as the door opened. Kim Sumi stood framed in the faint light of the doorway. She said nothing but stretched out her hand, holding a sheet of paper. He took it without a word. The door closed, but the key did not turn. Eisener realised he was no longer locked in. He thought he heard the softly departing footsteps of the young woman as she went back along the corridor and up the stairs. From outside came the noise of the truck's engine turning over; the English major and his *kommandos* were getting ready to leave, he realised. He smiled to himself.

Eisener's heart almost stopped when the cell door suddenly swung open again. The tall, rangy figure of Ziegler appeared. He had been hiding unseen in the darkness of the corridor.

'Hello, Colonel,' whispered Ziegler menacingly. 'I'll take a look at that piece of paper, if you don't mind.'

Kim Sumi hurried back outside, clutching her North Korean Army uniform cap. 'I'm sorry about that,' she said to Howard.

'No harm done,' replied Howard, helping her into the cab. As she climbed up, he glanced behind him and saw the shadowy figure of Ziegler emerge swiftly from the building.

As Ziegler approached the truck, his eyes met Howard's. He gave a slow but definite nod. Then he disappeared behind the truck and Howard heard him climbing on.

Howard pulled himself up into the cab next to Sumi

and closed the door. 'OK, Tony,' he said, his voice calm and neutral. 'Let's get going.'

In the back of the truck Harris discreetly nudged Zeccara. 'Him or her?' he murmured. 'It's got to be the girl, hasn't it?'

'Reckon so. But the boss knows what he's doing – he'll have her covered.'

Treacherous bitch, thought Harris. *I never trusted her from the start.*

There was a crunch of gears and the truck began to pull away.

54

The jeep bumped, swerved and rattled its way northwards from Kumhwa, nearing the end of its journey. In the front seat, Colonel Max Goodale hung on to the grab-handle for dear life, comforting himself with the knowledge that there wasn't much further to go. The rough dirt track had not been improved by the passage of heavy military vehicles on their way to and from the Demilitarized Zone; it was heavily rutted and potholed, with some water still in evidence from the previous night's rain. At least, thought Goodale, the rain had dampened the dust down, even though the ground was still bone-shakingly hard.

The jeep's driver, a purposeful-looking South Korean army captain, was obviously familiar with the route; he was driving well, if too fast for Goodale's taste. Johnny Bourne, in the back seat, was leaning forwards between them; Bourne's sense of urgency had been infectious and the South Korean captain had responded to it.

There had been no stopping Bourne after he had received Howard's last message confirming his route.

Throughout his time in Seoul, Bourne had behaved like a caged tiger, snarling his frustration and pacing ceaselessly back and forth; now unleashed and free, he was a different man. In a way, Goodale preferred him like this. Bottled up, the young man had been almost impossible to deal with. His hunger for action – any form of action – now looked like being partially satisfied. At last he had something to do, something concrete to organise, even if it was not action of the sort he knew Howard and his companions would be facing when they attempted their crossing of the DMZ.

Goodale was keenly aware of his own promise to Juliet, Bourne's wife. He had given her his solemn word of honour that he would not allow Johnny to involve himself in any hazardous activity. At the time there had appeared to be no danger of that happening – he and Johnny would be in Seoul the entire time, just manning the radio link and liaising with the embassy. Things now appeared a little different, and Goodale felt apprehensive at the thought of the younger man in such close proximity to the front line.

But Bourne had a job to do, Goodale told himself, and it was strictly limited to liaising with the South Korean army and their American counterparts on the ground. Ever since that last message, he had been decisive and clear about what he wanted, issuing concise requests and instructions, impressing the American and South Korean forces' personnel with his grasp of detail and sense of urgency.

There had been only two matters over which he had had to seek Goodale's help in overcoming or bypassing obstructive bureacratic regulations, and Goodale had not hesitated in either case to request the US Embassy's help in getting what he wanted. To be fair to the officials concerned, thought Goodale, their hands were very much tied by the necessity for due caution – the DMZ, the border between North and South Korea, was potentially one of the world's major potential flashpoints, and extreme care was exercised to prevent full-scale military confrontation. The US ambassador, though, was well aware of the recent deeds of Ed Howard and his team. He knew they had been instrumental in obtaining information that provided his government with the chance to prevent an assassination that would be a catastrophe. The ambassador wasn't about to throw such men to the wolves by sitting on his hands and doing nothing to facilitate their escape from the North, and if he needed any further encouragement in the matter Goodale had provided it by informing him that two of Howard's team, Mike Ziegler and Kim Sumi, were American citizens. The ambassador had responded with enthusiasm to Goodale's requests and the previously reluctant officials – especially the South Koreans, had responded too, with evident glee. Everyone, it seemed to Goodale, had been itching to give the repressive P'yŏngyang régime a figurative poke in the eye, and the opportunity now to do just that had brought eager smiles to many faces.

The jeep braked to a halt. The South Korean Army captain, Lim Chong-hui, dismounted. 'We will need to walk the rest of the way,' he announced in fluent, American-accented English. 'We mustn't do anything to attract attention from the North.'

Goodale strapped on the US Army helmet he had been loaned. It felt strange to be in uniform again after so many years, and he had certainly never before worn that of an American Military Police major; but he realised that the subterfuge was necessary. 'Is it far, Captain Lim?' he asked.

'Not far, sir,' said the captain. 'Twenty-five minutes, no more. We will keep in cover, and if we are careful we will not be observed from the other side. I will lead the way. I repeat that as we get nearer, the area becomes very open and exposed. We will need to take care that our arrival at the edge of the Zone is not visible from over the border. The North is always vigilant, and their forces are there in large numbers.'

Bourne nodded in agreement. He suppressed a shudder at the mention of how open and exposed the DMZ was along this particular stretch of its length, and he winced at Captain Lim's reference to the massive strength of the North Korean Army. Ed would somehow have to lead the others through all that, without being detected . . .

'Mr Bourne, may I help you with your case?' Captain Lim was asking.

'No, thanks, Captain,' he replied. The request was meant kindly, Bourne knew, but he resented it. The South Korean had obviously noticed his injured leg and was aware that the equipment case was heavy; but limp or no, Bourne resolved, he would carry it himself. They set off along a path through the scrub.

Fifteen minutes later Bourne was limping heavily. The strain on his damaged limb of carrying the case containing the lights and heavy battery-packs was telling on him. *It can't weigh more than seventy pounds,* he thought, trying to ignore the ache in his leg. *I used to be able to run, not just walk, carrying heavier weights than this, and think nothing of it.*

The scrub had now thinned. Captain Lim announced that they were now less than half a mile from their destination, a dug-in command-post on the southern edge of the DMZ. They entered a system of trenches winding forwards. The South Korean bent double to keep his head below ground level; Goodale and Bourne followed his example. Sweat began beading on Bourne's brow. Arriving at the command-post, he sank to the ground gratefully, setting down the heavy equipment case and flexing his leg to relieve the pain. 'Phew,' he sighed, breathing hard. 'Well, colonel, if I needed any evidence that I was out of condition, I've just had it.'

'Here, buddy,' said an American voice, proffering a steaming mug, 'have a cup of coffee. You look like you could use it.'

Bourne looked up at the US Military Police corporal standing over him and nodded. 'Thanks,' he said gratefully. He sat back and relaxed.

Goodale took his own coffee mug and went forward to the edge of the below-ground shelter. Cautiously he raised his head and looked out to the north.

The scene that met his eyes was an empty and desolate one. Away in the distance across the open ground he could make out the main fence that marked the actual border. He raised a pair of binoculars to his eyes and scanned the area.

The cover was pitifully sparse. Apart from a few stunted bushes and some slight rises and falls in the ground, there was almost nothing to provide concealment. Anyone out there would be dreadfully exposed, he realised, frowning anxiously. What chance did Howard and the others have of crossing such terrain undetected, even if they did somehow manage to sneak past the massive numbers of North Korean troops concentrated in depth on the other side?

He glanced sideways at Captain Lim. 'It's madness,' he muttered to the South Korean. 'How can anyone hope to . . .'

'I know, sir,' conceded Lim. 'But the real problem is not the open ground – it's the landmines. You see, this is the only place on the whole DMZ where we know there is a dead straight path through the minefields on both sides. It's an absolutely straight line, right from the north through to this exact spot. Two years ago a North Korean defector, a senior Army officer, gave us the information. He brought with him a map, and our CIA realised its potential value. We began clearing the mines on our own side too, continuing the straight line. Although it took much patient work, we knew it might one day make a useful escape route. But,' he shrugged, 'speaking for myself, I rather agree with you. If I were a North Korean, I would certainly choose an easier way to try to escape.'

'How?'

Lim sighed. 'Not easy,' he said. 'Some have escaped through Russia, but they are not always . . . trustworthy. For a normal person in North Korea, someone with no influence, it is impossible. But if one could get oneself into a position of privilege, perhaps with access to restricted areas near the border, to an aircraft, or perhaps to a submarine . . . Not easy, though.'

Bourne had joined them. He too was scanning the open ground through binoculars. 'Jesus,' he muttered. 'Anyone out there would be like a moth pinned to a board. There's hardly any cover at all.'

'I'm afraid so, Mr Bourne,' said Captain Lim.

'Well,' said Bourne, 'at least the beacons should be visible the whole way along the route. Point out the exact line, would you?'

As the South Korean began indicating the precise features, Bourne busied himself with his GPS satellite navigator, a large-scale map and a prismatic compass. Finally he was satisfied. 'OK,' he said eventually, 'we'll set out one IR right here, on the roof of the command-post. Will there be any objections to that?'

'I don't think so,' said Lim. 'There are sometimes lights here at night, and I doubt that one more will make any difference – especially if it is infra-red.'

'Fine,' said Bourne. 'Let's go and site the other one.' They moved to the rear of the command-post facing back southwards. 'The second one needs to be set quite some distance back,' he said. 'Say four or five hundred metres, on a bearing of . . .' He read out the back-bearing and handed the compass to Captain Lim, who in turn peered through the prismatic compass lens. 'What do you think?'

Lim frowned. 'Well,' he said, 'it will of course have to be on that bearing – I appreciate that. It's just . . .

'What's the problem?'

'Well, I can't see a problem with actually having a light there, but you will need to take great care not to be seen setting it out. It's very exposed back there, as you can see. We are being watched the whole time. That's why we approached through the trench system. But the trench is not on that line. We will already have been seen looking at them through binoculars, but that is a normal daily activity and they will not consider it unusual. But when you go to set out that beacon . . .'

'Don't worry, Captain,' grinned Bourne. 'I won't be seen. As well as the beacons, I've got plenty of old scrim-nets and hessian sacking in that equipment case. All I'll need in addition is some water, to make lots of nice sticky mud to smear everywhere. By the time I'm dressed up in that lot, you'll have difficulty spotting me crawling ten yards away.'

An hour later, Bourne was ready. The second beacon and the heavy lead-acid battery that would power it were now in a canvas rucksack. Inside his smock were the compass, map and GPS. He was covered from head to foot in filthy, mud-smeared tatters and strips of sacking and scrim-net; the US and South Korean occupants of the command-post turned out to look with interest at the strange, shapeless apparition. He nodded at Goodale, slithered up the bank and began crawling slowly away on the bearing he had taken.

Captain Lim watched him go. True to his word, by the time he was ten yards away, moving slowly and carefully, Bourne had become almost invisible, his shapeless form merging with the ground.

Lim turned to Goodale. 'Colonel Goodale, sir?' he asked politely. 'I don't want to sound too inquisitive, but . . . who exactly is Mr Bourne?'

Goodale smiled. 'He was once a captain in the Special Air Service,' he said.

'Ah,' said Lim, nodding in understanding. 'Of course. That explains a great deal.'

'Yes,' said Goodale. 'But that leg-wound of his . . . Well, you've seen yourself what it has done to him. It was a very serious wound.'

'He was wounded in action?'

'Yes,' said Goodale. 'It was one hell of an action, too.' He paused, reflecting. 'Once, Johnny Bourne was just about the best there was. The best . . .' He shook his head slowly. 'But not any more, I'm afraid. Johnny's active service days are all behind him now.'

55

Levy's cab pulled up; he paid the driver and got out. Hurrying inside, he pressed the button for the elevator and stood waiting, a slight frown on his face. Joanna had been slightly mysterious on the telephone, asking him to come by taxi rather than be driven by Ronald as usual. *Oh well*, he thought with a sigh, *never mind. It must be another of her little surprises.* He grinned with anticipation.

The elevator arrived; a slightly-built, fair-haired man in his early thirties appeared and got in with him. Levy pressed the button for the seventh floor.

'Hi!' said the man, smiling. The lift started up. 'You going to seven too?'

Levy nodded politely without replying.

'I'm Jim Garrett. My parents live in apartment 705,' said the man brightly.

'Oh,' said Levy, smiling. 'Yes, I've met them. Nice people.'

The lift stopped and they got out. The fair-haired man paused, bending to tie his shoelace, then followed Levy down the corridor. A large trolley with a packing case on it was standing near Joanna's door; Levy glanced idly at it as he pressed the door-buzzer. The door opened immediately, and he felt a sudden push in his back. He stumbled through the door, nearly falling over, vaguely aware that there was a black plastic sheet covering the floor in the hallway. His briefcase fell from his grasp and skidded across the plastic. He heard the door close behind him and looked round. The fair-haired man who had called himself Jim Garrett and another, a stocky, dark-haired individual dressed in overalls, were pointing silenced pistols at him. There was no sign of Joanna; it had been the stocky man who had answered the door. Levy gaped at the two of them.

'Sit down on the floor,' snapped the fair-haired man from the left, his voice cold. Peter Kramer was angry; he had received very little notice of Levy's visit to Joanna Stone. The last few minutes had been a bit of a rush, and being rushed always annoyed him.

Levy's mouth was still hanging open in shock. Carl Berman punched him hard in the solar plexus; Levy collapsed to his knees, winded and gasping.

'Sit,' commanded Berman.

Too stunned to think, Levy remained kneeling, fighting for breath. A few seconds later fear took over and he did as he was told. The black polythene beneath him made a rustling noise.

'Some questions,' said Kramer, who was pulling on a pair of overalls. 'First one: who else have you talked to about the White House security pass for McKinley?'

'McKinley . . . pass?' Levy did not understand. 'I . . . Who are you? What have you done—'

'Shut up. Answer the question.'

Levy tried to think. He suddenly remembered the name. 'Oh . . . McKinley. The technician. Yes. My secretary arranged it. I helped . . . Look, I'm sorry. Maybe I shouldn't have done it. I'm sorry.'

'Just you and your secretary?'

'Yes! I mean, no! Joanna . . . my fiancée . . . she asked me to fix it up as a favour. I'm sorry if I've done anything wrong . . . Where is Jo—'

'Shut up,' said Kramer, snapping on a pair of surgical gloves. 'Just answer the questions, or Carl will hurt you very badly. Next question. Who else knew you were coming here?'

'No one,' said Levy, trembling. 'No one! I came straight here to see Joanna. This is her apartment. She can explain—'

'Not even your secretary? You didn't leave a contact number?'

'N-no,' stammered Levy, shaking his head. 'We wanted to spend a quiet night together. Joanna asked specially . . .' Levy fell silent, mindful of the man's warning. He was badly scared. Something had obviously gone very seriously wrong. These must be Secret Servicemen, he decided, and that guy McKinley must have stepped way out of line. What had the man done? Joanna had said that McKinley would just be installing an Israeli surveillance camera in place of one of the US-made ones, to demonstrate conclusively how much better the new Israeli technology was. It was no big deal, Levy told himself. In fact, it would ultimately have benefits for security at the White House. But now it looked like he, Levy, was being held responsible for McKinley's actions.

His legal mind addressed the issue. What was the alleged crime? Sabotage, perhaps, or tampering with US government property? Technically, he admitted, there might be a case to answer on the tampering charge, but in this particular instance it could hardly be a serious matter. The replacement video unit would actually be an improvement on its predecessor, which would in due course be handed back anyway. Or, in his own case, could the supposed 'offence' be that of obtaining a security pass under false pretences? What nonsense! Plenty of White House staffers did that, for their 'research assistants' and other cronies.

But the Secret Service, Levy knew, didn't go round punching people or pointing guns at them without good reason. He must be in bad trouble. For the time being, anyway, it would be inadvisable to argue with these two.

He would sort the bastards out later, and by God would he then hang their balls out to dry! In the meantime, he told himself, he would just do exactly as they said. They were hard, vicious-looking, frightening individuals.

Kramer kicked Levy's briefcase across to him. 'Open it.'

His hands shaking, Levy fumbled hurriedly with the locks and opened it. Inside were two fat folders of documents, a small dictating machine, some pens and a yellow legal pad.

'Empty it onto the floor.'

Levy did so.

Kramer produced a folded sheet of paper and handed it to Levy. 'Tear this up into small pieces and drop the pieces in the briefcase.'

Confused but terrified by the pistol Berman was holding close to his head, Levy did as he was told. He was then ordered to put the other items back inside, on top of the pieces of torn paper, and close the briefcase. The locks snapped shut again.

'Lie down on your back and open your mouth.'

Levy gulped; he complied, not understanding.

'Wider.'

Berman leaned down with a quick motion and squeezed the pistol's trigger. There was a soft thud. The bullet passed between Levy's expensive white teeth and through the back of his throat, smashing into the second cervical vertebra and lodging there. The hydraulic shock pulverised Levy's spinal cord and he died instantly, his body giving one brief, convulsive jerk. Berman knelt to check that there was no exit-wound from the low-power 6.5mm pistol. He looked up at Kramer, who was finishing zipping up his overalls. 'Do you think he was telling the truth?'

'Yes. Come on. We haven't got much time.'

They swiftly wrapped Levy's body and the briefcase in the heavy black polythene sheet and lifted it into the packing case on the trolley outside, pulling the door of the apartment shut behind them. They closed the lid of the packing case and wheeled it away down the corridor. Passing the main elevator, Kramer paused briefly to remove the wooden wedge that he had used to jam it open and immobilise it. The doors closed; Kramer heard the muted whine of the motor as the empty elevator began to descend. Five yards further on, the corridor turned left, towards the service elevator which would take them down to the rear entrance of the building.

Two minutes later, Kramer and Berman were loading the packing case and trolley into a small delivery van parked outside the building's rear entrance. Berman closed the rear doors of the van and climbed into the passenger seat. Kramer fired the engine and pulled away into the Washington traffic.

Behind them and seven floors above, Joanna Stone emerged from her bedroom, dressed only in her silky, cream-coloured wrap. She moved around her apartment, checking that everything was ready for the visit she expected. There was no hurry, she realised, wiping the door-latch with a cloth; it would be at least an hour before anything was discovered in the park. Maybe another hour after that . . .

She paused in the hallway, sniffing the air. She frowned, wrinkling her nose at the faint but distinctive odour of gunsmoke. *That won't do*, she thought, heading back towards the bathroom. A minute later, a liberal squirt of air-freshener had masked the smell. Maybe a bit too obvious, she decided, frowning again. Time for some cooking.

In the kitchen she began preparing spaghetti with a strong tomato, onion and garlic sauce. Better make it for two, she thought, humming softly to herself as she added more ingredients. One can't be too careful.

The aroma began to fill the apartment as Joanna

Stone waited patiently for the police to arrive with the news of her fiancé's death. They might be suspicious, but she doubted it. Even if it wasn't a very convincing suicide, she knew she had covered her tracks well.

56

The busy military traffic proved to be a help rather than a hindrance. Emerging from the *Stasi* compound on to the main road, Ackford simply slotted the truck in behind an empty transporter vehicle heading south-east. After a mile Howard indicated a turning to the left, going north-eastwards, which would bypass the town of Yŏngbyŏn some three miles away. Wherever possible, he intended to avoid centres of population. There were numerous small unnamed villages marked on his map, and they would have to pass through some of them; but the road and track network was extensive and he had provisionally worked out a route which would bypass larger places. The danger, Howard knew, would be military road-blocks or checkpoints.

'How far is it altogether, boss?' asked Ackford, his jaw methodically chewing his customary wad of gum.

'To the DMZ? About two hundred miles as the crow flies, to the spot we're aiming for. By road probably twice that and more.'

'Are the roads all like this?'

'I don't know, Tony, but I very much doubt it. Some of them are more like mountain passes, and I expect they'll be very slow going.'

'They will,' said Kim Sumi, who had been looking at the map. 'The gradients are very steep and some stretches will be very slow indeed – first gear, or second at best. I hope we've got enough fuel.'

'Full tank plus twenty jerricans in the back, miss,' said

Ackford. 'I don't know how many miles this heap does to the gallon, but that should be more than enough.'

'If we're lucky enough to get that far without being stopped,' added Howard pointedly.

The journey to Hŭich'ŏn took nearly two hours. Approaching the outskirts, Howard saw that the town was larger than he had expected. 'Damn this map,' he muttered. 'It's way out of date. This main road is new. Take a right, Tony. We'll try and get round.'

A mile further on, before they could rejoin the minor road leading south-east across the Yŏngbyŏn river, they came across the first military checkpoint. As they approached it Howard tapped on the rear of the back to alert the others. 'Over to you, Sumi,' he said grimly as Ackford pulled up at the barrier.

In the back of the truck, through a tiny gap in the canvas canopy, Harris trained his weapon on her back as she jumped out of the cab and began talking authoritatively to the checkpoint commander, who straightened up and stood stiffly to attention. Howard too kept his hand on his AK, out of sight in the vehicle footwell. He listened to the sound of Sumi's conversation with the soldier, whom he guessed to be the equivalent of a sergeant. The Korean language had a strange sing-song cadence, but at the same time it was obvious that Sumi was expressing herself forcefully. Howard saw from the sergeant's subservient attitude that the man was not going to defy her authority, and he began to relax a little. Then Sumi abruptly turned and came back to the cab. She snapped her fingers peremptorily at Howard, and to his astonishment spoke to him in fluent German. 'Show me your identity papers and travel permit.'

Recovering from his surprise, Howard handed them over. Sumi showed them to the checkpoint commander, who briefly glanced at them, gave them back to her and saluted. Sumi returned to the truck and climbed in; the barrier was moved aside and they were waved through.

'Do you know any other languages that might come in useful?' asked Howard drily when they were clear.

'I also speak Japanese and Russian,' Sumi replied, 'but I don't think they will be required here.'

'Russian?' asked Howard in surprise. 'I didn't hear you talking any Russian while we were flying in on the Antonov.'

'No,' she replied. 'It's better that way. If people don't know that you understand their language, they're less guarded about what they say to each other in your presence. You learn more that way. Besides, I wasn't prepared to trust the Russians at first.'

Howard was stung by the remark. 'They were my friends!' he snapped angrily. 'They died trying to help us!'

'I know,' said Sumi, her voice now soft. 'I regret my suspicions. I quickly realised they were good people. I . . . I am very sorry about what happened to them.'

Howard glanced at her. Her expression had not changed; it hardly ever did, of course. 'Why did you speak German to me back there?' he asked, curious.

'That man had come across *Stasi* people before. Maybe even this truck. There's a uranium mine north of here, and *Stasi* personnel used to go there on security matters. I didn't want to run the risk of that sergeant understanding the difference between English and German, and becoming suspicious.'

'I see,' said Howard. They sat in silence for a while as the truck jolted along the rough road; then his eyes fell to the map again. 'Tony – another right turn up ahead, at the junction. Then we start climbing up into the Myohyang and Nangnim mountains.'

'Crafty, that, miss,' said Ackford as he made the turn, still chewing his piece of gum. 'Not letting on you know all those languages. Crafty,' he repeated admiringly. Crafty, she might be, he thought, but his money was on the sodding scientist as the one who'd betrayed them. But there was no chance to ask Howard yet.

For the five men being roughly jolted about in the rear of the truck, the journey was not a comfortable one. The experience was made no better by the powerful smell of diesel from the jerricans; the neoprene seals on the caps were leaking badly. As the truck began its steep haul into the granite peaks, Ziegler told Halliday and Zeccara to get some rest; they spread themselves out on the floor and within minutes were asleep. He and Harris stayed awake.

Weatherill had already had some rest, and while he was asleep Halliday had nudged Ziegler and nodded in the scientist's direction. 'Do we trust him, Mike? I don't think I do.'

'Boss says to keep a close eye on both of them,' came the whispered reply. 'But don't give anythin' away.'

Now awake again, Weatherill was feeling nauseous from the diesel fumes; he realised he had still not fully recovered from the gut-wrenching stink of the rotting animal corpse he had had to crawl past on that nightmarish journey through the drainpipe. He moved to the front and undid one of the canvas straps to let in some fresh air, stuck his head through the opening and inhaled gratefully.

'Feeling sick, doc?' called Harris, grinning.

Weatherill turned and smiled weakly. 'I've never been a very good passenger,' he replied, 'and I must admit I don't like the smell of diesel.'

'You should look on the bright side,' said Harris, drawing fiercely on a cigarette. 'It would be a hell of a lot worse if this truck ran on petrol. I wouldn't be able to light up, would I?'

'I'm not sure it's entirely safe for you to do so,' said Weatherill. 'The flashpoint of some diesel fuel mixtures can vary to the extent that—'

'Yeah, yeah, yeah,' said Harris. 'You tell me when we get to the flashpoint, all right? In the meantime, I'm having a nice smoke. Sure you don't want one?'

Weatherill turned pale and thrust his head back

through the gap in the canopy.

Up front in the cab three hours later, Ackford tapped the fuel gauge. 'We'll need to refuel soon, boss,' he said to Howard. 'Tank's getting low.'

'OK, Tony,' said Howard. 'Find a place where we can pull well off the road.'

'Call this a road, boss?' grumbled Ackford. 'Shagged-out donkey-path, more like.'

Ackford was exaggerating, thought Howard, but not much. The road was atrocious, and progress, especially for the past hour, had been very slow. The forty miles since leaving Hŭich'ŏn had not been too bad; the road into the mountains had been slow and tortuous, but it had followed the river valley south-east to Saench'ŏn and the climb had been a gradual one. It had been after the village of Yaksuch'am that the road had deteriorated. It was now little better than a rough track; but it was navigable, and there was little other traffic about. Their progress had drawn some dull, incurious looks from the locals as the truck passed by the small villages dotted along the valley. But the only people who had shown any interest were the soldiers at a small military outpost at Sosung, who stared at them as if they had come from Mars. Howard wondered whether they had ever seen Westerners before.

Kim Sumi's authoritative manner had cowed the outpost's commander into obedience, but her expression was worried as she climbed back into the truck. 'I don't know how many times we're going to be able to get away with this,' she had muttered to Howard. 'We shall certainly be the talking point of that Army post for the next day or two. They are only used to local traffic.'

'Do they have a radio?'

'No, thank God,' said Sumi, 'but there's a telephone. I think I may have convinced the sergeant that he's been in dereliction of his duty in failing to take note of the orders warning him of our arrival, so I hope he won't phone to double-check. The problem is that, the further we get from Yŏngbyŏn, the less likely it will be that people know there's a legitimate *Stasi* presence in this country.'

'You've done all right with them so far,' said Howard.

'Maybe,' muttered Sumi, 'but I'm not looking forward to coming across someone who outranks me. It's bad enough being a woman anyway. That man had never seen a female officer before.'

Ackford pulled off the track and switched off the engine; everyone got out to stretch their legs. Six jerricans of diesel were unloaded from the back and emptied into the truck's fuel tank.

'Pete?' Howard called Halliday. 'Take over the driving from Tony for a spell, will you?'

Ziegler and Howard moved off a few yards and sat talking for a while, their voices low. Eventually Ziegler shook his head. 'I don't like it one bit, Ed,' he said. 'I'm all for settlin' this thing here and now. The boys ought to be told, at least.'

'You know we can't do that, Mike,' said Howard, 'for all sorts of reasons. Look, we can handle it – no problem. The potential advantages are enormous. I'm afraid I must insist on it. Remember, I feel our traitor's just as anxious to get out of this goddam country as we are – but just in case I'm wrong we go on treating both our companions as if nothing had happened, OK? Just make sure that all six of *us* keep our wits – constant vigilance is our best plan. We'll settle things soon enough.'

'You're the boss, Ed,' Ziegler shrugged resignedly. 'I'll go along with you. I see your point, but I want to be on record as sayin' it's just askin' for trouble. As if we ain't got enough already,' he added.

The road wound its way south through the mountains. The Nangnim range was followed by the Ŏnjin, then the Masiknyŏng, as the road climbed to the watershed and then fell away again into the next valley. The valleys were steep-sided and in places spectacular, with mountain peaks rising up to five thousand feet on either side. Just short of the village of Kudang, they crossed the Imjin river as it wound its way tortuously towards the south-west. The name 'Imjin' was not lost on Howard, and he thought of the famous action fought by the Glosters in the Korean War during the early 1950s, when he himself had been a small boy.

He had been apprehensive about crossing the Imjin; at this point the road was close to the town of Kudang. To his surprise there was no military presence visible anywhere. The road crossed the river three times; finally they were clear, climbing again for the last time. On the far side of these mountains lay the huge Ch'ukanjŏng rift valley. They had been on the road for ten hours, and it was now late afternoon. When they were well clear of the town Howard ordered another halt for refuelling; Ackford took the wheel again.

'We're only about thirty miles from the DMZ now, Tony.'

'Do you want to push on now, boss, or lay up until dark?'

'We'll go on as far as we can. When I said thirty miles, that probably means sixty by road. It will be dark by the time we get within striking distance of the border, which is how we want it.'

'Nik-Nok Army permitting, boss.'

'Quite right, Tony – unfortunately,' said Howard.

The truck ground its way up the side of the mountain pass, as steep as any they had yet negotiated. The final descent into the Ch'ukanjŏng valley, towards the large town of Sep'o and its neighbour Hyŏn-ni, came as a relief for Ackford; but Howard was by now becoming increasingly apprehensive. The closer they approached to the DMZ, he knew, the more likely it would be that they would run into major concentrations of the North Korean Army. Three-quarters of a million men . . .

As they bypassed Sep'o, they began to encounter more traffic. All military, Howard realised. In a way, it was a comfort. If theirs had been the only vehicle on the road it was more likely to have been stopped; but there was some safety in numbers. Most of the traffic seemed to be heading towards Hyŏn-ni airfield. Eventually it thinned as they left the airfield behind them. *Only about another hour,* thought Howard. *Please God, let our luck hold . . .*

It was almost nightfall when they rounded a corner in the road and saw the checkpoint ahead. To Howard it was a perverse relief. After the long hours of doubt and uncertainty, here at last was something certain, something to focus on. As Ackford pulled up at the barrier and Kim Sumi once again jumped down to talk to the checkpoint commander, Howard could see straight away that these soldiers were of a different calibre from those they had encountered before. This was no forgotten outpost in the middle of nowhere. It was just over twelve miles from here to the DMZ, and these were alert, well-trained soldiers.

The checkpoint commander was outranked by Sumi but he was highly suspicious. He gave as good as he got as they remonstrated with each other. His voice became shrill and staccato, matching Sumi's. Then the commander abruptly pushed past her in an unmistakable act of defiance and rudeness. He strode up to the cab and barked a sharp order at Howard, gesturing threateningly with his AK-47. The barrel was less than three feet from Howard's face; behind the officer he could see other soldiers slowly raising their weapons, uncertain what to do.

There was a sudden scream of violent invective from Sumi. Howard had no idea what she said, but it had the effect of making the officer turn round. Howard immediately raised his own AK and shot the man in the back of the head, then threw himself out of the door of the truck. Rolling over, he brought his AK to bear on the other soldiers. Before he hit the ground he heard gunfire from behind him. Ziegler and Halliday were already out and firing, well clear of either side of the truck. Zeccara and Harris had dropped the canopy and were shooting over the top of the cab. As he rolled clear, Howard had felt a blow to his left arm; then he was steady and returning fire. Sumi, caught in the middle, had rapidly dropped to the ground and was lying still.

The firefight was brief but devastating. Within six seconds of the first shot being fired, all ten North Korean soldiers manning the checkpoint were dead.

'Mel? Angelo?' called Howard. 'Is there any more movement?'

There was a single sharp crack as Harris fired at a body that hadn't quite stopped twitching. 'Not now, boss,' he said.

'OK,' said Howard, levering himself to his feet. 'Let's get this place cleared up, and quick.'

Sumi was sitting up, clutching her right arm below the shoulder. 'I've been shot,' she said.

'Pete!' called Howard. 'Medical bag over here! Mike, Angelo – get those bodies off the road. Richard give them a hand.' He bent to examine Sumi's wound, which was bleeding profusely. He put down his AK. 'Can you bend your elbow?' he asked Sumi.

She did so. 'Yes,' she said. 'I don't think it's broken. Can you bend yours?'

'Huh? Why?'

'Because you've been shot too,' she answered.

Howard glanced down in surprise to see his left sleeve running with blood. 'Damn,' he muttered. 'Sod it.' He clutched his arm to staunch the flow of blood.

'Truck's fucked, boss,' reported Ackford. 'It must have taken some shots – won't start.'

'There are two jeeps parked up just ahead, boss,' said Zeccara. 'They must have belonged to these guys.'

Howard stood up and looked around. 'I think we've done enough motoring,' he said. 'Get all the bergens out and off the road. Load all the NK bodies and road-block kit on to the truck and the jeeps, and push them off the end of the road down into the river.' It was getting dark. He peered down at the water in the bottom of the ravine. 'It doesn't matter if they don't sink completely. They won't be noticed until morning. Quickly, before anyone else comes along.'

'Hold still, boss,' said Halliday, who had finished tending to Sumi and was now binding a shell-dressing round Howard's wounded arm.

'Come on, Pete, let's get off the road and do this,' he said.

It took the combined force of all of them to shove the heavy truck off the road. Howard put his good shoulder to it and, with the others pulling and pushing, it slowly tipped forward and began to roll down the steep slope. There was a grinding, scraping noise of disturbed earth and undergrowth, and a rattle of loose metal as it gathered speed. The fuel cans began to clank around inside the back. The truck hit a large boulder with a dull thump; there was screech of tearing metal as it slewed sideways and toppled over. It began to tumble, picking up momentum. There was a series of crashing thumps, then finally a loud clanging splash as it hit the water.

'If this was the movies, boss,' observed Ackford, 'that old truck would have blown up halfway down the slope and caused a bloody great fireball.'

'Just as well this is real, then,' responded Howard drily.

The two jeeps followed the truck. Howard hoped it would be a while before evidence of their destruction, or the bodies of their former occupants, were washed up somewhere downstream. Having watched them go he sat down abruptly, realising that he was in mild shock from his wound. The arm ached a little, but it was not yet painful. That would come later, he knew. *Get the bergen on first, and get moving.* 'Let's go.'

Despite his wound, Howard set a fast pace, anxious to get well clear of the place as quickly as possible. Keeping well off the side of the road, he pushed on relentlessly. His left arm began to throb painfully, and the hand felt cold and slightly numb. After an hour's progress he heard the sound of traffic on the road, now far below them, and ordered a halt.

'Mike,' he breathed to Ziegler. 'I think you'd better take over the lead. I can keep going OK, but my left hand's not much use and it makes navigation difficult.' For a few minutes he and Ziegler discussed the route to take.

'What do you reckon on that traffic, Ed?' asked Ziegler. 'Do you think anyone could have heard our firefight back there?'

Howard considered. 'I doubt it,' he said. 'If anyone was near enough, they'd have been there much more quickly. It's more likely that those soldiers have failed to report in on schedule, and the alarm's been raised. They're bound to be a bit jumpy when something goes wrong this near to the DMZ.'

'Boss?' whispered Ackford. 'What did you say the name of that place was, where we had that contact? Was it 'unchon?'

'Something like that.'

'*Har, har,*' chuckled Ackford coarsely.

'Hunch'ŏn,' whispered Sumi, correcting Ackford's pronunciation.

'*Har, har,*' chortled Ackford.

'What's so funny?'

'Don't worry about him, Sumi,' sighed Howard. 'He hasn't gone completely mad. He's just doing what he always does on night marches. He's thinking up a silly rhyme. He claims it keeps him alert.'

'It's one of those Nik-Noks I shot back there,' rumbled Ackford. 'Got him straight through his front teeth. *Har, har.*'

'All right, Tony, belt up, will you?' said Howard tiredly. He turned to Sumi again. 'How's the arm?'

'The same as yours, I expect. But I'm not carrying a heavy pack, so it's easier for me. Why not let Richard take yours?'

'Because the nearer we get to the DMZ, the more careful we'll have to be with noise. It's less easy to move quietly with a big load on your back, and I've had more practice at it.'

Ziegler kept up a steady pace, slowing down only when they neared signs of human habitation. For the first three hours they managed to keep to a routine of an hour's march followed by five minutes' rest, but the sightings of military installations became more frequent and their progress became slower as they were forced to make wide detours, taking rests only when they were clear and it was safe to do so.

Richard Weatherill had at last begun to understand the enormous difficulties of night patrols in hostile territory, and the extreme care that had to be taken to avoid being seen or heard. He was no longer puzzled by the fact that they didn't follow roads or tracks, or walk over bridges; he understood the long pauses silently signalled by Ziegler so that he could reconnoitre the best route round an obstacle.

Weatherill's first sighting of a major North Korean Army unit had scared him badly. Zeccara had silently pointed out the various installations to him, and he realised that if he had been by himself he would have blundered straight into the middle of it. There must be hundreds of men there, he thought. As he looked through his night-vision goggles and followed Zeccara's pointing finger, the outlines of vehicles, big artillery pieces, command posts and sentries seemed to leap into focus. One particular sentry, although he was nearly a hundred yards away, seemed to be staring straight at him. Weatherill froze, then slowly subsided into the ground. For some odd reason he suddenly thought of television films of big cats stalking their prey in Africa. Their slow stealthy movements were perfectly controlled and almost imperceptible, and the cats had used every bit of cover available in order to conceal their advance. Ziegler and the others were like that, he knew now. They were predators themselves, completely at home in this world, even when surrounded by thousands of lesser men who would overwhelm and kill them all, immediately and without any hesitation, if they were discovered. At last he understood. He needed the protection of his companions, and the best thing he could do was emulate them, and think like a cat himself. *The North Koreans don't know how close we are,* he thought. *But if they find out, they won't stop to ask questions.*

For a further four hours Ziegler led them cautiously past innumerable North Korean military positions. At one point, Weatherill was convinced that Ziegler had gone mad. He seemed to have brought them right into the middle of an enormous, sprawling encampment surrounded by tents, bunkers, vehicles and lethal-looking objects pointing skywards. It took nearly an hour to crawl less than two hundred yards until they were finally clear; after this, Weatherill was exhausted. He wondered briefly what it must be like for Sumi and Howard, with their wounds – especially Howard, with the added burden of the bergen on his back. He carefully pulled his watch from inside his smock, shielding the luminous face so that it could not be seen by hostile eyes. He glanced at the time; it was nearly two o'clock in the morning. In his tiredness, he understood the crucial importance of the emphasis that the SAS placed on physical fitness. That mind-numbing, muscle-torturing flog over the Welsh mountains – no brain-power required, other than the little that was needed for accurate navigation – now made sense. He even understood why Harris had accompanied him, carrying a heavy bergen himself. It wasn't that Harris needed to get himself fit again. It was all to do with the state of mind that was essential for Special Forces soldiers. The pain, the ache, the discomfort, the boredom – none of that mattered. What mattered, in truth, was that these things *didn't* matter – the discomforts had to be routine, things that simply had to be ignored and endured. *That word . . . Endurance . . .*

As the eight of them crept slowly forward, they gradually became aware of someone speaking in a loud, monotonous drone. The voice was tinny and distorted; Howard realised it was being amplified through loudspeakers. The closer they approached, the louder the voice became, until it practically drowned out all other noise.

'What the hell is that bloody awful racket, Sumi?' asked Howard.

'Chairman Kim Il Sung's voice,' she said. 'Probably his latest speech. "Harangue" would be a better word. Boring propaganda, from start to finish. The North Korean Army blasts out his diatribes all day and night, all the way along the border, loud enough for the South Koreans to hear it over the other side. As if they would be likely to pay attention to it,' she added with a grimace. 'I hoped I would never have to hear that voice again. The Americans think they invented "political correctness", but they should listen to this garbage. Kim Il Sung invented PC half a century ago – and look where it's led his country.'

'Well, it's doing us no harm,' remarked Howard. 'No one's going to hear us with that crap blaring out – however much noise we make ourselves.'

As they continued, Kim Il Sung's voice became almost deafening. They passed within fifty yards of one of the loudspeakers; it was clearly visible, a huge conical horn mounted high on a wooden pole. Harris, whose ears were still suffering from his near-miss with the MiG-25, found it almost intolerable; he longed to put a bullet through the thing to silence it.

Ziegler was conferring quietly with Howard. Some distance away to the south a small flashing beacon was now visible, pulsing out a faint, short-long, short-long signal. Weatherill thought he saw a fainter reflection of the same signal, slightly to the left and below, through his night-vision goggles; he wondered if there was something wrong with the goggles. He switched them off and raised them. The beacon was still visible, but its synchronous reflection had gone. When he put them back on the reflection reappeared. He shrugged, assuming it was an optical distortion caused by the goggles.

Ziegler now began moving to the left. Weatherill saw that he and Howard were glancing frequently in the direction of the flashing light; to his puzzlement, the reflection was gradually coming into line with it. He gave up trying to understand it. Finally, the two flashing lights were precisely aligned. Ziegler stoped. Weatherill switched off his goggles and raised them again; once more, only the one light was visible. Short-long, short-long . . .

'OK, we're here,' whispered Howard. Despite his tiredness and the pain from his arm, he was elated and relieved that the beacons were in place as he had hoped. 'We head in a straight line, keeping those two synchronised lights exactly in line. *Exactly* in line, understood? A few yards to either side and we hit mines, especially on the South Korean side. There will be barbed wire and fences, but we'll deal with those as we come to them. It will be a very long, slow crawl for four kilometres, all the way from here. And I mean slow. Any sudden movement will be spotted. Any questions?'

'Why can I only see one light without the goggles on?' whispered Weatherill.

'The nearer of the two is an infra-red signal,' breathed Howard. 'I'm hoping the North Korean IR monitors will think it's just a trick of the light.'

'Where are we?'

'Can't you hear the music over old grapefruit-head's monologue?'

'What music?'

'Listen,' said Howard.

Far off in the distance Weatherill faintly heard music

playing, but he couldn't make out the tune over the blaring of the North Korean loudspeakers. Then Kim Il Sung's voice paused for a moment between two sentences; in the temporary silence, to his incredulity, Weatherill recognised the Rolling Stones' rendition of 'Sympathy for the Devil'.

'What the hell's going on?' he asked. 'Has the world gone bloody mad? Where's that coming from?'

'An appropriate choice of music, in the circumstances,' muttered Howard. 'That's the South Korean response to Kim Il Sung's propaganda. He drones on about Communism, and they belt back the Stones and Beatles at him. In case you hadn't guessed, we've reached the DMZ.'

57

Marvin Jefferson could not have picked a worse day for a comprehensive search of the White House, and he knew it. In normal circumstances Sunday should have been a relatively quiet day, with many of the staff away for the weekend break; but the level of activity on that particular Sunday was frantic – at all levels. Everyone seemed to be hard at work, and people were swarming and scurrying everywhere like ants. The Uniformed Division guards were overstretched with official visitors, the switchboard operators were being swamped with calls, the domestic staff were moving furniture into position, electricians were setting up public address systems, secretaries were chasing around on errands, aides were yelling into telephones or at each other, there were press briefings, meetings, conferences . . .

The whole place had gone mad, Jefferson decided. He was glad he wasn't George Reynolds, whose responsibility it was to keep track of it all. He had seen that his deduction that IRIS had somehow been smuggled into the White House had hit Reynolds hard. It had been to the Secret Serviceman's credit that he had accepted the irrefutable logic of Jefferson's conclusions and swallowed his pride. Reynolds had known what to do; the Uniformed Division had already been there in more than usual strength, but Reynolds had ordered the numbers doubled again, with every sniffer dog they could lay their hands on being drafted in to help with the search. All Jefferson could do, until something else occurred to him, was to let Reynolds and his men get on with their jobs. He decided to go for a walk and take a good look round.

Reynolds had provided him with a colour-coded Secret Service lapel pin and a radio set with an earpiece. The radio was tuned to Charlie channel, the one reserved for the Secret Service, as well as to the primary channel. Apart from his FBI shield in its wallet and his supporting identification documents, that was all he carried. He had surrendered his gun at the entrance, knowing that to carry it would be pointless and would only result in extra delays when he was challenged by security. He was reassured by the number of times he was challenged as he walked around; the uniformed guards, and the occasional US Marine, were polite but firm, and it seemed that people were being stopped every few yards to check their authorisation to be in that particular part of the building. The regular White House employees, Jefferson noticed, were already becoming exasperated by the increased security, and he saw a couple of them lose their temper. It made absolutely no difference to the guards, who refused to be browbeaten. *No one with an ordinary gun would get ten yards in here without being stopped and arrested,* he thought. *With something like the IRIS weapon, he wouldn't get ten feet.* But that wasn't the point, Jefferson knew. Someone already had; and the first thing to find out was how he had actually got into the premises. He made his way to the north-east gate.

For ten minutes Jefferson stood and watched the procedure as cars, vans and delivery trucks entered and left. The number of guards on duty was impressive, and the sniffer dogs, Geiger counters and metal detectors were used on every person, and on every item being brought inside. Most of the vehicles contained individual officials, many of them from the State Department, but he was interested when a small truck drew up at the entrance and an engineer climbed out.

Jefferson wandered over to watch, and flashed his badge at the uniformed guard. 'Don't mind me,' he said. 'You carry on. I'm just trying to get an idea of procedure here. But it would be a help if you explained it.'

The guard checked Jefferson's ID. 'OK, Mr Jefferson,' he said politely. 'Well, this is a routine job. Dan Zelinski here is a regular GSA engineer—'

'GSA?'

'General Services Administration,' said the guard.

'Hi, Dan,' said Jefferson amiably.

'Hi,' replied the engineer.

'Sorry to butt in,' said Jefferson, 'but could you tell me what your job entails?'

'Yeah, well, the GSA is responsible for systems maintenance, right? I have some parts here for a failed air conditioning unit. Happens quite a lot.'

'I see,' said Jefferson. He watched the guard fill in an entry in his log; then a sniffer dog was brought over to the vehicle. It showed no interest. The engineer unloaded the parts and was accompanied away by another guard. Inside, Jefferson knew, the parts would come under further scrutiny from the magnetometers, X-ray machines and Geiger counters. The whole procedure took less than five minutes and seemed thorough.

He turned to the guard again. 'What happens to your log sheet at the end of your shift?'

'It goes to the main office. They used to just file the

logs, but now they all go on to a computer record.'

'So everyone coming in and out is logged? Even officials?'

'Everyone – no exceptions. Take a look, Mr Jefferson.' The guard handed him the log sheet.

Jefferson glanced down the list of entries. There were columns for date, time in, name, vehicle number, vehicle make and type, purpose of visit, items in, items out and time out. Under 'purpose of visit' most visitors simply entered the name of the person they had come to see, and they left the 'items in/out' columns blank. Zelinski, the engineer, had given the room number where he would be working, and details of the machine parts he had brought in.

'Comprehensive,' said Jefferson. 'Is the procedure the same for people working on the exterior of the White House?'

'You mean like painters, National Park gardens people, those sort of guys?'

'Yes,' said Jefferson.

'Exactly the same. Even the cans of paint get screened. So do new plants for the garden. Everything.'

'And everyone is escorted?'

'Workmen, yeah. Someone like Dan normally wouldn't be, as he's a regular, but there's some sort of security blitz going on today, so he is. I mean, Dan works here full-time. He only went out to pick up these parts. A contractor would always be escorted. He wouldn't be left unsupervised at any stage, even if he had a pass.'

Jefferson nodded thoughtfully. He looked around, as if searching for something. His glance fell on a steel post, discreetly mounted back from the gate. On top of the post was a metal casing; behind the glass front cover, he could just make out the circular outline of a camera lens. As he watched he saw the lens move, sweeping in an arc to cover the gate and the parking area every few seconds. 'That closed-circuit TV unit,' he asked, pointing, 'is it on the whole time?'

'Day and night,' answered the guard. 'Never blinks, never sleeps.'

'It's monitored the whole time too?'

'Yes – and recorded on tape, in case there's an incident and evidence is needed.'

'How long are the tapes kept?'

'I don't know,' said the guard, 'but I think it's a couple of weeks before they're reused. You'd have to ask at the main office. They keep all the records.'

'Are there logbook records and video coverage of all the entrances?'

'Yes,' replied the guard. 'The old Executive Office, Treasury building, the lot.'

'You've been very helpful,' said Jefferson. He smiled at the guard and walked away, reaching for his radio. He called Reynolds on Charlie channel. 'George?' he said. 'I think we may have something.'

'What is it?' asked Reynolds.

'Our assassin,' said Jefferson. 'Somewhere in the Uniformed Division gate-logs there'll be a record of his entry. And somewhere on the videotapes, there'll be footage of him unloading IRIS from a vehicle.'

Reynolds immediately grasped the significance of what Jefferson was saying. 'Of course!' he agreed. 'Why didn't I think of that?'

'We'll need a team of people to start scanning back through the logs and the tapes,' said Jefferson. 'The more people you can assign to it, the quicker it will be.'

'I'll get on to it right away!' said Reynolds.

'There's a problem, of course,' added Jefferson.

'How come?'

'Well, if he fooled the guards in real life, he's certainly going to be convincing on paper and on video, isn't he? But we can probably eliminate everyone on the log records who doesn't have an entry in the "items in" column. That should save some time.'

'Yeah, we'll check those ones first,' said Reynolds enthusiastically. 'Once we've got our man from the log and the gate video, we can cross-check with the videotapes from other cameras to see exactly where he went and where he planted this thing. There are cameras everywhere, covering every angle.'

'All we have to do is concentrate on places we know Flagman will be tomorrow morning. Inside the White House itself, and of course outside in the grounds. My guess is outside, but we can't be sure.'

'Either way, we'll find it,' said Reynolds confidently.

Patrick Donovan's initial twinge of unease had turned to a feeling of sick fear. He had known from the start that he shouldn't have done the 'favour'. He still insisted to himself that it was just a favour, nothing more, and he had done similar things before. Anyway, five hundred dollars was a good incentive. He had told himself there was no harm in what he had been asked to do. It happened all the time, didn't it? Everyone falsified records from time to time, and no one ever checked these ones.

But now someone *was* checking them. To be more accurate, no fewer than forty officers were checking them, under the instructions of Mr Reynolds himself. He had never seen so many people crowd into the records office. The log records had been downloaded from the mainframe on to a battery of Apple Macs and people were poring over them, checking every entry.

That was not what bothered Pat Donovan. What bothered him was the videotape archive. The log was easy to deal with, but the video archive was quite another matter.

Donovan realised he was sweating. He forced his mind off what was going on around him, and thought back to the 'favour' he had done. It had seemed innocuous enough, at the time. That big-shot aide, what was his name? Yeah, Levy. Tom Levy. It was always the same, thought Donovan. *A big-shot aide finds himself a new piece of tail, but he's having difficulty getting inside her panties. So, he waits until the President and First Lady are out of town, and he sneaks his piece into the White House. He's already talked to a White House butler – promised him a ride on Air Force One, something like that. So the butler gives the aide the run of the Lincoln bedroom for the night. The eight-foot bed and the President's bedroom impress the hell out of the piece of tail, and the aide gets laid. She's not to know the President himself doesn't actually sleep there, of course. But it works, every time. And, of course, the aide wants to cover his tracks afterwards, so he pulls the records – or, at least, he gets good old Pat Donovan to do it. If not Pat, then whoever's on duty. They all do it.*

There wasn't anything wrong with that, was there? Donovan asked himself. Well . . . no. Not normally, anyhow. But there was something a little odd about this one. He had known it at the time. In the first place, it had been a daytime job. That wasn't normal – it was usually at night. In the second place, he had found out later that the President and First Lady weren't away at all at the time. Levy's story didn't tally. Third, he knew from general White House scuttlebutt that Levy already had a perfectly compliant bimbo. By all accounts neither of them could keep their hands off each other – so why did he need the Lincoln Bedroom to clinch it?

It didn't stack up, Donovan realised, but he told himself that Levy must just have been camouflaging some other equally harmless reason for wanting the records pulled. After all, Levy *was* a big-shot. He was one of the President's closest and most trusted associates, right? And you didn't argue with guys like that if you wanted to keep your job, right? So he hadn't argued. He had taken the five hundred and done as he had been asked.

But he knew there was something not quite right about it. He just *knew* it, instinctively, however far he tried to push the thought into the back of his mind. And now it had surfaced, with a vengeance. Forty guys, going over the log and the videotapes.

They would never find it from the log, thought Donovan. The original papers had been shredded. Once the daily records were entered into the computer, there was no requirement to keep them. Then it was a simple matter of just deleting one entry. Levy had given Donovan the vehicle number to search for; he had found it straight away using the search facility on the computer, and then . . . delete entry. Simple. One keystroke and it was gone. Repeat the procedure with the back-up copy on the disk, print out a new hard copy with the entry no longer there, and there you were. It had never existed. Undetectable.

The videotape was the problem. Donovan had switched the tape that included the time of the deleted log entry for an older tape that was due to be reused. The older tape had genuine coverage by the same camera, the one at the gate entrance; but it was two weeks old. Donovan had just relabelled the tapes and swapped them round. The newer one, with the incriminating evidence, had already been reused. The old one – showing activity at the gate a fortnight ago – was labelled as being more recent.

So where was the problem? Donovan asked himself. Not in the date, thank God. The tapes did not feature the date in the picture – only on the label, and he had changed that. And not in the time, either. Or at least, not in a way that would be immediately apparent. In the bottom right-hand corner of the picture, the video imprinted the exact time of each frame. In one sense that was OK, because Donovan had taken care to use a tape that had been recorded at the same time of day. But that wasn't the whole story. There was one major, *major* problem, and Donovan now found himself sweating hard as he thought about it. What would happen if one of the guys checking through the log wanted to double-check an entry against the corresponding time on the videotape? He would see immediately that the log and the tape didn't tally – the vehicles shown on tape arriving and leaving would bear no resemblance to the entries in the log. It would be obvious that the tape had been switched.

Donovan had already decided to bluff it out, to feign complete ignorance. Even if the switch came to light, there was no way they could know that a log entry had been deleted. They couldn't even pin the tape switch on him. It could have been anyone, couldn't it? It could have been . . . Yeah. An accident. Someone switched the tape by mistake. An accident, that's what it was. An accident.

Donovan looked up. Over in the corner by the door he saw a big, hefty-looking guy in a dark blue suit, standing next to Mr Reynolds. He hadn't seen him around before. Reynolds was talking to him, but the big guy didn't seem to be paying much attention. Instead . . . he was looking in his direction! There was a strange kind of expression on the big guy's face. *Shit!*

Pat Donovan hurriedly dropped his glance and tried to concentrate on his work. You're imagining things, he told himself. He can't possibly know. Anyway, it was an accident . . .

'How can I help, Mr Jefferson?' asked David Gergen.

'It's good of you to see me, Mr Gergen,' began Jefferson. He was glad the Director had told him about Gergen. The man was as rushed off his feet as everyone else, but like most efficient people he seemed to have the knack of remaining calm and relaxed. 'I know how busy you are.'

'No more than anyone else,' said Gergen, 'and what you're doing is more important than the crap I'm dealing with right now. What can I do for you?'

'Well, sir, I have to tell you that we're no further forward with this search than when we started. You'll have seen all the dogs and extra security people we've had on the job. So far, we've found nothing at all, and there's no trace on the gate logs of any unusual occurrence. We've still got people going through the video records, but it will be quite a while before we finish checking them all. My point is, sir, there's a good chance we aren't going to find this IRIS thing in time.'

'Hell,' muttered Gergen. 'You've looked everywhere?'

'Everywhere,' said Jefferson. 'The roof, the walls, the portico, the grounds, the lobby, the gate – everywhere.'

'Have you checked all the surveillance cameras?'

'We thought of that, sir. IRIS would have to have some sort of video capacity to identify its target, and to disguise it as one of the video surveillance cameras was a fairly obvious choice – it could even have been hooked up so that the camera could work as normal until Flagman appeared. We've had GSA maintenance technicians taking the covers off every single one of them and poking around inside. Nothing. All absolutely standard, none of them interfered with.'

'So – what next?'

'We'll keep looking sir. The Secret Service are doing the best they possibly can. But the fact remains, there is a chance we won't find this thing. We have to think now about what happens if we don't.'

Gergen shuddered briefly at the thought. 'What do you have in mind, Mr Jefferson?'

'This is where I need your help, sir. As I see it, we have three options. The first is that we postpone the scheduled program. I am assuming that to cancel it would be unthinkable.'

'You're right there,' said Gergen immediately. 'Cancellation would be a disaster. I'll have to ask State about postponement, but I think even that would put the whole thing at risk. You've no idea how finely-balanced this thing is.'

'I can guess, sir. I figured it wouldn't be possible. In any case, even if we postpone for twenty-four hours, there's no guarantee we could find IRIS even with the extra time.'

Gergen nodded. 'Your second option?'

'We relocate, sir – move the meeting anywhere but here. I would strongly urge you to consider this, sir.'

Gergen shook his head. 'Again, I'll have a word with the President and the Secretary of State, but I can't see it happening. This business is incredibly delicate. To move it elsewhere would seem like a deliberate snub. I can't see Flagman agreeing to it.'

'Believe me, sir, I know what I'm asking. I can imagine what a disaster it would be if Flagman felt he was being slighted by us, but I would submit that it would be an even greater disaster if he was shot, right here in the White House.'

'You don't need to tell me, Mr Jefferson. It would be . . . well, there's only one word for it – catastrophic. There would be a gigantic international upheaval, a bloodbath . . . Jesus, I don't even like to think about it. But what is your third option?'

'Sir, I can't guarantee it will work, but I must emphasise that it is our only remaining option. Our only one.'

'I understand your point, Mr Jefferson. We have no choice in this, right?'

'No choice at all, sir. Let me explain. From what we have been told, this IRIS machine is not absolutely foolproof. The computer program was still in development when it was stolen. There is no guarantee that it will work. Do you follow me?'

'Yes, but we can't take a chance on . . .'

'The point is, sir,' said Jefferson, leaning forward, 'we're told that the *Stasi* knew perfectly well that IRIS was not completely reliable, but despite that, they were still one hundred per cent confident that in Flagman's case it would work. Furthermore, we know *why* they were so confident. It is all to do with Flagman's distinctive appearance.' Jefferson explained what he meant. 'In that one respect, Flagman is absolutely unmistakable. Everyone in the world recognises him because of this one feature – and that's how IRIS will recognise him too.'

'Are you suggesting we ask him to change his appearance?'

'That's exactly it, sir. We have to get him to do it. Everyone will see who he is, but with that one thing changed, IRIS won't recognise him. It's absolutely vital that he agrees to do this, sir.'

'You're right, Jefferson!' said Gergen decisively. 'My God, you're right! I'm going to get straight on to this. I'll talk to the Secretary of State and ask him to put this to Flagman in person. It'll have to be done tactfully, but we'll find a way. Leave it with me. I'll let you know what he says.'

'Thank you, sir . . . If I may, I'll get back to the search.'

'Thank *you*, Jefferson. And good luck – I hope to God you find this thing in time.'

'We'll do our best, sir. But if we *don't* find it, and if Flagman doesn't agree to change this one thing . . . then he's as good as dead.'

58

Howard motioned Halliday forward and signalled to him to lead the way, keeping the two lights ahead dead in line. As the slight figure began crawling slowly forward, Howard found himself wondering once again at the man's unusual energy and stamina. Halliday seemed little more than skin and bone, with that unhealthily pale complexion and those large, protruding eyes. Howard had met few people so unprepossessing in appearance, but he knew that Halliday could carry the same weight as everyone else, just as fast and for just as far. Certainly he was showing no signs of tiredness now. *Unlike me,* he realised. *I'm getting too old for this game. Slowing down . . .*

He motioned to Sumi to follow Halliday, then set off himself behind her; the two wounded near the front of the line. He crawled on his right side to protect his injured left arm, and could see Sumi in front of him doing the same. He knew she had lost a fair amount of blood, like himself, but she was tough and determined. *Extremely determined . . .*

The ground was hard and stony, and the long hours of crawling they had already done, passing through the North Korean lines, had rubbed his right elbow and both knees almost raw; but it was the same for the others, Howard knew. Through his night-vision goggles he could see the landscape stretch ahead in a seemingly interminable, almost featureless drabness. There was little cover – just a few stunted bushes and the occasional slight rise and fall in the ground. The larger trees had presumably been chopped down. One part of his brain had been hoping for better cover – perhaps even enough to allow them to cross most of the DMZ on foot, rather than on their stomachs. But he knew that was entirely unreasonable. This route was ideal precisely because it was relatively flat – otherwise the beacons would not have been visible. The mines would be only yards away from each side of the line they must take . . .

Harris was next in line behind him, semi-wounded, his ribs cracked from the hard parachute landing. The crawling would be every bit as painful for him, Howard knew, yet he was making no sound. Howard recalled the bitter protests Harris had made eighteen months before on being told he was to be left behind in Saudi Arabia when the main team crossed the Iraqi border; but he had managed to get into the action towards the end – it had been he who had shot down the Hind helicopter gunship. *I hope you're satisfied this time, Mel,* he thought. *You've certainly had your fair share on this mission, and I doubt it's over yet . . .*

Behind Harris would be Weatherill, then the massive

frame of Tony Ackford. Big, genial, easy-going Tony, whom Angelo Zeccara had once memorably described as having a head like a King Edward potato set on a body like a collapsed shit-house. Ackford had taken a swing at Zeccara that would have knocked him cold if it had connected; but with his boxing experience he had known that Zeccara was quick enough to dodge out of the way. Both men had then simply carried on drinking their pints. Ackford was never rattled, even if he was often noisily indignant about the small things in life. He grumbled endlessly about minor inconveniences, but Howard had seen many times that the big man was tireless and uncomplaining when things became really difficult. *Dammit*, he thought, *this arm is really beginning to hurt* . . . He tried to force his mind away from the pain.

He had not had much personal contact with Zeccara prior to this operation. Zeccara had come to XF Securities highly recommended by both Harris and Halliday, and had soon established himself as a valuable asset to the company. His notorious reputation for seducing women and then dumping them soon afterwards had not impaired his operational effectiveness; he had made no play for Kim Sumi, so perhaps he did have a degree of self-control after all. His one foray into matrimony had quickly foundered due to his serial infidelity, but Howard knew he was in no position to criticise the man on that score – he could hardly claim to have treated the few women there had been in his own life particularly well. *Too remote, too aloof, too much of a loner; and too late now to change* . . .

Inch by inch, the line of eight figures crawled slowly forward into the DMZ, gradually leaving the North Korean positions behind them. For the three injured it was painful – and painfully slow. The two synchronised flashing lights did not appear to draw any closer. Howard concentrated on the figures of Sumi and Halliday in front of him, confident in Halliday's ability and alertness. Guarding the rear of the line, he knew, was Mike Ziegler. The tall, rangy American was his greatest friend, and in his opinion the finest soldier and most fearsome fighter of them all. Howard had many times witnessed Ziegler's deadly proficiency in combat, his deceptively relaxed, laconic manner literally exploding into a blur of controlled violence when circumstances required it. *True to his friends; terrifying to his enemies. That would be a good epitaph for Mike*, thought Howard. Morbidly, he began to wonder about a suitable one for himself, then snapped out of it, wrenching his thoughts back to the present. *This is no time to think of dying*, he told himself grimly.

After three hundred yards they came to a multiple-coil barbed-wire fence. Howard waved Ackford and Zeccara forward; they took long minutes to check the fence for alarms and trip-wires, then began silently snipping through the strands. Ackford held each strand with wire-gloves and Zeccara used the cutters. There was only a faint click as each strand was cut, then a slight rustle as Ackford slowly released the two ends; the noise was drowned out by the loudspeakers.

'It'd be quicker if you chewed your way through, you little pisspot,' whispered Ackford. 'That metal fang of yours ought to make short work of it.'

'I've got a better idea,' grinned Zeccara as he continued snipping. 'You do your King Kong act and lift the whole fucking fence up, then the rest of us can crawl under it.'

'I'm not having a nasty little thing like you crawling between my legs,' rumbled Ackford.

'Why not? There are hundreds of beautiful women just panting for me to get back home and do just that.'

'Nasty little pisspot.'

After twenty minutes they had cut a narrow diagonal passage through the wire coils, which Howard hoped would not be visible from the north. Slowly, careful not to snag clothing on the wire, they crawled through the gap as Ackford and Zeccara held the wire coils aside. When Ziegler, the last of them, was through they closed the gap again, twisting some of the strands back together to restore an appearance of normality. It would certainly be noticed in the morning, thought Howard, but by then . . .

The pain from his arm was now affecting his concentration. He gestured to Halliday for the medical bag. Halliday had been expecting it. He thrust two tablets into Howard's hand and offered a further two to Sumi. She waved them away at first, but at his insistence relented and swallowed them. Fifteen minutes later, the ache began to recede and she realised she should have accepted the painkillers long before.

There was a hollow, metallic *thump* from behind them, a long way back, and the sound of real voices just audible above the noise of the loudspeakers.

'Keep down and don't move!' Ziegler whispered fiercely to Weatherill. They pressed themselves flat into the ground.

A few seconds later a mortar flare burst into brilliant light several hundred feet above them, lighting up the entire area for hundreds of yards around. Any movement would be instantly seen, but the shifting shadows of the flare as it slowly descended on its parachute would make stationary objects difficult to distinguish. There was a low whistling noise as the empty canister fell to the ground, an unearthly cat-call to Kim Il Sung's thin drone. Howard felt his heart thumping, waiting for what would come next. Had they been heard? Had they set off some sensor, alerting the North Koreans?

A second flare followed just before the first one burned out. They lay still; Weatherill closed his eyes, breathing hard, grateful for the rest. Then it was dark again.

Howard waited for a full two minutes before moving on again, now taking the lead. He was even more cautious than before, convinced that the North Koreans must believe something was amiss. Slowly, the eight of them covered a further two hundred yards. Howard saw they were approaching a slight rise in the ground, strewn with rocks and boulders.

His hand touched a wire, and he froze. It was a single strand of thin steel piano-wire. Thankfully, it was loose, not taut. A trip-flare, or maybe some sort of jumping-jack mine. *Dammit!* he thought savagely. *This route is supposed to be clear!* At both ends of the wire, maybe ten or fifteen yards away, would be small metal stakes. One stake would simply be an anchor, but on the other one the wire would pass through a small swivelled screw-clamp to a spring. Pulling the wire would jerk the clamp, but so would cutting it – the spring would tug it back the other way. Either way, the motion of the swivelled clamp would trigger the device. If it was a jumping-jack, a powder charge would fire the mine-pot into the air on the end of a five-foot chain. The chain would jerk the firing mechanism and it would detonate instantly – death for everyone within fifty yards. *Thank God the wire is loose*, he thought. After what might have been many years since it had been laid, the wire had gradually stretched and slackened, and the spring too . . .

He clicked his fingers softly, and Zeccara crawled forwards. He nodded as he saw the wire and slowly moved off to the right, following it.

After a few minutes he returned silently, shaking his head. 'Trip-mine, boss,' he whispered. 'I wouldn't advise touching it. The spring is still tight. The lever could be corroded solid – but if it isn't, the slightest movement could set the bastard off.'

The Rolling Stones and 'Jumping Jack Flash', thought Howard. *The South Koreans ought to be playing that one.* 'How about cutting the wire?'

'Might work, but there's still some tension on it. I wouldn't risk it. Better to crawl round the other end.'

Howard nodded and added, 'Watch out for other

wires.' He let Zeccara lead the way. Ten yards along the wire to the left, he saw the sharp outline of the small steel anchoring stake. Then he was round it, moving back to the right, back on to the line of the flashing lights.

But the lights had disappeared. Howard's pulse raced until he discovered that the small rise just ahead had temporarily obscured them. Zeccara was still in front, crawling slowly upwards now, towards the rocks.

There was a slight twang from somewhere behind him. *Oh, shit, someone's snagged . . .*

A hooter sounded raucously, far away behind them, and within seconds there came the dull thumps of mortars being fired. 'Up into the rocks, quick!' Howard called urgently. They scrambled forwards towards the cover of the rocks, knowing they had perhaps only fifteen seconds before the mortar bombs began falling, each one blasting shards of steel in every direction, lethal to anyone caught out in the open.

They tumbled into the chaos of the rock formation and flattened themselves to the ground. Howard kept his head raised slightly, peering through a crack between two rocks, back in the direction of the North Korean positions. *A cigarette,* he thought. *That's what I need now.* The brief rushing noise of the falling bombs came from away to the side. *No danger, yet. Time of flight approximately twenty seconds,* Howard reckoned. His eyes glittered darkly as he watched the flashes of the explosions. *Way off target,* he thought dispassionately. *Add two hundred, right four hundred.* The shock waves of the detonations assaulted his ears. *Sod it, I want a cigarette.*

He recalled the advice he had been given many years before by a brother officer, a veteran of many battles and a man he greatly respected. By then Howard had been shot at a few times himself, and had been on the receiving end of ineffective artillery and mortar attacks on more than one occasion, but he still knew himself to be a relatively inexperienced novice. He had never quite understood what had drawn the two of them together – Sean, the veteran, an Irish mercenary, and himself, the English novice, a youth who had hardly yet begun to live, let alone understand how to die.

The older man . . . *older?* Howard sighed. *Sean was barely thirty at the time* . . . had an understanding of life that only ever came to those who had been in close proximity with death. *Touching distance . . . reach out, and it's yours . . .*

He and Sean had found themselves sitting together quietly at a boisterous party. Both were bored with the noise, and despite the fact that they hardly knew each other they had begun talking. Howard had listened, fascinated, to Sean's stories.

'Sean?' he asked eventually. 'What is it like to be in a real battle?'

'You can't describe it properly,' Sean replied slowly, drawing hard on a cigarette. 'D'you want one of these?' he asked, proffering his pack.

Howard declined with a smile. 'No thanks, I gave up a couple of months ago. I found I couldn't keep up with my soldiers climbing hills.'

'Take the pack, Ed,' Sean had said quietly. 'Keep it.'

Howard did so, puzzled. He put it in his shirt pocket.

Sean was talking again. 'I'll tell you one thing. Just a piece of advice that may come in useful one day, if you ever have a big enemy contact.'

Howard was staring into the older man's eyes. They seemed far away, flitting through past experiences.

'When you get a real contact, light up one of those.' He patted Howard's shirt pocket. 'Spend five minutes smoking it, just looking around and thinking. Everyone else will be going frantic, shouting and yelling at each other and trying to get things done. The fact is, for five minutes nothing much *can* be done, unless there's an obvious emergency. By the time the five minutes are up, you'll know what has to be done – and if you don't, at least you'll have put five minutes more thought into it than anyone else.'

Howard had never forgotten Sean's advice. The following day, he had given him a lift to the airfield; Sean was leaving on another operation. He was killed in action just a few days later, trying to save someone else's life . . .

A cigarette . . . Decisions. *Are the North Koreans going to adjust fire, or have they just been guessing?* There were lights now, probing out towards them, sweeping from side to side. Then a further volley of thumps in the distance as the mortars were fired again. Howard began counting slowly. *Fifteen, sixteen, seventeen* . . .

The whistling was overhead. 'Incomers!' hissed Howard urgently. The ground shook with the detonations as the mortars burst a hundred yards short of them. *Shit, they adjusted after all . . . Time to move? Yes.*

Crack-crack-crack-crack-crack-crack-crack-crack. A heavy machine-gun, probably 12.7mm, firing high, over their heads and to the left. 'Move out! Keep down, and keep the lights in line!' he yelled above the noise of the gunfire punctuating the music of the Boomtown Rats now thumping out of the South Korean loudspeakers way off in the distance.

A distant *thump-thump-thump-thump-thump-thump-thump-thump*; the report from the machine-gun. Then the lower, hollow thumps of the mortar tubes again as they scrambled away through the rocks. A barrage this time, continuous. Grey-black smoke from the high-explosive detonations was already swirling round the position.

'Jesus!' whimpered Weatherill.

'Shut up and move!' grated Ackford.

The night was lit with the concussive flashes of the explosions. Mercifully, Howard realised, the North Koreans hadn't adjusted fire again and the mortar bombs were still falling short. The smoke was thick and choking, and he fervently hoped that Ziegler would still be able to catch occasional glimpses of the flashing beacons. The heavy machine-gun, now firing continuously, had been joined by a multitude of other automatic weapons and the noise was deafening. The sharp cracks of the passing supersonic bullets were frighteningly disorientating and Howard knew what Weatherill, and maybe Sumi too, would be feeling at their first experience of battle. Ahead of him he could see that Ackford had one hand firmly on Weatherill's collar, unceremoniously dragging the scientist along with him. At the front, he could make out the figure of Sumi, wisely sticking close to Ziegler. The rocky outcrop, now behind them, was still giving some cover; they were now in a slight dip, temporarily safe from the machine-gun fire. Two hundred yards ahead was another, similar rocky area . . .

Howard only briefly heard the new noise over the explosions of the mortars behind him. It was a terrible, roaring, whooshing sound that he knew only too well. He had less than half a second to react. *'Down!'* he yelled.

The 122mm Katyusha rocket exploded less than fifty yards away. The blinding force of the explosion hit them like a heavyweight punch. Pieces of rock and earth were blasted into the air and came showering down around them. 'Go!' yelled Howard. No one seemed to have been hit. They were nearly at the second rocky outcrop.

There was another barrage from the 82mm mortars – closer, this time. The eight figures flattened themselves to the ground again as the bombs burst. Howard tried to count them; there had been about forty in the last barrage – say five rounds fire-for-effect from eight tubes. That made sense. But this time they were closer . . .

Thirty-five, thirty-six . . . There was a brief cry from Sumi.

The barrage ceased. '*Go!*' yelled Howard above the cracking of the machine-gun fire.

'Fuck,' grunted Ackford crossly as he clambered awkwardly to his feet, one arm hanging limply by his side.

Halliday bent down and picked up Sumi. He slung her over his shoulder in a fireman's lift and staggered after Ziegler as they ran the last few yards to the second group of rocks. There was another whoosh of a Katyusha. As he dived to the ground, Howard saw Ackford pulling Weatherill down with him. The explosion was closer. *Any minute now, they'll let the whole lot rip, all forty of them . . . No, that's wrong, Sumi said only thirty . . .*

They heard the whooshing noise far away as Howard dived into the rocks after them, and then the whole world seemed to light up. Even though their heads were hugging the ground and their eyes were tight shut, the flashes of the Katyusha explosions seemed sharper than lightning. The air burst and thundered, the earth leaped and shook beneath them, and the rocks seemed to crack and split. Someone was making a thin wailing noise of terror or pain . . .

Johnny Bourne was frantic with anxiety as he stared out into the darkness of no-man's land. The night was lit by the sharp, neon-flickering flashes of the explosions away in the distance, the dull, booming thumps of the reports reaching his ears seconds later.

There could no longer be any doubt about what had happened. His friends – Ed, Mike, Mel, Tony and the others – had been seen by the North Koreans and they were now under attack, fighting for their lives.

Bourne tried to imagine what it must be like for them, scrabbling for shelter from the mortar and rocket barrages. He had experienced shell-fire himself before, but not on anything like this scale or intensity. Ed and the others would be exposed, helpless, almost naked – they had no trenches or shelters to dive into for cover. Rocked, shaken almost senseless by the power of the explosives, shredded by shattered fragments of metal blasted from the warheads, they would be wounded, dying, perhaps even dead already, out there in that hellish, empty killing-ground. So near to safety . . . *they had been so near* . . .

'Oh God,' he muttered despairingly. 'Oh *God!*'

'I'm sorry, Johnny.' Colonel Max Goodale was at Bourne's elbow, his voice sad and low. 'I'm very sorry. Perhaps . . .' His voice tailed off bleakly.

'We must do something,' said Bourne, his voice cracking with emotion. 'We must help them.'

'There's nothing we can do,' replied Goodale quietly. 'This is a battle that they have to fight alone. We can't do anything from here.'

'We can't simply stay here in this bloody command-post and do nothing!' Bourne yelled suddenly, shouting his fury into the night. 'I can't stand and look on while they're being killed! I just *can't!* Anyway, I bloody well *won't!*' He twisted away from Goodale, moving awkwardly on his withered leg. 'Even if no one else is going to do anything, I *am!* I'm going out there, right now, to try to help them!'

'*No!*' Goodale seized the younger man's shoulder and pulled him round, staring fiercely into his eyes. 'Listen to me, Johnny! *Listen!* If you go out there, you'll only get yourself killed too! I won't allow it! Apart from anything else, just remember your promise to Juliet! There's nothing you can do! Damn it, Johnny, you're a cripple! Face up to it, for God's sake! What the hell do you think you could achieve, in your condition?'

As suddenly as the barrage had started, it stopped. There was nothing except the ringing in Howard's ears. Even the machine-gun fire had ceased. Thick, grey-black smoke swirled in silence round the position, mixed with heavy, choking, stone-dust; the long-familiar acrid smell of burnt explosive stung Howard's nostrils and left a dry, bitter taste on his tongue. He heard someone behind him cough weakly, gag and spit. Dazed, he reached for his water-bottle and began to lever himself up into a kneeling position, then slumped back as the sharp pain of grating bone seared through his right leg. *Oh, damn* . . . He grimaced, clutching his thigh, feeling blood seeping out wetly from the wound. *Femur smashed*, he thought dully. *Damn! Must have missed the femoral artery, though, or there would be a real fountain of blood* . . . 'Mike?' he called. 'Are you OK?'

'Yeah,' bawled Ziegler conversationally, 'but my left hand's taken a heavy knock. Can't use it. Also, somethin' smacked me in the ribs, but I'm still breathin'. Pete, hand me a shell dressin' or two, will you, when you have a moment? I'm losin' a fair bit o' blood here.'

'Anyone else hit?'

'Sumi's taken a hit in the left foot or ankle,' called Halliday. 'Can't tell how serious yet, but it doesn't look too good. She certainly won't be able to walk.'

'My right shoulder's knackered, boss,' grunted Ackford. 'Lump of shrapnel. And the doc here seems to have gone fucking catatonic or something.'

Harris, Zeccara and Halliday were unhurt. *Oh God*, thought Howard. *Five wounded already, out of eight.* 'Mike,' he called, 'the NKs may be preparing for an assault. Get going, and quick! Take some PE charges to blow the main fence – it's only about three or four hundred yards on from here. Pete, you carry Sumi. Tony, you take Richard. We'll cover you – Angelo, Mel and I. Go!' He tossed a small package to Ziegler, who caught it in his good hand. '*Go!*'

Ziegler understood. He gave Howard a brief nod and led the other four away, leaving their bergens behind. 'Claymores are in mine, Ed, grenades in Tony's,' he yelled back over his shoulder. Ackford's AK was now slung; his one good hand gripped the collar of the terrified Weatherill, forcing him along.

Howard clutched his leg and watched them disappear southwards. The slackening of the mortar and rocket barrage had given them a welcome respite, but he was fairly sure what would come next. 'Angelo, get the spare ammo and grenades out of Tony's bergen. Mel, set out the claymores.' He bent to bind a shell dressing tightly round his thigh. *This is where we could use a couple of GPMGs or Minimis*, he thought, *or better still an M19 . . .*

Zeccara rapidly distributed hand-grenades and spare AK magazines as the three men spread out, facing back the way they had come. With each second that passed without a resumption of the mortar barrage, they became more certain of what would soon happen.

Harris quickly set out six claymore mines on their stands, ten yards in front of them in the open, spread out wide apart from each other. He kept two more in reserve. Each claymore consisted of a curved slab of high explosive, about eight inches by four, and one inch thick. On the convex side hundreds of steel ball-bearings were embedded into the surface; when the mine was detonated, the steel shot would be blasted forward over a wide arc, mowing down anyone who was out in the open. A wire ran back from each one to a small hand-held pulse generator. When squeezed, it would send an electric charge down the wire and detonate the mine immediately.

Howard tried to concentrate, aware that he was fast losing strength because of his shattered leg. Shaking his head fiercely to thrust away the feeling of dizziness, he resigned himself to the fact that he would not be able to move again. He must fight to stay conscious. He must fight . . .

Go, Mike, go! he thought weakly. *Goodbye, old friend . . .*

Then came the sound he had been dreading. Shrill, urgent shouts, much nearer now, from the North Korean side. They were coming. There would be another mortar barrage, followed immediately by a full-scale assault. Howard's heart sank. Glancing briefly at

Harris's face, he saw a sadness there that he had never seen before. *Mel knows too*, he thought. Hope was deserting them, stealthily vanishing away into the dark. Only three of them left to try and hold off the entire North Korean Army . . .

Flickering patterns of light and dark began to swim into Howard's fading vision. It was the loss of blood, he knew. He forced his head up, his eyes glittering dully. *Time to die, after all.*

Then came the hollow thumps of the mortars firing again. It had begun.

Time to die.

59

Jefferson felt groggy and light-headed from lack of sleep. From his vantage point on the roof of the White House he gazed down on the scene below. Already guests were arriving, taking their seats and waiting expectantly, the first in a gathering of three thousand heads of state, diplomats and other VIPs from all over the world. The media were already there, crowding the allotted spaces in huge numbers. There were more television cameras than Jefferson had ever seen in one place, there were TV anchormen, radio reporters, photographers, newspaper journalists, columnists, commentators . . . it was perhaps the most important and momentous thing that had happened here in decades, and here he was, Marvin Jefferson – still in his rumpled Sunday blue suit on a Monday morning when he should have been in the dark grey one – powerless to prevent it turning into a total catastrophe.

He had done everything he could think of. With less than an hour to go, he could do no more unless something turned up. *Flagman will agree*, he comforted himself. *He'll agree to make the necessary change to his appearance.* As he watched the crowd below swelling, the murmur of their voices drifted up to the roof. A band was playing; there was a sense of anticipation, of excitement, of history in the making . . .

Around him on the roof were dozens of armed men in black uniforms, concealed behind the parapet, all with their weapons trained discreetly on the scene below. The usual Special Weapons team had been quadrupled in strength, and further augmented by four individuals armed with cumbersome-looking devices that Jefferson had never seen before. These had been Reynolds' idea; they were laser guns which could cause permanent blindness to an enemy at the same distance at which a rifle could kill. The Dazer, as it was called, was silent in operation, punching out a pencil-thin coherent beam of 10.6-micron blue-white light in ultra-rapid pulses. Each pulse lasted only nanoseconds, allowing the laser to recharge itself instantly – the cyclic rate of fire of the pulses was faster than that of any machine gun in existence. The entire energy of the beam focused on a spot less than an inch in diameter at a range of one hundred yards. On a misty or rainy day, or if there was smoke in the air, the laser beam would simply punch through it, vaporising the water or smoke particles in a flash, although doing so would absorb much of the beam's energy. This vaporising effect could be seen by an observer, but in clear conditions – unless one was unfortunate enough to be its target, in which case it would be the last thing one would ever see – the beam was virtually invisible.

If the Dazers worked on a human eye, Reynolds had reasoned, they should work on the CCD cell in IRIS's video camera, unless IRIS had a 'hardened' camera that had been specifically developed for battlefield use. 'But it's unlikely it has a hardened camera, because of the extra size that would entail,' Reynolds had said. 'Anyway, the Dazers may give us some extra time. If we only spot IRIS when the crowd has gathered, I doubt we'll get authorisation to shoot it out with a rifle, even one with a silencer.'

That was all very well, thought Jefferson. But none of this goddam hardware would be of the slightest use unless they knew what to aim it at – and no one yet had any idea what the IRIS device looked like or how it had been disguised.

People were now pouring out on to the grass. There were maybe over a thousand already and more were arriving all the time and being ushered to their places. Jefferson tried to imagine the gigantic problems faced by the Uniformed Division officers on the gate. Every available man had been drafted in to help, he knew. And IRIS still hadn't been found . . .

'Marvin?' his earpiece crackled. It was Reynolds on Charlie channel.

'Yes!' responded Jefferson tersely.

'We've found a switched videotape. It didn't tally with the log. The label says it's three days old, but we've checked back and it fits exactly with traffic that was logged in and out of the same gate two weeks ago.'

'Could the switch just have been a mistake?'

'Could be, but I doubt it. There are strict procedures for reusing the tapes. My guess is that it's been deliberately relabelled.'

'Right!' said Jefferson quickly. 'That tape must cover the time IRIS was brought in. Find out who was on duty at that gate during that period. Grab him and quiz him about what came in. It will have been a delivery of some kind. And get hold of the escorting officer for that delivery, to find out what it was and where it went.'

'I've already got people working on that. They're looking back through the rosters right now to see who was on duty.'

'Good.' Jefferson frowned briefly, thinking. 'George?'

'Yeah?'

'Last night, when we were up there in the records office. You remember – around seven o'clock. The guy on duty when we arrived. Small, skinny guy with red hair and metal-framed glasses.'

'Doesn't ring a bell with me. What about him?'

'Find out who is he and pull him in.'

'OK, but why?'

'A dollar gets you ten he's the one who pulled the switch on the videotapes. I bet he deleted something from the log too, to cover it up.'

'Why him?'

'It was quite cool in that room, but he was sweating like a spit-roast hog. He looked nervous as hell.'

'He did, huh? I wish I'd noticed it.'

'My fault. I did notice it, and I should have said something.'

'Never mind. We'll get him.'

'Fine,' said Jefferson. 'And don't bother to read him his goddam rights before you start asking him questions, OK?'

'I'll read the bastard something out of the official Bosnian Serb handbook on prisoner treatment.'

'Fine,' said Jefferson, signing off.

Damn! he though angrily, kicking himself. *I should have followed my instincts and grilled that little creep last night.* He glanced at his watch. *Oh, God! Only twenty minutes to go. Where the hell is Gergen?*

As if on cue, the earpiece crackled again. 'Jefferson, are you there?'

'Yes sir, Mr Gergen. Has Flagman agreed?'

'I'm afraid he's said it's completely out of the question.'

Oh shit oh shit oh shit . . .

'It's practically his trademark,' continued Gergen. 'He says it would be unthinkable for him to change his appearance in the way you suggest. So it's a flat no, I'm afraid. Warren Christopher has tried his hardest, but things are very touchy down there right now and there's nothing more he can do.'

'Goddammit!' yelled Jefferson into the radio. 'Doesn't Flagman realise he could get shot? Hell, I'll rephrase that. Doesn't he realise he *will* get shot?'

'He does,' said Gergen. 'And do you know what his answer was? he said he was prepared to put his trust in us. That was what he said.'

'Oh, God,' moaned Jefferson. 'Listen, Mr Gergen. You've got to delay things. You've just *got* to! It doesn't matter how, but you *have* to do it. I think we're on to something – a gate entry log has been falsified, and we're pulling in the guys responsible for questioning. Give me a little more time, and we'll have it.'

'I'll try,' said Gergen simply.

The earpiece went dead.

Down below in the crowd, way back from the most important seats in the front, a man in a thick suit was sitting next to his wife, a dark-haired, vivacious and attractive woman in her mid-thirties. The man, some years older, had brown hair that was just beginning to go grey at the temples, and a kind, gentle face. They were a good-looking couple, obviously devoted to each other. There was a keen sense of expectation in all those present, but none felt it more keenly than these two. They were clutching each other's hands tightly. The man was beginning to wish he had worn lighter clothes; under the blazing sun and cloudless sky he felt hot and uncomfortable.

He sighed. 'I hope everything will go well, Mona,' he said softly, tiredness and strain audible in his voice.

She smiled up at him and squeezed his hand. 'It won't be long now, darling,' she whispered to him. 'This is your day. You've worked harder for this than anyone. It will all go well. Try to relax.'

'It's your day too,' he said. 'I could not have played

my part without you there to help me.'

They watched together silently as the last seats began to fill up. There were just a few minutes to go . . .

'We've got the bastard, Marvin.'

'Who?' snapped Jefferson.

'Your spit-roast hog,' said Reynolds. 'Name of Patrick Donovan. We're working on him.'

'We're running out of time!' said Jefferson desperately. 'We need the guy on the gate too – he can tell us what was brought in. Have you got him?'

'Not yet,' said Reynolds.

'Then we've lost it! There's only a couple of minutes to go! Can you do something to delay things? Tell them there's a bomb scare, a hurricane alert, an air-raid warning, World War Three, any goddam thing – but for God's sake, get them to wait!'

'I'll do my best,' muttered Reynolds.

Jefferson ran his hands through his hair and began pacing back and forth on the roof. He envied the SWAT team members their calm. Their commander, Scott Hazeldine, was moving among them, issuing last-minute instructions in an unflappable voice, double-checking that all fields of fire were clear. Jefferson listened with half an ear.

'. . . your arc of fire,' Hazeldine was saying to one of his men. 'Can you see everything OK?'

'No problem, in this sun,' said the black-clad figure. 'Pity it isn't always like this. We won't need the flood-lights today. Do you remember last winter, when it was so overcast they had to light the place up to make it look like it was a nice day?'

'Yeah,' smiled Hazeldine. 'Raining too, wasn't it?'

'It sure was.'

Jefferson had been praying hard, throughout the night, that there would be a torrential downpour that would force the ceremony inside. But there wasn't a cloud . . .

He froze. '*What* was that you just said?' he hissed, whirling round.

The SWAT commander turned his head, startled. The big FBI man standing over him looked as if he had been stung by a hornet. 'Just discussing the lighting conditions,' he said evenly.

That's what we missed, thought Jefferson. 'Floodlights! Floodlights! Where are they?'

'They're all round the grounds, Mr Jefferson. Some up here on the roof, others on poles, others mounted in the trees . . .'

Jefferson was already shouting into his radio. 'George! It's in one of the goddamn floodlights! Get some men out there to disable them, quick!' He turned again to the SWAT commander. 'Get some of your people to take off their black overalls and drape them over the ones up here on the roof! And get those guys with the lasers to start zapping every goddam floodlight they can see out there in the grounds! Hurry!'

Hazeldine barked out instructions. Riflemen swiftly began to rip off their uniforms and scurried along the roof, bent double to avoid showing themselves above the parapet. Hazeldine was already directing the fire of the Dazer guns. 'Taylor!' he yelled over his shoulder to one of his squad leaders. 'How many floodlights out there on this side?'

'A dozen or thereabouts, sir.'

'Fifteen, sir,' said another voice. 'I counted them one night.'

'Get your ass over here and help point them out!'

Jefferson grabbed a pair of binoculars and began to sweep his gaze around the grounds below. One of the lights sprang into view. As he watched, he saw a flash of bright light hit the glass cover of the rectangular black casing. *One of the Dazers just zapped that one . . . But there was no reaction. Hell – what will IRIS do if it is hit? Will it go crazy and fire anyway?* 'How many have you hit?' he shouted.

'Four, so far!' replied Hazeldine. 'We're giving them a concentrated blasting. These things have a narrow beam, and we want to make sure we hit a key component.'

'Sing out each time you finish one!'

Jefferson was suddenly aware that something new was going on below. The crowd had fallen silent. Dimly he heard an announcement being made. He lowered the binoculars and peered over the edge. 'Oh, God,' he muttered. The Vice-President, Al Gore, was walking out on to the grass, with his wife beside him in a pink dress. There was applause from the gathered crowd. Behind the Vice-President came a procession of other VIPs. 'Oh God,' Jefferson repeated despairingly. 'Why couldn't they have waited? Just a few more goddam seconds!'

'Six down now!' called Hazeldine.

Jefferson had the binoculars to his eyes again. The public address system was making a further announcement, the one Jefferson had been dreading.

'. . . and the President of the United States!' concluded the announcement.

The applause from the crowd surged and a hundred television cameras began to roll, broadcasting the dramatic scene live to viewers worldwide. Millions of viewers watched in near-disbelief. Few had thought that what was about to happen could ever have been possible.

In the back of the crowd gathered on the lawn, Terje Larsen clutched his wife Mona's hand tightly. The two Norwegians were close to tears. *It is actually happening*, thought Larsen . . .

President Clinton, Israeli Prime Minister Yitzhak Rabin and PLO Chairman Yasser Arafat emerged from the White House and walked out into the bright sunshine bathing the South Lawn.

The television cameras were rolling, all concentrating

on the three men as they walked out on the red carpet, past the two US Marines standing stiffly to attention. Hundreds of camera flashguns began to fire, capturing the first of the extraordinary pictures that would soon be winging round the world. Some of the spectators in the crowd thought they glimpsed brief reflections of the flashguns from the windows and glass surfaces of the White House. They were unaware that these were blinding pulses of laser light being fired over their heads, zeroing in on the floodlights, one by one.

Twelve feet up in its tree at the far end of the lawn IRIS had had a busy morning, scanning the vast crowd of people at the rate of twenty faces a second. Now it took in the three new arrivals.

IRIS instantly recognised Yasser Arafat as the target it had been programmed to kill. Arafat's black-and-white patterned *kaffiyah*, the unmistakably distinctive head-dress that over the years had become his personal trademark, confirmed it beyond doubt. *Positive identification . . . Ready to fire . . .* IRIS centred its sight on Arafat's forehead, just below the carefully folded point of the *kaffiyah*, and tracked his movements, waiting for him to stop as it had been programmed to do. The electric servo motors made frequent minute adjustments to keep the image of his head centred in the picture. *Tracking . . .*

On the roof, Jefferson's heart was pounding. He had braced himself for the shot, but none had come. Could IRIS have failed? He could see Flagman now, walking beside the President and Yitzhak Rabin along the red carpet, down towards the lawn . . .

Nineteen paces out from the door, still on the red carpet, Yasser Arafat showed just one visible sign of the mortal danger he knew he faced from the assassination machine he had been warned about. His hands went in a reflex motion to his head-dress. He adjusted it nervously, but his steps did not falter and his smile remained in place.

'Eight down!' called the SWAT commander, his voice urgent.

Oh God, it's waiting for him to stop, thought Jefferson. *That's why it hasn't fired. It's not over yet . . .* He raised the binoculars again. *There's another one, up in that tree. Could that be the one?*

'Nine!'

Still six to go . . . Not enough time . . .

Something caught Jefferson's eye. It was a slight flickering reflection of light from the floodlight in the tree. The glass front cover was shimmering, moving in the slight breeze . . . It wasn't glass! It was something more flimsy!

'Scott!' yelled Jefferson, diving down beside the SWAT commander and pointing. 'That one over there, about twelve feet up in that tall tree at the far left-hand end of the lawn. That's the one – it's moving!'

'I see it!' said Hazeldine tersely. He rapped out a quick target indication and fire control order to the four Dazer gun marksmen.

Down below on the lawn, President Clinton, Yitzhak Rabin and Yasser Arafat had stepped off the end of the red carpet and were now out on the closely mown grass, approaching the four steps leading up on to the white-painted platform, only five yards from where they would stop. They mounted the steps. Three yards; two; one . . .

Arafat reached his position and stopped.

At that exact moment IRIS registered brilliant blue-white light as the laser beam struck its camera's charge-coupled-device receptor, then total darkness as the CCD burned out. *Incorrect image. Malfunction.*

On the roof, Jefferson was still looking through his binoculars. He saw a wisp of smoke curling from the front of the floodlight unit; as he looked closely, he saw a score of puncture marks in the flimsy glass-substitute where the laser guns had burned through. Cellophane, or something like it, he thought dully. He lowered his binoculars and looked down. The ceremony had started. Yasser Arafat was still standing, he realised. IRIS hadn't fired. Jefferson knew he had succeeded. Suddenly, his hands began to shake violently.

Blinded but unaware of it, IRIS patiently began searching once more, for the image it would never see again . . .

Two things happened over the next few minutes which went largely unobserved, even though they both effectively occurred in full view of the millions of people watching. The pictures and video footage of the famous handshake, between the smiling Arafat and the somewhat embarrassed and awkward-looking Rabin, would be watched again and again; but of all the millions who saw it, only one man spotted a tiny detail.

Robert Lucas was a professional photographer. Like all the other photographers crammed into the press enclosure, he was hoping to capture the one definitive picture which would be syndicated worldwide. In the event there were so many similar ones for newspaper editors to choose from that his photographic record was just one of dozens – remarkable pictures, but no different from many of the others. In one respect, however, Robert Lucas did indeed differ from his colleagues. He was almost totally deaf.

As Arafat moved forward and shook Rabin's hand, Lucas saw the Israeli Prime Minister say something out of the side of his mouth. Rabin's lips hardly moved, but because the long lens on his Nikon camera acted like a telescope Lucas just managed to catch it. He saw it in well-defined detail – better than anything that could be captured by the television cameras; because of this, no one else would spot it later. Lucas frowned briefly as he saw it; then, professional that he was, he continued to fire off pictures. Rabin turned to face Shimon Peres, his Foreign Minister, and this time the television pictures would clearly show his lips moving as he said, 'Now it's your turn,' to Peres, as he too moved forward to shake Arafat's hand.

Puzzled, Lucas nudged his neighbour. 'That's strange,' he said, frowning.

'What is?' asked the other photographer.

'What Rabin just said to Arafat. It seemed an odd thing for him to say.'

'You can lip-read?'

'I'm deaf.'

'Oh. I'm sorry, I didn't know. So, what did Rabin say?'

'He said, "You are a brave man, my little brother." Why would he say that to Arafat? He hates him.'

'Hell, I don't know,' said the other, losing interest.

The second incident, too, passed largely unnoticed. It occurred during Yitzhak Rabin's speech, following the signing and the handshake. Rabin spoke for just over one minute, his voice echoing the suffering and anguish caused by the decades of bitter conflict between the Israelis and the Palestinians. Understandably, all eyes were on him as he spoke; everyone was concentrating on his words. Few noticed what happened behind him, just a few seconds after he started speaking. 'The time for peace has come . . .' Rabin was saying. 'This signing of the Israeli-Palestinian declaration of principle here today . . .'

At that precise moment Yasser Arafat, standing behind and to the left of Rabin, turned his head sharply to his left. Someone nearby was trying to catch his attention. Arafat didn't see him at first, but then the man caught his eye. Arafat leaned over to hear what he was saying. He listened intently for a brief moment, then nodded in understanding and straightened up again, facing forward once more as Rabin continued with his speech.

Arafat seemed to take a deep breath. His head bent in brief contemplation of what he had just heard from the man on his left, and then he looked up again. His expression remained serious for a few seconds, after which the tension seemed to leave his body and he relaxed. His smile, which had earlier seemed brittle and forced, suddenly sparkled like the sun.

That smile marked the moment when Flagman knew that the threat from IRIS had at last been neutralised. It was over.

'. . . We who have fought against you, the Palestinians,' continued the Israeli Prime Minister's voice, low, reaching the end of his speech, cracking with emotion. 'We say to you today, in a loud and a clear voice: enough of blood and tears! Enough!'

60

The flashing lights beckoned Mike Ziegler as he and the four others stumbled their way towards the South Korean border. Tony Ackford drew level with him, hauling the lurching figure of Weatherill. 'Give us a hand, Mike,' panted Ackford. 'My right arm's knackered.'

'Sure,' gasped Ziegler, grabbing Weatherill under the other arm. He winced at the pain from his own ribs. 'What's wrong with him?'

'Just deaf, I think,' gasped Ackford. 'A few of those 122-mil Kats landed quite close. Bugger's gone flaky on us, whatever it is.' Between them they broke into a run, bent forward and dragging Weatherill with them. The young scientist appeared to have lost his mind – he was moaning and staggering, but not quite a dead weight.

Behind them Halliday forced himself along, carrying Sumi in his arms. She felt as light as a child, but it was an exhausting run across the rough terrain, and it seemed to go on for ever. Sumi remained conscious, staring up at his face. The jolting of her wounds must have been painful, Halliday knew, but she did not utter a squeak of pain or protest.

'There was a young Nik-Nok from 'unchon,' gasped Ackford.

'What?'

'... Got shot in the mouth after luncheon,' continued Ackford.

'Hunch'ŏn,' murmured Sumi.

'*Har, har!*' laughed Ackford. 'Before—'

'Leave it out, Tony,' gasped Ziegler. 'Anyway, it was nearer supper-time.'

'*Har, har!* Before the bloke died—'

'Aw, shit, Tony—'

'I said open wide—'

'Jesus,' panted Ziegler, grinning, 'Do I have to put up with this?'

'Here's a couple of bullets to munch on. *Har, har, har!*'

'Tony, you're an asshole, you know that? It's goddam painful, laughin' with busted ribs.'

'*Har, har, har!*'

Behind him, Ziegler heard Sumi and Halliday giggling.

Suddenly they were at the main fence. 'Down!' shouted Ziegler. 'Stay back while I set the charges to blow it! Pete – give me a hand here!'

Ninety seconds later the plastic explosive charges erupted, blasting a jagged hole in the chain-link fence and toppling two of the big steel posts with the Y-shaped branches holding coils of razor-wire on top. They scrambled through the gap. Ahead, nearer now, was the first of the two beacons, the infra-red one. Not too far to go, now . . .

A few minutes later they reached the beacon. Suddenly they tumbled forward, down an embankment into a large dug-out. There were lights, faces . . .

Ziegler grimaced in pain; he had landed awkwardly on his injured hand, and the wound in his ribs stung like fire. Disengaging himself quickly from Weatherill and unshouldering his AK, he saw the face of Johnny Bourne bending over him. Behind him in the trench stood Colonel Max Goodale; a few yards away was a South Korean Army command post, dug in below ground level.'

'Mike!' yelled Bourne. 'Are you OK?'

'Hi, fellas,' panted Ziegler, exhausted. 'No. I am *not* OK. As a matter of fact, I'm in terrible, blindin' agony. Tony's just finished tellin' the worst joke in the whole world.'

'*Har, har!*' laughed Ackford weakly, his arm hanging at an unnatural angle from the shattered shoulder.

Ziegler struggled painfully to his feet. 'Colonel, a word in your ear, please.' He drew Goodale to one side and began talking in a low voice, out of earshot of the others. The conversation was brief and urgent. At one stage Goodale glanced sharply back towards the others. Ziegler fished in his smock and handed over the small package Howard had given him. Goodale briefly grasped his hand; then he turned towards the command post. 'Medical orderlies!' he called. 'This man needs help! Quickly!'

A South Korean medical team was already tending to Sumi's and Ackford's wounds. Ziegler sank to the ground. His face was grey with pain, but he was still clutching his AK. Two medical orderlies cut away his shirt and smock and began attending to the deep gash on the side of his ribcage, while two more dealt with his smashed wrist. Sumi had passed out. Goodale was once again looking anxiously out over the open ground of the DMZ.

The mortars had stopped again; now came the sound of gunfire. Ziegler tried to struggle to his feet. Bourne restrained him. 'You're in no fit state, Mike,' he said. 'You've been pumping out blood like a broken fire-hydrant. You wouldn't last ten yards.'

Ziegler slumped back down, exhausted, his head

spinning. 'Maybe you're right, Johnny,' he said weakly. 'But we must do *somethin'* to help . . .' He thought briefly, then his eyes flashed. 'Hey – get hold of that officer over there and give him my Magellan sat-nav unit. The GPS has got the four nearest NK positions plotted on it, plus our last two, accurate to ten metres. Get him to arrange for some nice, persuasive ordnance to drop on all of them except the last one, where Ed and the boys are now. Tell him I don't give a shit if it starts World War Three.'

Bourne nodded. 'I'll ask Colonel Goodale to see if he can arrange it. He carries a lot more clout than I do.' Thirty seconds later he was back. 'He says he's going to see what he can do.'

Ziegler nodded, closing his eyes.

Goodale approached the command post, a determined gleam in his eye. 'Captain Lim,' he said to the liaison officer, who had been watching from the narrow doorway, 'would you be kind enough to arrange to put me through by telephone, on a secure line, to the US Ambassador in Seoul. In person, please, and at once.'

Something about Goodale's expression told the South Korean captain that this was not a facetious request. 'Yes, *sir!*' he said, grinning. He saluted and went inside. Goodale followed him, frowning grimly at the sound of the further barrage of mortar-fire coming from the middle of the DMZ.

Bourne rose awkwardly to his feet and limped back towards the edge of the dug-out, gazing out once more over the demilitarised zone. The gunfire was intensifying; there was an expression of anguish on his face. He kicked his withered leg hard against the earth bank of the dug-out, as if willing the damaged limb back into full life.

Glancing around him, he realised that Goodale was still inside the command-post. He seemed to straighten. Snatching Weatherill's night-vision goggles from his head, he put them on; then he picked up Ackford's rifle and belt order, swiftly checking the magazines. He turned to Halliday. 'Come on, Pete,' he beckoned fiercely. 'It's you and me.'

'I'm with you, boss!'

The two men scrambled up the embankment and raced out and away into the open ground of the DMZ. Bourne ran, jinking fast from side to side, oblivious now of his old leg-wound. Halliday ran with him, following his lead. The gunfire ahead of them became more intense, and stray bullets cracked, buzzed and whined above their heads. The dull, thumping sound of hand-grenades punctuated the automatic fire. The years seemed to fall away from Bourne; he felt as if he was back in his early twenties, spurred on by an urgent anxiety for his friends.

As he and Halliday ran forward, the gunfire rose to a vicious crescendo; the loud *crump* of an explosive detonation was followed by three more. The gunfire slackened. There was one final burst of firing and two more explosions as they approached a rocky outcrop. Finally the gunfire dwindled . . .

'*Ed!*' roared Bourne. 'Hold on! We're coming!'

Harris had completed the setting out of the claymore mines in good time. The boss was badly wounded in the leg, he knew, and wouldn't be able to move. The claymores might keep the first wave of an assault at bay, if that was what was coming next, but he wished he had an M16 203 in his hands instead of an AK . . .

Shit! 'Incomers!' he yelled, hearing the 82mm mortars again. Once more the barrage burst around them, very close. They could do nothing but ride it out; immediately it stopped, a direct assault would come.

Finally it ceased. Harris immediately raised his head, his fierce blue eyes gazing intensely down the line the enemy would take.

'Mel . . .' Zeccara's voice was weak, hardly audible.

Harris glanced to his right. Zeccara's left shoulder was a mass of blood.

'Shit!' Harris pulled a shell-dressing from the medical bag, tore it open and threw it across. 'Just keep it pressed tight into the wound, Angelo. I'll fix you up in a minute.'

'Bastard nose-plug from one of those 82s, I think,' managed Zeccara. He pointed weakly. 'Look, the boss . . .' His head fell forward as he lost consciousness.

Turning towards Howard, Harris saw that he was slumped face-down. He crawled quickly towards him. A fragment of one of the mortar bombs had smashed him in the head and there was blood everywhere.

Zeccara, badly hit, out of action, unconscious. And now the boss, out of the picture for good. Dead.

Harris was alone.

Right at that moment, he saw movement in front of him. Scuttling bodies, heading forwards in his direction. Little bastards. Dozens of them. Time for a bit of bowling – give 'em a few no-balls. Pull the pin, sod that shit about lobbing it – chuck it. Give it a bit of wrist. *Ping*, *crack*, as the lever flew away. OK, Dickie? All right, Shep? No good hopping about on 111 – count to four instead, and keep your head well down at square leg. Next one. Pull, chuck. *Crump*, the first one. Nothing. *Crump*, the second one. A thin scream. *How was he?* Finger up please, Dickie: *Out!* Yorked the fucker. Three, four and five already in the air. *Fast over, this.* Six.

As his hand-grenades began to burst forty yards in front of him, Harris heard one or two satisfactory screams and cries. Then the North Korean AKs and RPDs opened up again, with the big DShKs thumping away off in the distance. *Bollocks to the background fire*, thought Harris; *but those assault troops must have just about pinpointed my position.*

Harris had made a brief estimate of their numbers.

He knew that he was in far more trouble than he had ever faced before. This was a company-strength attack, with heavy machine-gun support. There were maybe a hundred of them, and there was already fire coming in from his left flank – fire that would cover the final frontal assault. It was now down to judgement. When to fire the claymores, and hope to God they hadn't been knocked over by the mortars . . .

'Back in the US, back in the US, back in the USSR!' yelled the Beatles over the South Korean loudspeakers.

A heavy concentration of AK fire came from directly ahead. Harris ignored it and briefly raised his head. He had got it right. They were coming! *Head down. I'll send you fuckers back to the USSR, all right. Claymore one!* Boom. *Claymore two!* Boom. *Three!* Click. *Shit. Fucking mortars must have zapped it. Four!* Boom. *Five!* Click. *Sod it! Six!* Boom. *Thank fuck for that one – it should have sorted out the NK platoon giving covering fire from the left . . .*

Quickly now, thought Harris. *Up, burst of fire, down, roll to the side, repeat. Two claymores left.* He had already prepared them. *Where to place them? To the left, where the covering fire came from just now, or ahead and slightly right, to cover another assault?* Decision! *First one to cover the front. Keep the last one in reserve.* He reached forward and jammed the claymore's stand into the ground. It would go off only feet from his head. He knew the concussive effect of the blast would be deafening – it could damage his lungs or even kill him . . .

There was movement in front. Harris rolled three yards to one side, then carefully raised his head. *Yes. Here they come again. Wait until they're all on their feet. There's the commander, gesturing. Slot him first, if the claymore fails. Shit! There are so many still left alive! Come on, you bastards! Thirty yards.* The AK fire started again, trying to force his head down, but aimed at the wrong place, because he had moved . . .

Head down, Harris shouted to himself *Seven!* Boom.

Head up! Fuck, that was too near for comfort. Ear-drums gone? Get number eight ready? Where? Devastation ahead, nothing but bodies, none of them moving worth a shit. AK ready, spare mags. Spray to the left. Thirty rounds, three-round bursts, moving between each burst to keep the bastards guessing . . .

Heavy automatic fire now splattered down at Harris from the left, pinging and whining off the stones all around him. A bullet slammed into a rock inches in front of his face and ricocheted viciously away; chips of stone stung his face and he spat out some pieces that had spun into his mouth. *Fuck. Mouthful of shit. Bust a tooth.* The left eyepiece of his goggles had starred. *Near one. Would have been blinded without the goggles.*

He was now aware that he had underestimated the group on the left giving covering fire. *Get the last claymore in place, facing left.* He heard a shrill command, then the crump of a hand-grenade, then another, falling well short. *Useless bastards. Get some bowling practice!* He thrust the claymore up and jammed its stand into the earth, aiming it towards the threat from the left. Wait until they move. Scream for effect, to encourage the bastards – '*Aaaa . . . !*'

Head up slowly, face left, Harris commanded himself. *There they are, on their feet now. Just a few more yards, until they commit themselves . . . Keep still . . . Yes, they're all up. Now!* He thrust his head down again, simultaneously squeezing the clacker of his last claymore. *Eight!* Boom. *Head up! Maximum fire! Long bursts! Down, roll! Reload!* He swept the ground to the left and ahead, firing, rolling to the side, popping up again a few yards away, trying to create the impression that he was not just one man, but many . . .

'Get about as oiled as a diesel train!' Elton John was now belting out of the South Korean tannoy system at maximum volume. 'Gonna set this dance alight! Saturday night's all right for fighting, Saturday night's all right – all right – *All right!*'

Harris had done well, he knew. He had killed dozens of them, but others were still coming. Some from ahead, and more from the left. Something smashed into his left hand, almost knocking away his AK. *Those four bastards in front,* he decided. *They're the threat.* Crack-crack; crack-crack-crack. *Shit. Left hand's gone dead on me. Missed two of them. Shit, I'm going down, here. Change magazine. Fucking left hand. No time!* He whipped out his knife and prepared to die.

The North Korean company commander and three other soldiers had been charging towards Harris, the bayonets on their Chinese AKs folded out, arrowing towards his chest. Two of them had fallen to his last two brief bursts of fire, but the commander and one other man came on, almost abreast of each other. Out of ammunition, Harris now faced them with nothing but his knife.

In that brief moment, facing death, Harris felt a sudden, overwhelming pang of grief that he would never see his family again. *Forgive me, Janet, my love,* he thought. *I'm so sorry, Ben. So sorry . . .*

There was a short, vicious burst of gunfire and the North Korean commander spun round and collapsed, dead. The second man hesitated briefly, puzzled as to where the fire could have come from. It was enough. Harris leaped at him. His knife went in, below the man's ribs, and then up. They fell together. The North Korean gave a dying groan and went limp. Out of the corner of his eye, Harris saw two more North Korean soldiers bearing down on him from the left. There was another long burst of gunfire and then everything went black.

'Mel!' Halliday shook Harris's shoulders. 'Mel! Come on!' He pulled out a water-bottle and emptied it over the man's face and into his mouth.

Harris moaned and spluttered and began to regain consciousness. Vomiting out the water, he clutched the side of his head with his good hand. 'Ohh . . . shit,' he moaned groggily. Slowly he opened his eyes and sat up. 'Pete,' he said, his eyes struggling to focus. 'Oh, fuck, my head.'

'You've got to get up, Mel,' said Halliday. 'We've got to move.'

'What? Can't hear you.'

'You've got to move,' shouted Halliday, realising that Harris had been deafened. 'I'll bring Angelo.'

'I wanna be your man!' yelled the Beatles idiotically.

'Angelo . . .' muttered Harris. 'He took a nasty one in the shoulder.'

'I know. He'll live. Now, come on – I've got to get him out of here and I can't carry both of you!'

'The boss was hit in the head,' said Harris bleakly. 'He's dead.'

'No, I think he's still alive,' shouted Halliday. 'Johnny's carrying him back.'

'Johnny? He's here?'

'Yes. *Come on!*'

Harris forced himself to his feet. 'The boss is really still alive?' he asked disbelievingly.

'Yes! Now *get going!* I'll bring Angelo.'

'OK. Oh, shit,' moaned Harris, holding his head. 'What the fuck happened?'

'You got smacked by a rifle-butt or something,' said Halliday. 'Johnny and I dropped the last three or four as they were coming at you. It looked like one of them fell right on top of you. Move it – quick!'

'What about the bergens? All the kit? We can't leave . . .'

'Fuck the kit!' shouted Halliday. '*Get going!*'

'Hang on,' said Harris. Swaying slightly, he kicked over the body of the North Korean he had knifed and pulled out the blade. 'I'm not leaving this,' he muttered. He thrust the knife back into his belt-sheath. 'Johnny's already gone, you said?'

'Yes. Follow the two lights and catch him up. *Go!*'

Halliday could see Harris was really in no condition to move anywhere. He was moving sluggishly, barely conscious, his will-power the only thing keeping him on his feet.

'Yeah. OK.'

Halliday watched as Harris began to stumble away, then picked up Zeccara's limp body and followed. 'Must have been a whole NK company there,' he muttered to himself, staggering after Harris. 'Mel Harris, you are one hell of a fine soldier . . .'

The mortar-fire began to rain down again.

Goodale was aghast. 'What do you mean, Johnny's gone out there?'

'Went back to help Ed,' said Ziegler weakly. 'Him and Pete.'

'But he promised! I . . .'

'You couldn't have stopped him, Colonel,' said Ziegler gently. 'Nothin' could have stopped him.'

'But listen to that!' Goodale's composure had been shattered and he gazed out desperately across the open ground. The noise of the North Korean mortar-fire was now deafening. Massive volleys of stupid explosions, going off at random . . . hideous, scorching flashes of light . . . shrieking fragments of metal, hurtling past unseen . . . choking, grey-black smoke . . . 'It's madness! Madness!'

Ziegler rose wearily to his feet in the trench. He stood there swaying, his face pale; then he leaned forward on to the earth embankment next to Goodale. He rested his chin on the bank, his eyes just above ground level as he stared out over no man's land. 'Yeah, Colonel, listen to it,' he said slowly. 'Those goddam Beatles got one song right, at least. "A little help from your friends." D'you get the picture, Colonel? You see, we don't like leavin' our people behind. Tony and me, we'll be the next out if Johnny and Pete aren't back in the next few minutes.' Ziegler glanced to his side and saw Ackford already standing up painfully, his shattered arm bound tightly against his side. 'You know who you have to keep an eye on when we're gone, Colonel,' he said quietly.

'No!' Goodale shouted, horrified. 'You're both mad! You're in no fit state . . .'

Ziegler was staring out through the smoke as it swirled and drifted lazily upwards into the dawn sky. There was a series of dull, booming reports of big guns firing, this time from the South Korean side. *At last, a real response*, he thought. *Good for you, Colonel.* The shells screamed overhead. *Artillery. 105s, maybe. Difficult to tell. Wish they were 155s . . . Too late, though . . .*

'Are we off then, Mike?' asked Ackford.

'We'll give it another minute or two,' said Ziegler. He stared out over the open ground of the DMZ. A brief frown crossed his face and he turned to Ackford again. 'By the way, Tony, what was all that shit about "luncheon"?'

'What? Oh, yeah – it's a sort of posh version of lunch,' replied Ackford. 'Roast beef, half a pint of port in a straight glass, that sort of caper. I read about it somewhere. You eat it wearing a tie.'

'Those goddam North Koreans weren't wearin' ties,' said Ziegler, 'and I bet they didn't even have a stinkin' old piece of boiled dog to eat, never mind beef.'

They've both gone completely mad, thought Goodale numbly.

'Yeah, well, it's the principle, see?' said Ackford. 'And "boiled dog" wouldn't have rhymed, would it?'

'Uh, no, but, "coiled frog", or maybe "soiled bog" . . .'

'Wouldn't scan though, would it.'

Barking mad, thought Goodale.

'How about "oiled hog"?'

'Mike.' Ackford's expression had changed. He was pointing with his one good hand.

At first Goodale could see nothing. Then, through

the swirling smoke, he thought he glimpsed some movement. The smoke obscured it again, and it was gone. Nothing there. He had been imagining it. But . . .

'I think it's them, Mike,' said Ackford.

'It's them,' said Ziegler.

Out of the grey-black smoke came a slowly limping figure, carrying a man's body. Behind were two more men, staggering and carrying another. Through the bawling of the loudspeakers and the crashing, thundering, booming explosions of the artillery shells now beginning to pound the North Korean positions beyond, Goodale dimly heard people near him begin shouting and yelling – yelling their heads off in encouragement, screaming like maniacs, cheering themselves hoarse . . .

Goodale felt his eyes smarting, and he knew the smoke had nothing to do with it. Dumbly, incredulously, he watched the agonisingly slow approach of the five men, and he knew that this was the most magnificent bloody thing he had ever seen in his life.

61

The American Army nurse put her head round the door. Seeing that her patient was wide awake and had finished his breakfast, she smiled and came in. 'Someone will be in shortly to see you, Mr Howard,' she announced.

Howard's eyebrows raised fractionally. 'Oho! So I'm considered well enough to receive visitors now, am I?'

'This one's been in every day, but Colonel Payne hasn't allowed him anywhere near you yet. I guess that means you're well on the road to recovery. Mind you, I could have told him that myself,' she added caustically, giving him a sharp look.

'Oh, come on, Mary-Ann,' said Howard. 'You can't blame me. That lump of metal must have done something to my brain. It's the starch in your uniform – it seems to have an effect on me. And stop calling me "Mr Howard". My name's Ed, OK?'

'There's no starch in my uniform,' said Mary-Ann Kelley with mock severity, 'and I'll thank you to keep your hands to yourself from now on.' She moved his breakfast tray to one side and began wrapping the sphygmomanometer cuff round his right arm to take his blood pressure.

'Hand me my cigarettes before you do that, would you, Mary-Ann. They're over there in the—'

'No I will *not* hand you your cigarettes,' she said, pumping the bulb. 'Smoking is bad for you.'

'Nonsense. I was wounded in the head, not the lungs.'

'That has nothing to do with it,' said Mary-Ann. 'There's no smoking in here, period. It's against regulations.' She listened through the stethoscope as she continued pumping.

'Ouch, that hurts!' said Howard. 'My arm's going numb. Let it out, will you? I hate that bloody thing.'

'Your language is a total disgrace,' she said in a bored voice, her eyes fixed on the meter on the wall next to the bed. 'And anyway, how can you complain about a little thing like this, with a bullet-wound in your other arm?'

'Stupid regulation, anyway,' said Howard, ignoring her comment. 'Who decided I'm not allowed to smoke?'

There was a hiss of air as she released the screw-valve. 'I don't know. This is a US Military hospital. It's probably the Secretary for Defense who makes the rules.'

'Tell him he's fired.'

'Tell him yourself,' she retorted tartly. 'Hmm. One hundred and thirty-five over seventy-five.' She made a note on his chart.

'Is that good or bad?'

'It's disgusting. Now, stop complaining. You're lucky to be alive.' She thrust a thermometer into his mouth and marched out of the room.

Max Goodale was with her when she returned a few minutes later. 'Good morning, Ed,' he said breezily.

'Mphm,' mumbled Howard, gesturing crossly at his mouth.

Mary-Ann leaned over and removed the thermometer.

'*Thank* you, Mary-Ann,' said Howard sarcastically. 'And good morning to you, Colonel.'

'Normal,' announced Mary-Ann severely, studying the thermometer. 'As I expected. There's nothing much wrong with *him* today, Colonel Goodale. I'll leave you two together.' She turned and left.

'I'm delighted you're on the mend,' said Goodale as the door closed. 'How do you feel?'

'Not even a headache,' said Howard. 'They say the bandages have to stay on for a few more days. I've been warned I'll look like Frankenstein's monster when they come off – my head was shaved, and there's a four-inch scar where they put the plate in. I feel fine, but I could use a cigarette. They're in that cupboard over there, if you wouldn't mind handing them to me. I'm not allowed to get out of bed because of my leg.'

Goodale handed him the cigarettes and matches and sat down in the chair near the bed. 'I don't suppose you're allowed these, either. I'll probably get a tongue-lashing from that nice nurse of yours for giving them to you.' He sighed. 'Have you seen the others?'

'I've heard they're all recovering OK, but I've only actually seen Mike,' said Howard, lighting up a cigarette. He drew on it appreciatively. 'Mm, that's better. Yes – Mike was allowed in for a couple of minutes just to tell me everything had gone OK in Washington.'

'It went very well indeed,' confirmed Goodale.

'Have you heard any details?' asked Howard. 'What did this IRIS thing look like?'

Goodale told him what he knew. Howard listened with interest; he whistled softly when he heard what a close-run thing it had been.

'Ingenious,' he muttered.

'Yes,' said Goodale. 'I must ask you to keep that to yourself, of course. There's been no release of information about the attempt on Arafat's life. As far as the public is concerned, none of this ever happened and he was never in any danger.'

'You do surprise me,' said Howard with heavy sarcasm.

'Well, you know how these things are,' said Goodale. He smiled thinly, then shrugged. 'Or, at least, you damned well ought to, by now. But . . .' He paused briefly. 'I feel I haven't been told the whole story. For example, how did someone manage to get that bloody machine past all the White House security people? Maybe I have a suspicious mind, but I couldn't help wondering about it.' He stood up and walked over to the window, his back to Howard. 'Have you heard of someone called Thomas Levy?'

Howard frowned. 'No, I don't think so. Who is he?'

'He *was* one of President Clinton's senior aides.'

'He's been given the sack?'

'No. He shot himself. At least, that was what they said, and I haven't heard any suggestion to the contrary. There were reports that he was depressed. But it happened shortly before the peace accord was signed, which is rather a coincidence . . . As I say, maybe I just have a suspicious mind.'

'You think he had something to do with it?' asked Howard.

'I doubt we'll ever know, but I can't help wondering.'

'Hmm,' said Howard, 'I can imagine the Americans would want to keep it pretty quiet, if he had.'

'You can hardly blame them,' said Goodale,

returning to the chair. 'Anyway, enough of that.' He sat down again and leaned forward, clasping his hands in front of him. 'Tell me all about Colonel Eisener. I've heard a bit from Mike, but I'd like to hear the whole thing from you. Eisener sounds a most interesting fellow.'

'Yes, he is,' said Howard. 'But I'd better start from the beginning.' He began to explain, skimming rapidly through the story leading up to their arrival at the *Stasi* base. He frowned as he recounted the details of the interrogation and death of General Erfurt. 'That was a bit of a drawback,' he said. 'I think the general would have cracked eventually. I think he would have named Arafat as the assassination target, but of course I don't know. He was a tough old sod. But I don't think that was why he was murdered. My guess is that the traitor in our team didn't care much about Arafat one way or the other – or perhaps didn't even know he was the target – but was simply afraid of being identified by the general. Anyway, it didn't matter in the end.'

'So it was Eisener who told you that Arafat was the intended victim?'

'No,' said Howard. 'In fact, I don't think he knew, although I can't be sure. But that remark he said the general had made to him about something being in "black-and-white" set me thinking. When I heard a BBC World Service news report about Israel's agreement to recognise the PLO, and that Arafat was on his way to Washington to sign the declaration, it all fell into place. The Iranians hate Arafat and regard him as a renegade, as you know. I immediately thought of his black-and-white head-dress, and that was that.

'Immediately after that, we found out that the radio wasn't working, and that it had probably been sabotaged. We didn't know for sure, but coming on top of the shooting down of the Antonov, I was suspicious. I took a closer look at the general's body, and found the syringe puncture mark. That was when I knew we had a traitor. The problem was, there was no evidence pointing to one particular person. It could have been Kim Sumi or Weatherill – either of them could have done it. What I still don't know is how the information about our connection with the Antonov could have been passed on to the North Koreans. I can't believe they would have shot down that plane unless they had hard information.'

'I think I can help you there,' said Goodale. 'The Americans picked up a radio-beacon signal, and they pinpointed its source to the exact spot of your parachute drop zone. I'm just guessing, but I expect there was a message attached to the beacon, telling the North Koreans about the Antonov.'

'A bloody TACBE,' growled Howard. 'I see. But why didn't the message attached to the beacon also warn the North Koreans where we were going, and what we were up to?'

'I expect your traitor was afraid the North Koreans would attack the *Stasi* base and kill everyone there, but reasoned that you'd probably surrender without a fight when you heard about the Antonov and had no hope of getting away. A turncoat generally prefers a reward for services rendered, rather than a bullet.'

Howard looked thoughtful. 'I suppose that must be it,' he said.

'So how did you find out who the traitor was?'

'It largely hinged on Colonel Eisner,' said Howard. 'He offered to help us, and the offer certainly seemed genuine, but I didn't trust him. The problem was, he identified different buildings on the Yŏngbyŏn map to the ones that Weatherill had shown me. Obviously, one of them had to be lying. I decided to test both Eisner and Kim Sumi at the same time. Just before we left the *Stasi* base I talked to her in private. I told her Eisner was now on our side, but that no one else must know about it yet. I gave her a partially encoded message and told her to pass it to Eisner and set him free, and that she must not be seen doing it. The part that was *not* encoded told Eisener to make sure the message somehow reached you at the British Embassy here in Seoul as soon as possible. I put Mike Ziegler in the picture, and told him to watch what happened. He confirmed that Sumi did exactly as I asked her. She went down to the basement, unlocked Eisener's cell door and gave him the message. Mike had a duplicate of the message, and he'd have given that to Eisener if she'd substituted a different one.'

'I see,' said Goodale.

'Kim Sumi passed the test,' said Howard. 'That was when I knew Weatherill was the traitor. Obviously Eisener passed too, otherwise you and Johnny wouldn't have received the coded message I asked him to send you.' He lit another cigarette, drawing deeply. 'I should have listened to Tony Ackford. He had a feeling about Weatherill, right from the start.'

The unspoken implication of Howard's words stung Goodale to the quick. He lowered his head. *I should have listened to Tony Ackford*, Howard had said. What he really meant was *I should never have listened to you, Colonel, when you asked me to take him*. He raised his head again and looked directly at Howard. 'I promise you, I had no idea . . .'

Howard's dark eyes glittered dangerously for a moment, then he shrugged. 'I suppose I have to believe you. But the only reason I do so is because it wouldn't have made any sense to jeopardise this mission by deliberately saddling me with someone you suspected – or knew – was a traitor. But you see, Colonel,' he drew on his cigarette and continued calmly. 'I am sure you must be aware that this is not the only issue about which I have had reason to doubt you. You haven't been straight with me, and you know that as well as I do.' Howard's eyes were studying Goodale's face intently.

Goodale sighed. 'I think I know what you are going to say,' he said.

'The old man I was supposed to kill, if I found him,' said Howard flatly, his voice now hard. 'Who was he? And why did you tell me to do it? That question comes from Mike, as well as from me.'

'You told Mike about him?' asked Goodale, alarmed.

'Of course I did,' said Howard impatiently. 'Some of the others knew too – mostly because there was mention of the old man in your signals. But Mike was the only one I told about being asked by you to commit deliberate murder. He was my second-in-command, so I had to tell him. He might have had to do it if I had been killed myself on the way in.'

'I see,' said Goodale slowly.

'You'd better be straight with me, Colonel. So far, you've given me ample cause never to trust you again. In fact, you'll need to give me a pretty good reason not to put in a report about this to Century, and let them sort it all out. Don't think for one moment that I wouldn't do it, or that I don't know who to go to.'

'That wouldn't do you any good, you know,' said Goodale softly. 'In fact, it wouldn't achieve anything at all.' He leaned back in his chair and stared out of the window for a minute or so. 'Give me one of your cigarettes, would you?' he asked eventually.

Howard tossed him the pack and the lighter, and watched him light up. He could not recall having seen Goodale smoke before. 'That's a pretty hackneyed delaying tactic, Colonel,' he said evenly. 'If you're trying to think up some fairytale to tell me, it had better be a pretty bloody convincing one. Try the truth, just for a change.'

Goodale's eyes flashed briefly at Howard, then his face settled into an expression of resignation. 'I'll tell you no fairytales, Ed. Actually, I never have. Delaying tactic? Maybe. But in fact, I was trying to think if there was anything at all that I *could* tell you about this. It would be easy to tell you a perfectly credible lie, one that you would swallow. Yes –' he gestured at Howard with his hand, '– even someone as cynical about life as you. I have been in this game long enough to know how to lie convincingly, when I have to. Ever since I asked you to deal with this, I have been wondering whether to lie to you or to tell you the truth. I decided to do neither, and I have not changed my view. In the past minute or so, I have been wondering whether it would be fair to give you some small hint as to the truth. In many ways, you do at least deserve an explanation.' Goodale paused for a moment, drawing on the cigarette. *I wonder whether Hislop is alive or dead,* he thought dispassionately. *One way or another, unless he or his corpse turns up somewhere within the next few days, the Prime Minister will be forced to make a public statement about the abduction.* He turned to face Howard directly. 'The answer is simple. I'm afraid I can tell you absolutely nothing at all. No name, no reason, no motive. Not even a hint. I'm sorry, but that is how it has to be.' *Given even a hint, Howard would eventually guess,* Goodale knew.

Howard remained silent for a few seconds. 'A brave answer, Colonel,' he said coolly. 'Either that, or a desperate one. Right now, I'm not sure which.'

'Might it be an idea for you and I to declare a truce of some sort?' asked Goodale. 'Perhaps on the basis that while you may not entirely trust my motives and actions in this matter, you don't actively *dis*trust them?'

Howard said nothing for a few seconds; then he sighed. 'Oh, I suppose so,' he said eventually. 'Perhaps I'm just getting a little tired. Yes – let's forget the old man for the time being.'

Goodale's face betrayed nothing of the relief he felt. Hastily, he changed the subject. 'Could we get back to the matter of Dr Weatherill?' he asked. 'Why didn't you kill him on the spot when you found out he was a traitor? It must have been one hell of an extra risk, bringing him back here with you.'

'I reasoned that by then he was probably just as anxious to get out of North Korea as we were, so he was unlikely to risk his life by trying to give us away. As you said yourself, he would probably have preferred it if we'd surrendered, but once it was clear we weren't going to do that, he didn't really have any option but to go along with us. He thought he hadn't been found out, and he could hardly have announced to me that he had decided to stay behind – that would have looked more than just a bit odd, wouldn't it?'

'I see your point,' said Goodale.

'He's a plausible bastard, though,' said Howard. 'He acted extremely disappointed when I said we wouldn't be able to install his monitoring equipment at Yŏngbyŏn. He had me almost convinced at the time, but I bet he was actually quite relieved. In fact, I don't imagine for one minute that the bloody equipment would have worked. If Weatherill had had his way, he would have planted it in the wrong place, or he would have sabotaged it, just as he did with the radio. It's still lying somewhere out in the DMZ right now, I suppose. My guess is that he had a hand in the illicit trade in nuclear technology, perhaps helping the North Koreans, and was afraid that this would come to light. But that wasn't really the point.'

'You had a particular reason for bringing him back?'

Howard grinned. 'I learned a lot from Colonel Eisener about the art of duplicity. Exposing Weatherill, or killing him there and then, would have been too straightforward. I thought if I could get him back here in one piece, still thinking that his secret was safe, you might be able to make good use of him.'

Goodale nodded. 'I'm extremely glad you did. We'll be keeping a very close eye on him from now on – without him knowing, of course. Every contact he makes will be monitored and recorded. I hope that within a few weeks or months we'll have sufficient information to take action against quite a few people involved in illicit nuclear technology transfer.'

'Good,' said Howard. 'That's exactly what I hoped.

Let me know when you finally decide to pull him in, will you? I'd like to see the bastard's face when he finds out we knew about him all along.'

'I will,' said Goodale. 'But tell me, how could you be sure Eisner would pass the message on?'

'I couldn't be sure at all,' said Howard. 'It was just a test of his good faith, nothing more. The message itself was relatively unimportant – the only new information it contained was to the effect that if you received it intact, Sumi was in the clear and Weatherill was the traitor. Eisner himself had no way of knowing what it said.'

'Well,' said Goodale, 'your gamble on Eisner seems to have worked. I'm damned if I would have gambled my own life like that,' he muttered, shaking his head. 'But never mind. I suppose you had no choice. He did indeed send the message as you asked. I don't know how he managed it, but an unidentified European woman turned up at the British Embassy that evening. She handed in an envelope addressed to me, then disappeared without saying a word. Johnny decoded the message with his one-time pad. The envelope also contained details from Eisner concerning how payments should be made for his services. Anyway, he did exactly as he had promised you – and the result is that we now have a new and extremely well-placed agent inside North Korea. With luck, and as long as we continue to pay him, he should be able to pass further vital information on North Korea's nuclear capability.'

There was a brief silence as Howard studied Goodale coolly, his dark eyes giving no hint of his thoughts. 'You know, Colonel,' he said eventually, 'it's strange.' He paused to light yet another cigarette, his fourth since Goodale had arrived. 'Gerhardt Eisner is a very clever individual – and a very dangerous one. He's utterly unscrupulous. He has no discernible moral values, and he's as slippery as a Teflon-coated eel. He doesn't seem to care a shit about anyone other than himself. He seems prepared to do absolutely anything if he is paid well enough for it, and I'm pretty sure he told me nothing but a pack of bloody lies. On a personal level I wouldn't trust him an inch. But despite all that . . .' He paused to draw on his cigarette again.

'Go on,' said Goodale quietly.

'Well . . .' Howard's voice was cold and distant. 'It's odd, but in some ways I still have a sneaking regard for him.'

'That's understandable,' agreed Goodale, his voice carefully neutral. 'One should always respect a capable adversary.'

'I know that,' said Howard, his eyes now hard.

Max Goodale nodded. He was once again struck by the intensity of Howard's dark, penetrating stare – there was no glimmer of warmth or humour there. Immobilised though Howard now was, flat on his back in a hospital bed and with serious arm, leg and head-wounds, he was still the most dangerous and frightening man Goodale had ever met.

'It's quite possible to hate someone,' continued Goodale, 'and at the same time to admire his abilities.'

'Oh no, Colonel,' said Howard softly. 'It wasn't like that at all. You see, what really bothered me about Eisener was that I actually quite liked the bastard.'

Max Goodale's face remained utterly impassive. *Are you just talking about Gerhardt Eisener, Mr Howard?* he wondered. *Or is it me that you have in mind? Or, perhaps, both of us?*

62

Gerhardt Eisener leaned back in the chair in the big office, satisfied. The notification from his Swiss bank had arrived; the payment he had been anticipating had been made by the British. There would be further payments to look forward to when he supplied more information.

It was nice to be in charge, Eisener reflected; he was now free to do as he pleased, without interference or obstruction from General Erfurt. He had disliked the general, and was glad he was now dead.

Weatherill had been useful, he decided. As soon as he had seen him, he had recognised him. After all, Weatherill was one of his own recruits. It had been a simple matter to turn the man's unexpected presence to his advantage, and warn him that the general might be about to reveal his involvement in the illegal nuclear technology trade. Weatherill had panicked and killed the general, as he had hoped. It had been an opportunistic move, but it had worked and saved him the trouble of killing Erfurt himself later.

He wondered about Howard. There was more to that man than met the eye, he realised. He had heard about the incident down on the DMZ, and Colonel Zang had been in a particularly foul mood the following morning when he had telephoned him in P'yŏngyang, fishing for information. Zang hadn't said so in so many words, but Eisener had read between the lines and deduced that Howard and his men had managed to make it over the border after all. He had been secretly rather glad about that, even though it did leave him with a minor problem to resolve.

He hadn't told Howard about Weatherill, but that odd charade with the Korean girl passing him the encrypted message had set him thinking. It had obviously been a test of some sort, with the tall American hiding there to watch what happened. But a test of whom? Of himself, obviously; but almost certainly of the girl too. Why otherwise would she have been sent to deliver the message? If her loyalty was being tested, then Howard must have realised something was amiss. Perhaps as a result of that test he now knew that Weatherill was a traitor.

The simplest and best solution, Eisener decided, would be to play safe; in his next message to British Intelligence he would disclose Weatherill's involvement. There was nothing to be lost by doing so. Either way, Weatherill had served his purpose and was expendable. It was interesting to have learned that Max Goodale was now back in harness following his retirement the previous year, but not altogether surprising. He was most definitely not a man to be underestimated. If Goodale now knew about Weatherill, Eisener concluded, it would reinforce his own credibility to confirm it.

Naturally, he had not been truthful with Howard. He had of course known perfectly well that Yasser Arafat was the assassination target; he knew all the general's other secrets, too. He had found the files when the general was away on one of his trips to Japan; they had been cleverly hidden, but not cleverly enough. Howard had not found them, but he must have guessed about Arafat and prevented the assassination; the news on the radio about the signing of the peace accord in Washington was proof of that, and Peter Kramer had confirmed it in his report. Eisener sighed; he had always had a weakness for riddles, and he hadn't been able to resist setting the 'black-and-white' one to try to distract Howard. Well, he thought, he had paid the price for it – there would now be no payment from the Iranians.

Never mind, Eisener told himself. There were other projects, and the Washington *Stasi* cell run by Peter Kramer was still intact. Joanna Stone's fate was less easy to predict, but now that Kramer knew who she was, he would be able to keep him informed if anything happened to her. Telling Kramer about her had been contrary to normal security precautions, but in the circumstances it had been not only excusable but necessary. It had been obvious that that fool Levy would have to be disposed of. Kramer was the obvious choice to do it. The general, stupidly, hadn't even considered that, and hadn't listened even when Joanna had voiced her own concern about it. He had exposed her to far too great a risk of being compromised. If he, Eisener, had not taken steps behind the general's back to rectify the situation, she would almost certainly have found herself in the position of having to kill Levy herself. He doubted whether she could have got away with it. As it was, she would have to lie low for a while, keeping out of contact. But she was careful, clever and resourceful, and Eisener considered that she had a very good chance of remaining in place. There was no evidence against her – Kramer had confirmed it.

All in all, Eisener decided, things had turned out pretty well. He was now rid of the general and had at last gained control, after many years of patient servility, of a lucrative commercial enterprise. The events of the past few days, he reflected, had not been risk-free; but then most worthwhile things, in his experience, involved some degree of risk. Howard and his *kommando* team had come; then, when they had gone, he had been left in charge – with a new source of income, too. The first order he had given, to the evident pleasure of the others, had been to put an end to the old method of address. There would be no more of the absurd 'comrade this' or 'comrade that' claptrap.

It was a pity about the Iranian contract, he thought, but all was not necessarily lost. Perhaps something could be salvaged. Arafat would probably be too elusive after this episode, but perhaps the Iranians would settle for . . . Yes – of course they would.

He pressed the buzzer on the big desk; after a few seconds his aide, Jürgen Kessler, knocked and entered the room.

'There are some files I need from the Yŏngbyŏn safe, Jürgen,' said Eisener. 'I want you to go up to the nuclear plant today with Dr Gerber and bring them back here.

You can leave the others to clear up the mess downstairs.'

'Certainly, sir,' said Kessler. 'Which files do you require?'

'All those to do with extreme right-wring Israeli organisations. The hard-line settlers, the most vocal anti-Palestinian groups, Jewish religious fanatics, those sort of people. There is one group in particular called Eyal that I want to have a look at – but bring everything there is, on all of them. You will need several boxes – the files are extensive.'

'I know the ones, sir,' said Kessler. 'Is there any urgency? Perhaps I should go right away?'

'No, no,' Eisener shook his head gently. 'There is plenty of time. Go with Dr Gerber in the normal way.'

'As you wish, sir,' said Kessler. 'Oh, by the way – a message has come through for you. It is in code.' He placed it on the desk.

'Thank you.' Eisener glanced at it briefly. 'I will let you know if there is to be a reply.'

Kessler left the room, and Eisener reached for his code-book. A few minutes later, he leaned back in his chair and considered briefly what he had read. It was a relatively minor bit of business, concerning a matter that was no longer of any importance to him, but which nevertheless needed attending to. It was time to wrap it up. A simple order, and it would be done. He wrote out the necessary instruction and rang again for Kessler, who appeared promptly.

'Please have this signal sent at once, Jürgen.'

'I will see to it immediately, sir.'

As Kessler disappeared once more, Eisener remained seated behind the big desk, alone with his thoughts. He dismissed the coded message from his mind and once again considered the matter of the Iranian contract. Was there any urgency there? No, he decided. Joanna Stone would be the one to advise on it and help set it up; but she would be keeping her head well down for a while – maybe for a whole year, or even two. In the meantime, there were plenty of other jobs on file. Business, from now on, was going to boom. The Iranians would, if anything, become more keen, not less so, to scupper this Middle East peace process. They would pay handsomely. It would be a relatively simple matter to find some stupid young Eyal fanatic, unable to see beyond the end of his nose, and put him up to doing the job. Close range, with a small pistol – no chance of escape afterwards . . .

For the first time in many years, Eisener's bland, expressionless face relaxed. Alone in the big office, he contemplated the future with just a very slight grin of anticipation. There was nothing personal in it, of course – he felt no animosity towards Israeli Prime Minister Yitzhak Rabin. But business was business.

63

A door opens, and an old man is shoved outside into an alley. The door slams shut behind him. The old man is unshaven and is wearing a shabby raincoat. He looks like a scruffy old tramp. For several minutes he stands motionless in the alley, no expression at all on his blank face. A young university student on a bicycle glances incuriously at him as he cycles past, late for a lecture.

Eventually, the old man shuffles away. He emerges into a busy shopping street at the end of the alley and wanders along, peering into each window. Television sets in an electrical retail shop show a weather map of southern England; the cheerful face of a forecaster mouths his prediction of further heavy rain in the region. The old man's face registers nothing. He passes a clothes shop, a newsagent, a jeweller, an optician; he shuffles on, hardly pausing.

Finally, something in a shop window seems to catch his eye. He stops. He gazes into the window, then turns and enters the shop. Ignoring a sales assistant, the old man reaches into the window display and grabs a large glass bowl. He sets the bowl down on the floor, then begins to undo his raincoat and lower his trousers. A woman screams, but the old man pays no attention to the sudden commotion around him. A store detective grabs him and hustles him into the manager's office in the rear of the store. The manager telephones the police.

Two police constables arrive in a patrol car; they take the old man away. At the police station he is searched and put in a custody cell. He has still said nothing, and his face remains completely expressionless. The police have found no clue to his identity, but the desk sergeant feels sure he has seen the old man's face somewhere before.

The old man sits alone in the cell, his face still blank. His mind has gone. As was its purpose, the treatment he received during his captivity has caused him irreversible mental damage. His memory is in fact now virtually dead – he can recall nothing of his past life. He cannot even remember his own name.

He has forgotten all about the East German general, Reinholdt Erfurt, who cultivated and recruited him all those years ago and turned him into the most important *Stasi* agent of them all; and he has no recollection whatever of Max Goodale, the MI5 officer who many years later interrogated him at length, confronted him with the damning evidence of his treason and forced him to resign as Prime Minister.

Buried in the shattered debris of the old man's mind, never to be recalled, are the identities of dozens of other traitors who over the years gradually and insidiously wormed their way into positions of influence in the

West – all of them determined, most of them ruthless, some of them clever, but many of them too greedy and stupid even to realise what they were actually doing. So many names, so many secrets – all now buried, erased, obliterated from the old man's memory . . .

The desk sergeant, still curious, goes to the cell to take another look at the old man's face. His footsteps echo slowly down the corridor as he walks along, frowning in thought. He stops outside the cell. He opens the small eye-level inspection hatch in the cell door and peers inside.

The old man hears the noise of the hatch opening. Slowly he looks up and mumbles, 'I can't remember anything.'

On hearing the old man's voice, the desk sergeant instantly recognises him.

THE END

HEAT
by Campbell Armstrong

Frank Pagan, Special Branch's counter-terrorist agent, is being observed, his every movement tracked and recorded. His flat is broken into. The only object stolen is a photograph of his dead wife, which is later returned to him grotesquely disfigured.

But it is more than Pagan's home that has been invaded. His dreams, his every waking moment, are filled with hot, obsessive thoughts of a mortally alluring woman. For it is the most critical assignment of Pagan's career, as well as his fate, to bring to justice the enigmatic and ruthless terrorist Carlotta, who is wanted the world over for her hideous crimes.

Indifferent to the horror and destruction she leaves in her wake, yet curiously fixated on Pagan, Carlotta sends emotional depth-charges into his life to the point where his pursuit of her crosses the line that separates duty from sexual obsession. In a deadly cat-and-mouse chase, Pagan is destined always to stay just a step behind Carlotta, until the fatal day he catches up with his nemesis.

Riddled with intrigue, violence and sexual tension, *Heat* takes the reader on a thrilling journey into the darkest reaches of a man's soul.

0 552 14169 0

ICON
by Frederick Forsyth

Russia, 1999, poised to collapse in an economic and social meltdown of hyper-inflation, chaos, corruption and crime. Elections loom and a single charismatic voice rings out across the land. Igor Komarov claims he will crack down on crime, eliminate corruption and restore the glory.

But a secret document, stolen from his desk, leaves those in the West who read it pale and shaken. If the Black Manifesto is true, this man is no saviour of the nation, but a new Adolf Hitler.

Jason Monk, ex-CIA, goes back to the city to which he said he would never return. He finds a world of poverty and luxury, of politicians, gangsters, private armies, prostitutes and priests. The American has a double task: stop Komarov and prepare for an icon worthy of the Russian people.

Icon is the master storyteller at his very best, a novel with all the Forsyth hallmarks of intricate political realism, stunning suspense and a narrative that will leave you breathless.

'Forsyth's narrative surges along with great power; the story is terrifying and timely; and the vendetta between Monk and Komarov grips you to the end'
Daily Telegraph

'One of his best works for a long time'
Sunday Times

0 552 13991 2

HAYWIRE
by James Mills

To former DEA agent Doug Fleming, it is the deal of a lifetime: carry $100 million in bearer bonds from Caracas to New York as a small favour for an old contact and get the chance to rebuild his life.

After all, he has the perfect cover: his nine-year-old son, Charley, whose toy lion easily conceals the bonds. But the small favour becomes a high price to pay when the boy goes missing en route . . .

With his son vanished into the nightmare vortex of the international airline system, Fleming is thrown into a race with federal agents and ruthless criminals . . . with Charley and $100,000,000 as the ultimate prize . . .

'A slam-bang thriller . . . even better than John Grisham's *The Client*'
James Patterson, author of *Along Came a Spider*

0 552 14389 8

A SELECTED LIST OF FINE WRITING AVAILABLE FROM CORGI BOOKS

THE PRICES SHOWN BELOW WERE CORRECT AT THE TIME OF GOING TO PRESS. HOWEVER TRANSWORLD PUBLISHERS RESERVE THE RIGHT TO SHOW NEW RETAIL PRICES ON COVERS WHICH MAY DIFFER FROM THOSE PREVIOUSLY ADVERTISED IN THE TEXT OR ELSEWHERE.

14168 2	JIGSAW	Campbell Armstrong	£4.99
14169 0	HEAT	Campbell Armstrong	£5.99
13947 5	SUNDAY MORNING	Ray Connolly	£4.99
14227 1	SHADOWS ON A WALL	Ray Connolly	£5.99
14353 7	BREAKHEART HILL	Thomas H. Cook	£5.99
14518 1	THE CHATHAM SCHOOL AFFAIR	Thomas H. Cook	£5.99
13827 4	SPOILS OF WAR	Peter Driscoll	£4.99
14377 4	THE HORSE WHISPERER	Nicholas Evans	£5.99
13275 9	THE NEGOTIATOR	Frederick Forsyth	£5.99
13823 1	THE DECEIVER	Frederick Forsyth	£5.99
12140 1	NO COMEBACKS	Frederick Forsyth	£4.99
13990 4	THE FIST OF GOD	Frederick Forsyth	£5.99
13991 2	ICON	Frederick Forsyth	£5.99
14293 X	RED, RED ROBIN	Stephen Gallagher	£5.99
14472 X	CONFESSOR	John Gardner	£5.99
14224 7	OUT OF THE SUN	Robert Goddard	£5.99
14223 9	BORROWED TIME	Robert Goddard	£5.99
13840 1	CLOSED CIRCLE	Robert Goddard	£5.99
13678 6	THE EVENING NEWS	Arthur Hailey	£5.99
07583 3	NO MEAN CITY	A. McArthur & H. Kingsley Long	£5.99
14249 2	VIRGINS AND MARTYRS	Simon Maginn	£4.99
14250 6	A SICKNESS OF THE SOUL	Simon Maginn	£4.99
14389 8	HAYWIRE	James Mills	£5.99
14136 4	THE WALPOLE ORANGE	Frank Muir	£4.99
14392 8	CASINO	Nicholas Pileggi	£5.99
13094 X	WISEGUY	Nicholas Pileggi	£5.99
14541 6	AMERICAN GOTHIC: FAMILY	William T. Quick	£4.99
14290 5	FALLEN ANGELS	Eddy Shah	£5.99
14143 7	A SIMPLE PLAN	Scott Smith	£4.99
10565 1	TRINITY	Leon Uris	£5.99

Transworld titles are available by post from:

Book Service By Post, PO Box 29, Douglas, Isle of Man, IM99 1BQ

Credit cards accepted. Please telephone 01624 675137
fax 01624 670923, Internet http://www.bookpost.co.uk
or e-mail: bookshop@enterprise.net for details

Free postage and packing in the UK. Overseas customers: allow £1 per book (paperbacks) and £3 per book (hardbacks).